PROTECTOR OF THE

REALM

SUPREME CONSTELLATIONS
BOOK ONE

What Reviewers Say About BOLD STROKES Authors

❧

KIM BALDWIN

"*A riveting novel of suspense* seems to be a very overworked phrase. However, it is extremely apt when discussing Kim Baldwin's [*Hunter's Pursuit*]. An exciting page turner [features] Katarzyna Demetrious, a bounty hunter…with a million dollar price on her head. Look for this excellent novel of suspense…" – **R. Lynne Watson**, *MegaScene*

❧

ROSE BEECHAM

"…her characters seem fully capable of walking away from the particulars of whodunit and engaging the reader in other aspects of their lives." – *Lambda Book Report*

❧

GUN BROOKE

"*Course of Action* is a romance…populated with a host of captivating and amiable characters. The glimpses into the lifestyles of the rich and beautiful people are rather like guilty pleasures.…[A] most satisfying and entertaining reading experience." – **Arlene Germain**, reviewer for the *Lambda Book Report* and the *Midwest Book Review*

❧

JANE FLETCHER

"*The Walls of Westernfort* is not only a highly engaging and fast-paced adventure novel, it provides the reader with an interesting framework for examining the same questions of loyalty, faith, family and love that [the characters] must face." – **M. J. Lowe**, *Midwest Book Review*

❧

RADCLY*f*FE

"…well-honed storytelling skills…solid prose and sure-handedness of the narrative…" – **Elizabeth Flynn**, *Lambda Book Report*

"…well-plotted…lovely romance...I couldn't turn the pages fast enough!" – **Ann Bannon**, author of *The Beebo Brinker Chronicles*

PROTECTOR OF THE REALM

SUPREME CONSTELLATIONS
BOOK ONE

by

Gun Brooke

2005

PROTECTOR OF THE REALM
SUPREME CONSTELLATIONS, BOOK ONE
© 2005 BY GUN BROOKE. ALL RIGHTS RESERVED.

ISBN 1-933110-26-0

THIS TRADE PAPERBACK ORIGINAL IS PUBLISHED BY
BOLD STROKES BOOKS, INC.,
PENNSYLVANIA, USA

FIRST PRINTING: DECEMBER 2005

CREDITS
EDITORS: JENNIFER KNIGHT, STACIA SEAMAN, AND SHELLEY THRASHER
PRODUCTION DESIGN: STACIA SEAMAN
COVER ART: TOBIAS BRENNER (WWW.TOBIASBRENNER.DE)
COVER GRAPHICS BY SHERI (GRAPHICARTIST2020@HOTMAIL.COM)

By the Author

Course of Action

Acknowledgments

Supreme Constellations, Book One: Protector of the Realm would not have become a novel without the assistance and support of the following people:

Pol, my best friend and the one who saw a potential in me and my writing, first of all. Thanks for beta reading, for letting me pick your brain, for helping with tactics, action, and anything science fiction. You're the best!

Glynis, my New Zealand beta reader who goes over everything with a fine-tooth comb and offers constant support and advice and finds logic gaps like no other. Thank you for your conscientious efforts to keep me in check! http://homepages.paradise.net.nz/glynisgriffinswriting/

Snowolf, my very good friend and beta reader hailing from Australia. Your humor, your candor, and your friendship, together with your beta reading, have me looking forward to your remarks in hot pink! http://www.wolf-fic.com/

Koile, my German friend, read and commented upon every chapter with a special European take on things. I found your views immensely helpful, dear friend. Your support and friendship mean a lot to me.

Jay, you read everything I write with such enthusiasm and always willingly discuss it when I need to.

Other people offered support and/or advice too: Elon, Lotta, Malin, Henrik, Mom, Ove, Wendy, and Åse!

At Bold Strokes Books

Radclyffe, publisher—for your passion, your drive, and your belief in your authors. Thanks for daring to take this journey with me—and for making it fun!

Dr. Shelley Thrasher, editor—editing with you is not only most informative and inspirational—it is fun too!

Jennifer Knight, book doctor—thanks to you, I now know much more about adding insight!

Tobias Brenner, artist, and Sheri, graphic artist—the cover is beyond my wildest dreams. Thank you for sharing your talent—Tobias, especially, for seeing my commodore the way I see her.

Stacia Seaman, editor—nothing escapes your Argus eyes. That makes for quality, and it makes my book look great!

Dedicated to:

All the men and women who risk their lives to live the adventure and pave the way to the sort of space travel that I have described in this novel.

Space Shuttle *Challenger*—January 25, 1986
Space Shuttle *Columbia*—February 1, 2003

Elon
Who loved science fiction even before I had heard of it

My children
Miracles that outshine any scientific breakthrough

Joanne
My best friend

Lotta
My best friend

My mother, Lilian
You've seen so many miraculous discoveries take place since you were born
You still claim my brother and I are your only true miracles

My brother, Ove
Best brother ever

CHAPTER ONE

Rae Jacelon felt the frigate *Ixis* reel as a new blast from the smaller spacecraft's torpedoes hit it, making her and all the officers on her bridge hold on to their computer consoles so they wouldn't lose their balance.

"Open comm channels! Unidentified space vessel, this is Commodore Rae Jacelon of the *Gamma VI* Space Station. By not responding to hails by an SC Fleet spacecraft and committing an act of blatant aggression, you are in clear violation of our space."

"So you claim," a woman replied in Premoni, the intergalactic language of the Supreme Constellations sector. She sounded unimpressed. Her low alto voice revealed a faint accent, a soft slur of consonants that suggested she hadn't learned the language within the SC.

"Take out their weapons array and propulsion system!" Rae seized the bar next to the captain's chair to keep her balance when the alien vessel fired a new round.

"Shields down to seventy percent, ma'am." The honey-skinned ensign at tactical clenched one hand around her console and punched in new commands with the other. "Firing torpedoes one and two now!" The space between them and the alien ship lit up.

"Report!" Rae ordered.

"Their weapons are down. The vessel's dead in the water, ma'am."

"Reestablish comm channels." Rae rose from her seat in the center of the bridge and tugged at her short black leather jacket, its tall collar adorned with rank insignia. She kept her anger in control as she spoke.

"Unidentified vessel, examine your computer readings and look at the identification seal on our transfers. It confirms our identity and our capabilities. Lower your shields and prepare to be boarded."

"We have video, Commodore," the ops ensign reported.

The large screen on the far wall of the bridge flickered, and a woman's face came partially into view. "This is the private vessel *Kithanya*. We have no intention of surrendering. Our shields are fully operational…"

Rae bristled and felt like kicking the wall with her tall black boot. She had suffered through an endless series of boring negotiations for the past two weeks and was in no mood to be diplomatic. If this woman was foolish enough to acquire outlaw status by firing her ship's full array of weapons after being hailed, she would be sorry.

Impatient, she smoothed down her short red hair and said, "Yes, but you cannot win. Nothing in your arsenal can prevent me from tractoring you in. You are not above the law."

"We have broken no laws." The woman's tone was dismissive, almost disdainful.

Seething at this unexpected insolence, Rae replied brusquely, "As a matter of fact, I can think of several. This is your last chance. Lower your shields."

"No."

"Congratulations. You've won a free trip to the *Gamma VI* Space Station. Enjoy the ride." Rae bent down, straightened the knife-sharp crease in her blue trousers, and gave the next order to her tactical officer. "Reel them in. Let's go home."

❖

"You and the boy in your care, Armeo M'Aido, will remain in custody until—"

Rae broke off as a transparent blue teardrop ran down Kellen O'Dal's cheek. So the blue tears really existed. She had heard of them, but never seen them firsthand. Crystal clear, reflecting the light in her office, the solitary tear left a damp trail on her prisoner's face.

"I understand if you are upset, Ms. O'Dal, but—"

"I am not upset," Kellen O'Dal hissed. "Do not mistake my tears for signs of fear. I am furious!"

A security guard moved closer, but Rae motioned him back to his post by the door. She stared at the tall, proud Gantharian woman who stood before her in her office aboard *Gamma VI*. The expression in her prisoner's brilliant blue eyes was impossible to read. Rae had never seen anyone go from volatile to complete blankness so quickly. It was like putting a lid on a volcano. And although she knew this woman was physically stronger than she was—in fact, stronger than any human, due to a denser, more tractile muscle tissue—she merely shrugged and circled her desk. She had stared down taller, more physically imposing individuals than Kellen O'Dal.

"I was trying to be civil," Rae said forcefully. "The boy is in custody, awaiting his relative. You are a prisoner, waiting to stand trial for kidnapping."

Kellen apparently tried to stay calm by clasping her hands behind her back and standing at strict attention. She breathed deeply and with obvious forced consistency. "I am *not* a kidnapper. His parents are dead, and his mother entrusted him into my care. He has lived under my protection his entire life, and I have raised him since he was five, when his mother was killed."

"The Gantharian ambassador sent files less than an hour ago, stating you've kept the boy from his father's relatives for seven years. It's your word against that of a diplomat." Rae folded her arms across her chest and leaned against the corner of her desk. She was curious to hear the other side of this story, having detected arrogance and a hint of threat in the ambassador's messages.

"Commodore, you cannot trust Ambassador M'Ekar's version of the facts. He is not from Gantharat. He's an Onotharian." Kellen spat the last word as if it tasted foul.

Rae scrutinized the impressive woman once more. Gantharians were blue-blooded in the truest sense of the word. Their blue-colored blood cells shimmered just beneath the skin, and the unusual tint enhanced the woman's statuesque appearance. According to her file, Kellen was thirty-two Earth years old, young for her race. Their life span was about thirty years longer than that of humans. A striking woman, she wore her blond hair in a long, severe braid down her back. A tight black leather suit accentuated her lean body.

Rae thought she detected a faint tremor in Kellen's hands and wondered what caused it. Was it more of her impressive anger? *Or is she afraid, or perhaps in pain?* "Do you have proof of what you say?" she inquired.

"Only her last words! When she was dying, she asked me to raise Armeo, and until a few lunar cycles ago, nobody cared either way. I won't give him up."

The defiant retort seemed to mask other, underlying emotions. Rae rubbed her neck, where an all-too-familiar tension reminded her of countless negotiations with Onotharians wanting to cross the border into the SC. Situations like this one were always stressful. "Take a seat." She pointed at one of the alu-carbon visitors' chairs.

Kellen looked as if she was about to refuse, but relented and sat down, flinching as she extended her left leg in front of her.

"Are you injured?" Rae asked.

"I'm fine."

"Very well. As you know, I've spoken with the boy. He's obviously very fond of you and would be upset if you were apart. That's why I haven't confined you to the brig without him. Yet. Fact remains, by firing on my frigate and refusing to obey direct orders, you violated at least a dozen Supreme Constellations laws."

"You were approaching me head-on. I had no way of knowing your intent."

"We identified ourselves as an SC spacecraft."

"You are not the first to present yourselves as representatives of the SC. I have come across several convoys of pirates with the exact same method of operation."

Rae knew this was probably true. The Gamma outposts were eternally trying to stamp out the pesky space pirates who infested intergalactic space and made it dangerous for traders and other small spacecraft. "My people are searching your vessel right now. They'll find any such incidents on record in the ship's computer log, if they exist."

"They will be there." Again, an expression of anguish flickered over Kellen's face.

Rae scanned the lean body before her for clues as to where the pain originated. She could see no outward signs, but she wasn't going to take any chances. "Before we commit you to your quarters, I'll send you and young Armeo through sick bay."

"Your scans will come out negative. We carry no disease."

"Perhaps, and our biological filter should've picked up any foreign agents already. However, we're many light-years from the nearest medical facility. We can't take any chances. Besides, someone needs to look at your leg."

Kellen rose without permission, glaring at her. "Have your doctors scan us, then. They can't be any worse than the bunglers the Onotharians allow to practice medicine on Gantharat."

Acidic, aren't we? Rae nodded toward the guard. "Escort Ms. O'Dal to Dr. Meyer. Pick up the boy on the way."

"Yes, ma'am."

As she returned to her chair, Rae watched the proud woman leave. Her stoic appearance and the arrogance that bordered on hauteur were hardly the demeanor one would expect of a prisoner. And she showed no signs of gratitude for her decent treatment at Rae's hands. Puzzled, and somewhat concerned at the thought that Kellen O'Dal could be injured, Rae returned her focus to her work. She had no plans to allow her captive to prey on her mind; she had more important things to think about.

Kellen gazed around sick bay, waiting for the chief medical officer to join her and Armeo where they sat next to each other on an elaborate-looking examination table. Two guards armed with laser-pulse rifles stood by the door.

"What's going to happen now?" Armeo sounded more curious than afraid.

"A doctor will make sure we're healthy and all right. It won't hurt."

Armeo looked at her with an expression of disdain that reminded Kellen of his mother. "I'm not afraid of anything."

"It's natural to fear the unknown." Kellen smiled fondly and let her gaze soften. "We don't know these people, but they won't harm you."

"The commodore interrogated you," Armeo pointed out.

"Yes, but she didn't hurt me." Kellen knew Armeo was worried by the rumors he'd heard about interrogations in the Gantharat System. "We only spoke together."

He scooted closer. "Honestly?" His dark blue eyes, framed by straight, black eyebrows, probed hers.

Armeo's face was thin below a shock of dark brown hair. Like his mother's, his features were finely chiseled, and he also carried the Gantharian blue-blood cells, making his dark eyes blackish blue. Despite this coloring, his skin possessed a clear olive tint that was inherited from his father, as were his broad shoulders and lithe body. He was lanky and tall for his twelve years, reaching almost to Kellen's shoulder.

Knowing he was also emotionally mature for his age, Kellen took his question seriously. "Honestly," she insisted. "The commodore only asked me questions."

The woman in command of this space station was unlike anyone Kellen had ever met. At first glance her form was unremarkable despite the flaming dark red hair, which seemed to be unusual for a human. She was shorter than Kellen, her eyes at the level of Kellen's lips.

She was also immaculate and had dealt with Kellen by the book, so she obviously valued correctness and order. Even the way she spoke—her pronunciation clear, each word distinct—suggested the commodore was meticulous.

However, Kellen sensed Jacelon was not an ordinary minion of the SC. She guessed her age to be around forty human years, which, she surmised, was fairly young for someone to achieve such a high rank. The woman's blue-gray eyes, piercing and relentless, never wavered. *They kept looking at me, as if they could sum up my strengths and weaknesses by simple subtraction. Perhaps a worthy adversary in this mass of human weaklings.*

The door hissed open, and a petite, wiry woman with short black hair stepped inside. Wearing a different version of a Supreme Constellations uniform, a light blue retrospun cotton shirt with the standard blue trousers, she strode up to Kellen and Armeo and gave them a brisk nod.

"I'm Dr. Meyer, CMO aboard *Gamma VI*. Call me Gemma. I hate titles."

Taken aback by the surprising request, Kellen exchanged glances with Armeo, noticing the curious look in the boy's eyes and hoping he wasn't afraid of this new experience. The few times she had been forced to take him to one of the clinics on Gantharat, he had been traumatized for days afterward. Now Kellen was relieved to see him meet the CMO's eyes without hesitation.

"I'm Armeo," he said, extending a hand in the human way of greeting. "How do you do?"

Gemma, about to reach for a handheld computer, turned around and shook his hand. "I'm fine, thank you. Why don't we start with you, Armeo? I want to make sure you didn't bring any germs we weren't prepared for. Also, you were in the middle of quite a scuffle in space, I hear. Were you hurt?"

"No, ma'am…eh, Gemma. I was strapped into my seat. Kellen's orders."

"Good." Gemma took a scanning device from a tray. "Now, let's see. Hmm, I detect scarring around your clavicle. I'd say you've been injured in the last year or so."

Armeo blushed faintly and cast an embarrassed glance toward Kellen. "Yeah, and it was all my fault. Kellen told me to wait for her when I wanted to go riding on her new *maesha*. I didn't listen to her. He threw me off and I landed on my shoulder."

"What's a *maesha*?"

"What you would call a horse," Kellen replied. "Only much bigger."

Gemma shot her a look. "Armeo's clavicle hasn't healed properly. Why didn't you take him to a physician?"

"We have no physicians working with this kind of technology on Gantharat. And if they did exist, they would not be accessible to Gantharians. We have what you could call doctors, but no bone-knitters or derma fusers. Since I refused to have these idiots carve on him, it had to heal the old-fashioned way."

"Didn't you at least wear a sling, Armeo?"

He squirmed, the picture of guilt. "Yes…sometimes."

Kellen raised her hand, ruffling the hair at the back of his head. "Sometimes, as in *rarely*, Armeo?" She felt her muscles relax marginally when he wrinkled his nose at her, looking so familiar in this stark alien setting.

Gemma shook her head and smiled. "Kids. You probably had to nag him about the sling the few times he actually wore it."

She's trying to act friendly, but I certainly don't trust her. They were in the hands of people working for the woman she'd fired her torpedoes at. She mustn't forget that. Their loyalties lay with Commodore Jacelon and the SC, not with a fugitive accused of kidnapping.

Kellen decided acting as if everything were normal in front of Armeo, making him feel safe, would help their case in several ways. If the *Gamma VI* commodore learned from her crew how wonderful Armeo was, Jacelon might be more lenient when she made her decision about Kellen's fate. "Yes," she replied, keeping her voice even. "He's very active and didn't want to wear bandages."

"I guess you're going to stay with us for a while. I can easily repair this if you want." Gemma scanned the rest of his body. "Apart from the injury, you're in great shape." She punched a few new commands into the handheld computer, then turned to Kellen. "All right. Any injuries or illnesses I should know about?"

"No." Wordlessly, she tried to communicate with Gemma by gesturing in the boy's direction.

The doctor nodded. "Listen, Armeo, why don't you go over there, to the main computer. I bet Ensign Dario can show you an interesting game while I finish." She motioned for one of the guards to accompany the boy and, turning her attention back to Kellen, said, "Go on."

"Thank you. It's nothing, but I don't want to worry him."

"I understand." Gemma ran the scanning device across Kellen's body. Reaching her left leg, she stopped, circling it over an area on Kellen's thigh. "Remove your uniform. I'm detecting bacteria in what appears to be an open wound."

"It isn't necessary. I've bandaged it myself."

"It's infected, and I have no way of knowing how bad it is without a visual inspection."

"Very well." Kellen straightened her back. "Could I have some privacy, please?"

"Of course." The doctor tugged at a curtain, partly obscuring the other guard's vision. "He can still see us, so don't try to fool me, Ms. O'Dal."

"I'm not."

Standing up, Kellen unfastened her leather suit and peeled it off her shoulders and down across her hips. She couldn't help but moan when it slid over the injury in her left thigh. She sat on the gurney, biting her lower lip to keep from whimpering when Gemma carefully peeled off the makeshift bandage.

"God," the physician murmured. "And you call this nothing? What the hell caused it?"

"Ambassador M'Ekar's way of dealing with me." Kellen ground her teeth at the searing pain.

"This isn't new. When did it happen?"

"When we left Gantharat twenty-two days ago."

Gemma scanned the infected area of the five-inch-long wound. "It needs treatment. How could you let it become so bad?"

"I tried to keep it clean, but we have a limited supply of medications aboard the *Kithanya*."

Gemma reached for an injection device. "This is for the pain and is also an anti-inflammatory. Further scans will determine which bacteria are causing this mess, and we'll give you an intravenous infusion of the right medication to help you heal and make it possible for me to close the wound later." She pressed the imbulizer against Kellen's upper arm. "I can't believe you tried to clean this yourself. Without the right pain relief, it must have hurt like hell."

"What, exactly, must've hurt?" a husky voice said from behind the screen.

"Commodore, come in and take a look at this." Gemma took a step back.

Kellen did her best to conceal her annoyance when the woman in charge of the space station rounded the screen to join them. She was reluctant to show any sign of weakness, even if it was merely a wounded leg.

Commodore Jacelon looked at the wound on Kellen's leg with a puzzling expression on her face. Kellen recognized anger mixed with something close to remorse, and she wondered why she would look at a perfect stranger with so much feeling. *Perhaps she doesn't realize how visible her emotions are to me?*

"I can't imagine how you've managed to move, let alone walk, with your leg in that condition." Jacelon shook her head.

"Ms. O'Dal shouldn't be on her feet at all until I've closed this wound. I'll admit her to the infirmary and—"

"No," Kellen objected. "I can't be away from Armeo. I will not have him incarcerated without me."

Commodore Jacelon looked affronted. "I've thought about your situation and…seeing this," she gestured toward the injury, "reaffirms what I've decided."

Kellen raised an eyebrow, unable to keep sarcasm out of her voice. "Do go on, Commodore."

"You're in SC custody and so is the boy. We'd never throw a child into the brig—and we don't do that to seriously injured people either. I will assign proper quarters for you both. Armed guards will be on duty at all times, so don't fool yourself that you can escape."

"Why are you being so kind?" Kellen immediately regretted how she had phrased the question, afraid she might sound as if she needed compassion from this woman.

"It may be hard for you to believe, but I'm not inhumane. A child's future is at stake, and by the looks of it, so is your health." The commodore turned to walk away. Stopping before she rounded the screen, she shot Kellen a glance. "This is a gesture of good faith on my behalf. Don't let me down, Kellen. You won't like the consequences if you do."

❖

"You gave that good-looking Gantharian woman her own quarters?" Rae's longtime second in command, Commander Jeremiah Todd, looked stunned. "What could possibly warrant that after she damn near blasted you out of space?"

"We apprehended her with a child in her care." Rae cut her vegetables into smaller pieces and speared one with a fork. As usual in the mess hall the food was passable, but little more. The rations included in the SC officers' credits left a lot to be desired in texture, taste, and composition. The giant BaDalchian asparagus was decidedly thready, and chewing it provided ample time to ponder her response. Glancing around, she was grateful that the officers' mess hall was almost empty, with only a few young ensigns occupying the bar at the far end of the room.

"A child she abducted," Jeremiah pointed out.

"Allegedly abducted. We don't have all the facts yet."

"What are you saying?"

"Since we apprehended Ms. O'Dal and Armeo, I've heard from Ambassador M'Ekar's attaché regarding 'formal inquiries,' as he calls it, stating a long list of reasons for us to more or less shoot Kellen

O'Dal on sight and ask questions later."

These so-called diplomatic questions had set her on edge with their overbearing attempts to dictate her actions. She would never do anything except follow SC laws to the letter. M'Ekar seemed to disregard whose jurisdiction Kellen O'Dal and young Armeo were under. She attacked another innocent vegetable, then dropped her fork impatiently. "There's something more here than the good ambassador is leading us to believe, if you ask me."

Jeremiah gestured at her with his glass and came dangerously close to spilling his water. "You might be heading for a diplomatic minefield, Rae. The Onotharians have governed Gantharat for almost thirty years, and the Supreme Constellations Council members are divided regarding their right to do so."

"I know. Earth leaders, for instance, have never fully acknowledged the Onotharian right to form a cabinet on Gantharat. Theoretically we're supposed to stay apolitical in the service, but I think our Council does great harm by not making up its mind."

"I couldn't agree more. So, what's this woman's story? I hear she's quite striking."

Rae gave her next in command an exasperated look. Jeremiah was the best XO she had ever had, but he was an unrepentant womanizer whose affairs were legendary. Oddly enough, though, all his exes defended him if anyone dared criticize him in any way.

"She seems extremely protective of the boy." Rae sipped her beer. "She would have skipped the infirmary altogether to stay with him if I hadn't given them their own quarters. I don't know how they do it on Gantharat, but she thought we'd throw both of them in the brig."

"The child too?" Jeremiah sounded incredulous.

"Yes. Makes you wonder, doesn't it? Her injury was the most painful-looking thing I've seen in years. Sure, I've seen bigger wounds, but they've been clean, new. This was infected, and together with the fact that her blood is blue…it was ugly." She shuddered, then gave a regretful smile. "Sorry, didn't mean to spoil your meal."

"I was done." He wiped his mouth with a napkin. "Sounds like she's not a stranger to toughing it out."

"Yeah. Still, it's hard to achieve that kind of self-control. I don't trust her." Rae raised her hand as Jeremiah opened his mouth to speak. "No, don't get me wrong. She's probably an honorable person deep down, but as long as that child's in danger of being handed over to the Onotharians, she's a loose cannon."

Jeremiah still looked doubtful. "Did she appreciate being given special quarters?"

Rae folded her hands under her chin, leaning her elbows against the table. "She seems very suspicious of our motives, as if she sees hidden agendas everywhere. Who knows? Perhaps for good reason."

"You like her." Her XO's voice softened, becoming personal.

Rae flinched, nailing him with her eyes. "What do you mean? I'm trying to stay objective despite the fact that she almost blew us up. You know me. I don't let personal feelings affect my actions."

"Kind of hard to stay objective when a child's involved and it's one woman against the entire Onotharian fleet." Jeremiah's face darkened. "From what I've heard, they aren't exactly famous for being big on mercy. And I find another fact curious. The latest tactical report says long-range sensors picked up twelve vessels heading our way. I don't like it."

"I know. Overkill, if their sole intention is to reclaim a little boy. They maintain they have the law on their side, so why send a whole flotilla? Speaking of laws, we'll know soon enough if they'll stick to the treaty they signed with the SC." Rae doubted it, thinking of the obvious arrogance in the messages she had received. "They will need to downsize to two ships if they want permission to approach."

Gamma VI, one of ten space stations located in the outer perimeter of SC space, boasted an extensive firepower and a vast fleet of ships. Together with six Betas and three Alphas located in three rings around Earth and the thirty-four other Supreme Constellations home planets, the installations protected Supreme Constellations space. However, as the final outposts between the SC homeworlds and intergalactic space, the Gamma stations were vulnerable. No more than two ships from any planet outside the SC were allowed within a two-light-year radius of the space stations without the station commodore's authorization.

"And I take it there'll be no exceptions to policy?"

"Damn straight, there won't."

"All right, then." Jeremiah grinned, raising his beer. "Here's to policy."

"To policy." Rae lifted her glass and met his in a toast. She knew her strict adherence to regulations and protocol was renowned, and she guessed Jeremiah looked forward to rejecting the Onotharians if they insisted on approaching *Gamma VI* unlawfully.

"By the way," Jeremiah asked, "what kind of quarters did you give Ms. O'Dal and the boy? It'd be tough to keep security tight enough around our regular guest quarters."

"I thought of that, so I put them in one of the VIP suites. It's fully monitored. Besides knocking out the around-the-clock security officer, she'd need a verified handprint and retina scan to leave the corridor."

"Do you expect her to try something? You have that cautious look on your face."

"I do?" Rae let her finger trace the rim of the glass as she thought about the mysterious alien. "You know what? She seems exhausted, despite her determination to keep the boy safe. As long as she believes we won't merely hand the child over, she might just behave."

"And when she realizes she and the boy have become pawns in a diplomatic chess game?"

Rae didn't hesitate. "That's when we'll see the true nature of Kellen O'Dal."

CHAPTER TWO

Kellen moved restlessly on the bed, tossing off the covers since they felt too heavy on her injury. The CMO had been to see her a few hours ago, but the pain relief had worn off and her leg felt worse than ever.

Pressing her lips together, she tried to stay calm and quiet. Armeo was asleep in the next room, also used as the sitting room, and she didn't want to disturb him. He had been through enough the last few weeks and needed to rest.

She forced back a moan and tried to shift onto her uninjured side. The new position worked for a while, but eventually the throbbing ache became unbearable. As she sat up in bed, an unexpected movement in the doorway startled her.

"Are you all right, Kellen?" Armeo asked.

She knew the anguish was visible in her face. Had it been anyone other than Armeo, she would have made every effort to mask her pain. "Actually, I'm in agony. Maybe the doctor would give me something more for the pain if we paged her. I'm keeping both of us awake."

"Let me call her. I can use the communication console on the desk next to my couch." Without waiting for permission, Armeo hurried off.

Kellen tried to rise from the bed. If the CMO had to be called, she'd rather do it herself so she could make her condition sound less serious than it·was. But the pain was severe, and she sank back down with a groan.

Armeo returned a moment later wearing a familiar broad grin. This was how he looked when he thought he might be in trouble. "I thought I pressed the correct commands on the machine. I'm not sure what I did wrong."

"What did you do, Armeo?"

"I pressed the command for sick bay, and then I don't know what happened, but the commodore responded." He shrugged, obviously trying to look casual. "She told me not to worry. She would take care of things. She didn't seem angry. She was nice."

Kellen tried to remain calm. She couldn't afford to let Commodore Jacelon see her succumb to pain. Granted, the commodore knew about the wound, but so far, Kellen had remained unfazed by it in Jacelon's presence. "Did you tell her I need more medication?" Slowly she sat up, breathing evenly so she could remain in control and not show just how bad it was. *I have endured pain before, and I can do it now. Some more of the medication and I'll be fine.*

"I did. She said she knew you must be in pain. Do you think she's a doctor as well?"

"I wouldn't be surprised," Kellen muttered, unable to stop her sarcastic comment.

The door in the outer room hissed open, and Kellen could hear voices talking quietly before it closed. Putting a hand on her knee, she tried to will her leg to stop trembling.

Commodore Jacelon stepped into the bedroom, squeezing Armeo's shoulder as she passed him. "Good job, kid. You did the right thing to page sick bay," she said.

"So I *did* do it the right way," the boy exclaimed. "Are you a doctor too, ma'am?"

The commodore gave a wry smile. "No. We had several casualties tonight. Since Dr. Meyer is busy taking care of them with her staff, I answered your call."

"Will they be okay? The people that were hurt?"

"Eventually. Gemma is a very good doctor. We're just lucky the trader made it here in time."

"Pirates?" Kellen asked, her voice husky from pain.

"Yes." Jacelon approached her, placing a bag on the small nightstand. Blue-gray eyes examined Kellen thoroughly while she pulled out an imbulizer. "Here, roll up your sleeve for me." Jacelon loaded a small metallic vial into the device, and it sank into place with a low hiss.

"It isn't necessary. I think Armeo may have overreacted a little. I'm quite fine," Kellen said in a low voice, out of earshot of Armeo, who lingered by the door. She looked straight at the commodore, determined to not let any of the almost unbearable pain show.

"I'm sure you're a resilient woman," Jacelon said in an objective tone. "But since I'm here, why risk it becoming worse?"

"I said it isn't necessary…" Kellen's eyes landed on Armeo, who had begun to look concerned. "Really. I can manage without your expensive SC medication." She forced her voice to be strong, not about to show her weakness in front of the other woman.

"But, Kellen…" Armeo approached the bed. "You were in so much pain just before the commodore came. You almost had tears in your eyes." His eyes grew moist and his chin trembled.

Jacelon remained silent, waiting with the vial containing the pain relief in her hand and a faintly mystified expression on her face.

"Very well. Since you're already here." Kellen gave in as the injured muscle began to spasm beneath the bedsheets. "It'll calm Armeo down. He's worried about me, about our situation." She felt the commodore's warm hand cup her elbow and press the cold imbulizer against the inside of it.

The quick, stinging sensation when the drug entered her vein was nothing. Instead, the strong hands adjusting her soft thinlinnen shirt unsettled Kellen for some reason she couldn't understand. "Thank you. Armeo was very concerned, or I wouldn't have allowed him to disturb the doctor." Kellen was determined to keep her voice from trembling. Pain was one thing, weakness another. She didn't trust anyone here, and certainly not the one who sat on all the power.

"I know. And he didn't disturb me." Jacelon reached for the bag. "Gemma asked me to check the wound while I was here. She's concerned about it."

Kellen looked pointedly toward Armeo, who still stood just inside the doorway. Jacelon followed her glance. "You must be tired, Armeo. Why don't you go back to bed? Tomorrow, I'll personally introduce you to our teacher. I thought while you're on the space station, you should attend school. Several of the kids who live here are your age."

Armeo's eye brightened. "Really? I can go outside the quarters?"

"With an…escort accompanying you at all times, yes," the commodore cautioned.

"Did you hear that, Kellen? I can go out and—" He suddenly stopped and swung around. "But *you* can't. You'll be here all alone when you're sick."

"I'll be fine." Kellen pushed herself farther up onto the pillows, the pain thankfully starting to ease. "I can rest while you're in school. Now do as the commodore says and go get some sleep."

"That's right," Jacelon said. "Hop into bed and I'll take care of Kellen, all right?"

"Yes. Good night, ma'am." He all but saluted the commodore, and Kellen easily interpreted the look of reluctant admiration on his face.

Armeo hugged Kellen, and she kissed the top of his head. "Night, Armeo." Her lips felt numb. *Is it the medication?* The pain reliever was definitely making her dizzy. Fighting against an overwhelming urge to reach out for support, she pressed her palms onto the bed to steady herself.

"Okay, lie back down on the bed," Jacelon suggested. "Let's have a look at that leg of yours."

"Why do you persist in being so nice to us?" Kellen lay down, flinching when she tried to raise her leg back up on the bed.

The commodore assisted her with gentle hands, somehow easing the pain by her mere touch, and began loosening the bandage. "You'd rather I treated you harshly?" When Kellen did not reply, she continued, "You're hard to figure out, Ms. O'Dal. But I don't punish children for the peculiarities of adults, so you will be well treated while you are on my station. However, I don't trust you. You might decide to grab Armeo and run, and even if I might sympathize with your situation, I cannot allow that."

Jacelon examined the injury carefully before she dressed it again with a clean bandage. "It doesn't look worse, at least. The interactive antibacterial suspension sometimes takes time to kick in, especially when the patient isn't within the normal demographic for this method. Hopefully by tomorrow you'll start seeing an improvement." She pulled the covers up. "Want to tell me how it happened?"

Kellen looked up into sharp, intelligent eyes. Their calm, unwavering expression made her think for a moment it might be possible to trust Jacelon, and she detected nothing but honest interest in the husky voice. The medication took the pain away, and with it, a little of her resolve to remain aloof.

"Take your time." Jacelon sat down on the edge of the bed.

Kellen knew the details she disclosed would be superficial, easy to check. She would still be safe. "Three weeks ago, several Onotharian men came to the estate and told me they had come to get Armeo, to take him to Ganath, our capital city," she said, finding she spoke more slowly than usual since her tongue did not quite cooperate. "They tried to emulate civil servants, but I could see they were OECS."

"What does OECS stand for?"

"Onotharian Empire Clandestine Service. Armeo's father was half Onotharian, but I had not heard from his relatives since his mother, my friend Tereya, died. I thought they weren't interested in him."

"Are you related to Armeo at all?"

"Not by blood. His mother, Tereya, was my adopted sister, my best friend all through school and later at the Gantharian Academy of Pilots. That's where she met Armeo's father. Zax was a wonderful person, and despite all our hatred and prejudice against the Onotharians, we adored him. Tereya and Zax fell in love, and the three of us shared a great friendship. We were the best pilots in our squadron."

"So you served in the Onotharian space force?"

Kellen made a face, wincing at the question. *I only joined for one reason, and I'm not about to tell you that, Commodore. Armeo's heritage, and the information regarding my sacred duty, cannot fall into the hands of strangers, no matter how benevolent. The day I have healed and can move more freely and protect Armeo, we will escape.* "No, it didn't turn out that way. We graduated, and when it turned out Tereya was pregnant, the two of us resigned. I had to stay with her...her pregnancy was not an easy one. Zax stayed on to fulfill his contract."

"What happened to him?"

Kellen swallowed. "He was killed six lunar cycles later. Tereya went into labor when they notified us. I was there when Armeo was born. I helped raise him and, when Tereya lay dying in my arms five years later, I promised her he'd always have a home with me. I'm all he knows."

Jacelon nodded slowly. "And how did you provide for the boy all alone during the past seven years?"

Kellen made sure she sounded calm and matter-of-fact. "I possess two skills. I'm a pilot for hire and I write music."

Jacelon looked surprised, then gave a broad smile. "Music? What kind of music?"

"Classical, folk music…anything that speaks to me. I've become quite famous, and I'm afraid that's what led Hox M'Ekar to my doorstep. Well, not him in person, naturally. He sent six men, and if it hadn't been for my training at the academy, Armeo would be lost to me now." Kellen closed her eyes briefly. "They carried laser-pulse weapons. Their leader fired and Armeo tried to protect me. I had no choice but to throw myself on top of him. The pulse cut across my leg. At first I thought he'd severed it."

She inhaled deeply at the memory. Flickering images, flashbacks, of how she had tugged Armeo with her, running toward the barn. The boy, white-faced, scared, screaming her name when more men appeared behind the stables. Searing laser-pulse beams split the air around them, and Kellen had feared any one of them would hit Armeo in the chest.

The doors to the barn jammed for a terrifying moment before they relented and let her and Armeo in. They ran toward the ramp leading into the *Kithanya,* and it was when they were almost by the large hatch that the leader of the OECS unit stormed in after them, laser-pulse rifle raised and aimed at her. Armeo tried to get in front of her, to shield her with his smaller body. Only by brute force did Kellen manage to toss him halfway through the hatch and herself on top. That's when the pulse hit.

At first she'd felt no pain, only numbness, and she used every bit of her strength to ignore what had just happened and struggle into the ship, pushing Armeo ahead of her. Calling out to the computer, she had initiated the emergency boot sequence, which meant locking all exits and then slingshoting the *Kithanya* more or less through the roof of the barn and into orbit.

"How did you escape?" Jacelon asked.

"Several lunar years ago, I used some of my credits to buy a small spacecraft. It was pretty run down when we brought it home, but Armeo and I restored it…"

"And fitted it with quite the weapons array," Jacelon noted.

Kellen shrugged. "Yes. Apart from the attack, we lived on occupied land. The Onotharian patrols would consider it a crime to own a heavily armed ship, of course. But I did what I had to do to get us out alive. Wouldn't you have done the same thing?"

Jacelon fell silent, her expression reflective. "If I had a child in my care, I might. I can relate on a different level too. I'm responsible for the people on *Gamma VI* and those who inhabit the space around here.

I'm prepared to use brute force to keep them safe as long as I abide by SC law."

Kellen realized she was slurring her words and losing her ability to pronounce Premoni properly, but she couldn't help herself. "Unlawful or not, the weapons came in handy when we kept running into bands of pirates."

"And this happened three weeks ago? You must have traveled at maximum field-distortion drive to get this far."

"I was trying to reach SC space before the Onotharians caught up with us. I had to. I can't possibly get a fair trial on Gantharat." Kellen yawned. "I'm sorry. It's the medication."

"I'm glad it's taking effect." The commodore rose. In a gesture that seemed close to tender, she tugged the blankets up around Kellen. "I can't guarantee the outcome, but this is my space station, my jurisdiction, and I'll make sure the Council considers everything you've told me."

Kellen wanted to believe her. She sensed compassion in Jacelon's gaze and warm hands, and something else, a hint of steadfast integrity. But she had learned the hard way not to trust anyone, especially someone like the commodore. Only by remaining on her guard, not confiding in a single soul, had she and Armeo managed to get away from that last close call. She was not about to relax her stance.

Feeling drowsy and weak, she cursed herself for giving in and allowing Jacelon to administer the pain relief. It could be the last mistake she ever made. "Understand this, Commodore," she murmured huskily, the medication beginning to take over. "I can't let them take him from me. Armeo's too good for them...He knows nothing about their world."

Jacelon looked as if she was about to address what Kellen had just said, but if so, she changed her mind. "Try to get some sleep, Kellen. The ambassador's vessels will be right on the perimeter of SC space tomorrow."

Kellen closed her eyes as sleep began to overtake her. "Armeo..."

"Is safe. Rest now."

The last thing Kellen heard was the door open and close when Jacelon left.

❖

Mr. M'Indo, the ambassador's attaché, was obviously displeased. A short, bony man with a distinctly protruding nose, he stood by an elaborate desk in an equally impressive room and twisted his long, skinny fingers around each other. He restated the ambassador's demands and glared at Rae from the large computer screen in her office. Nearly paper-thin, the screen sat on slim titanium rods and almost hovered above her desk as she placed her left index finger on the fingerprint scan.

"We must have proper escort when we enter Supreme Constellations space," the attaché demanded. "The ambassador is dependent on his cruiser, four destroyers, and seven frigates."

Rae tapped her fingers on her thigh beneath the desk and addressed the pompous little man. "Listen to me, Mr. M'Indo. Your nation has signed a treaty with the SC that clearly states that no nation may approach any of the Gamma stations with more than two vessels. This safety precaution is nonnegotiable."

"So is the ambassador's request that you make an exception. The treaty also states that you as a commodore can do so." The Onotharian smiled smugly, clasping his hands behind his back and rocking back and forth on his feet.

"I don't see why he needs such a large entourage." Rae slowly crossed her legs as she sat in her command chair in her office, making sure she looked relaxed and confident in order to irritate the attaché. Her office was located behind circular transparent aluminum walls in the heart of the triangular mission room on Deck 1. Outside, twenty-two traffic controllers and security officers worked at their consoles. Rae studied the view screen. The Onotharian seemed frustrated, his jaw muscle clenching and releasing over and over when she did not yield to his demands.

"You show a remarkable disregard for the ambassador's situation. We have enemies out there, exiled Gantharians who would stoop to anything when it comes to using terrorist methods to make political statements."

Rae knew he was partially correct. Outside the SC, small cells of Gantharians resorted to violence as they struggled to free Gantharat from Onotharian occupation.

"So far they have only targeted military installations. Why would they care about a personal matter like Ambassador M'Ekar's?" She feigned innocent puzzlement.

"Because he's a prominent figure in the Onotharian administration on Gantharat. They might see this as ample opportunity to strike against him and what he represents."

"We have an excellent and well-equipped security force at the station," Rae assured him. "If the ambassador wants to discuss the matter of Kellen O'Dal and Armeo M'Aido, he'll abide by SC laws, exactly like everybody else."

M'Indo sighed, a quick puff of air, and looked irritated. "I think you are making a great error in judgment, Commodore. I will forward your position to the ambassador and get back to you shortly. I will also remind you that when and if the ambassador comes aboard the station, he enjoys diplomatic immunity."

Biting back a harsh suggestion regarding what M'Ekar could do with his diplomatic immunity, Rae spoke curtly. "Until later, Mr. M'Indo. Jacelon out."

The screen flickered momentarily before it showed an overview of the space station. Looking at the triangular concave structure, Rae saw ships of all shapes and sizes arrive and embark, delivering goods and people or taking them away. She had commanded *Gamma VI* for eight years and loved most aspects of the job, especially the encounters with people passing through and the tactical challenges of outsmarting pirates in her ongoing struggle against them. The view calmed her and helped clear her mind, as usual. Nothing was as breathtaking as the vastness of space around them.

Her communicator beeped, a low, husky two-tone alarm, and she tugged it from its place on her left shoulder. "Jacelon here. Go ahead."

"Terence de Brost here, ma'am. We have a situation in the school quarters."

Rae uncrossed her legs and rose quickly. "Have you alerted security?"

"Eh, ma'am? It's not that kind of situation. Are you free to pay us a visit?"

Terence was a civilian who had worked as a teacher and librarian at the station since before she took command. He was a well-read, versatile man who came across as low-key with his gentle voice and thoughtful way of speaking. However, Rae had seen him lead classes in the martial arts and was well aware he could be lethal.

"On my way. What's this about? Oh, don't tell me. It concerns Armeo M'Aido. Right?"

"Yes, it does. Thank you, Commodore."

Rae strode out of her office, handing over the conn to a dark-haired lieutenant standing at the tactical station. "I'll be in the school quarters."

"Aye, ma'am," he replied smartly, saluting before he switched his screen to overview mode. "I'm relieving you, Commodore."

Rae walked to the closest rail gate, located to the left outside the mission room. The rail system, consisting of tubular cars, would deliver her only minutes later at the school, which was situated between the residential and commercial sections of the station. *Gamma VI* could house 1,200 permanent residents—and four times that many including temporary residents in hotels and aboard moored ships.

Divided into three sectors—military, commercial, and residential—the station comprised forty-five decks and three major ports. Deck 1 hosted the mission room, with the commodore's office located in its center.

The commercial area boasted several shopping areas, which catered to trade between homeworlds. A multitude of restaurants offered a variety of cuisines from the different Supreme Constellations worlds. Hotels were prosperous, especially their casinos, since gambling had become legal five years earlier.

The residential sector's lower decks served as housing for the lower-ranking military staff and the permanent residents working in the private areas. Rae resided on Deck 3, and so did her XO and a few other senior staff members.

She stepped out of the car two stations and two minutes later, crossing an intersection full of people before she entered the school. Only seventeen children resided on the station, but occasionally generational ships would linger, and then Terence would work long hours to prepare lessons for them all. Right now the children, ages six to sixteen, were working in small groups at different projects.

She saw Terence waiting for her at the entrance, and he waved her over while he walked toward his office.

"What's up?" Rae asked when the doors to the inner room closed behind the two of them.

"Armeo arrived this morning with a security guard, and Dorinda and David immediately introduced him to the class. They're both his age, and he seemed thrilled and settled into their group easily." Terence scratched the back of his neck, a gesture Rae recognized as signifying his uneasiness. He looked regretful. "It's my fault, Commodore. I should have realized..."

"Go on." Rae wondered with increasing concern why the seasoned teacher looked so distressed.

"This particular group is studying trials and legal procedures in various parts of space. Since the six children in this group all belong to different homeworlds, they find this topic particularly interesting and were helping Armeo catch up when suddenly Dorinda came and got me." Terence paled and slicked back his thinning gray hair. "Armeo was sitting by the computer, shivering all over. For a moment I thought he was going to be sick."

"Oh, God. What was wrong?"

"Because he's quite intelligent and curious, he looked up the different punishments for the same crime on several worlds. When I saw the screen, I noticed he was reading about Onotharat's punishment for abduction and kidnapping. He must've figured out what his guardian is suspected of."

Icy fingertips tapped down Rae's spine. "And?"

"It's an ancient, barbaric law, and it's incomprehensible why any nation would cling to such cruelties. The punishment for these offenses is death by starvation."

Slumping into the teacher's chair, Rae felt her lungs cave in. Forcing oxygen back in, she steeled herself at the images her imagination sent flickering through her mind. "Are you sure about this?"

"Yes, ma'am. I double-checked while Dorinda took care of Armeo. He seemed to respond well to her, so I decided to keep him here until I spoke to you."

"I should have researched this, but I haven't had time yet," she said, angry at herself for not studying this case as meticulously as she usually did. "Damn."

"I know. It's unfathomable, ma'am. It also brings another question to mind."

Rae could read his mind. "Heavens, yes. Does Kellen O'Dal
know? And what will she do now that the boy knows?"

"I don't envy you having to deal with that." Terence regarded her
with kind blue eyes. "Will you take Armeo back to his guardian?"

"Yes, I have to tell her what happened." Rae rose from the chair
and looked through the window facing the classroom. "What's Armeo's
educational level?"

"He seems to be keenly interested in math and research. He's well
educated in all general subjects for his age. Whatever the circumstances,
Ms. O'Dal has provided him with a proper education. He's also polite,
with excellent social skills, and his sense of humor has struck a chord
with his peers. If we hadn't been studying this particular subject, he
would have probably enjoyed his first day at school thoroughly."

Pleased, Rae filed Terence's report away for future reference,
knowing Kellen would need all the plus points they could sum up when
M'Ekar arrived to claim him. Having provided Armeo with a good
education and appropriate social skills were important points in her
favor. "I'll return him to his quarters now. Thank you for contacting
me, Terence."

She found Armeo with his perpetual guard sitting on one side of
him and a girl with a long blond ponytail on the other. The girl was
gripping his hand and talking to him quietly. Looking up, she smiled
at Rae, her relief obvious. "The commodore's here now, Armeo. She'll
take care of *everything*. Don't worry."

Rae inhaled deeply at Dorinda's unreserved trust in her,
unexpectedly touched and hoping she'd never let the girl down. "Hello,
Dorinda. I'm going to escort Armeo back to his quarters. He'll be back
in class tomorrow, all right?"

"Yes, ma'am." The small, slender girl rose and stood close to Rae.
"He was very upset. Can you help them, Aunt Rae?"

Dorinda, the daughter of her closest friends, usually called her
Aunt Rae only when they were in private. The small slip betrayed her
genuine concern for Armeo. "I'll try, Dorinda. You've been a good
friend. I'll remember this."

Armeo was silent on the way back. Rae noticed that he looked
pale, which emphasized the faint bluish tone of his skin. When she
looked into his dark eyes, she could easily recognize his Onotharian

heritage in his oval-shaped irises, common among his father's people. More so, something new, a burning anguish, or perhaps anger, made his unusual irises sparkle.

"You would never let that happen to Kellen, would you?" Armeo suddenly said huskily.

His desolate tone, tinged with a futile hope, was almost more than Rae could bear. Unprepared for the emotions surging through her, she acted without thinking, taking Armeo's hand and squeezing it. Rae couldn't remember feeling this mix of tumultuous emotions ever before. The thought of Armeo fearing for the life of his guardian, the only mother he knew, stung deeply.

"I'm sorry you stumbled upon this information," she said, biting the inside of her cheek at how formal she sounded. "It's an awful punishment. I'll do everything I can to make sure this doesn't happen to Kellen."

"It shouldn't happen to anyone." Armeo scowled. "It's horrible. If I can return to Gantharat when I'm grown, I'll make sure it's forbidden."

A little perplexed at the boy's solemn tone of voice, Rae noticed that he didn't let go of her hand. Instead, he walked closer to her, and it took her a moment to diagnose the sudden ache in her heart as profound tenderness.

When they entered the living area, Rae released Armeo's hand and gently nudged him toward the bedroom door. He stepped just inside, lingering by the doorway. Rae stood back a little, out of sight. Kellen sat propped against the pillows with a computer close to the bed. Apparently deep in thought, she stared at the screen.

"Kellen…" Armeo's voice was barely audible; still the tall blonde flinched.

"Armeo? What's wrong?" Kellen made a move to get out of bed, but fell back onto the pillows with an expression of pain. Instead she reached out for the boy with both arms.

"Is it true, Kellen? Can they sentence you to death?" Armeo whispered, refusing to step closer. "Can they?"

For the second time, Rae watched brilliant blue tears rise in the other woman's eyes. Anger and distress were so transparent in her face, Rae was awed. If she had ever doubted the Gantharian's feelings for

Armeo, she now put those trepidations to rest, witnessing how quickly Kellen switched from the stoic aloofness she confronted everyone else with to being openly wracked by conflicting emotions in the boy's presence. "Please," Kellen whispered, "I don't know who told you this, but you have to understand that I couldn't share something so awful with you. You know it's my duty to protect you, child."

"I'm not a child anymore!" Armeo's voice was harsh. "I can deal with reality."

Kellen slowly lowered her arms. "Maybe…but maybe *I* couldn't. I couldn't face telling you this, in case it—"

"It's like lying, Kellen." Armeo's voice broke. "Not telling the whole truth is like lying."

Rae found it difficult to witness the pain in the other woman's eyes. The torment reflected something inside herself, a dull resonance from the countless times of being the one to make the hard decision and later be the bearer of devastating news. Unable to remain passive anymore, she moved into the room and rested her hand on the boy's shoulder.

"Armeo, calm down. Trying to protect the ones you love by not scaring them isn't lying. Surely you know Kellen would do anything to keep you safe and happy?" She glanced up at Kellen, who seemed frozen in place, her blue eyes the color of dark fjords. Still, it wasn't hard to distinguish the pain behind the frosty appearance.

Armeo went rigid under her hand. "Do they have a case against her? Can they do this to her…because of me?"

"I won't lie to you. Ambassador M'Ekar thinks he has a strong case against Kellen. He believes she kept you without having the right to do so."

"It's not true." Armeo whirled around and faced her with tears of fury in his dark eyes, his back ramrod straight, chin raised. "I was young when my mother died, but I *heard* her make Kellen promise to keep me when we sat with her at the clinic—several times. I heard it!"

Looking over Armeo's head, Rae saw that Armeo's words affected Kellen profoundly. She flushed a faint blue and clutched the bed linen, twisting the down-woven sheets as she apparently struggled for composure. Her obvious inability to harness the look of utter distress on her face pierced the layers of Rae's professionalism. Suddenly she felt a totally new urge to protect someone instead of something.

"Kellen, listen to me carefully," she said. "I know it's hard to stop once you start running. It's difficult to trust anyone. Something tells me this is what's going through your head right now. But if you stay, I'll do my best to make sure you get a fair trial. The ambassador may be powerful on Gantharat, but he's out of his jurisdiction here."

"You can't give me any guarantees," Kellen growled. "You heard. Armeo knows what will happen if I'm found guilty. The SC will extradite me to the Onotharian authorities, and they will force Armeo to go back to live with strangers. It goes against everything—and trust this: I will *not* go back on my word or disgrace my word of honor."

Letting go of Armeo, Rae walked up to the bed and sat down next to Kellen. "I hear you. However, you're under Supreme Constellations jurisdiction, and since this is a Gamma space station, special laws apply. If you want guarantees, you have only one option. Have faith in my advice, and Ambassador M'Ekar can't touch you."

Rae's mind reeled as she gazed at Kellen and tried to make sense of the unfamiliar emotions flooding through her. She wasn't sure what was going on and, automatically recoiling, she slipped back into the comfortable role of authority, distancing herself from her turbulent feelings. "If you go along with what I'm about to suggest, you and Armeo can never go back home. At least not for a long time."

Kellen wiped quickly at her wet cheeks. Her long hair hung loose like a golden cloud around her well-developed shoulders, and her thinlinnen shirt clung to her tall, lithe body. Temporarily incapacitated and obviously distraught, she still radiated a feline strength, her eyes relentless when she locked them on Rae. "What are you talking about? What would Armeo and I have to do?"

"Anyone who enters SC space, no matter their origin, can ask for political asylum. And until an SC court of law evaluates and resolves your situation, nobody can do anything to you."

"No, we can't…" Kellen began to object but stopped when Armeo walked up to the head of the bed.

Tears as clear blue as his guardian's welled up in his eyes. Taking deep breaths, he wiped moisture from his cheeks. "I'm scared, Kellen," he whispered.

"Come here." She hugged him tightly and rested her chin on his dark hair. "For now, we're safe, Armeo. We're safe." Lifting her gaze, she looked at Rae with shimmering blue eyes. "Let's say it was possible.

Where would we go afterward?"

"Once they grant you asylum, you can apply for citizenship among any of the homeworlds within SC."

Armeo stirred in Kellen's embrace. "Remember what you said when we left Gantharat?" he said huskily. "That we had burned our bridges and might never return. I have accepted it—for now. This could be our chance, Kellen. Listen to the commodore."

Rae could detect a tone of hope in the increased animation of his voice, and it stirred something old and forgotten, a longing for closeness with another person that made her almost dizzy as she tried to navigate around her rampaging emotions.

She decided to support Armeo by leveling with them. "You were right in your assumption, Kellen. With this threat hanging over your head, you can't return. Not now. But you and Armeo can still have a life and a future together." She hesitated, then placed her hand over Kellen's, wondering at herself for being so uncharacteristically spontaneous. "It just can't happen on Gantharat."

CHAPTER THREE

Jeremiah turned to face Rae when she entered the mission room early the next morning. "Commodore, we have a bit of a situation."

Another one. Go figure. "Report." She strode up to her next in command where he stood in front of a view screen.

"Ambassador M'Ekar still insists we allow his ships to approach the station. All twelve of them."

Rae snorted with contempt. "He must be mad. Doesn't he realize we'll enforce the laws? Request denied."

"It isn't that simple. As you know, the ambassador has connections in high places within the SC Council."

Leaning against a railing behind her, Rae glared at Jeremiah and felt her jaw tighten. "And he thinks this makes him exempt?" she huffed. "Not unless he has a declaration from the Council. But it does complicate our lives."

"We just finished the background research you requested. Perhaps the report contains some useful information we could use to persuade the ambassador to be more…diplomatic in his approach."

"Good idea." Rae led him into her office and motioned for him to sit. "Go ahead. Begin with Kellen and the boy."

"Kellen O'Dal graduated from the Gantharian Academy of Pilots with honors and moved to the countryside with her friend, Tereya M'Aido, the spouse of Zax M'Aido. A few months later Zax was killed in the line of duty, but the follow-up investigation was inconclusive. Around the same time, Tereya gave birth to Armeo, a Gantharian/

Onotharian hybrid. The two women stayed in the countryside and brought the boy up together until Tereya died in a vehicle accident when her son was five."

Jeremiah looked up at Rae, and she could tell from his pensive expression that he suspected something. "No one witnessed this accident, and the subsequent investigation was also inconclusive."

"Two parents gone, both of their deaths unexplained. Go on."

"Ms. O'Dal enrolled Armeo in a nearby school, where he did very well, especially in science and math. She's never tried to conceal his whereabouts."

"So far, everything she's told us checks out." Rae tugged a lock of her short red hair as if she were trying to uproot the truth. "Now, the ambassador. Why is he so interested in this boy? Are they related?"

"The ambassador's late wife was born a M'Aido. She was from a very wealthy family, with long-standing political connections. The M'Aidos have long served in the Onotharian government."

"Hmm. The ambassador could be using the M'Aido name to pressure us. Go on."

"M'Ekar's wife died seven years ago and..." Jeremiah looked up from the computer screen. "Quite a coincidence."

"Same year as Armeo's mother," Rae mused. "Interesting."

"Only four weeks later, actually."

Rae leaned forward on her desk. "Kellen risks capital punishment for running with the boy." She shook her head. "I can't believe she would do that unless she had a very good reason."

"The political complication is tricky. If M'Ekar circumvents your authority..."

Rae knew Jeremiah was right. If the Council decided to extradite Kellen, she would starve to death in a prison cell on Gantharat, away from the boy she'd raised.

"I need to discuss this with Kellen. I told her she'd be safe if she applied for asylum. Now I'm not so sure. The M'Aido name carries a lot of weight, and I'm sure the ambassador intends to use it."

Jeremiah nodded. "You can't let it happen, Rae."

"I wish I could think of an alternative solution." Rae closed her eyes briefly and pictured a scene with Kellen that she'd rather avoid. "I'll go talk to Kellen again. How about approaching one of the civilian lawyers? He might see things from another angle."

"Good idea." Jeremiah brightened, the corners of his eyes crinkling. "I have a friend in the new business section who just moved to the station. He owes me one, and he can keep a lid on things."

"Excellent. Report back soon." Rae rose from her desk.

Jeremiah rose also, but stopped halfway to the door. "By the way, about those ships…"

"I haven't forgotten. If the ambassador brings them into our space without proper documentation, he'll find a warm welcoming committee."

"In other words, you'll blow him out of the skies."

"Damn straight."

"So much for my career."

"Cheer up. It hasn't come to that yet. And you can always look back at your career and say it was short and eventful."

"Thanks, ma'am, I'll remember that," Jeremiah said with a pained expression.

Rae had to smile. "Dismissed."

Jeremiah walked out of the center office, leaving Rae to gather her thoughts. She didn't look forward to disappointing Kellen.

❖

Because Kellen's leg didn't hurt so badly, she could sit at the desk in the other room. However, her head was spinning from trying to absorb all the research she had done since four o'clock that morning, when she couldn't sleep. Armeo was back in school, having insisted on rejoining his new friends. Kellen was proud of how he'd bounced back.

A rattle came from the other side of the room, and the door hissed open. Commodore Jacelon stepped inside.

"Kellen, I'm glad to see you up and about. How's the leg?" She strode up to the desk and leaned her hip against it, her arms folded.

"Much better, thank you. Dr. Meyer was here an hour ago. She seemed pleased." The sight of the commodore made Kellen's stomach clench. Uncertain why the other woman spurred such a reaction, she forced herself to appear unfazed.

"Good. May I sit down?" Jacelon gestured to a chair next to Kellen, who hadn't realized it was up to her to grant the Gamma station's commodore the privilege of sitting.

"Forgive me. Of course."

Jacelon sat down, leaned back, and crossed her legs. "This morning Ambassador M'Ekar asked to bring his entire fleet of ships here, despite our laws."

"Surely he can't do that?" Kellen felt her tongue betray her as her mouth went dry. Licking her lips, she pressed herself hard against the backrest of the chair.

"Normally he wouldn't, but the ambassador may have some connections tied to the M'Aido name. His late wife was a M'Aido."

"I know. She was Zax's aunt. They had very little to do with each other because Armeo's father settled down and married on Gantharat. Zax's father was a colonel in the Onotharian space force." Kellen examined the impenetrable expression on Jacelon's face and suddenly recognized it as similar to her own reflection sometimes. At once she felt uneasy. "Something has come up, hasn't it?"

"Ambassador M'Ekar has a connection high within the SC Council and won't hesitate to use it." Jacelon leaned against the desk on one elbow. "I'm sorry, Kellen, for getting your hopes up yesterday. He might persuade the Council to extradite you even if you do apply for asylum."

A cold hand dug its nails into Kellen's heart, and sudden vertigo made her cling to the armrests of the chair. "Armeo would be devastated." She felt furious yet afraid. "I'm forced to beg, for his sake, Commodore. Can't you do anything?" Swallowing hard against the dryness in her mouth, she stared at the other woman and forced the next word over her lips. "Please."

"Yes, I can," Jacelon assured her. "I'll be damned if I'll turn over a woman and her foster son to someone out to destroy them, no matter who they are. Kellen, listen to me. Why is the ambassador so determined to get his hands on Armeo?"

"Armeo is the last in the M'Aido dynasty. He's the heir to all their assets, including a seat in the Onotharian government once he's old enough. The M'Aidos were almost royalty on Onotharat for centuries. When the family died out with Zax and his aunt, I knew the Onotharians would hunt Armeo down if they knew of his existence too early. I never meant to rob him of his inheritance, Commodore. I merely wanted him to be old enough to take care of himself before he claimed it."

During a brief silence, Kellen watched the different pieces fall into place in Jacelon's mind. "So if he were under the ambassador's influence, M'Ekar's power would increase…"

"Tenfold. More than tenfold."

The two women looked at each other in silence. "And any influence you have on Armeo is diametrical to the ambassador's interests." Jacelon nodded as if she was thinking carefully.

"Armeo deserves to grow up and be loved for who he is, not because of his heritage or his political usefulness." Kellen tried to rise from the chair, but the searing pain in her leg made her utter a muffled cry and lean forward, holding on to her thigh.

"Don't move," Jacelon ordered. "What did you do? Let me look at it."

Kellen glanced up at the other woman and saw nothing but concern in her eyes. "It's not necessary. I just moved too quickly, that's all." She dismissed her pain with disdain.

Jacelon apparently wasn't about to be rebuffed. "I know you're resilient, but don't turn down help when it's offered, Kellen. Let me see. You didn't tear it, did you?"

Her hands trembling, Kellen slid the loose-fitting retrospun cotton infirmary trousers down her hips, awkwardly leaning from side to side to get them off. Jacelon leaned over her and lifted the bandages to examine the wound on her upper thigh. The soft touch didn't surprise Kellen, who had felt how careful Jacelon was two nights earlier, but today it created a totally new shivering sensation that startled her, although it faded quickly.

"Oh, it looks much better. Did Gemma say when she would close it?" Jacelon smiled warmly up at her in a way that caused a faint echo of the shivers to appear.

"Tomorrow, probably, if it improves like it has been. She assured me it would be much less painful after the derma-fuser treatment."

"Gemma is wonderful at emergency medicine."

"She's a true professional," Kellen said as Jacelon covered the wound up again. "She's never made me feel like a prisoner, and she's very considerate of Armeo." Still surprised and suspicious of any perceived friendliness, Kellen had to admit the CMO had not made any untoward remarks or hinted at Kellen's situation as a prisoner.

Kellen found she missed the warm and careful touch when Jacelon let go of her after she helped her pull up her baggy trousers. Not counting Gemma's professional touch, no one had touched her like that for a very long time. *With care and kindness, but anyone can fake that.* She couldn't allow herself to relax around Jacelon. A commodore in the SC was only a short step away from a promotion to admiral. Playing Kellen for a fool, and using her, could be part of a career shortcut plan.

"Your status might change soon, since all the evidence so far backs your story. I know you don't have the freedom to roam the corridors, even if you could actually walk, but these quarters aren't so bad, are they?"

Looking seriously at Jacelon, Kellen wondered if she realized how eager to reassure she sounded. "These quarters are more than sufficient. It's a relief to be able to stay with Armeo and not be confined to the brig."

"That's what they would have done to you back at Gantharat or on an Onotharian prison asteroid?"

"You've heard of their prison asteroids?" Kellen was surprised that the commodore cared enough to find out about the harsh conditions of a subject nation.

"My lieutenant provided me with extensive research. I'm aware the asteroids orbit one of the moons, which in turn orbit Gantharat. The Onotharat penal system is appalling and nothing the SC Council condones. I guess that's one reason why Onotharat is not a full member yet. We have diplomatic liaisons, but that's all."

"I'm sure the Onotharians would see it as a political triumph if they could use the M'Aido name to gain membership. The ambassador has great ambitions."

"I'm starting to understand that. I'm going to—"

A distinct beep came from the communication device attached to Jacelon's shoulder. Pulling it to her lips, she spoke quickly. "Commodore Jacelon. Go ahead."

"Commander Todd here, ma'am. Are you free to talk?"

"Not quite yet, Commander. I'll let you know when I'm back in the mission room. Jacelon out."

Turning toward Kellen, Jacelon reached out halfway, only to let her hand fall back down again. "I'll have to go take care of this.

Hopefully Commander Todd has found something that will help your situation."

Kellen felt a mixture of emotions surge to the surface as she leaned back to regard Jacelon. She knew she had let her guard down more with this woman than she had done with anyone in a long time. She felt terrified, since it was too great a risk, and relieved at the same time to allow another adult to take charge, if only for a moment. "May I ask you something, Commodore?"

"Go ahead."

"I fired my weapons at you, and you had every right to be angry when you brought me aboard the station. Why do you go out of your way to personally assist us?"

Jacelon sat quietly for a moment. "A great injustice is in progress. One woman and a little boy against twelve spaceships. Armeo's testimony and your own, together with the facts my staff dug up. The barbaric capital punishment Onotharat employs. Armeo losing the person he sees as his parent. These things all play a role." Jacelon shrugged. "I can't sit idly by."

"This might cause you problems professionally. You may step on toes belonging to someone powerful."

Jacelon smiled, waving a dismissive hand in the air, an elegant gesture. "It wouldn't be the first time. Now, I have to leave. Get some rest and hurry up the healing process."

How utterly attractive she looks when her arrogance manifests itself like that. Kellen's foolish heart picked up speed at the sight of Jacelon's smile. She rebuked herself for being nearly taken in by a few kind words and a simple smile. The Onotharians were not this subtle. This woman also wanted to control her and Armeo. She was just using a different tactic. Kellen nodded, as if in submission. "Good idea. I'm tired."

As Jacelon helped Kellen raise her leg onto the bed, Kellen reluctantly absorbed the feeling of Jacelon's kind hands.

"Thank you, Rae," she murmured without thinking. Seeing the other woman's surprised look, Kellen bit her lower lip. "I'm sorry. Commodore."

"Don't worry about it." Jacelon's smile appeared again. "You can call me by my first name when we're alone, all right?"

"Thank you."

"Sleep now. I'll come by later."

As Kellen obediently closed her eyes, she heard the door close. Examining the possibility that the commodore might find a way for her and Armeo to stay together, she put her arm over her eyes and breathed deeply to relax. Jacelon's resourcefulness utterly impressed her, but she didn't reflect on her ingenuity or humane attitude. *The way she touched me, smiled at me...Why should it matter? Such things have never been important to me before and they aren't relevant now. If she's warming up to me—so much the better.* Kellen had spent the day devising several backup plans. Because her duty toward Armeo was all-important, she needed to be able to act immediately if she had a chance. She also had to regain her strength. As long as Jacelon thought she was incapacitated and grateful for any favor, Kellen would have the advantage.

Riding back to the mission room in the rail system car, Rae thought about her own reaction to Kellen's pain. When the alien woman cried out, Rae had almost jumped out of her skin and her chair to come to her aid. Her sudden urge to comfort Kellen unsettled her. Rae was used to keeping an empathetic and protective distance from the individuals in her care or under her command. This compulsion to erase anguish from a stranger's eyes, and to console a distraught child, was simply not her method of operation. Distracted, Rae stepped out of the rail car and headed for her office.

Wearing the SC fleet uniform for twenty-four years did not make it only her work. The fleet was her life. At one point, a dismissed lover had in frustration and anger told Rae that she wore her uniform around her heart as well.

For a few seconds, for the first time in years, I forgot about my uniform today. The notion startled her, making her lengthen her stride as she walked briskly toward the door where the security guard on duty called out, "Commodore on the bridge!"—an ancient tradition since the tall-ships era more than four centuries ago. Nodding to her crew, Rae entered her circular office, setting the aluminum walls to semitransparent. Still a little on edge, she wanted some privacy while she read her messages.

Several messages from official SC sources were flickering on her computer. But before she read them, she paged Jeremiah on a secure line.

"Todd here, Commodore."

"Report."

"I've spoken to my friend, who's an expert at civilian law when it crosses over to military law. He's not very optimistic about finding loopholes in the military law."

Rae bit back an impatient reply. "What does he suggest?"

"We switch our attention to civil law." Jeremiah's voice held an odd tinge. "My friend has one suggestion that can keep Ms. O'Dal and her foster son within SC space, but it's controversial."

"Go on."

"If she marries a citizen of a Supreme Constellations homeworld, she immediately gains citizenship, and with that comes SC protection and the right to try a custody case in any of the SC sectors."

Rae wasn't sure she'd heard the commander right. "You're kidding."

"No. But she has to act right away. If she stays more than a few days longer without getting married, she risks extradition. M'Ekar is pulling his strings with several of the Council members who want Onotharat to become a full member because of its natural resources."

"Damn. And Kellen is caught in the middle of this crap? How the hell do we solve this situation?"

A brief silence. "I think you have to tell her, Rae." Jeremiah's voice softened, and his use of her first name, unheard of during duty shifts, made it clear he knew how this situation troubled her.

"Yeah. I know. Of course, we'll have to prove the marriage is for real, not just a means to an end."

"Yes, it has to last more than five years. And the happy couple needs to live together during this time."

Rae tucked her hair behind her ears, something she'd done since her younger days when she was nervous or excited. "Any suggestions?"

"For potential spouses?" Jeremiah sounded surprised. "I could offer, I suppose."

"You're not serious?" Rae balked at the idea.

"She's one of the most stunning women I've ever seen. A man would be lucky to have such a wife." Jeremiah sounded way too serious for Rae to merely ignore him.

"You don't even know her. As far as I know, you haven't even talked to her once."

"The language of love is universal. I'm sure I could—"

"Jeremiah!" Rae groaned out loud at her next in command. She never could quite tell when he was joking. *Am I entirely devoid of humor? That's what Father always says.*

"Rae, I'm kidding. She's not really my type—too tough." Jeremiah laughed, which flustered and annoyed Rae.

"How droll, *Commander*."

Jeremiah stopped his needling. "How *do* we solve it, ma'am?"

"Are you sure this is her only chance?"

"Yes."

"All right. I'll take care of it. Send all the relevant documentation to my personal computer station."

Rae signed off and stared out the view port. Outside, vessels moored and debarked; people of all species and races went through *Gamma VI*, the last bastion between the SC and interplanetary space. As the highest-ranking military official, Rae commanded not only the station but also eight sectors of the surrounding space.

However, her usual burden of responsibility seemed easy compared to the current dilemma. No matter how hard it was to make clear-cut decisions involving the destiny of a multitude of people, she preferred them to her current emotional turmoil when dealing with Kellen O'Dal.

She watched a ship large enough to be a generational vessel dock with *Gamma VI*'s longest extendable tube. The captain was skilled at his job; the vessel gently made contact, and long cables emerged to hook themselves to the space station. Once the ship was attached, the crew and passengers could safely go through the bio-filter screening and enjoy what *Gamma VI* had to offer.

Rae's thoughts returned to her current situation. She was willing to bet a credit or two that the alien woman would try to escape once she learned of the limited options.

Rae couldn't put it off. It was time to discuss marriage with Kellen.

CHAPTER FOUR

Gemma ran her diagnostic scanner over the wound in Kellen's leg. After she punched commands into it, she said, "We can begin the preliminary procedures today. We'll start by fusing the torn muscle fascia."

"Thank you, Doctor." Kellen regarded Gemma with well-hidden disdain. She knew this woman was an accomplished physician, and it infuriated her to think how many people on Gantharat would never enjoy any sort of competent medical care. Instead, callous Onotharian doctors who'd been sent to Gantharat for crimes committed on their homeworld subjected them to rudimentary treatments. Many Gantharians suffered needlessly or died at the hands of these uncaring butchers.

Kellen wanted to object to Gemma's excellent therapy, feeling like a traitor to her people for accepting it. However, she needed to regain her health as quickly as possible to be able to care for Armeo. This would probably mean fighting her way off *Gamma VI* at the first opportunity.

"You'll still have to be careful, but you'll be able to move around much easier and with a lot less pain. The torn muscle worried me most, but the infection is gone. I'm surprised it cleared up so quickly."

"You have access to sophisticated medication." Kellen tried to keep the resentment out of her voice. "I noticed a difference after twelve hours."

"Great. All right, let's do this." Gemma reached for a small device attached to a machine next to her. "This is a deep-tissue fuser, and it won't hurt. You'll feel a slight tingle as it heals the torn muscle and then the fascia."

While Gemma moved the fuser just above the wound, Kellen leaned back, then felt faint warmth spread through her thigh.

"Just relax," Gemma said. "Good. That didn't take as long as I thought it would. At first I was afraid you'd need a transplant, which would have been difficult, since you and Armeo are the only Gantharians on board."

"And Armeo may not be a fit, since he's half Onotharian," said Kellen. "I'm grateful for your work, Doctor."

"Gemma."

"Gemma," Kellen repeated, faking obedience.

"One more day without treatment and you could have needed an amputation. Granted, with a prosthetic…" Gemma said. "Sorry, I shouldn't talk about worst-case scenarios that won't happen."

It was indeed a miracle that she and Armeo had reached SC space at all. Kellen closed her eyes and thought of their difficult space journey. She'd slept less than thirty minutes at a time and squeezed everything out of the old, rebuilt spaceship she and Armeo had outfitted back at the farm.

Kellen had installed a holographic device, able to display fake biosignatures and make it look like four more crew members were aboard. She barely hid a smile, remembering how surprised Commodore Jacelon had looked when Kellen and a young boy turned out to be the only ones on the *Kithanya*. Her eyes ablaze, the commodore had ordered the guards to escort them to the mission room.

Rae Jacelon was a fascinating enigma—unbending and intimidating when she ensured the safety of the space station and its inhabitants, compassionate and caring when Kellen least expected it. No matter the situation, she was always in command. The way she moved, poised yet forceful, fascinated Kellen. She thought of how she had leaned with casual elegance against the door frame the previous evening and gazed at Kellen with eyes that seemed both curious and all knowing. Kellen would never forget going toe to toe with her.

"They told me I'd find you here," a voice said, making Kellen snap her eyes open. Rae stood next to the gurney, as if Kellen's thoughts had summoned her there.

"Hello, Commodore," Gemma said, not taking her eyes off her task. "Almost done."

"Good. Is everything all right?"

Kellen wondered if her ears were playing tricks on her, or if the other woman's voice really did sound concerned. *Of course not. Why should she? I wonder why she's acting like this. I've given her nothing but trouble.* Watching the other women discuss her as if she weren't present, Kellen tried to interpret Jacelon's tone of voice.

"She's doing very well. We were able to start the procedure one day early."

"Excellent. I need to talk to you, Kellen, and it's urgent. I have some new information, and time is running out…"

Rae's communicator came to life with a loud beep, and Gemma looked up and stopped what she was doing.

"Jacelon here."

"Commodore, we have a Code H82. We need you right now." Commander Todd's voice was quiet, but urgent.

"Any new decrees from the Council?"

"No, ma'am, no new orders. We operate under standard rules and regulations."

"Good. On my way. Ready the destroyer and the frigates. ETD in fifteen minutes."

"Very good, ma'am. Todd out."

Rae turned to Kellen, her eyes a dull gray. "We have an emergency. Normally I wouldn't discuss it at the infirmary, but it concerns you. Gemma, how long before Ms. O'Dal is mobile?"

"Five minutes, to close the fascia and dress the wound."

"Good. It's important. I'll use your office in the meantime."

Rae disappeared and Kellen looked at the physician, uncertain what was expected of her. "Do you know what's going on, Doctor?"

"I can only guess. Code 82 means that someone's invaded our space."

"Why does this concern me?" Kellen asked, and the only plausible explanation hit her. "M'Ekar." The name chilled her like a wet blanket around her heart. *He's here for Armeo. And to throw me into an asteroid prison to wither away. Thank the Gods of Gantharat the doctor fixed my leg. It's time to get out of here. The commodore will be busy defending her station and won't have her eyes on me. This is our chance, Armeo.* She would have to find a way for them to reach the *Kithanya,* but she could deal with that once they were ready to leave.

"The commodore will take care of this situation." Gemma obviously supported her superior without hesitation. "There. Let's get this bandaged. I'll work on the skin tomorrow."

Kellen inhaled deeply as her stomach twitched. Was she going to be back here tomorrow, or would she be on her way to prison? Gemma and Jacelon's close association reminded Kellen that she and Armeo were alone on this base. These SC citizens had sworn their allegiance to Jacelon and the power she represented, which made Kellen the outsider, and this was yet another dangerous position.

Rae returned and quickly crossed the floor. "All set? Come with me." She helped Kellen off the gurney and looked her over with sharp eyes. "You okay?"

Carefully trying her leg, Kellen was delighted that she was once again able to put weight on her leg without any searing pain. "Yes."

"You need to change clothes." Rae glanced at the guard. "Take Ms. O'Dal back to her quarters and give her a neutral uniform. Gemma, make sure Armeo knows his guardian isn't here. Arrange for him to stay with someone he knows."

"Yes, Commodore."

"I won't leave without Armeo," Kellen objected, refusing to move. "I'm not going anywhere or changing into anything until you tell me what's going on." *And enough time to lose the guard, find Armeo, and leave before you guess my intentions.*

Rae had begun to walk toward the door, but now she stopped and whirled around with an impatient look on her face. "We don't have time," she said. "Ambassador M'Ekar has passed our outer markers with twelve of his vessels. He's violated SC law. I have to deploy the fleet and prepare for battle."

"Why do I have to be there?"

"You're the reason he's here, and you're in danger. I don't have time to explain the details yet." Rae's glance softened a fraction. "Trust me, Kellen. If you want to keep Armeo safe and in your life, you need to come with me now."

Rae's voice and her gaze were both steady, leaving no room for objections. Kellen examined every one of her reasons to remain suspicious of her motives and found them all valid. Nobody in authority had ever proven trustworthy in the past.

Still, another part of her, something buried deep within the rarely visited caverns of her soul, insisted Rae was what she seemed, trustworthy and protective. To Kellen's amazement, this persistent inner voice threatened to drown out her suspicions. She snapped her head back, her contempt still simmering. "Very well. I will do as you say."

"Be ready in ten minutes. See you at Port 1."

As Kellen changed into a plain SC military uniform, she made a disdainful face at herself in the full-length mirror, unaccustomed to wearing such attire. Like most Gantharians, she connected the practice of wearing a uniform with the Onotharian occupational forces.

She straightened the leathermix jacket. Her security guard had explained the materials, probably guessing how alien they were to her. The jacket's synthetic material felt soft against her fingers. The blue trousers were made of thermilon, able to keep their wearer comfortable regardless of outer temperature. Kellen stuck her feet into the knee-high, black leathermix boots outfitted with an auto-refreshing thermo-lining. She remembered with a smirk how the guard pointed out their self-cleaning feature. *Never anything but shiny boots in the SC fleet.*

Five minutes later, at Port 1, Kellen saw the docks filled with crewmen on their way to the ships.

Large portholes overlooked the vessels moored outside. The largest ship, a destroyer, was anchored to her left, and her guard guided her to the entry gate. "Kellen O'Dal is the commodore's guest," he said. "Permission to come aboard."

The ensign stationed at the gate checked his computer. "Affirmative. Permission granted."

The security guard checked his chronometer. "You have less than four minutes to report to the bridge, Ms. O'Dal."

Kellen was not unaccustomed to being aboard a tightly run ship and lengthened her stride, moving faster than her guard as they hurried through the gate and rushed down a corridor with transparent walls. They reached the ship's main door, where they repeated the procedure and once more obtained permission to come aboard. A tall, muscular woman wearing a security officer's insignia walked up to Kellen.

"Ms. O'Dal, I'm Lieutenant Owena Grey, chief tactical officer on *Gamma VI.* I have orders to escort you to the bridge. Come with me."

"Thank you."

Kellen followed the dark-haired woman through long corridors. All around her, crew members scrambled to reach their posts as one message after another boomed over the shipwide comm system. They saluted Lieutenant Grey with hurried movements, which she acknowledged with a brisk, "Carry on, please." Of the same height as Kellen, Grey moved with the pantherlike grace of someone trained in combat skills and the martial arts. She wore her black hair pinned up in a tight twist, and her uniform was immaculate. Her eyes were dark blue under black eyebrows and straight bangs. Sharp angles and planes helped form a strong, formidable face.

The bridge, on Deck 1, was controlled chaos. Ensigns manned the posts along the semicircular wall, standing behind computer consoles and talking in low voices into their communicators all at once. Lieutenants manned four more consoles within the outer circle. One was empty, and Kellen guessed it was Lieutenant Grey's post on the bridge. The main view screen on the far wall depicted the vast space outside *Gamma VI*.

Kellen took in the scene, listened to the intent voices, and felt the rising tension before battle. Suddenly taken back in time to her years in the Gantharian Academy of Pilots, she found it amazingly familiar to observe these people prepare as a team for the same goal. Once she had thought she would pretend to cooperate with the Onotharians and try to change the system from within. Her life had not worked out that way. Instead she had lost not only her chance to make a difference, but also everyone she'd ever cared about, except Armeo. A part of her connected now with the unique mix of exhilaration and dread that preceded a space mission.

"Three minutes to launch." A voice pierced through the conversation, and everyone scrambled.

The two command chairs sat on a dais between the four stations. Although a couple of lieutenants obscured her vision, Kellen recognized the voice the moment the woman occupying the chair spoke.

"Ms. O'Dal, ma'am." Lieutenant Grey rounded the consoles and approached the chair.

"Thank you, Lieutenant." Rae stood, stepped off the dais, and glanced at Kellen, while Lieutenant Grey assumed her duties at the vacant computer console.

"Can I help?" Kellen asked as the commodore approached. "After all, I am a pilot."

"That would be a breach of protocol, but how are your navigational skills?"

"Quite good, ma'am." Astounded at how easy she fell into the crisp military language, Kellen feared she sounded impudent.

She waited for Rae's disapproval, but to her surprise, Rae nodded. "All right. Join Ensign S'hos at the navigation console. He's as new as you are on the *Ajax*."

Kellen nodded. "Yes, ma'am." She noticed several officers furtively watching her when she walked over to the young man's station. Kellen wondered if they realized they were deploying because of her actions.

❖

Rae sat in the command chair. As the commodore of the *Gamma VI* Space Station, she did not have to captain destroyers herself, but she preferred to take the conn while in space.

"Our XO is aboard, in engineering. On our way, people. Release locks."

"Aye, ma'am. Locks away."

"Take us out, Lieutenant D'Artansis. Thrusters only."

"Aye, Commodore." The pilot punched commands into the computer and maneuvered the small joystick skillfully.

Rae watched her favorite pilot get to work. The young-looking Cormanian, Leanne D'Artansis, was a divinely gifted pilot who handled any vessel as if it were an extension of her slender arms. Her strawberry blond hair, secured by a SC Fleet–issued hairclip, ran like fresh water down her back and reached well below her shoulder blades. Rae knew every one of the pilot's peers loved and treasured her. Her laughter was contagious, and her glittering personality automatically drew people in. Leanne was rare—a truly kind person.

The *Ajax*, equipped with the best technology and weaponry the Supreme Constellations could assemble, glided by the six smaller frigates waiting to accompany the vessel on an intercept flight to Ambassador M'Ekar's fleet. Each frigate carried eight small assault craft, each manned by a pilot and a navigator.

"We've passed Gamma's outer perimeter, Commodore," Ensign S'hos reported.

"Very good. Wait for the frigates and go to half-impulse until we're at a safe distance, then field-distortion drive six."

"Aye, ma'am," Leanne replied smartly.

Rae checked the small computer console next to her chair. She still didn't see any new information from the Council. That meant Kellen was still safe but also that they were going into battle. Though Ambassador M'Ekar had insisted he had connections in high places, so far he hadn't produced a shred of proof.

"All frigates in position, Commodore."

"All right. Leap to field-distortion drive six."

Stars became streaks of light as the destroyer leaped to field-distortion drive. Rae felt a slight tremor reverberate through the vessel as the dynamic vibration absorber, the DVA, engaged. She glanced over at the navigation console. Kellen held a small computer and was making calculations. Ensign S'hos glanced over Kellen's shoulder, asking questions in a low voice. Rae hid a smile. She wasn't surprised Kellen had taken over and was in fact more knowledgeable than the young ensign. She watched Kellen demonstrate something to S'hos, earning a vigorous nod from him.

"How long before we reach our destination, Ensign S'hos?" Rae asked.

His yellow eyes shimmered. "Two hours and forty minutes, ma'am."

"Very good." She heard someone occupy the XO's chair next to her. "Good of you to join us, Commander Todd."

"Sorry, ma'am. The problems in engineering took longer than expected."

"You have the conn. I'll be in my office." Rae stood up and glanced at the view screen in front. "Page me when we're within range of the ambassador and his fleet."

"Aye, ma'am."

"Ms. O'Dal, join me in my office."

She walked across the bridge toward a door at the far end and waited as Kellen put the small computer down and followed her. Inside, she pointed toward the visitors' chair on the opposite side of the desk. "Take a seat. How's the leg?"

"Fine. I prefer to stand. Can you tell me now why I'm here? Have you changed your mind about me after all and intend to hand me over to M'Ekar?" Kellen stubbornly remained on her feet, which reminded Rae of their first face-to-face encounter.

She recognized the fear and anger behind Kellen's arrogant tone. Examining Kellen's posture, she sensed how uneasy she felt. Her blue-tinged fingers tapped against her thighs, and she seemed to be forcing herself to breathe evenly. It was as if all of her feelings simmered just beneath her skin, ready to erupt and cause havoc at a moment's notice.

"Please, do take a seat, Kellen." Rae watched Kellen finally relent after a few seconds. She sat down and carefully extended her injured leg. Rae joined her and sat down behind the desk. She wasn't quite sure why it felt appropriate to keep the piece of furniture between them. "And as for your question, absolutely not. That's the point of this whole display. M'Ekar is trying to place himself above SC law." She paused for effect. "*No one* is above the law. I mean to stop him. It's that simple. We're treating him as we would treat a pirate.

"The law is fascinating, with many facets. For instance, if Ambassador M'Ekar has connections within the Council and obtains supporting documentation, legally I would have to turn you over."

Kellen paled. "What?"

"Of course, there's usually a loophole. We have means to ensure you cannot be extradited, and if you have to stand trial, you could do so in an SC court of law."

"What do I have to do?" Kellen spread her hands in a wide circle that emphasized her words. "Just tell me, I'll do it."

Rae could tell Kellen had taken a leap into battle mode in one effortless moment. She paused, then said, "You have to marry a Supreme Constellations citizen and remain married for at least five years."

Kellen looked stunned. Her shoulders slumped, and a desolate expression spread over her paling features as she sank back into the chair. "It's hopeless, then," she murmured. "If he uses his connections, and he will, I won't stand a chance. Who would marry me? I don't know anyone within SC space."

Rae leaned forward, resting her elbows on the desk. She didn't see any blue tears yet, but she knew they weren't far away. Suddenly, she had a strong urge to keep them at bay no matter the cost.

"Commodore…Rae, please." Kellen's voice sounded raw with emotion. "Send me back to the station and give me access to my ship. Now. Armeo and I will have to take our chances. I can't allow M'Ekar to get his hands on Armeo and use him as his puppet. You know that!" Placing one hand over her heart, she reached the other one across the desk, palm up. "You've guessed what kind of man M'Ekar is. Armeo and I still have a chance to get away if you stall him. If it means running and hiding, I don't care. We'll just have to do it."

"No, you won't. I've brought a civilian judge on board the *Ajax*. You can get married right now, before we rendezvous with the ambassador. No matter what happens then, you'll be a SC citizen with all its benefits and obligations."

Kellen looked shocked. "But…who would marry me? I told you. I don't know anyone."

"Hear me out. You've met several people on the station, and of those people you've had the most interaction with me."

Kellen crossed her arms and leaned back in her seat. Rae could tell from her hardening expression that she still hadn't grasped what she was saying.

"With my occupation, I've never had time for, or wanted to form, a family unit," Rae said in a matter-of-fact voice. "However, it makes sense to do it now. Since no other suitor for you comes to mind, the most realistic option is that you become my wife."

CHAPTER FIVE

Kellen stood by the porthole in the commodore's office and watched the stars turn into silver streaks. Her inner turmoil had settled into a false calm, as if her life were that of a stranger.

Only a few weeks ago, she and Armeo had lived happily in the quiet countryside on a planet light-years from here. What twists of fate had taken the son of her heart and placed him in such danger? She had to be pragmatic. She and Armeo were fugitives, refugees at the mercy of strangers. Their life on Gantharat was over and her options limited. Rae's route offered the best possible outcome, but damn, the woman overwhelmed her.

The commodore's solution to her situation disconcerted Kellen, and an inner voice clanged, warning her not to trust Rae. *H'rea deasav'h!* The Gantharian curse flashed through her mind, relieving some of the pressure. *She's a member of the damn ruling class. High up enough in the hierarchy to have power over an entire sector. Everyone on Gantharat knows it's only a matter of time before the SC recognizes the Onotharat occupation. No matter how you look at it, she's part of all that!*

Kellen pressed her nails into the calloused palm of her hand, trying to remain collected. She had to play along; right now she had no options. *She's damn sure of herself, manipulating me this way. Well, two can play that game, Commodore.*

"Kellen, this is Judge Trijjani." Rae's calm voice broke her out of her reverie. Turning around, Kellen faced an extremely tall man dressed in a long black robe. His handshake was strong when he greeted her the traditional human way, and the gleam in his brown eyes was alert and observant.

"Ms. O'Dal, I'm glad to make your acquaintance," he said in a deep voice. "I believe we have an urgent ceremony to perform."

"So I understand." Kellen glanced at Rae, trying to judge what she was thinking. Rae merely nodded, her eyes darker than usual.

Turning her attention back to the judge, Kellen scrambled for something polite to say in Premoni. She had to prevent them from noticing her true feelings regarding this charade. Searching her brain, Kellen wanted to curse out loud when the alien language eluded her. She clenched her hands harder and attempted a common nicety, almost choking on it in the process. "Thank you for helping me...for..." This was not going well.

"For assisting us in this matter," Rae filled in, moving up to stand next to Kellen. "I have summoned two witnesses, as required, Your Honor."

"Excellent. I know we must hurry." Judge Trijjani walked over to the desk and placed a folder and an old scroll on it.

The door hissed open again and Lieutenant Grey entered, followed shortly thereafter by Commander Todd.

They exchanged formal greetings and shook hands with Judge Trijjani.

"Thank you for coming." Rae gestured for her crew members to stand by the porthole. "You are here to witness a legal procedure."

Kellen thought she detected a glimpse of understanding in Commander Todd's eyes when he shot her a look. Refusing to lower her gaze, she returned his glance with defiance. He surprised her by smiling and winking discreetly, which took her off guard, since she expected him, and everyone else around Rae, to disapprove.

"Let's begin," Judge Trijjani suggested. "Commodore, please stand in front of me and take Ms. O'Dal's hand."

Kellen and Rae moved in front of the impressive man, looking up at him. Kellen tried to remember all the objections to Rae's solution to her problem that she hadn't listed out loud yet. *We don't know each other. We're from different worlds. And we certainly don't love each other. And who knows what the commodore's agenda is.*

Kellen knew she should feel grateful for Rae's sacrifice, and she did, but her emotions were tangled as she tried to fathom Rae's real motives. Was she being absurdly overprotective? Would Kellen become a political pawn for Rae's future promotions? Or was she being what she seemed—caring and unwilling to let Kellen die a slow, agonizing death on an Onotharian prison asteroid?

Kellen had agreed to marry Commodore Rae Jacelon only because she had no other choice. She would be trapped in a loveless marriage for five years, but that was a small price to pay if it guaranteed Armeo's safety. Standing in front of the judge, she felt a hand claim hers. She refused to look at Rae but found she clung to the hand nevertheless. No matter how she distrusted the commodore, right now, she was her only solution.

The judge began the ancient ritual. "Dearly beloved, we are gathered here to join these two women in a civil partnership, the bond acknowledged and revered by the Supreme Constellations and all its inhabitants. They have agreed to form a family unit, forsaking all others and staying true to each other until life expires."

Kellen listened to the strange words, unable to take them in, aware only of the sound of her thundering heart. She was about to commit to a stranger, someone who'd hauled her in like a common space thug. To spend five years in this woman's presence, acting to the world like her spouse, seemed undoable. Her throat constricting, Kellen held on to Rae's hand with ice-cold fingers. She wanted to yell to the friendly judge to stop, it was all a mistake and they could find another way. But it was too late for objections. It was time to repeat their vows.

"Rae Jacelon, do you take Kellen O'Dal to cherish and care for, as long as you both shall live?"

"I do."

"Kellen O'Dal, do you take Rae Jacelon to cherish and care for, as long as you both shall live?"

Kellen flinched, her voice betraying her. Rae squeezed her hand and forced her to focus.

"I do."

"You have now, in the presence of these witnesses, agreed to the terms of matrimony. By the power vested in me by the Supreme Constellations Council, I hereby declare you partners in life. You are now responsible for each other and obligated to pursue mutual happiness. All worldly assets are now your common property. You may embrace."

Startled, Kellen turned to Rae, who smiled. "It's tradition." She leaned forward and placed a soft kiss on Kellen's cheek. "Now you."

Oddly comforted by the small caress, Kellen allowed the feeling of Rae's lips on her skin to warm her just like kisses from loved ones had done in the past. Finally able to take an unlabored breath, Kellen turned her head and kissed Rae's cheek.

"Congratulations to the both of you." Commander Todd said. "May I call you Kellen? I'm Jeremiah."

She nodded, dazed at how quickly everything had transpired. Unable to take in the fact that she was now married to a woman who was little more than a stranger, Kellen refused to let go of Rae's hand when she felt Rae tug on it. Their connection seemed the only thing of substance at the moment.

Owena Grey joined them. Radiating strength, she extended her hand, first to Rae and then Kellen, who reluctantly let go of Rae's hand. She recognized the calluses on the outside of Lieutenant Grey's hand and wondered if Owena's training equaled her own. The lieutenant moved with controlled force, even in this private setting.

"Ms. O'Dal, Commodore, congratulations. I hope you will be very happy." Owena's intense blue eyes examined them but revealed nothing.

"Thank you, Owena. We'll do our best." Rae checked the time on the computer screen on the wall. "We don't have long before our rendezvous. Return to your stations." Turning to the judge, she gave him a warm smile. "Thank you for joining us on this mission, Your Honor. You better return to your quarters now. Things might heat up soon."

"My pleasure, Commodore. I just need you to sign the scroll, please. Ms. O'Dal as well. I'll register your marital status on my computer as soon as I'm back in my quarters."

Kellen took the proffered pen, made of titanium and sculpted like a bird's feather, and signed her name, watching Rae do the same in unfamiliar letters as the ink sizzled against the paper, scorching it. Judge Trijjani rolled up the scroll, gathered his belongings, and left after once more wishing them well.

Todd and Lieutenant Grey returned to their duty stations, leaving the two women alone in the office. For a moment it looked like Rae didn't know what to say.

Hoping to avoid another awkward moment of losing her voice, Kellen reached out and took her hand. "Thank you," she murmured, determined to hide her mixed emotions of gratitude and resentfulness.

Armeo was one step closer to safety, but the feeling that Rae had maneuvered her into a situation not of her choosing lay like smoke over Kellen's soul. "You have sacrificed five years of your life with two words and a signature."

"Let's look at this more optimistically, Kellen. Our marriage is one of convenience, but we can get to know each other and be friends. You're younger, and if you think about it, you may have sacrificed more than I have. You might have found someone to love. After all, you're very beautiful." Rae seemed uneasy and freed her hand.

"All I care about is Armeo's happiness and safety."

"And your own happiness?"

"It's secondary. If Armeo's happy, I'm content." Kellen clasped her hands behind her back, regretting her harsh tone of voice. Rae was obviously trying to bridge the gap between them. "I would like to be friends, though."

Rae leaned against the desk, arms folded over her chest, and Kellen wondered if the reality of signing away five years of her life had struck the commodore as it had her. "Let's try for that, then. But right now, it's time to offer our warmest welcome to the ambassador."

❖

The ambassador's cruiser, surrounded by six destroyer-class vessels and five frigates, floated motionless, apparently waiting for the SC fleet.

"Comm channels. Audio on," Rae ordered.

"Go ahead, Commodore," her operations officer said.

"Onotharian vessels, this is Commodore Rae Jacelon of the *Gamma VI* Space Station. You have unlawfully violated Supreme Constellations space. If you fail to rectify this infringement, we will view it as a hostile act and deal with it accordingly. Over."

A short silence filled with faint static permeated space.

"Commodore, there is no need for these hostilities. This is Deputy M'Indo, Ambassador M'Ekar's aide. The ambassador has permission to enter SC space with as many of the Onotharian fleet as he chooses."

"Do you have proof of such a claim?"

"The ambassador's good name and well-known connections in the SC Council should be proof enough." M'Indo's supercilious tone indicated that this assertion should be obvious. "We take offense to your attitude, Commodore."

Unimpressed, Rae sighed inwardly at the little man's pomposity. "Deputy M'Indo. Turn all but two of your ships back to the outer border immediately or I will be forced to take actions against you and your fleet. You have one minute to comply."

"Commodore, they're charging their weapons," the tactical officer said.

Rae gestured to the ops officer to cut the audio. Using voice command, she opened the comm system for the SC fleet. "*Gamma VI* vessels, this is your commodore. Man your stations and prepare to engage the enemy. Deploy fighters and raise shields. Do not fire. Confirm."

"The fighters are deployed and shields are up," Owena acknowledged from her work console.

"Stand by for Tornado Alpha attack maneuver on my mark."

"Standing by," said Owena.

"Deputy M'Indo. I wish to speak to the ambassador or the commander of your fleet immediately. Take your weapons systems off-line and begin to redeploy ten of your ships out of this airspace."

"They're not responding, Commodore."

Rae watched with astonishment as the ambassador's cruiser opened fire. "Mark!"

The SC fleet established a *V* formation with a destroyer in the lead, the frigates and assault craft taking up the flanks, and the *Ajax* falling back to assume the command position.

The *Ajax* reeled from explosions around it. Rae felt her vessel lurch underneath the soles of her boots. "Evasive maneuvers!"

"Aye, ma'am. Evasive maneuvers, Tornado Beta," Leanne replied. Punching in commands and handling the joystick as if it were a plaything in her hands, she threw the *Ajax* into a spiral dive, avoiding the torpedoes fired by one of M'Ekar's frigates.

Rae's eyes never left the screen. "Damned Onotharians! What are they trying to do? Start a damn war?"

Ten or more of her assault craft engaged the ambassador's cruiser, skillfully avoiding its antispacecraft defense systems. It took them three daring rounds before holes in the hull appeared in the lower decks. Two SC frigates moved in from the left flank, firing torpedoes at one of the Onotharian destroyers.

"Their shields are down to sixty-five percent," said Lieutenant Gray.

The *Ajax* shook from a series of explosions. Rae clung to the armrests of her chair as she glanced over at Kellen. Her new wife held on to the navigational console and fed it commands at a furious pace. "Damage report!" Rae barked.

"Shields down to eighty-five percent. Hull microfractures on Decks 6 and 7. No casualties," Jeremiah read from his computer console.

"Good. Work on the shields. This is far from over and we're going to need them." Rae raised her voice. "All right everyone, look sharp. The *Infinity* will start attacking their rear while the rest of the force attempts to flank them—a Tornado Epsilon attack formation. We'll begin when the *Infinity* initiates its attack."

"Yes, ma'am," Owena responded. "All ships have acknowledged and are standing by."

The Onotharian vessels were attempting to retaliate, but their assaults were disorganized. When the *Infinity* and the *Ajax* pressed the advantage and managed to divide the alien forces in half, the Onotharians couldn't regroup.

The *Infinity* opened fire, engaging one of the frigates.

Rae activated voice command. "All SC vessels, commence Tornado Epsilon."

"Aye, ma'am, Tornado Epsilon," Leanne confirmed.

The assault craft encircled the Onotharian ships. The rest of SC fleet began to envelop the intruders from above and below, firing in intricate patterns from port and starboard cannons. The Onotharians' erratic defense made Rae wonder if they were having a communications failure or were merely incompetent.

Suddenly a large explosion and a blinding flash of light filled the screen.

"Report!"

"Our frigates just destroyed one of the Onotharian vessels," Owena answered.

"How's the rest of their fleet doing?"

"Less than fifty percent combat-effective."

"Enough of this stupidity. Have the fighters lock onto their shield emitter and weapons. I want them incapacitated." Rae watched as the Onotharian vessels scattered, obviously trying to avoid the attack of the smaller craft, only to be confronted by the larger ships of her fleet.

The *Ajax* approached M'Ekar's cruiser.

"Firing torpedoes, full volley." Owena's voice sounded calm as she performed her task.

Searing through space, the torpedoes tore at the diminishing shields of the cruiser.

"The cruiser's shields are down."

Rae rose from her chair. "One more time. Target their weapons again."

They all watched a large gaping hole form in the aft of the cruiser.

A panicked voice came across the communication array. "Deputy M'Indo to Commodore Jacelon. Cease fire. Cease fire."

"Tell your ships to stand down at once, or I will continue this fight."

"All Onotharian vessels stand down."

Rae punched her communication console. "*Gamma VI* vessels, this is your commodore. Cease fire. Remain on red alert and stand by. Confirm. Jacelon out." She paused for a moment. "Tell me, Deputy M'Indo. Are you and the ambassador in charge of these forces? Are you the senior personnel on the scene?"

"Yes, we are."

"Then by the powers of the Council, I place the two of you under arrest. Prepare to be boarded."

"You cannot arrest us! We enjoy diplomatic immunity and have obtained special permission from the SC Council to approach the *Gamma VI* Space Station with the forces we deem fit to carry out our mission. I have the documents here. Transferring them now, as well as our credentials."

Biting back a curse, Rae watched the documents in question appear on her and Jeremiah's computer screens.

"Deputy M'Indo, you and Ambassador M'Ekar might, and I do mean might, enjoy diplomatic immunity for the moment, but your fleet does not. It lost that standing when it opened fire on my vessels. Your actions were an act of aggression, if not an act of war, but I leave that to the Council to decide."

"How dare you! It was you who forced us to act in our defense. We will see how your superiors react when they learn how you handle such a minor border skirmish. Of course, Ambassador M'Ekar might be willing to forget the entire matter if you turn over Kellen O'Dal and Armeo M'Aido."

Rae shook her head at his choice of words. She had to hand it to him; M'Indo didn't waste any time.

"Onscreen," she ordered, and the image of Ambassador M'Ekar's aide appeared in front of them. "That last explosion must have left you delusional. I am in charge of this battle space on behalf of the SC. You obviously do not understand your situation at the moment."

"And neither do you."

"I will not hand over anyone, let alone Kellen O'Dal and her foster son, to you."

"You have to. SC law is clear on that point."

Rae found it almost amusing at how conveniently the deputy now quoted SC law, when only moments ago, he had blatantly ignored it with his unlawful approach.

"I *am* following the law. Unlike you and the ambassador, I *always* follow it—to the letter. Kellen O'Dal stays here and, until an SC court settles the custody issue, so does the boy."

Deputy M'Indo seemed to waver for a moment at her confident tone. "You can't do this! SC law states you must carry out this extradition immediately."

"Pretty hard to carry out extradition when you don't have a ship to stand on, so to speak. Better talk to the captain of your vessel and check out your fleet. You'll find you're not going anywhere unless it's in my custody."

"Of all the—"

"While you're at it, check out your computer screens and reports for the message I'm about to send you about Ms. O'Dal. You'll find it a fascinating read."

Growling orders to someone offscreen, M'Indo shot Rae a disdainful look while he drummed his finger on the console in front of him. "If this is another one of your tricks, Commodore..."

"I don't know what tricks you could possibly be referring to. As I said, legal and aboveboard."

A crew member walked up to the deputy and mumbled something inaudible. Slowly raising his eyes to look at Rae, M'Indo snarled. "You married her! A marriage of convenience, so you can get your hands on a boy who is not of her blood. We will contest this," he spat.

"You can try." Rae realized she sounded more casual than she felt. "Kellen is now my wife and enjoys all the benefits and obligations of SC citizenship. Armeo will stay with us while an independent court, which the ambassador cannot intimidate, coerce, or otherwise manipulate, will try the custody case. You should point out to your boss that he will not have diplomatic immunity when the trial starts. He will be merely one of the parties involved, unless he's serving time for this fiasco. Check the SC law book again and you'll see I'm right. That's called equality under the law."

Rae glanced at Kellen, who stood next to Ensign S'hos, her hands clasped behind her back, a stance Rae had come to interpret as her way of keeping composure. She looked into brilliant blue eyes and, before she could analyze her own intentions, she reached out. "Kellen?"

Her wife shook her head and looked dismayed, perhaps at having to face an Onotharian, but walked across the bridge to stand next to her. Placing her arm around Kellen's waist, Rae looked steadily at M'Indo. "My fleet is standing by to assist in the rescue-and-recovery efforts. I will validate those that cannot make it back to Onotharian space safely and approve their docking at the space station for medical and repair assistance. We will escort the rest of your fleet to the border."

"You will be sorry for this," M'Indo replied, but he sounded shaken.

"It might take your ship a while to go anywhere," Rae informed him. "Seems it needs a great many repairs. I would prefer, since you profess to have diplomatic immunity, to deal with the senior officer in charge. That way we will have no misunderstandings. Jacelon out."

When she'd cut communications, she looked at Kellen with concern. "Are you all right? How's the leg? You're trembling."

"My leg's fine. It's just adrenaline."

Rae squeezed her arm. As she turned her attention to the officers on the bridge, she smiled faintly. "Thank you all for a successful mission, and for keeping *Ajax* and the other vessels intact. Let's go back to *Gamma VI*. Commander Todd, you have the conn. Make sure enough frigates remain to assist. I'll be in my office. Kellen?"

The newlyweds walked across the bridge to the office, where Rae finally let go of her spouse so she could enter it. After striding over to the porthole, Kellen turned around, her face serious.

"Commodore...I mean, Rae...we have to talk."

CHAPTER SIX

Rae sat down on the corner of her desk, her outstretched hands on her lap.

Kellen regarded her, trying to grasp that this dynamic human was now her wife. "You should know some of the things that happened when Armeo and I escaped from Gantharat."

"Go on."

Kellen slowly exhaled. "The men, the ones the ambassador sent, I believe they had orders to destroy any evidence regarding my custody claim. Armeo and I ran for the spaceship. It was well hidden in the barn, which I had outfitted with hydraulics to open the roof. When we took off…they were burning down the house, the stables, everything."

Rae rose and walked up to her. "They killed your animals?"

"Yes, without hesitation. I'm a coward. I haven't told Armeo the truth about that yet." Kellen slid her hand along the transparent aluminum in the porthole. "But this is secondary to something else I've kept from him. When we blasted through the half-open roof to the barn, it was already ablaze. If it had been a regular barn, we would have died in the fire."

Rae's eyes hardened, turning slate gray. "In other words, M'Ekar ordered you both to be eliminated. He's trying to get his hands on Armeo, but if that fails, he's not above murder."

"That was my deduction also."

Rae cupped Kellen's chin, turning her face toward her own. "Was that why you blasted my vessel with everything you had when we ran into you?"

"I can't trust anyone." Kellen found the words hard to say now that she felt a burning hope for the first time in years that they weren't true anymore. "M'Ekar has many allies."

"You're wrong on the first one. You can trust me. I'll do my best to keep you and Armeo safe."

"You don't understand," Kellen murmured huskily. "I will not risk Armeo. If I ever have the opportunity, I'll deal with M'Ekar myself. He's a dead man."

Rae grabbed Kellen by the arms. "Now you listen to me. You will *not* go off like a loose cannon. We are fighting this man by the book. We will battle him in a court of law, not by becoming exactly what you're accusing him of."

"He will stop at nothing! If Armeo is dead, all the M'Aido estate will go to M'Ekar. Or if he has Armeo at his mercy, he will control it through the boy," Kellen growled. "I cannot let this happen."

"I know. It won't, but you're going to have to trust me and do this my way—by the law." Rae gently shook her by the shoulders. "Give me your word."

Her jaw squarely set, Kellen did not avert her eyes. "I can't lie."

"I'm not asking you to lie. I'm asking you to trust me and the plan we've set in motion."

Kellen stared into Rae's uncompromising eyes, and her heart contracted painfully. She realized Rae meant every word. "It's a lot to ask." She drew a trembling breath. As far as she knew, Rae had been honest in every instance since they met. *Or is that what she wants me to think? For all I know, she could be paving the way for more far-reaching plans than keeping Armeo and me on the station.*

The commodore was obviously using her resourcefulness, together with her strong claims that she was doing what was right, to reassure Kellen, but she might also be keeping herself open to other options. *She doesn't strike me as an opportunist, but what do I know? Her strength is obvious and may well turn against me at a moment's notice. Right now she's dangling Armeo's well-being before me. Very well. I'll play along for his sake.*

"Your actions speak in your favor," Kellen said. "I will do as you suggest. For now."

"All right. Fair enough." Rae released Kellen's shoulders. She opened her mouth to speak, but the comm system interrupted her.

"Bridge to Jacelon. Onotharian casualties coming in."

"On my way." Rae walked toward the door and glanced over her shoulder. "Are you coming? If your leg isn't hurting too badly, we can use an extra pair of hands."

Though the idea of helping Onotharians repulsed her, Kellen found herself nodding in agreement. "Of course."

As much as she resented the people they were about to help, being alone with her jumbled thoughts didn't appeal to her. In fact, being alone even under close surveillance made her uneasy in a way she could not explain. For some reason she knew she would feel safer if she remained close to her spouse.

❖

The cruiser docked at the brightly lit port, and medical personnel and crewmen scurried to assist the injured. Kellen observed from the porthole in Rae's onboard office as more than twenty wounded Onotharians were carried off the *Ajax*. Kellen had watched Rae oversee their care en route for *Gamma VI* before a security guard had escorted her back to the commodore's office an hour ago. Rae had joined her shortly before the *Ajax* reached the station.

"What happens now?" Kellen murmured. "Armeo doesn't know anything. I have to prepare him, even if our arrangement is one of convenience and won't affect us on a daily basis."

Rae looked surprised. "What do you mean, won't affect us? Didn't you understand what I explained?"

Uncertain what Rae was referring to, Kellen mentally reviewed the tumultuous day. "Obviously not. I thought Armeo and I would return to my quarters, like before."

"No, you have to go pack immediately." Rae checked her chronometer. "It's early in the morning. Armeo will join us when he wakes up. You can talk to him then."

Kellen wasn't sure she liked where this was going. "Pack? Explain. I don't understand."

Rae rubbed the base of her palms against her eyes, suddenly looking fatigued and impatient. "You and Armeo need to stay with me in my quarters. We have to live together for five years, as spouses, sharing everything. Ambassador M'Ekar won't hesitate to use any sign of fraud against you."

Kellen flinched. She hadn't thought of that. The idea of five long years under the same roof as Rae gave her a feeling of *tindras* in her midsection. "So it's not enough we're married on paper? I have to stay in your quarters and pretend to…"

"You don't have to pretend anything." Rae's eyes took on a frosty expression, going from soft gray to dark ice. "We'll live in the same household, but you can rest easy, because I'm rarely there. I'm on duty around the clock."

Taken aback by the coldness in her so-called spouse's voice, Kellen forced herself to take a deep breath. "I'm sorry. I don't mean to sound ungrateful, but everything has happened so quickly. I really appreciate your sacrifice for me…and Armeo. I'll try not to disturb your routine."

Rae glared at her. Then her expression changed, and she surprised Kellen with a slight smile. "And raising Armeo, a child who needs to feel safe and wanted by both parent figures, can you guarantee he won't disturb me?"

"He's polite, with good manners…Ah. You are being facetious." Kellen returned the sharp look. The unexpected case of nerves increased at Rae's smile.

"I am. I'm sorry. I know we have a lot to work out. But facts remain. We have to make this work. Talk to Armeo when he wakes up and explain the situation to him. If you wait, he'll hear it from somebody else first. News travels fast on a station."

"Is that an order, *Commodore*?" Kellen asked pointedly. "I do not foresee a happy marriage if you regard me as a subordinate. My parents' marriage was one of equals. They shared each other's lives, and neither of them outranked the other."

Rae bit her lower lip, as if pondering what to say. She studied Kellen for a moment, then visibly made a new effort to communicate. "I meant it as a suggestion. Speaking as if I'm giving orders is an occupational hazard. I didn't intend to boss you around."

Kellen's attitude mellowed at Rae's slightly awkward statement, and she donned a cautious smile. *I have to think before I speak. I can't afford to alienate her.* "Apology accepted. And you are correct about informing Armeo immediately. Rae…" Calling the commodore by her first name would take some getting used to. "If you have time, would you accompany me? It would make more sense to Armeo if he sees us together. He's a child, and he can't know the truth."

Rae dug white teeth into her lower lip. "Damn it, you're right. If he told anyone this was a marriage of convenience, we'd be in trouble. As much as the ambassador may suspect it, he has to have proof or a living witness to testify to it. We can't ask Armeo to lie."

Kellen leaned back against the bulkhead. The vast number of details and potential traps to keep track of was making her dizzy. Something similar to regret permeated her, and she held out her right hand, palm up. "I'm sorry I've caused you so much grief."

Rae's expression softened. "Our paths are shifting, taking us to unexpected territory," she mused. "I admit, a few days ago I didn't expect to suddenly gain a beautiful wife and a son. All things considered, I know several people who would envy me." She gave a wry smile. "The very same people would also offer you their condolences."

Not sure what she was referring to, Kellen only nodded. "I want you to know, I *am* grateful."

Rae placed a hand on her shoulder. "People know we just met. They won't expect us to be too romantic right away. We have time to ease into that kind of display."

"Armeo will be observant enough to notice that we don't treat each other romantically," Kellen said. "That curiosity of his is going to make him want to know how and why we married so suddenly."

"Then we'll have to come up with something."

"And quickly," Kellen agreed.

As she looked down at her new wife, Kellen saw strength combined with something else that intrigued her—an aura, an indescribable essence. The woman she had just married carried herself with authority and a rare presence. In some ways, she reminded Kellen of her father. Rae met her eyes the way he did, head-on, never wavering. The way Rae expressed her viewpoints, in almost the same manner as her father, comforted Kellen. Her father's frankness and Rae's blunt, yet kind, approach seemed woven from the same unbreakable *paeshna*-silk filament.

"We'll tell him we fell in love at first sight." Speaking on impulse, Kellen felt her cheeks get warm. "He'll understand we had to marry quickly because of his and my situation, but he'll think we did if for ourselves if we tell him it was…love."

To her surprise, Rae tossed her head back and guffawed. Feeling discouraged by her mirth, Kellen opened her mouth to take back what she had said.

"Brilliant," Rae said. "Now, anyone looking at you wouldn't have any reservations. But they would certainly wonder how you could instantly fall in love with me. It's the best explanation we have, though, so we'll go along with it. Love at first sight it is." She checked the chronometer and motioned toward the door. "We better go."

Feeling light-headed, Kellen followed the commodore onto the bridge where Commander Todd was getting ready to leave. As she leaned against the bulkhead by the elevator, she tried to find her bearings while the two senior officers spoke briefly to each other. She had never been anything but honest with Armeo. How was she supposed to pull off such a blatant lie?

❖

Rae would rather have faced any armada of space vessels in combat than stand in front of Armeo with Kellen.

"Did the mission go well, Commodore?" he asked, sounding interested. "The kids in school talked about it."

"It did. In fact, it went very well."

"I heard a lot of people were wounded. Did anybody die?" He looked concerned.

Rae gestured for all of them to sit down in the living room. Armeo sat on the couch beneath the porthole, and Kellen started to join him, but caught herself and took a seat next to Rae on the other couch.

"Some of the Onotharians were killed," Rae said. "They lost one of their ships."

"The Onotharians." Armeo seemed lost in thought, then said, "I don't want anybody to die, but I wish they would leave everybody alone. They shouldn't be on Gantharat, for instance. And I bet they'd take over more worlds if they had a chance."

Impressed with the boy's compassion and insight, Rae responded, "You seem to dislike the Onotharians a lot, but you're half Onotharian yourself."

"My grandfather was a colonel in the Onotharian occupation, and my father was a starship pilot in the Onotharian fleet, but I don't feel Onotharian. And at times I've almost wished I weren't. The kids in my old school used to tease me for being a hybrid."

Rae felt Kellen flinch next to her. "What did you do about that?" she asked.

Armeo seemed to consider his answer, tilting his head. "I told them we don't choose our parents, but if I could have, I wouldn't change a thing."

Rae smiled at the young man, delighted with his keen mind. Clearing her throat, she glanced at Kellen. "We, your guardian and I, have some news for you. You may find it a bit sudden and startling, even…"

"Are we going back to Gantharat?" Armeo did indeed look startled. "Oh, please, Commodore Jacelon, don't make us leave the station."

"You don't want to go home?"

"If things could be just like before, but they can't, can they? Those men will always be after us, and they want to throw Kellen in prison and kill her." His lips trembled, and Rae had to remind herself he was actually younger than he looked.

"Well, you don't have to worry, Armeo, because you're not going back to Gantharat. You and Kellen are going to stay here with me."

The boy seemed baffled. "You mean here?" He looked around the spacious quarters.

"Yes. When Kellen joined me on the mission last night, we had a judge perform a ceremony." Rae dug deep for much-needed courage. "Kellen is my partner now. We're married."

Armeo's jaw sagged. "Married?" His eyes grew wide, and he turned sharply to Kellen. "Is this true?"

"Yes, it is. Rae and I were married on the *Ajax*. Apart from the witnesses, you're the first to know." Kellen squeezed Rae's hand between them on the couch as she told the white lie.

"But why? Why would you marry someone you hardly know?"

"I fell in love with Rae the moment I saw her," Kellen said in such an effortless manner Rae felt as if her heart took a detour to her mouth before it raced back to her chest. "Marrying her also helps protect you and me, so we decided not to wait."

"What about what I wanted?" Armeo jumped up from the couch and stormed over to the porthole. "Why didn't you tell me before you left? Don't we tell each other everything?"

Rae wanted to reassure him but knew this was up to Kellen.

"I didn't know of the possibility then, Armeo," Kellen said, her voice infinitely soft. "I would have told you if I could. When I heard about this unexpected solution, I seized the opportunity, and so did Rae. Sometimes you don't need to know someone very long to realize she's right for you. Still, Rae and I understand we have to familiarize ourselves with each other. We'll stay with her here on the station, you'll go to school with your new friends, and I'll make myself useful somehow."

Locking a steadfast gaze onto Rae, Armeo asked, "And why did you marry Kellen, Commodore?"

Rae found it impossible to lie to the boy, so she took a different approach. "I found something in your guardian that I haven't found in any other person. Courage, loyalty, beauty, intelligence, all wrapped up in one very special person. I wanted her, and you, to be safe. With all this in mind, I offered Kellen marriage. She agreed, and since everything happened so quickly, we'll have to slowly learn more about each other. You're an important part of this new family, Armeo."

Several expressions chased each other over the boy's features. His normally smooth forehead wrinkled, and his perfectly chiseled lower lip disappeared under his top teeth. Rae studied him closely, hoping he'd concluded this was worth pursuing. Since she didn't know him very well, she could not read his true feelings from his expression.

With hesitant steps, he moved closer to the two women on the couch, stopping next to Rae. "You want me too, then? Not just Kellen?"

"As I said, you're important too. Without you, Kellen would be miserable, and the more I get to know you, the more I realize how special you are. I'd like to become your friend."

This reassurance seemed to untie whatever knot had formed inside Armeo. He smiled carefully as he sat down on the couch next to Rae. "So nobody can make us leave here?"

"No, not now." Rae leveled with him. "The ambassador still wants you, so there'll be a custody hearing soon. We'll put some really good legal people to work and come up with proof of your mother's wish. I'll do everything I can to keep you with Kellen...with us."

"Armeo," Kellen said huskily, her voice betraying her.

Rae glanced at her, afraid she would crumble and tell Armeo the exact circumstances. Determined to stifle any such inclinations, she put an arm around her new wife's shoulders. "I think you're tired, Kellen," she interrupted. "Why don't we send Armeo off to have breakfast in the mess hall while you rest? Gemma can come by later and check your leg, and when Armeo's back from school we can all go out to dinner."

Kellen looked as if she were going to object, then nodded. "Very well."

Rae swallowed a sigh of relief. "Your escort is now also your bodyguard, Armeo," she said. "I want you to be aware of the situation. Several Onotharians are present on the station, and we don't know who we can trust. I'll inform your escort and make sure he stays at a proper distance. I'll have maintenance move the rest of your things from the guest quarters too. You'll have your own room. It's not big, but I think you'll like it. I'll give you a personal tour later, when you come home. All right?"

Armeo looked pleased; apparently she had found a way to communicate with him that worked for now. As he left for the mess hall with the guard, Rae turned to Kellen. "Would you like a tour of the place now? Goodness knows when I'll have time again. I have a lot of work waiting."

Kellen rose, looking unsteady on her feet. Rae stepped closer and placed her right hand under her arm. "Whoa, easy there. Maybe we'll take the grand tour later. Let me just help you into bed." As she guided Kellen toward the bedroom, Rae hoped she'd made the bed before she left. Seeing ruffled sheets, she groaned inwardly. No such luck. "Sorry for the mess, Kellen. I'll straighten up later."

"Don't worry. I can help." Kellen yawned. "Later."

"Much later, by the looks of it," Rae teased, desperate to keep their conversation light.

Kellen lay down and jerked at the covers. "I'm so tired all of a sudden."

"Stop, stop, let me take your boots off." Rae unfastened the buckles on the black combat boots. "There you go." She tucked the covers in around her wife, not thinking how her thoughtfulness might seem to Kellen. "You take a nice nap. I'll page Gemma and have her come over this afternoon when things settle down in the infirmary."

"Thank you." Kellen's voice was dreamy but her grasp tight as she caught Rae's left hand in hers. "I mean it. Thank you."

An unfamiliar feeling constricted Rae's throat. At a loss for words, she held Kellen's hand until her delicate eyelids covered the blue brilliance of her eyes. Tucking her hand in under the covers as well, Rae straightened her aching back. As she looked down at her wife, a sudden paresis in her throat made it impossible to swallow. "You're welcome."

She left the bedroom and headed for the small kitchen area. Reaching up for the big jar of Cormanian coffee, she tapped the dispensing sensor twice, wanting her beverage strong. Water boiled instantly in the safer-glass jug in its niche in the wall, and she poured it over the condensed coffee.

Rae drew a trembling breath, her hands unsteady as she raised the rounded titanium Keep-Hot cylinder-mug to her face and blew on the steaming beverage. *The look on Armeo's face almost did me in.* Rae shuddered at how close she'd come to botching it with the boy. *Still, he seems okay for now. Kellen's done a good job raising him.* Armeo seemed secure in his approach to things, not afraid to show emotions. *What if I end up keeping him at the same distance my parents kept me? What if I'm just not cut out for parenthood? Five years is a long time in a child's life. And Kellen...*

The look on Kellen's face when Rae suggested marriage might very well haunt her for a long time. Rae knew she'd given Kellen very little time—hardly any—to think things over. But what choice did she have? M'Ekar would've been able to demand her extradition on the spot, more or less.

Stirring her habitual coffee even though she didn't take synth-o-sweet in it anymore, Rae wandered into the living room and stood looking out the view port. The incredible vastness of space ought to have made her feel small and insignificant, but it didn't. Instead it filled her with a sense of adventure, a desire to explore and encounter new worlds, species, and...She shook her head. *I do love the element of danger. That's another thing that makes me unsuitable for being part of a family unit.*

She was completely without experience in this matter. Emotionally distant from her parents for as long as she could remember, and later married to her work, Rae considered herself a poor candidate for this assignment. *I'm not exactly a catch, Kellen. I'm too old for you. I'm too busy.*

Suddenly Maeve's face appeared before her inner eye—their maternal, nurturing cook who'd taken her parents' place in being there for her. When she was sick, or upset, or merely wanted to share something exciting, it was Maeve who listened, comforted, and rejoiced with her. *I can draw from that. I can try to be a Maeve to Armeo. Damn it, I'll just have to find a way to do it. He deserves nothing less, now that he's lost his home.*

As for Kellen, she was at a loss how to compensate the beautiful woman. *I can make sure she wants for nothing. I have enough credits to buy her anything.* Appalled, Rae stopped her train of thought, putting the mug down on the small ledge beneath the view port with a loud thud. *Damn it, I'm not going to buy her affection.* Her parents used to come home with expensive gifts after their travels, and they had collected dust on Rae's shelves. She had never liked the presents but was too well brought up to say so.

If Kellen ever grew to like her, if they stood any chance for friendship, affection would have to develop naturally. *I just have to bite my sarcastic tongue and not hurt or confuse her. She's strong and can fend for herself, but in many ways, she's at my mercy. I must never forget that.*

Taking a large gulp of the bitter drink, Rae swallowed, feeling it warm her belly and energize her system almost instantly. *I don't fear many things. Right now, I fear I'm simply not good enough.*

Rae walked out into the kitchen, ran the mug through the dish-cleanser, then placed it on its shelf. Duty called, and in this case it was a blessing. She would have to think about her private situation later.

❖

The mission room was boiling with activity. Rae found Jeremiah standing with a communication device pressed to his ear, evidently trying to hear over the buzz. She raised her hand to greet him, only to see him frown and shake his head, pointing at the communicator and then back at her.

With a sharp twitch just beneath her sternum, Rae walked up to him just in time to hear him say, "She'll be with you in a minute, sir." He pressed a sensor and let the communicator rest on the desk while he looked at Rae. "I have a subspace call for you, ma'am. It's the admiral."

Several admirals served in different capacities throughout Supreme Constellations space, but everyone referred to only one person as "the admiral," without any other designation.

"Oh, God." Rae reached for the communicator, suppressing an exasperated grunt before she pressed the sensor. This was turning out to be her life's most challenging day on a personal level. "Jacelon here, Admiral."

"What the hell's going on out there?" Admiral Ewan Jacelon barked. "I've had several dispatches arrive, not to mention inquiries by foreign nations and media. Are you trying to start a damn war with the Onotharians?"

"No, but they seemed to have their hearts set on one."

"What are you talking about? My information says you blew them out of the water."

"I did, but only when they fired up their weapons after they broke at least three different SC laws."

"The ambassador enjoys diplomatic immunity."

"It expired the minute he used weapons toward military targets within SC borders. I know what the law says, Admiral."

He muttered something inaudible. "Then I heard some other surprising news, girl. What on earth possessed you to get married all of a sudden, at your age?"

"Is this official business or a private call, Admiral? If it's private, I really don't have time right now. If it's official, refer to me by my title."

"I think it's both! You've always gotten yourself into trouble. I don't know who this person you lured into marrying you is, but I hope he's strong enough."

Rae knew it wouldn't do much good to respond to the admiral's tirade, but she still tried. "She. And yes, she's very strong. In fact, I think you'd like her."

"We'll see soon enough. The Council is sending me to settle some business at *Gamma V*, and now they also want me to calm down the situation you've created."

Her stomach lurched, and Rae felt like screaming. "What a surprise, Father. Not that I've created any sort of situation, but you're always welcome to visit. Is Mother coming too?"

"No, she's on vacation in the Reposa System. I don't expect her home for another three weeks."

"I hope she enjoys herself. Now, I don't have time to talk anymore…"

"See you in a few days, then. Jacelon out."

Staring at the communicator, Rae steeled herself and glanced to Jeremiah, who stood at his console next to her. "You heard him. He's on his way here."

"Why?"

She had to laugh at Jeremiah's startled expression. "He's going to 'calm down' the situation *I* created. Honestly, all things considered, I'm not sure if things are looking up or down."

How she hated when her father always assumed she was at fault. When she was growing up, no matter the circumstance, the admiral— back then a captain—seemed unable to give her the benefit of the doubt. If someone from school complained, Ewan Jacelon, who never found the time to socialize with his only child, would suddenly make time to scold her without listening to her side of it.

Rae had quickly understood her father's greatest disappointment— she wasn't the boy he had dreamed of. Even though she chose typically masculine extracurricular activities and early on decided to follow in his footsteps, he declared the next best thing would've been if she formed a family unit and provided him a grandson.

Her mother, illustrious diplomat Dahlia Jacelon, with a far-reaching reputation for her skills, also had little time for her daughter. Absentmindedly, she'd pat Rae's hair, comment in passing on her perfect grades, and then fly off on another planet-saving mission. Knowing full well that her own minor problems or worries couldn't compete with the lives of millions, Rae went to Maeve. The cook, having worked for the Jacelons since before Rae was born, was always there.

Rae looked up at Jeremiah, who still seemed stunned. She knew her father liked her next in command, and also her friend, Captain Alex de Vies, who lived aboard this station. She couldn't help but wonder how differently the admiral would have reacted if either one of these men had defeated M'Ekar's fleet or gotten married.

Over time her nonrelationship with her parents had made Rae distance herself from them, knowing she could never please her father or really matter to her mother. Some would say heading for deep space was overdoing it, but she disagreed. It was by far the best solution. Here she served a purpose, and she knew she was damn good at her job. Living on Earth, in the shadow of her parents, was no life for her.

CHAPTER SEVEN

The commercial section of *Gamma VI* buzzed with activity. Most civilians were coming off duty and shopping in the multitude of stores that lined the six-meter-wide corridor. Unlike those in the military section, the materials used to construct and decorate this part of the station were luxurious and aesthetically pleasing. The floor was made of D'Tosorian silver-marble that shimmered underfoot. Transparent aluminum windows showed displays of the goods for sale, and Kellen marveled at the high-tech equipment available, as well as the multitude of garments, food stuff, and jewelry. Armeo stopped in front of a window where games and toys overflowed the moving shelves, his eyes huge and darting.

Proud of him for not begging either her or Rae to buy him something, Kellen glanced at Rae and wondered if she noticed. Half expecting her new spouse to make Armeo choose a gift, she was surprised and relieved when she didn't. Rae didn't need to buy Armeo's affection.

As they approached the Food District, mouthwatering scents hovered in the air, and Kellen noticed the crowd around them became denser. The ones who recognized the commodore in civilian clothes nodded respectfully and looked at the three of them curiously.

Kellen walked closer to Rae. She was concerned for Armeo's safety, as usual, and draped an arm around his shoulders. Armeo glanced at her, apparently surprised, but smiled and hugged her around the waist. The contented, curious look on his face as he obviously tried to assimilate all the new sights and sounds made her smile in return. Looking down at Armeo, she wondered if anyone could possibly mistake the two of them for the fugitives who had been towed to *Gamma VI* three days ago. *Three days? I can't believe it's only been three days.*

Having retrieved more of her things from the *Kithanya*, Kellen was relieved to find the bag she'd packed a long time ago with a few sets of clothes, just in case she needed them. She wore a simple white suit with long sleeves made of retrospun cotton, and wide-legged trousers. Armeo had insisted on wearing his new school uniform—nuevosuede blue trousers, a short reversible twillmix black jacket, and brand-new nuevoskin shoes.

Rae was dressed in black trousers of the same material as Armeo's and a long gray Cormanian fairy-silk tunic with a black leathermix belt.

"People are staring," Kellen murmured out of earshot from Armeo, who was walking in front of them. She did not recognize the awkward shyness that flooded her, making her feel vulnerable. Also, she wondered if any of the many eyes turning their way belonged to anyone out to harm Armeo.

"I've noticed," Rae replied dryly. "We're probably the talk of the town right now. As I said, the grapevine here is unbelievable. Ah, here we are—Hasta's, my home away from home."

Kellen looked through the windows into the crowded restaurant. "It looks full." The thought of pushing through a room packed with staring strangers almost made Kellen insist they return to their quarters.

"I have my own table. Commodore's privilege." Rae's glittering eyes took the arrogance out of her words. "And there's Hasta herself. She owns the place and is also a famous chef."

A woman of unfamiliar alien descent approached them. Small-boned and barely as tall as Armeo, the chef wore her almost glowing white hair in a tall, elaborate style. A reddish tattoo adorned her face, creating intricate patterns along her hairline, down in front of her ears, and curling in waves along her long, slender neck. Hasta's skin was nearly as white as her hair, making the bright red of her lips and the blackness of her eyes all the more noticeable. She wore a long, light blue tunic over black trousers, both with golden threads woven into the unknown, shiny material.

"Commodore, your table is ready as usual," she said. "I see you brought your family. How nice to meet you. Young man, I'm sure I can whet your appetite with my egg rolls. Just come with me."

Armeo glanced over his shoulder, clearly seeking Kellen's approval before he hurried after Hasta.

"He's always hungry." Kellen smiled, starting to relax. "Most boys his age are."

"He seemed pleased with his room," Rae said. "When he's had time to personalize it with his own things, he should begin to feel some sense of home. The main ingredient for that is already there."

Kellen raised an eyebrow, not quite following.

"You," Rae explained. "Without you, Armeo would be lost. You're his mother in every sense but the biological."

"Oh." The unexpected words of understanding ignited a warm flame somewhere in Kellen's stomach. "That's how I feel," she said.

"Here they are." Rae pointed toward the kitchen entry. "You were right. Armeo's already chewing."

Hasta showed all three to a corner booth with a *U*-shaped couch that bordered three sides of an oval table, making quite the spectacle of arranging their napkins and pouring iced water into tall blue glasses. "Now, since it's your first time here together as a family, everything's on the house. Pick anything you like and I'll prepare the food myself. The commodore will tell you, you've never tasted anything like my cooking."

"I can also tell you, you've never met anyone with such a healthy dose of self-confidence," Rae deadpanned, and Armeo giggled. "Truthfully, Hasta's skills as a chef are legendary throughout the Supreme Constellations."

"Thank you, Commodore. Nice save." The tiny chef walked back toward the kitchen as they reached for the small computers displaying the menu.

Kellen glanced furtively around the busy restaurant, noticing how the inhabitants of the space station kept staring in their direction. Though it bothered her, she decided not to let it spoil the evening. It was far too important for them to be off to a good start.

"Kellen?"

Startled, Kellen realized she hadn't paid attention to the other two at the table. "Yes?"

"How did Gemma's visit go?" Rae asked. "I was worried you might have put too much strain on your leg."

Relieved that Rae had distracted her with something pragmatic, Kellen replied, "No, it held up well during the mission. In fact, Dr.

Meyer was able to close the skin, and I'll only have to see her every other day for scar-reduction therapy."

"Excellent. I'm relieved."

"Gemma called Kellen a real trooper," Armeo said, his eyes on the computer. "She offered to take her to the infirmary for proper anesthetics, but Kellen refused. I think it hurt, though."

Kellen groaned inwardly at the inquisitive look on her wife's face. *And here everything was going so well...Now she's worried and probably questions my motives. Thanks, Armeo.*

"It made sense," she defended her decision. "The infirmary is full of casualties in critical condition. My injury was minor compared to theirs."

A human woman accompanied by a man and a young girl stopped at their table and stood smiling down at them. "Look who's here. Good evening, Rae."

"Gayle, Alex, I thought you might pop in." Rae rose and hugged her. "It's been a while, Gayle. You and Dorinda came back only several days ago, right?"

"Yes, and I have presents for you from Earth." The woman looked back and forth between them. "I understand congratulations are in order."

"They are." Rae turned toward Kellen and made the introductions. "Captain Alex de Vies and his wife, Gayle. And their daughter, Dorinda." She took Kellen's hand. "This is my wife, Kellen O'Dal, and her foster son, Armeo."

Dorinda wrinkled her nose. "I know Armeo from school, Aunt Rae."

"Of course, I forgot." Rae looked suitably apologetic.

"Congratulations, Kellen. It's nice to meet you." Gayle extended her hand. "Please call me Gayle."

"The pleasure's mine, Gayle." Taking the other woman's hand, Kellen appreciated her steadfast grip. And even if Gayle scrutinized her unabashedly, she didn't make Kellen feel awkward, oddly enough. Gayle was an elegant woman who looked slightly younger than Rae. Golden brown hair ended just at her jawline, framing a thin face. Kellen thought the warm colors seemed to fit her personality. *She reminds me of Tereya. Same strength, same warmth.*

Alex de Vies stepped closer and studied Kellen closely. "I think I'll offer congratulations to Rae and my condolences to you, Kellen," he said. "I don't know what she possibly could have done to deserve someone like you."

Before Kellen had time to respond to the strange remark, the tall man turned to Armeo. "Hello, son, I remember you from the school yard. That's some arm you've got there."

Kellen thought they were speaking in code. Rae must have picked up on her bewilderment because she kept Kellen's hand in hers. "Alex is an FX counterpoint-ball freak. He must have seen Armeo pitch."

"That means to throw the ball," Armeo informed her. "Kind of like how we play *duchus* back home, but here the ball is digital, and the person batting makes different scores, depending where and how you hit it with the laser rod."

"Why don't the three of you join us?" Rae asked.

"We'd love to." Gayle immediately opted to sit next to Kellen. "I've always wondered what kind of person our good friend would fall for. Now I know." She wiggled her eyebrows.

Kellen realized she had never seen anyone move their facial muscles this way and made a mental note to observe these humans in private social settings. Her Gantharian sense of etiquette was only useful so far.

"Darling, don't scare the poor woman. She's not used to you." Alex winked at his wife and sat down next to Rae as Dorinda joined Armeo. "You *have* been known to overwhelm people, I'm told."

His wife wrinkled her nose. "I'm not overwhelming, am I, Rae?"

"Like the old steamrollers, my dear."

Kellen found the arrival of Rae's friends a reprieve from having to explain to Rae why she had avoided full anesthesia. The name *Alex* seemed familiar, and she tried to remember where she'd heard it. "You're the captain of the *Infinity*," Kellen said as it dawned on her, recognizing his voice as well. "You were on the mission earlier. It is nice to meet you and put a face to someone with such great command skills."

"Thank you," Alex said, sounding surprised. "The *Infinity* has been my vessel for three years now." He turned his attention to Rae. "I knew you'd go for a person with brains and an excellent sense for other people's qualities."

"She saw *my* qualities, didn't she?" Rae's voice suggested she was serious, but her eyes gleamed and she smiled. Kellen found she was starting to lose track of the conversation.

"How long have you known Rae?" Gayle rested one arm along the backrest and looked at Kellen with friendly eyes. "Tell me all about it."

"We haven't known each other very long, only three days."

Gayle opened her mouth, but promptly closed it again, which apparently was hilarious to these humans because her husband and daughter broke into a fit of laughter. Though Gayle glared at them, she didn't really seem angry, Kellen realized, only glowering in what she assumed was facetious annoyance.

"Not many things in this universe render you speechless." The captain was obviously teasing his wife.

Sticking her tongue out at him, Gayle turned her attention back to Kellen, who wondered if perhaps this particular gesture was appropriate in this informal situation. "Don't listen to this fool. I think it's wonderfully romantic for the two of you to find love like this. I for one know Rae wouldn't have taken such a step without knowing exactly what she was doing. Right, Rae?"

Kellen slowly turned her head, waiting for her spouse's response and half expecting Rae to deny everything and tell the truth. These were her friends, and perhaps Rae wouldn't keep the secret of their marriage of convenience from them. After all, the de Vies couple put up a friendly front, but surely they must think the commodore mad to marry a half-illegal fugitive from Gantharat.

"You're always right. I know exactly what I'm doing, and marrying Kellen is no exception." To Kellen's surprise, Rae's eyes were a warm blue-gray that reflected the old-fashioned tea lights burning in the middle of the table. Kellen's blood warmed at the loyal reply, and beginning to relax, she leaned farther into the backrest.

"Rae and I go back more than twenty years, since we attended the Academy," Alex said. "She's found her own path ever since. I can testify to her stubbornness and also swear that nobody has *ever* forced her to do anything she didn't want to. Not even—"

"Here's Hasta now," Rae interrupted. "Hasta, add my friends' tab to my account, please. They're our guests tonight."

"Certainly, Commodore. Have you all punched in your orders, or would you like me to surprise you?"

Kellen observed Rae as she glanced around the table and wondered what she was thinking. Rae had asked the de Vies family to join them without consulting her. Perhaps she was going to order food for them too. *Well, she's paying.* Kellen gave a mental shrug. "Why don't you surprise us, Hasta? Somehow you can always figure out what suits everyone's palate."

"Very good. It'll be ready soon."

Pleasantly surprised, and curious, Kellen laced her fingers and placed her hands on the table while she observed the others.

"Aunt Rae, is Armeo going to stay with you now?" Dorinda asked. The girl had her mother's amber eyes and her father's blond hair, a striking combination. Kellen recognized that Dorinda was genuinely fond of Armeo, and she began to understand why Armeo couldn't stop talking about his new friend.

"Of course. I gave him the room just inside the door."

"It overlooks most of Port 1," the boy enthused. "I can see everything coming and going there."

"Cool," Dorinda said. "Our place is several floors beneath yours, on Deck 16. I have almost the same view. Do you have a computer yet?"

"Not yet, but Commodore…I mean, Rae, has ordered one for me."

Dorinda leaned back, looking pleased. "Good. We can set up a three-way communication so we can do homework with David."

The children reminded Kellen of herself and her best friend Tereya at that age. Armeo seemed able to form relationships and map out his new life much better than she'd been able to. He wasn't aware of the dangers still lurking, and she didn't want him to be. Suddenly the restaurant seemed full of shadows and strangers. Feeling her throat constrict, she looked for signs of malevolence in the unfamiliar faces around her.

"Kellen. Kellen?"

Rae's husky voice reached her on the second attempt. She didn't ask her out loud if she was all right, but her eyes expressed concern. Kellen forced a faint smile. "Yes?"

"Our drinks are here. You wanted a nonalcoholic too, didn't you?"

"Yes. I'm still on medication."

"Are you ill?" Gayle looked concerned.

"A minor injury, which requires me to abide by the treatment Dr. Meyer prescribed for a few more days." Kellen dismissed the issue gently. "I'm fine."

"Good. I didn't mean to pry. You look like health personified, but you never know. Looks can deceive." Gayle squeezed Kellen's arm, and the surprising ease with which the other woman touched her made Kellen have mixed feelings. Part of her wanted to withdraw and keep her distance, but a stronger reaction was to enjoy the camaraderie. *I didn't know how much I've missed having adult friends. Having anyone, really.*

"I agree." Kellen nodded. She was beginning to like Gayle de Vies. Her no-nonsense personality was refreshing.

The food arrived and silence fell around the table as they began to eat. Kellen furtively checked on Armeo, glad to see him eating with a healthy appetite despite the alien food. Glancing suspiciously at a tall sort of vegetable, she took a careful bite, relieved that it was palatable. Most dishes were vegetarian and any meat was synthetic, using the latest technology, which made it practically impossible to detect any difference between it and the real thing. Still, Kellen knew that if any of her dinner companions were ever treated to real meat from Gantharat, they would be able to make the distinction between that and synthetic meat in the future.

"If Hasta decided to relocate to another station, we'd have to ask for a transfer too, Rae," Alex said.

"Typical for a man to follow where his stomach leads him." Rae shook her head and looked at Gayle.

"Speaking of cooking, since Rae refuses to even program the Compu-Cook, do you cook, Kellen?"

Kellen quirked a disdainful eyebrow. "Is that a polite way of asking if she married me for my skills in the kitchen?"

Gayle looked startled. "No, of course not."

Glancing at Rae, who had stopped with her fork halfway to her mouth, Kellen offered her first genuine smile since she had come to *Gamma VI*. "I was only joking, Gayle. Yes, I do cook. I may have to adjust to learning about ingredients common in SC space, but I can assure you I won't poison the commodore."

Alex stared at Kellen for a moment and then chortled, making heads turn throughout the restaurant. "That's it. I think you've met your match here, Rae. Kellen, now you've managed to convince me once and for all. Rae's definitely the fortunate one in this marriage."

Gayle looked as if she'd need some time to recover from the unexpected sign of humor coming from Kellen. "God, you scared me," she said. "I thought I'd offended you."

"I don't offend easily. But I might commit a faux pas, since I'm unaccustomed to your culture."

As if she had sensed the worry behind the light tone of voice, Gayle smiled reassuringly. "I think the ones you can count on as your friends will give you the benefit of the doubt, if any such situation arose. I doubt it, though. You carry yourself better than anyone I've met on this station."

Flattered and surprised at the praise, Kellen felt her skin turn a faint ice blue. Rae hadn't taken her eyes off her throughout the conversation, and Kellen was curious to know what she was thinking. *Am I charming enough to your friends? Fortunately it isn't hard since they're nice people. I just can't risk anything at this point.*

After another hour, Gayle rose, gently tugging at her daughter's hair. "It's way past your bedtime," Gayle told Dorinda, who seemed too tired and too full of ice cream to object.

Kellen watched Rae rise also and reach out for Armeo, who hesitated for only a fraction of a second, then took Rae's hand. *You trust too easily, Armeo. Have you fallen for her act of protection?* H'rea deasav'h! *I didn't foresee Armeo bonding with Rae. It's evident that he admires her.* Kellen wished she could take Armeo aside and warn him to guard his heart. She had a feeling they wouldn't last long on this station.

Rae held Armeo's hand for a moment. "I bet you're tired too. Tomorrow isn't a school day, but still…"

When Kellen tried to get up, she realized her pain relief had worn off. Forcing herself to her feet, she winced at the stinging sensation in her left thigh. Suddenly she felt Rae encircle her waist and hold her close. *She's doing all the right things. If I didn't have to lean on her for balance, I'd show her just how superfluous these gestures are.*

"You seem a little unsteady. Time for us all to get some rest."

"Yes," Kellen agreed, determined to play her part. "It *has* been a long day."

They accompanied the de Vies family to the rail system, watching as they boarded a car. In another minute, a car bound for Deck 3 arrived, and Kellen was grateful to sit down again.

"You're in pain, aren't you?" Rae asked in a low voice.

"It's not too bad."

"You don't have to be brave around me. If it hurts, you're supposed to tell me. I'm your wife." Rae looked surprised at her own words. "Guess what I'm trying to say is, we're responsible for each other now, for better and for worse."

Kellen considered Rae's words, glancing at the half-asleep Armeo who sat opposite them and leaned his head on the window. She was used to hiding discomforts from Armeo and not worrying him. However, between adults, candidness *was* the road to understanding. *I'm just not used to it.* "Very well. My thigh stings, but Dr. Meyer said it would, as part of the healing process after the derma fusion. It's normal."

"But still painful. I have some ointment she gave me for a similar injury. I'll give it to you when we get home."

"Thank you."

After a brief silence, Rae spoke again, her voice soft. "He's almost asleep."

Glancing at Armeo, Kellen smiled. "He had a long day too, and a lot of new information to deal with."

"He took it well. You're doing a wonderful job of raising him." Rae lifted her chin a fraction and looked determined. "Kellen, I know you still have doubts, but I'm going to do everything I can to make sure he stays with us."

For the first time since she had come to *Gamma VI*, Kellen began to feel a glimmer of trust. Something in the way Rae looked at her, the steadfast gaze, reminded her of Tereya. Armeo's mother was completely devoid of deceit, and Kellen saw the same loyalty and honesty in Rae. *How easy it would be to just give in…To trust her, and let her help me. I can't. It's something I can never do.* She felt sad and resentful, and her throat ached as she spoke.

"I can't lose him."

Rae nodded. "I know. Believe me, I know."

❖

Rae rummaged through her cluttered medicine cabinet, scowling as she found one outdated container after another. Silently promising to sort through her old medication later, she sneered at her own delusion, knowing something more pressing would make her forget.

Triumphantly she grabbed the ointment she had promised Kellen and returned to the bedroom. "Here. I found it." She wiggled the tube. "This should take the worst pain away."

Kellen was sitting on the side of the bed, an odd expression on her face. "Thank you."

"What's wrong?" Rae sat down next to her. "Want me to help you?"

"No, I'm fully capable of rubbing ointment on my leg."

"Then what is it?"

"This is…awkward. I feel I'm invading your personal space. It was not so bad when I took a nap here earlier today, but now…"

"We're both here. Kellen, listen to me. Go take a shower, and then I'll help you with the paste. I'll use the guest bathroom to get ready for bed. We have to share a bedroom for appearances. I honestly don't mind." Rae was surprised how true the last statement was. She was used to having these quarters to herself, yet having Kellen and Armeo here didn't bother her.

Kellen had taken up a lot of her thoughts during the day, and having her in close physical proximity was logical. Armeo was endearing, someone she'd instantly felt protective about, and having him in her quarters would make this task easier. And unexpectedly, she enjoyed his company. After all, she wasn't used to dealing with children, not counting Dorinda.

The entire evening had been interesting and pleasant. Rae was happy that Gayle and Alex had readily accepted Kellen and Armeo. They would make it easier for her wife to acclimatize. Gayle de Vies was pivotal to the important social life on the station. She worked as a coordinator among the civilians with family members in the military and knew everybody.

Kellen rose from the bed. "If you're sure?"

"Very sure."

After her shower Rae stopped by Armeo's room and peeked inside, finding him fast asleep. The night-light shone dimly, and Armeo had tucked the covers close around himself.

In her bedroom, the sight of Kellen reclining on the left side of the bed made Rae stop on the threshold. She wore a fairy-silk mid-thigh shirt and rested her head against the bulkhead behind the bed, looking breathtakingly beautiful. Rae quietly observed her for a moment, trying to wrap her mind around the fact that they would share this bedroom from now on. Rae's past lovers had never reached "sharing bedroom" status, but now she had a wife, someone with as much right to this room and its bed as she had.

Kellen turned her head and gave a short nod.

"Armeo's fast asleep. I checked on him." Rae shrugged at Kellen's surprised look. "So while I'm on a roll, why don't I help you with the paste? It needs to go only on the scar, since it's pretty strong."

"Very well." Kellen pushed the covers down, nudged the shirt out of the way, and removed the bandage.

Rae grabbed the tube and a tissue, flipped open the lid, and squeezed a string of the white paste out on the tissue. Leaning over Kellen's leg, she gently applied the paste, cautious to rub it only on the scar. "There. It should last you all night." She attached the bandage again.

"Thank you." Kellen cleared her throat. "Do you prefer this side of the bed? I can move over…"

"No, it's fine. I usually sleep in the middle, but any side is fine." Rae climbed in between the sheets, ordering the lights to zero percent.

Lying there, she thought how her life had changed. She was now caring for two refugees who were fighting almost unbeatable odds, and she was not about to let them down. Kellen stirred next to her, her slender fingers ending up on Rae's shoulder. It sounded like she was already asleep, her breathing slow and deep. Determined to not disturb her new wife, Rae remained still, looking out at the stars.

In a few days her father would arrive. Admiral Ewan Jacelon was the highest-ranking officer in the fleet and set on running her life. Though she had never allowed it, he kept trying.

She turned on her right side and watched the woman next to her sleep. This was the person she would spend the next five years of her life with. The pale light shining in through the porthole illuminated Kellen's exotic beauty. Thoughts whirling, Rae gazed at her, dwelling on her soft, full lips, recalling how they felt against her cheek.

Kellen looked peaceful, but Rae was intensely aware of the barely harnessed force within this alien woman who now shared her bed. Fully unleashed, Kellen could become very dangerous. *Will I be able to communicate with her on a daily basis? Will she understand what her new position as the spouse of a high-ranking SC fleet officer entails?* Rae herself had a reputation for being a maverick, no matter how by-the-book she was, but she was also devoted to protocol. Was Kellen going to follow her example, or could Rae expect professional embarrassment when her wife disregarded rules, as she was prone to do?

Kellen stirred, and Rae held her breath, hoping she hadn't disturbed her when she shifted in the bed. Whimpering, Kellen contorted her face while she slept, and her fingertips trembled where they lay against Rae's shoulder. Afraid her wife was having a nightmare, Rae reached out and placed a hesitant hand gently on her cheek. To Rae's relief, Kellen's breathing slowed and the trembling ceased.

This is part of living together. Closeness, offering comfort, supporting each other. Can we do it, Kellen? Rae knew the cultural differences between them were oceanic. Kellen's main objective was to keep Armeo away from the ones out to use or harm him. Rae's role was multifaceted. On a personal level, it tied in with Kellen's, but professionally, it was more complex. The SC Council's orders dictated her actions, and the political aftermath of her victory in space was just beginning.

Kellen, now looking soft and relaxed, might be the best and most intriguing thing that had ever happened to her, but she could also mean Rae's downfall. *Will I be able to keep my word to you? And will keeping my word to you be the end of my career?*

CHAPTER EIGHT

The crew in the passageway snapped to attention as Admiral Ewan Jacelon entered Port 1. Rae stood in the middle of the passage and saluted him as he approached.

Admiral Jacelon returned the salute. "Commodore."

"Admiral."

"Permission to come aboard."

"Permission granted, sir."

Rae looked up at her father, who was more than a head taller than she was. He was impeccably dressed in his SC fleet uniform, as usual, with a few more impressive insignia on his collar. White, short-cropped hair and a neat mustache and beard accentuated his commanding persona, which impressed even Rae. So did the dark gray eyes beneath bushy, gray eyebrows. He looked as fit as he had the last time she saw him, and she felt a secret pride that he looked much younger than sixty-nine. If only he looked happier to see her. Instead, his eyebrows slanted at a foreboding angle, and he had that down-turned expression at the corners of his mouth that she recognized so well.

"Rae." Admiral Ewan Jacelon took her smaller hand in his. "You look well."

"Thank you, Father. So do you," she replied calmly. "If you'll come with me?"

"Lead on."

"I take it your trip was uneventful." Rae escorted him toward the mission room, where they took the elevator up to Deck 1 and to her office.

"Compared to what you've been up to, downright dull." His face looked solemn.

"Don't start, Father, until I get a chance to explain."

Jeremiah saw them coming and rose to salute.

"Admiral, you remember Commander Jeremiah Todd, my next in command."

"Of course." The two men saluted and then shook hands. Jeremiah had met her father on several occasions, and she knew the admiral liked the younger man a lot. It was more than obvious to her now when Ewan Jacelon shot Jeremiah a broad grin. "Always good to see you, Commander. Carry on."

"I'll brief you in my office, Admiral." Rae fought to keep her voice even. "After that, Kellen's offered to cook dinner for us. You'll be staying in the VIP suite." She showed her father inside the circular room and adjusted the transparency of the aluminum walls to a minimum, obscuring them from the mission room.

"All right, Rae, let's knock off the chitchat and get to the point. I'm here to see if we can work something out, since your actions seemed to have ignited an intergalactic incident." The admiral sat down in the visitors' chair. "What the hell's going on, Rae? The Onotharian government has inundated the Council with official protests regarding this latest stunt of yours."

Rae felt her anger rise like a solar storm. "And what stunt are you referring to, Father? My defense of our territory or my defense of my family? M'Ekar violated our rules and engaged in hostilities because of a little boy who is now in my care. Diplomatic immunity or not, he broke the law."

"What the hell are you talking about?"

"What M'Ekar wants, and I have, is Armeo, twelve years old and sole heir to the M'Aido estate. At your level, you should have heard of this dynasty."

Not many things fazed her father, but the name made him lower his lighter before he lit his cigar. "A M'Aido is still alive?" He sounded incredulous. "The Council believes this particular Onotharian dynasty is extinct."

"Well, it's not, and Armeo is very much alive. Kellen has been his sole guardian since he was five. The Onotharian authorities attacked them back on Gantharat and forced them to escape. Kellen is a trained fighter pilot and managed to get within range of *Gamma VI*."

"Does she know who he is? Does she claim anything of his?"

Though Rae realized these were valid questions, she still became angry. Kellen could be infuriating in her tenacious stance, but nothing she'd said or done hinted of greed. Rae knew in her heart she was concerned only about Armeo. "No. His biological mother died seven years ago. If Kellen wanted anything to do with his inheritance, she'd have filed a claim long ago. She's utterly devoted to him and was seriously wounded when they escaped."

"That's something M'Ekar made sure the Council never heard," the admiral huffed. "Damn. This complicates things." He shot her a sharp glance. "Why did you marry her?"

"To legally keep her in SC space. If they'd extradited her, the Onotharians would have found her guilty of kidnapping—and the penalty is death…by starvation." The words hurt her throat, and sudden images of a broken, emaciated Kellen flickered through her mind, making her briefly clamp her eyelids shut, to try to erase them.

"Barbaric." The solitary word displayed his contempt. "The SC Council has worked with the Onotharians since they applied for full membership, but their laws conflict with ours and their occupation of Gantharat is also controversial. Some members are more indulgent in their attitude toward Onotharat, but most are against membership unless they change their laws."

"If M'Ekar is an average representative of his country, I don't see that happening any time soon."

Ewan Jacelon lit his cigar. Rae wrinkled her nose and pressed a button on her console to boost the ventilation.

"I haven't told Kellen about the latest development yet," she said. "Before you arrived, the *Dalathea* responded to my request. They'll be here within five days."

The *Dalathea* was a court ship, one of several traveling through the SC sectors. The judges aboard these ships handled interplanetary law and legal disputes between SC citizens and non-SC aliens. Inside SC borders the court ships' rulings were beyond appeal.

"Have you discussed this situation with a lawyer, Rae? You need legal counsel."

"I know. Jeremiah's friend in our civilian legal department on the station says our chances are good, but…" Rae paused and pressed her fingertips against her temple in an attempt to align her erratic thoughts. "I want them to be more than good. I want to go into that courtroom knowing Armeo and Kellen will be safe when we leave. Right now, I'm not so sure."

The admiral bit into his cigar and leaned back into the chair. "What did the lawyer suggest?"

"He says we need someone beyond reproach, someone who can convince the court we're doing what's in Armeo's best interests. If the court thinks for one minute I'm after his inheritance or, like M'Ekar, using him as a political pawn, they might take him away from us. They might not give him to M'Ekar. Probably wouldn't. But they may give him to someone who can't protect him. Besides that…Kellen has taken care of him all his life. They'd be devastated without each other."

"I see." Ewan Jacelon rose from the chair and removed the cigar from his lips. "All right, let's go to dinner, then. I'm curious about this Kellen. You care about them, don't you?"

"Yes, I do, Father. Kellen loves that boy. She was willing to sacrifice her own life to save his. And Armeo, he's great. He's smart and has grit, but no child should have to deal with the things he's had to face."

"I see."

Rae tried to interpret the look in his eyes but failed, as usual, since her father had the best poker face in SC space.

He rose from the chair still gripping his cigar between his teeth. "All right, let's go to dinner so I can meet your new family."

Rubbing her sweaty palms furtively on her trousers, Rae sighed in relief. Talking with her father had been easier than she expected. He drove her crazy because he always assumed the worst when she was involved, but he was fair when it came to others. She needed his help desperately, even if she cringed at having to ask for it.

The admiral towered over her and tapped her shoulder. "What are we waiting for? I'm hungry. Let's go."

❖

Kellen came out of the kitchenette carrying two pots and placed them on the dining room table. The thermo technology would keep the food hot until they sat down to eat. Preparing food had calmed her temporarily; the mundane chore made her feel grounded. Unfortunately she had pictured the kitchen in her now-destroyed home, where she and Armeo had shared most of their meals. The thought of how the Onotharians had burned her estate and killed farmhands and her *maeshas*...Kellen tried to force the harsh memories to the back of her mind. *I have to focus. One of the highest-ranking officers of the SC will dine at this table. Armeo's future depends on his benevolence.*

She lifted the lid of the pot closest to her. She had made a version of her favorite vegetarian casserole, finding similar ingredients in the grocery stores aboard the station. Having tasted "new potatoes" for the first time two nights ago at the restaurant, Kellen had opted to serve them on the side. *Surely this scene, domestic and harmless, could fool him? I just have to bide my time and see where all this leads.* She had little knowledge of what a traditional marriage within the SC entailed, but she suspected nobody expected her to.

Jacelon and her father were due any minute, and Kellen hurried into the bathroom to check her appearance and make sure she looked the part. She made sure her blond hair was flawless, then glanced at an unused makeup kit, but it was too alien to even attempt. Hoping she would pass scrutiny, she examined herself in the full-length mirror attached to the door. She wore the same white suit as the other evening, since her wardrobe was limited.

Hearing the door hiss open in the living area, she held her breath for a few moments, pressed her palms hard against her thighs, and left the bathroom.

A tall, graying man boasting a neatly trimmed beard stood next to Rae, looking at her with familiar gray eyes. Rae's voice was polite and emotionless as she made the introductions.

"Admiral." Kellen nodded, extending her hand, which he accepted, taking it in his. "I'm honored you could join us for dinner." Reluctantly she admitted he seemed an impressive individual, with an unfaltering gaze and as much charisma as his daughter. Admiral Jacelon wore an SC uniform with elaborate rank insignia adorning the black jacket and had a distance in his eyes when he looked at his daughter.

His expression struck Kellen as odd. She could not fault him for looking at her with suspicion, but why would he regard his daughter with such obvious trepidation? Her own father had showed his pride in her freely and without hesitation. When he took Tereya under his wing as well, he'd extended his affection to include the orphaned girl.

The admiral let go of her hand. "It's good to meet you. And call me Ewan."

Kellen tried to guess the appropriate answer and decided to merely nod and reciprocate the unexpected familiarity. "Then call me by my first name too." Rae looked startled at her father's words, making Kellen wonder if she had done anything wrong. "Would you like something to drink, Ewan?"

"A beer, if you have one."

"Of course. Rae, do you want anything?" Kellen scrutinized her new spouse, sensing an unfamiliar tension.

"No, thanks. I'm fine."

"Kellen, have you seen my...Oh. Hello." Armeo rushed into the living room, stopping so fast he almost toppled over when he saw Rae and the visitor. He quickly regained his equilibrium after a glance in Kellen's direction and approached their guest. "I'm Armeo M'Aido, sir. You must be Rae's father."

"I am. Nice to meet you, Armeo. I've heard a lot about you."

"You have?" He glanced at the commodore. "From Rae?"

"Yes, we talked about you and your mother on the way here. I hear you're settling in well at school. Made any friends yet?"

"Yes, sir. Dorinda de Vies and David Grotny are my best friends here."

"Good. So, glad to be on *Gamma VI?*"

Kellen held her breath, not sure where the admiral was going with his questions. She was certain her own father would not have interrogated Armeo in this manner, no matter how subtle. Kellen was glad Armeo was straightforward and not easily intimidated.

"Very glad, sir. Rae and Kellen were married only a few days ago. They fell in love at first sight. That makes me happy, because the Onotharians can't make me go back...and nobody can hurt Kellen." Armeo's eyes were shadowed as he momentarily faltered.

Kellen didn't have to look at Rae to know she would have liked to put a hand over Armeo's mouth. Still, this was their official story.

"Why don't we sit down to dinner?" Rae said, to Kellen's relief. "Armeo, go wash your hands."

They sat down and sampled the casserole. After a first, tentative bite, Ewan gave Kellen a genuine smile. "This is great. How can I go back to mess-hall food after this?"

"I don't intend to cook every day," Kellen warned, knowing that she sounded haughty. "Perhaps a few times a week. I don't mind preparing food, but I don't want it to become a chore."

"Smart girl," the admiral remarked before sipping his dark red De-Te-Valhian beer. "Rae doesn't seem able to boss you around like she tries to do with everyone else. Mind you, that could easily become a problem unless you put your foot down right from the start."

Kellen snapped her head up at the implied criticism in Ewan Jacelon's words. She saw Rae clutch her fork. "I'd think for someone responsible for thousands of lives on this station, and ultimately millions on the closest planets, being bossy would be a desirable trait," she said, carefully enunciating every word without raising her voice.

"True, but she's been like that since she was born."

Kellen smiled faintly, making sure the admiral met her eyes before she continued. "Ah, I see. It must be genetic, then. She clearly resembles you."

Rae quickly hid behind a napkin, wiping her mouth.

The admiral looked taken aback. "Me? Really." He shot his daughter a look. "I suppose that could be true."

Rae met Kellen's glance with something resembling gratitude.

After refilling his plate twice, Armeo declared he was full. "Kellen, may I go to Dorinda's quarters? David's coming too."

"For an hour or two, but I have to call security. In the meantime you can help me take the dishes into the kitchen."

Armeo grimaced, but stacked their empty plates and carried them out of the dining area. Kellen contacted the security detail, then returned to the table. "Anything more to drink, Ewan?"

"No, thanks, I'm fine. I take it Armeo doesn't go anywhere without security?"

"Rae arranged for it our first day here. Now, with several recuperating Onotharians on the station, I fear for his safety."

The admiral leaned back and produced a cigar. "On my way here I reviewed the initial mission report. You did everything by the book, Rae, as usual."

"Meaning what? Every captain's log on every SC ship at the battle will validate that report." Rae's voice was short. She tossed her napkin on the table and rose from the chair. "Unless you're going to let anyone accuse me of coercing my crew into lying…" Putting her hands on her hips, she looked daggers at her father.

"Wait a minute," Ewan Jacelon barked, "I never said—"

"You didn't have to," Rae interrupted, setting her jaw and folding her arms. "You insinuated—"

"What's wrong?" a small voice asked from the kitchen.

Looking over her shoulder, Kellen saw Armeo, his face white. She was about to answer when Rae walked over to him. To her surprise, her wife drew him close and draped her arm around his shoulders.

"Nothing's wrong, Armeo. This is how my father and I exchange information." Her tone was vaguely sarcastic. "We sometimes don't see eye to eye on things, but you know what? We usually end up agreeing one way or another." The door chime beeped twice. "Here's your escort now. You can visit with your friends for two hours, all right?"

Armeo looked up at Rae, his face serious. "You weren't arguing because of me, were you?"

"No. In fact, my father thinks you're a splendid young man. Isn't that so?" Rae stared at the admiral, her eyes uncompromising.

"Absolutely." The admiral produced a new cigar. "Armeo, before you go, may I ask you a question?"

"Yes, sir."

"Are you worried that Rae won't be able to protect you and Kellen?"

Armeo began to shake, and Rae tightened her grip on him. "I... I..."

"Listen to me, young man. If anyone can deal with the situation, it's Rae. She may not always do things the way I would, but the results are the same. She'll know what's best for you."

Kellen saw a look of surprise mixed with something vulnerable pass over her wife's features. Finally, Kellen saw a similarity between Rae's father and her own. It had taken Armeo's pain to bring it out in the open, but there it was. *I wonder if Rae sees the tenderness in his eyes when he looks at Armeo.*

The tone of his voice was the same as that of her own father's when he'd left that last evening: *I'll be back early tomorrow morning, Kellen. Many lives are at stake. I don't have a choice. Don't wait up for me.* Of course she had waited. Sitting by the large fireplace in the grand room on the first floor, she'd waited until Tereya woke up. Two days later, a hover vehicle had driven up to the farmhouse. Bondar O'Dal's body showed no visible signs of violence until they turned him over and she saw the plasma burn on his back through the hole in his clothes.

"There, you see?" Rae said, and ruffled Armeo's dark hair, breaking Kellen's journey into bleak memory. She raised her voice. "Enter."

Ensign Y'sak, a familiar security officer, stepped inside. *Good, Armeo will feel safer and more at ease with someone he's used to.*

During the awkward silence after Armeo left, Kellen picked up the last of the dishes and carried them into the kitchen. She wondered if she should close the door, but before she had time to do so, she could hear father and daughter talking in the dining room. Suddenly the loss of her own father stirred and reminded her how much Bondar had loved her. He'd shown it so easily. Unconditional love, something she would never experience again.

"Thank you for treating Armeo so well, Father." Rae's voice was low, but sounded sincere.

"He's just an innocent kid. You can tell he's been through a lot these last few weeks, though he puts up a brave front. You're right, he's courageous."

"Yes, he is. Kellen's taught him well."

"She seems remarkable." The admiral spoke in a less certain voice. "It's none of my business, but how do you feel about her?"

Kellen held her breath while she waited for Rae to reply. It took so long, she wondered if her new wife would refuse to answer.

"She's a mystery to me. I don't know how I feel, but I do know this. She's put her and Armeo's lives in my hands, and I'm not going to fail them. Granted, she fired at me when we ran into their ship in space, but she had her reasons. I feel…protective and responsible."

"And how does she feel about you?"

Rae gave a low laugh. "I'm not sure. One minute she seems to despise everything I stand for—the power, command, everything. Next, she's defending me against my own father. I sprung this marriage on her as the only way to keep them safe. We're strangers, and yet she has to share my quarters. I expect her to trust me, and I think she's low on trust right now. She's prepared to take Armeo and disappear if she thinks it's called for."

Kellen shuddered. She felt naked where she leaned against the door frame, not realizing until now how well Rae had pegged her.

"I guess you don't trust her?"

"I don't know. It's not that clear-cut. I trust in her love and devotion to Armeo. But that might make her decide to grab him and run if I can't convince her they're better off here. She's wild." A brief silence.

"Father, I know we've had our differences, but I need your help."

"Let me guess. You need someone beyond reproach to testify on Armeo's behalf and possibly act as his guardian, so you can keep him with you and Kellen."

"Yes. Let's face it. Kellen's dependability is not exactly impressive. In the eyes of the SC and the court, I might be just as bad, for marrying her so suddenly."

"True. So that's where I come in. You don't trust her to live up to her end of the bargain, and you need me to vouch for you."

"Yes."

Furious at their reasoning, Kellen moved quietly to the doorway, glancing out at the two who stood opposite each other. The admiral had rested his cigar on the dining room table and was now raising his hands, placing them on his daughter's shoulders. Memories of how her own father had done just that, and how she missed having someone to share her burden, fueled her anger even more. They dared criticize her without having a clue what they were talking about!

Rae placed her hand on her father's arm. "Would you do it? For Armeo?"

The admiral's smile made Kellen close her fingers around the door frame. He looked so much like Bondar at that moment, as he gazed down at his daughter. Witnessing the similarity, she felt as if all of her intestines had wound up in a tight knot.

"Yes. You're not the only one with a passion for the law and ethics. Besides, Armeo's political dynamite. When you get full custody of him within SC territory, M'Ekar will probably try to kill him once he learns he can't get his hands on him."

Kellen felt bile rise in her throat, and she slammed her fist into the door frame, her breath gushing from her lungs. "No," she snarled, making Rae turn her head at the tormented sound.

❖

"Damn." Striding over to her pale wife, who seemed ready to tear the door frame from the bulkhead, Rae extended her arms toward her. Kellen evaded her touch and glared at her with eyes of blue fire. Rae realized this was Kellen unleashed, and made a new, more guarded, attempt to reach her. "Listen to me. When my father announces his offer to be Armeo's guardian, no one in his right mind will even consider trying to kill him. Instead, people will look out for him, wherever he goes."

"*H'rea deasav'h!* This is a nightmare," Kellen thundered, her voice carrying loudly through Rae's quarters. Blue tears rose in her eyes. "M'Ekar will never give up, and Armeo will never be safe." She breathed deeply and rapidly as she paced back and forth.

"Yes, he will." Rae reached out and took her wife gently by the arm. Kellen turned around, slamming a strong hand down on Rae's wrist. Rae had started to pry it off when she suddenly stopped and stared down at their joined limbs.

Rae tried again, not about to admit how painful Kellen's grip was. "Listen to me! He'll stay with us, and we'll protect him until he's old enough to manage his estate and heritage. We'll keep him safe, Kellen." She lifted her eyes and gazed into Kellen's eyes without blinking, determined to convince her.

"It's hard to believe." Kellen's jaw worked spasmodically as she searched Rae's face, as if seeking the truth. Tears clung to her dark eyelashes, quivering before they dislodged and ran down her cheeks. "In fact, it's impossible to believe when M'Ekar risks starting a war with the SC to find him. He didn't hesitate, sacrificing Onotharian ships and soldiers…"

The admiral walked up to them and stood next to his daughter. Rae glanced up and noted the compassion in his eyes, amazed to see this kind of emotion so visible on his face.

"You're right, Kellen." The admiral's voice was unyielding. "We'll need to deal with M'Ekar on several levels. He's dangerous, not only to Armeo. If he keeps this up, he'll become a political liability to Onotharat. They're seeking membership in the Supreme Constellations, and it's to our advantage that his illegal actions may make that impossible."

"I wish I could be sure of that." Kellen looked at the two standing in front of her, her breathing still labored.

"Let's deal with things one at a time," Rae said, knowing Kellen was still on edge, her volatile nature rampaging behind her mask of restrained fury. "I've requested the *Dalathea* to rendezvous with us in six days, and until then we can start preliminary hearings and exchange documents over secure links with the court officials." She turned to her father. "If you're unable to stay until the court ship arrives, we'll need your testimony for guardianship on record."

"No, that won't be necessary. I don't feel comfortable leaving until this is settled. It's not that I don't trust you to handle the situation, Rae."

Rae's first reaction was to insist she could handle station business without his interference. Opening her mouth to let him know, she gazed at Kellen and recognized the standoffish disdain the other woman had initially displayed when she first came aboard *Gamma VI*. Hoping they were not back at square one, she said, "I'm not offended. In fact, I can use you. The station is incredibly busy, and I'm expecting two generational ships entering SC space to arrive soon."

Not sure if she had imagined her father's surprise, Rae switched her attention back to Kellen. "Forgive me for saying this, Kellen, but there's more to this than Armeo's safety. We're caught in the middle of a rapidly escalating political game that can get out of control if we're not careful. We can't afford to lose our heads."

Kellen quickly swiped all traces of her blue tears away and straightened her back. Now that she was apparently calming down a little, Rae could see her left leg was trembling.

"Why don't you sit and relax that leg of yours while I finish clearing the table? Father can help." Rae shot him a mock glare, trying to ease the tension for Kellen's sake. She would deal with her father later. She truthfully needed his assistance and expertise, but she would never allow him to sweep in and start running her station.

Rae made sure Kellen elevated her leg with a cushion underneath her knee and carried out the last of the pots, noticing that the expression on the admiral's face at the prospect of household chores apparently even made Kellen smile warily. She gave her father a pointed look, and he rolled his eyes at her, removing the napkins and thermo plates before he joined her in the kitchen.

Rae placed the pots on the counter and turned around, leaning against it. "Thank you." She fought not to show any emotion, knowing her father disliked such displays from her.

"No need for thanks. It's the prudent course of action." The admiral placed his load on the counter. "If we don't neutralize M'Ekar, and quick, a mere custody case will turn into a diplomatic and political nightmare."

"You realize I did everything by the book. I had no other choice but to engage." *Did that sound as pleading to him as it did to me?* Rae wanted to thud her forehead against the bulkhead.

"My dear, you never do anything if it's not by the book. And if there's a loophole, I'll trust you to find it too."

Rae smiled. "True. I'm sorry. I didn't mean to go off like that." *Damn, why do I always fall into this trap of seeking validation from him? To date, he's never genuinely approved of anything I've done.*

"Rae, listen to me. I still have to go through all the reports and records. The next six days will give me time to do this. I never doubted your actions or your word, but I need to make sure we have everything in order. Besides, how would it look if I went easy on my own daughter?"

"Oh, the stars forbid it ever be said you were easy on anything," Rae replied sardonically. "That would be a miracle."

"At ease there, crewman, or I'll have you cleaning port ways."

Rae smiled reluctantly.

"I'm going to the VIP quarters now," he said. "It's been a long day."

"And I'm going back to the mission room. I have a lot of work to do."

"Kellen seems upset. I think you better work from home this evening. Perhaps everything's catching up with her."

Astonished, Rae said, "She'll be fine. She doesn't expect me to sit around and hold her hand."

"Armeo will be gone for at least another hour. Take my advice and stay here."

Smoothing her hair behind her ears, Rae nodded. "All right, if you insist."

"I do. Good night, Rae."

"Sleep well. Will you be at our 0800 meeting?"

"Yes. See you then."

The admiral left his daughter's quarters, pausing to say good night to Kellen. Rae took a few minutes to put the last dishes into the recycling machine. When she returned to the living room, she found Kellen sitting on the couch, reading from a small computer screen. She had taken the pins from her hair, and her long tresses formed a golden cloud around her shoulders. Rae noticed a tired line between Kellen's eyebrows, which worried her.

Walking over to the couch, she sat down next to her and gently touched her arm. "What are you reading?"

Kellen glanced up. "It's not a book. It's a photo album with every picture taken of Armeo since he was born. I never go anywhere without a copy. Luckily, I had put one in the *Kithanya*." Her voice wavered. "Everything I owned…We lost it all when they burned our home."

When she saw the emptiness in Kellen's eyes, Rae felt sorry for this woman who had lost so much. "I know." She cradled her hands over Kellen's where she clasped the computer. "You have Armeo, and you have these. You can use the computer here to make as many backup copies as you like."

"Thank you." Kellen leaned against the backrest. "I have a question."

"Go on."

"What will my function be at *Gamma VI*—apart from being your spouse?"

The stark tone in Kellen's voice caught Rae's attention. "Function? What do you mean?"

"I want to work. I have useful skills."

When she heard Kellen's sullen tone of voice, Rae wanted to kick herself. "Are you thinking of your ability as a pilot or your artistic skills?"

"Either."

"I suggest you think about which one you want to pursue. Once we've settled the legal arrangements for Armeo, you'll be free to do whatever you want. We can always use pilots with your experience."

Kellen relaxed visibly. "I know it may sound silly, but I was afraid of becoming…redundant. I'm not sure what being the commodore's wife entails."

"That makes two of us. I have no clue either." Rae laughed, making Kellen's eyes sparkle with indecipherable emotions. She thought she detected a sly look on Kellen's face but wasn't sure.

"We might have to make it up as we go along," Kellen suggested with a casual flick of her wrist.

"Sounds good to me. Why don't you show me some of these pictures of Armeo? He'll be home soon, and once he's gone to bed, I have some more work to do. For now it can wait, though." Amazed at her own words, Rae tried to mask her feelings by leaning over the album. She couldn't remember when anything had been more important to her than work.

"You sure you want to see these?"

"Yes. When was this one taken?" Rae pointed at the screen.

"He was six here and had just lost a front tooth…"

As Rae listened to the wistful, loving voice reminisce about days gone by, she found herself looking as much at Kellen as the many pictures of Armeo. Unmistakably, this woman was the boy's mother in every sense that mattered. *I thought I understood it, but it's…more, and such a simple, unbending truth.* Breathless with the impact of this realization, Rae vowed to do everything she could to not rob Armeo of the only parent he had.

CHAPTER NINE

Kellen walked toward the infirmary. She had her last treatment today and looked forward to returning to her *gan'thet* training program. Skilled in the ancient Gantharian martial art, she was the proud carrier of the Ruby Red Suit, which designated her as a master.

Her guard, now her bodyguard, walked two paces behind her. Kellen found his presence offensive. After all, she wasn't a child like Armeo who needed protection, but Rae had insisted, obviously not trusting her ability to protect herself, or…not trusting *her.* Kellen strode as briskly as her wounded leg allowed, trying to put more distance between herself and the security officer, but he had no problem keeping up with her.

When she stepped inside the waiting area, a nurse informed her Dr. Meyer was running late, so Kellen took a seat. Her guard stayed within sight, but kept a considerate distance.

Taking out a handheld computer, she logged onto *Gamma VI's* information channel. She was determined to find work as soon as she was back in shape, so she scanned the ads for both civilian and military personnel, pleased to see Rae was correct—pilots were in high demand. She didn't want to work as a trade ship pilot, since she would have to be away from the station and Armeo for months. Also, she knew she couldn't afford to be away from Rae at this point.

Kellen had woken up before Rae in the morning and found her wife curled up in the middle of the bed, a slender arm wrapped around Kellen's waist. Holding her breath, Kellen looked down at the tousled red hair sticking up on Rae's head. Seeing her looking so young in her sleep ignited a quick stab of tenderness before she reminded herself of what Rae represented. She was a power to be counted on within the SC, and so was her father. Images of her parents and Tereya, ripped from her life, leaving her to carry out her duties alone, flickered through her mind.

Rae stirred next to her but only buried her face in Kellen's neck and continued to sleep. Kellen realized how fragile a human body was compared to her Gantharian strength, and still Rae's heart was beating steadily; she could feel it against her upper arm. *She's beautiful.* Utterly ashamed for even noticing such trivial facts when Rae was part of a vast power that might be on the verge of acknowledging and endorsing her enemy, Kellen froze. She didn't know whether to move away or just lie still until her wife woke up. Eventually the chronometer's soft female voice recited the time, and Rae's eyes snapped open.

For a moment, she clutched Kellen even tighter, squinting against the faint starlight coming from the porthole. "Alarm off." Her voice was even huskier in the morning.

Kellen shifted a little, freeing her long hair where it was stuck under Rae's head.

"Kellen?" Rae sat up, looking down at her. "Oh, damn. Did I crowd you?"

"It's all right. We'll get used to sharing quarters…and this bed, eventually."

"Yes, I suppose so." Rae rubbed her eyes, still looking vulnerable and so much softer than Kellen had seen her. The thinlinnen shirt had twisted around her, baring Rae's left shoulder. Her lips seemed fuller and had yet to find their usual austere expression. "We'll just have to give it some time. I hope you slept okay, despite…" Rae gestured toward the wrinkled area in the center of the bed.

In fact, Kellen had slept better than she had before leaving Gantharat. Unsure what that implied she recoiled, raising her chin. "What do you expect from our union?"

Rae looked at her with obvious bemusement. "What do you mean? Union?"

"Our marriage. What do you hope to gain from it? Since this is for convenience, for appearance only…will you take lovers?"

"I'm not about to commit adultery," Jacelon hissed, her eyes suddenly dark gray slits. "That's not my style. Besides, it would be like confessing to the court that our marriage is arranged."

"That's why I asked." Kellen fought to remain calm. To her dismay, Rae's angry reply caused her more relief than she was comfortable with. *Take as many lovers as you like, Commodore. I couldn't care less.* Her thoughts echoed hollow in her mind.

"I see." Rae's eyes held Kellen's without wavering.

Kellen was struck by the contradiction between Rae's elegant features, enhanced by the pale light, and her tousled hair. "I don't even know if you find me attractive," she said, wishing she had never started this discussion. "You've labeled me beautiful, but that's not important. We have to have more than that between us if we're going to make this work."

Rae nodded. "I agree. But you haven't said if you think I'm attractive either. I'm older than you, by quite a bit."

Kellen thought she detected a trace of vulnerability in the way Rae fiddled with the bedsheet, as if to cover herself, but wasn't sure. The odd little gesture tugged at something inside Kellen, stirring a need to reassure her. "You're very attractive. Any man or woman would consider themselves lucky to marry you." She felt her mouth go dry, and a sudden bout of nervousness made her voice hesitant. Unaccustomed to such closeness with another adult, and certainly in such an intimate setting as a bedroom, Kellen struggled to find the appropriate Premoni words. "Your touch is soft and pleasing." She held her breath, knowing full well how uncertain she sounded.

"My touch?"

"You've tended to my wound several times. You've also touched me on several other occasions. You're a strong woman with a soft touch."

Rae averted her eyes, glancing down at her hands. Looking back up at Kellen, she reached for one of hers. "We're in this together. We've signed a document, promising each other allegiance. I won't break my vow. No matter what kind of relationship we have, how it may or may not develop, I want you to know you're the most beautiful woman I've ever seen."

Kellen swallowed. *What's she playing at now? Does she really think simple flattery will make me lower my guard when I need it the most?* "You don't find me too alien?" Kellen wanted to kick herself for continuing this unproductive conversation. What did she care if Rae found her attractive or not?

"No more than you find me alien." Rae had smiled then, her eyes glittering when they met Kellen's.

"Dr. Meyer will see you now, Ms. O'Dal." A nurse interrupted Kellen's train of thought, and she rose and followed her to the examination room. As she waited for Gemma, the memory of Rae's eyes lingered. So too did Rae's declaration: *I want you to know you're the most beautiful woman I've ever seen.*

"Hello, Kellen, you're hardly limping at all. Excellent. Come with me, please." Gemma stood in the doorway to the examination room. "You're healing much quicker than I expected."

Wondering if she was supposed to feel proud of her obedient flesh, Kellen removed her trousers behind a screen before she sat down in a chair. Looking where the inflamed wound used to be, she had to concede that it had healed beyond her expectations. Her mind flickered yet again to earlier in the morning, Rae's hand around her own, and she wondered how it was possible for her to allow such an intimate act. Only a few days ago, she would have recoiled with a disdainful snarl. *Instead I sat there, compelled to reassure Rae that she's indeed beautiful.* Angry at herself for her weakness, Kellen leaned back on her hands and glared at the doctor.

Gemma traced the pink scar tissue with her fingers and looked pleased. "I'll use the deep-penetration fascia fuser, to ensure the strength of the muscle. After this treatment, I also want to use the derma fuser one more time. And by the way, you can resume normal everyday activities."

Not about to get on her knees and thank the CMO, Kellen pinned Gemma with her eyes. "Can I get back to my physical training?"

"Sure, as long as you don't overdo it or use heavy workout tools. You may feel a tightness, which is okay, but if the sensation becomes more like burning, you'll have to stop what you're doing and see me. You know your own body's limitations. Pay attention, and you should be fine." She cleaned the skin and ran the first fuser along the scar. "I'm relieved we didn't have to graft any muscle tissue. You'd have been in the infirmary while we cultivated the tissue from cells from your uninjured leg, and that takes weeks."

"Because I'm the only Gantharian here." Kellen kept her eyes on the other woman's hand, which slowly moved the piece of technology along her thigh.

"Yes."

The tingling sensation bordered on pain, but was far less painful than the treatment the day before. Kellen assumed this was a good sign. Reluctantly, she admitted to herself that *Gamma VI*'s trauma physician far exceeded the Onotharian butchers who treated Gantharian citizens with inferior technology. Gantharian physicians were not allowed to practice medicine independently any more. Demoted to working as orderlies, once-distinguished medical professors and docents worked for minimum wages in humiliating circumstances. Kellen glowered at Gemma, knowing that she would become one of these oppressors once the SC acknowledged Onotharat's dirty business on her homeworld.

"There, that's it." Gemma put the instrument away and peeled off her surgical gloves. "My assistant will give you some scar-reduction tape and show you how you align it with the scar. Then you're ready to go."

"Thank you, Doctor." Cold politeness was all Kellen could muster. She rose and, to her astonishment, felt no pain at all, not even a small reminder of how excruciating the throbbing had been only days ago. Half admiring, half resenting the Supreme Constellations technology available to the *Gamma VI* military installation, she stood indecisively, her hands by her side. Her people back home had no such help, she reminded herself again.

"Please, call me Gemma," the doctor reminded her. "We're going to be running into each other frequently since Rae is a good friend of mine. I look forward to hearing more about Gantharat."

Kellen felt a sudden sorrow erupt in her stomach, making her bite hard into her lower lip. Visions of the rolling green hills around her estate sent shivers through her, and she knew from the sympathetic look in Gemma's eyes that she could spot the desolation on her face. *This woman's a friend of Rae's.* Kellen made an effort to answer politely. "Armeo and I will do our best to describe it to you. It'll be good for him to talk about his homeworld."

"I know you can't go home. I didn't mean to sound insensitive."

"You didn't. I'd rather people not walk on glass around me. Things are as they are. We're lucky to be together, no longer fugitives."

"And we'll benefit from knowing you." Gemma rose. "Take care, and don't hesitate to contact me if you have any questions or experience discomfort."

"I guess 'discomfort' is a good word. I'll use some more of the paste Rae gave me last night. It helps with the sting from the derma fuser."

Gemma covered her eyes with one hand. "God, that woman has half of my medical supplies in her cabinets."

"Why is that?" Kellen suddenly felt concerned. Did Rae's seemingly healthy appearance lie? "Is Rae ill?" *She's my only anchor here. What if something happens to her?*

"Fit and strong as a racehorse. The thing is, she insists on going on missions herself, despite her rank, or perhaps because of it. She's worn out more derma fusers than anyone else on this station. I have to run. Take care now."

Gemma disappeared out the door, leaving Kellen to get dressed. She frowned as she carefully donned her trousers. Was Rae as reckless as Gemma's words suggested or merely dedicated to her work? If her spouse risked her life at any given time, she and Armeo might end up stranded without her. *I can't keep Armeo around anyone who's not careful.*

❖

Sitting through an extended morning meeting because everyone on her craft wanted to impress her father was not what Rae had in mind. As she endured the ensign who sounded even more solemn than usual while he submitted his report, she had to bite her lower lip to keep from cutting him off. Shifting in her chair, she stealthily punched in a few commands on her handheld computer and checked the status of the three ports. Unfortunately she couldn't find even the smallest skirmish anywhere that demanded her attention. Damn.

The admiral seemed to listen attentively as the staff gave their reports, his expression unreadable. Rae knew this was a deliberate technique, meant to rattle any subordinates who didn't know what they were talking about. She hid a smile when the pompous ensign finally sat down, obviously relieved.

"I believe that was everything for now." Rae leaned forward on her elbows, knowing it was time to brief her senior staff on the new developments. She dreaded it, anticipating her father's scrutiny and criticism at the end of every sentence. "Commander Todd, Lieutenant Grey, I want you to stay. The rest of you are dismissed."

Ensigns and junior lieutenants literally scurried off. Then the admiral turned his steely gray glance to her.

"Commodore, I take it you have an update on the Onotharian situation?"

"Yes, sir. Commander Todd briefed me earlier. Go ahead, Commander."

"The twenty-two injured Onotharian crew members brought aboard the *Ajax*, and later onto the *Gamma VI*, are still here. Dr. Meyer's report shows we can return thirteen of them to the Onotharian vessel docked at Port 3. We can't move the remaining nine yet, two of whom are in critical condition. They were the only survivors of the ship we destroyed."

"I see," the admiral said. "Have you communicated further with the ambassador?"

Rae took over. "Yes, sir. We provided legal documents regarding Kellen and Armeo's citizenship status, as well as copies of the preliminary application for custody. Ambassador M'Ekar knows when the court ship will arrive, and we have informed him this is his opportunity to respond through legal channels."

"And his response?"

"Ambassador M'Ekar is not corresponding with us directly, but through Deputy M'Indo. The deputy maintains we attacked the Onotharian fleet unprovoked and is demanding to speak with someone in authority. When they learned you were aboard, Admiral, M'Indo seemed impressed. But once he learned of your relationship to me, he broke communications after telling us he would confer with the ambassador. This was earlier today, and we haven't heard back from them yet."

The admiral chuckled. "It's amazing how little background research they did before they blew in here. Don't you find that odd?"

"What do you mean?"

"Think about it. You're well known throughout the sector, and still they come charging in. At first they seem pleased that the admiral of the fleet shows up to set things straight and then taken aback by the fact I'm your father. Wonder what their next move will be."

"I'm sure we won't have to wait long to find out." Rae turned to Owena. "And our security detail?"

"We've changed the duty roster to SEC 5. Twice as many security officers are doing rounds on the station, and double the usual number of patrol ships are guarding our outer perimeter. I've emphasized two locations on the station—the infirmary and the guest quarters where the recuperating Onotharians stay. Security also accompanies Armeo M'Aido and the commodore's spouse at all times."

"And your assessment, Lieutenant?" the admiral demanded.

Owena directed her sharp glance at him. An obsidian hairclip kept her long black hair back and emphasized the sharp angles of her jaw and cheekbones. Her brilliant blue gaze homed in on the admiral. "Two patrol ship pilots reported increased activity at several places outside our borders. I redirected two frigates to investigate, but this is probably a diversion. The Onotharians want the boy back on their territory, so they will presumably attempt to create a small skirmish or a series of feints along the border. If that occurs we will have to reduce the number of resources available here at the station, and in this situation, we can't afford to do that.

"Several Onotharians are present on *Gamma VI*, and we know their ultimate target—the boy. Judging from their past actions, they really don't care if they take him dead or alive, so the station is as much at risk as the child and the commodore's spouse. An Onotharian ship is docked at Port 3, ready to launch when all of its people are aboard. The risk of them trying something stupid is great. The threat is very real. We must be prepared for any possible contingency."

The admiral was silent for moment. "Contingency, eh? Well, Lieutenant, I agree with your assessment, and I'll add my piece to it. We're dealing with the possible political and no doubt monetary greed of one man, as well as the much greater machinations of a planetary system out to cause a political meltdown. But for what purpose?" The admiral leaned back in his chair. Rae recognized his impatience as he drummed his fingertips against the conference table.

"Let's assume we're dealing with the greed of one man," he mused. "I don't foresee any major issues at the preliminary custody hearing. The ambassador isn't familiar with our legal system and will use this meeting as practice for when it really matters. I've spoken to one member of the Council who carries a lot of weight and explained about M'Ekar's actions at our borders." Rae felt his stern gaze. "I spent most of last night reviewing your logs once again and those of the ships under your command. This mission was a textbook example, Commodore. Irreproachable."

Surprised, she tried to conceal her reaction by shrugging dismissively. She didn't want her senior staff to witness how her father's unexpected praise sent her heart racing. "I'm glad the logs confirm my report." Rae paused and hoped her face didn't betray the commotion in her mind. "You're right. This situation can still blow up in our faces. Given the situation, Lieutenant Grey has placed more guards at Port 3 as well. The Onotharians may not be able to demand we extradite Kellen O'Dal, but her son's safety and the political climate depend on how we handle this situation."

"Yes, ma'am."

"Once our legal system rules in our favor, nobody within SC space will assist the ambassador. All right, I'll talk to Ms. O'Dal and the lawyer to make sure we cover all our bases before the court ship arrives. We can't have any last-minute surprises."

"Good." The admiral rose and the other three followed suit, standing at attention. "I have several subspace conferences to attend. I'll see you later, Commodore. Commander, Lieutenant."

Rae relaxed back in her chair as her father left the conference room. His brief, cropped praise still reverberated inside her. *Do we ever stop seeking validation from our parents?* Her thoughts brushed past the memories of how she had tried throughout her years in school to live up to her father's expectations by joining in some of the extracurricular activities appropriate for a commodore's daughter. She remembered art classes where her inability to even draw a straight line became humiliating among her talented friends. Later she tried music lessons, where she realized she'd never learn to master any instrument known to mankind. *All I wanted was for him to recognize my capability for what I really wanted to do. Was that what I just saw?* Angry with herself for not being able to shake the bitter thoughts, Rae pressed both palms against the titanium conference table. *Why such benevolence now, Father? A little late, isn't it?*

"All right, I'd better locate Ms. O'Dal." Rae stood, her command settling like a cloak around her shoulders, shielding her from personal sorrow as it always did. As the commodore, she was untouchable. "She and I will be at the law firm in the commercial section, if there's an emergency."

"Yes, ma'am," her subordinates answered in unison.

"Dismissed."

Leaving the room, Rae took a right and headed for the elevator. She pulled the communicator from her shoulder and paged her quarters. When nobody answered, she hailed the officer in charge of security.

"Yes, ma'am, go ahead."

"Where is Kellen O'Dal right now?"

"One moment, Commodore." A brief pause. "Ms. O'Dal and her security guard are at the physical training facility, section 10D."

Rae signed off and stood motionless by the elevator door, mulling over the unexpected information. She wondered what Kellen was up to and decided to investigate. After she rode the elevator to the tenth level, she took the rail car to the gym section. *What the hell's she doing there? Surely Gemma hasn't cleared her for such activities already?* Rae wanted to page the CMO to ask but refrained from doing so. She wanted to see for herself first.

Several officers saluted her as she strode toward the part of the facility designed for combat practice. What kind of training could Kellen be participating in? She found her wife so unpredictable that having her in this part of the military section worried her.

Rae heard muted thuds and grunts echoing from a room to her right. Nodding to the security guard on post, she peeked inside, her breath catching in her throat at what she saw.

Dressed in a skintight red suit made of what looked like real leather, a blond figure vaguely recognizable as her wife whirled through the air, one leg like a sword ahead of her, the other curled up underneath. Stretching her arms out as she landed, she produced two long metal objects, twirling them in intricate patterns as she dived into a roll. Slicing through the air with precise movements, she moved with feline grace, forceful and deadly in her display.

The red suit accentuated every part of Kellen's curvaceous body, and her hair was slicked back in a tight braid. Rae felt the small hairs on her arms stand up as she watched her move in ways that seemed to defy gravity. After a somersault, Kellen landed on slightly bent legs, her metal staffs describing a cross. When she didn't move for a moment, Rae stepped inside the room.

"Kellen?"

The blond head snapped in her direction, staffs moving into what Rae assumed was a defensive position, one in front of her, one above her head, ready to launch. Kellen's eyes raked along Rae's body until a look of recognition appeared. Lowering the staffs, she said, "Rae. What brings you here?"

Still oddly breathless from watching her, Rae walked closer. "I came to let you know we have a meeting with the lawyer. Are you up to this kind of exercise? I thought you had an appointment with Gemma this morning."

"She gave me the go-ahead to resume training."

"Did she know that your training entailed…this?" Rae gestured toward the staffs.

"No, but she said any method not involving tools." Kellen walked over to a long, sleek casing sitting on a bench. Sheathing what Rae had to surmise were weapons, Kellen glanced over her shoulder. "I assumed she meant the machines in the gym I passed on my way here. My security guard described their purpose to me."

"You better clear this with Gemma before you engage in another training session. What's this sport called?"

"*Gan'thet*. But you're mistaken. This isn't a sport. It's an ancient Gantharian martial art."

"So you don't compete?" Rae started toward the door.

Kellen hoisted the casing onto her shoulder and gave her a wry smile. "If I did, and won, my opponent would be dead."

Rae flinched, the truth dawning on her. This was no recreational activity to stay in shape. She was married to a woman who could turn into a lethal weapon in a second. "So no holding back, huh?"

"No."

"And the outfit?"

"The Ruby Red Suit shows I'm a *gan'thet* master. It's made of *gindesh* skin, from a large quadruped animal hunted on Gantharat for its tender meat and its prized skin. The red stands for the blood that my opponents would shed…"

"Too much information, I get the picture." Rae held up her hand to forestall any more. "Why don't we go back to our quarters so you can shower? I can check some things on the computer while you get ready."

"Of course."

Rae punched her code into the elevator controls. "I usually come down here late in the evening to work out, mostly because I have trouble sleeping sometimes."

"Maybe I can accompany you next time?" Kellen glanced at her.

Rae quirked an eyebrow. "Sure, but only if you don't intend to use me for target practice." She meant it as a joke, but she could not disregard the fact that watching Kellen in action confirmed her worst suspicions. A flick of her wrist with one of those rods would break a human bone, possibly a person's neck. This was, however, not the worst part. She shuddered at the memory of how Kellen, when she was in full battle mode, had not recognized her. That vacant look haunted her.

Walking along the corridor next to her wife, Rae had never been more aware that she had married a dangerous stranger.

CHAPTER TEN

R ae, is this dress appropriate for tonight's activities?" Kellen's voice sounded matter-of-fact, but Rae thought she detected an impatient tone beneath the cool surface.

As she grabbed her own black cocktail dress from the closet, Rae glanced at her wife and caught her breath at the vision before her. Kellen wore a deep blue, sleeveless dress made of silver-coated Cormanian fairy-silk under a thin grid of Savorian Karma pearls glimmering in all shades of blue above her waist. The skirt flowed around her legs, ending at mid-calf.

"You look wonderful," Rae answered truthfully, watching Kellen's hair take the shape of a sleek wave of moonlight down her back.

"Thank you for providing me with credits to buy it."

"You're welcome."

"I'll repay you when I find a job."

"It isn't necessary," Rae said absentmindedly.

"Yes, it is. I don't need you to support me financially." Kellen's face took on a stubborn look by now becoming familiar to Rae.

"All right, all right. You can pay me back, then." She didn't have time to argue about such insignificant details right now.

Glancing back at her old, well-used black dress, Rae bit the inside of her cheek in exasperation. "I would have bought something new too, if I'd known Gayle was going to invite us for dinner. Should I go with the black?"

Kellen walked closer and scanned the hangers in the closet. "I'm sure black suits you, but what about this one?" She took out a dress still in its protective nylon mesh bag.

"Oh, I've never worn that." To her surprise, Rae felt her cheeks warm. "I bought it off a merchant vessel a while back. I don't know what I was thinking. I'm a tad old for white." Rae was well aware that SC Fleet tradition insisted that officers wear the dress uniform at social functions, and usually she adhered to this custom. *Hence my meager wardrobe.* Tonight, she decided, was not an official event—it was a private party. Rae scrutinized the white dress. *Why not?*

"Try it on."

Rae hesitated. "If you insist. You'll understand what I mean, though." She slipped the winter-crinkled retrospun cotton dress with intertwined silver-gloss filaments over her head and adjusted the tiny buttons on her left side before she turned toward Kellen, feeling utterly self-conscious. "There, you see?"

"I see it fits you perfectly. Look." Kellen took her by the shoulders and turned Rae toward the full-length mirror.

The white dress, also sleeveless, caressed her curves without being tight. Rae saw it added more femininity than she was comfortable with and was about to take it off when she noticed the look of admiration in her wife's eyes. "You really think I should wear this?"

"It's beautiful and fits you well. Of course you should wear something you're comfortable in." Kellen's voice was noncommittal, while her eyes were not. Rae noticed a spark in the midst of the crystalline blue that she hadn't seen before, as if Kellen really saw her for the first time.

Suddenly jittery, Rae reached for a hairbrush and straightened her short hair out. "It needs a necklace or something." She reached for a small box on the dresser, browsing her modest collection of jewelry, and chose a three-strand freshwater pearl collar. "Perhaps this?"

"Excellent choice."

Without thinking, Rae turned her back, expecting Kellen to help her put it on. Their domestic image that she saw in the mirror made her press a hand to her midsection. This was dangerous. *I can't fool myself into thinking this is for real. Kellen's married to me because it was our only option. Stay sharp, Jacelon.*

Kellen slowly placed the necklace around Rae's neck, fiddling briefly before she closed the clasp. Her fingertips touched bare skin and sent small shivers down Rae's spine.

Stepping into white knee-high, mesh-covered nuevoskin boots, Rae turned around to face her spouse. "Guess we're ready, then. Where's Armeo?"

"Already there. Dorinda paged him and asked him to join her and David for a game of…I forget what it's called." Kellen looked embarrassed. "Some new terms pass me by."

"Don't worry about it. You haven't been here that long."

"It feels like a long time already."

Stepping closer to Kellen at her solemn tone of voice, Rae touched her arm. "Are you okay?"

"Of course."

Rae suddenly realized she was getting to know Kellen better than she thought. *How cool she sounds when she tries to cover up. Something's disturbing her and she's not about to tell me.* Rae didn't want to get into a discussion with Kellen just before a dinner engagement. Instead she gently squeezed her bare arm for emphasis. "I know you've seen too much change over the last month. I'll do my best to help you think of me as your friend and our quarters as your safe haven. Yours and Armeo's."

Rae winced at her own spontaneous words and wracked her brain for something to say that would put them into a sensible context. "I mean, it's important for Armeo's case that the two of you acclimatize as quickly as possible."

"I know. Right now…I feel stateless." Kellen's mouth became a fine line after the last, revealing words.

About to say something consoling, Rae stopped to think how she might feel if she had to leave everything she knew and cared about for an uncertain destiny in an alien environment. *What if I were at the mercy of Onotharians who wanted nothing but to send me to an asteroid prison with the prospect of wasting away?* It was an unfathomable vision.

Not sure where her intense urge to reassure Kellen came from, Rae pulled her into a friendly embrace. Smiling inwardly at the surprised gasp followed by a stiffening of muscles, she spoke softly. "Have faith in me, Kellen. You'll find your place here at the station, just like Armeo is beginning to. It's easier for a young person, but you'll get there, trust me."

Rae felt Kellen slowly relax in her arms. Tentatively she returned the hug. "Thank you."

"We better get going. Gayle is rather big on punctuality."

"The way you say that tells me it's not always your strong suit."

Rae smirked. "Have me pegged already, huh? Let's just put it this way: I've only been late to the home of Alex and Gayle once." She gave an exaggerated shudder, which turned into a pleasant thrill when Kellen returned her smile.

❖

"Surprise!"

Lights suddenly switched on, and people jumped out from behind bulkheads and furniture, startling Kellen enough to make her raise her arms in a defensive *gan'thet* pose. Among the smiling faces of at least twenty people, she recognized Alex and Gayle de Vies, Gemma, Commander Todd, and Lieutenant Grey. Dorinda, David, and Armeo giggled at the stunned couple in the doorway.

"You didn't suspect a thing, did you?" Gayle chuckled as she hugged Rae. "I thought Armeo might have slipped."

"You knew?" Rae grimaced toward Armeo, who merely laughed.

"Yes, I did."

"Traitor." Rae ruffled his hair. "I'll get even with you." Looking at her wife, she shook her head. "Look at poor Kellen. She must think you're all mad."

Gayle hooked her arm around Kellen's. "This is one of our traditions. We knew you didn't have a proper wedding reception, so I decided if anyone deserves it, it's the two of you."

"So this celebration is for our union?"

"Of course! Now let me introduce you to the people you haven't met yet." As Gayle led Kellen around the room, she wondered if she was supposed to remember all the names. However, shaking hands and smiling seemed to do for now. After they went through this repetitive ceremony with everyone, the hostess guided Kellen toward a large *U*-shaped table decorated with flowers and ornaments.

Around her plate, as well as around Rae's, tiny pink flowers were tied into the shape of hearts. "Is this also tradition?" Kellen gestured toward the decoration.

"Yes. It symbolizes how you two are not only joined legally, but also in your hearts." Gayle's eyes glistened with unshed tears. "I can't believe how mushy this is making me."

"Aw, you're always mushy," Alex said, hugging her from behind. "Let the lovebirds take a seat so we can get down to the essentials. Food."

Swatting at him, Gayle wrinkled her nose. "So much for romance. He's right, though. Places, everyone!"

"Can you tell she's married to a military man? She's used to giving orders." Rae smiled at Kellen, who followed her example by sitting down on the adorned chairs.

"So much of the decoration is in pink," she mused. "Why is that?"

"Because this is a same-gender marriage. Pink for women, blue for men. *Very* ancient tradition."

Kellen looked around the table and noticed several other familiar faces. *They're here to celebrate my union with Rae. Do they truly accept me, or is this, as our marriage, merely for appearance?* Careful to keep her features neutral, she glanced to her left. A few seats down, a young woman sat next to Lieutenant Grey, involving the tactical chief in what looked like an intense conversation. "Lieutenant…D'Artansis, isn't it? Wasn't she piloting the *Ajax*?"

"Yes."

"She seems so young."

"Don't let Leanne's youthful looks deceive you. She's my pilot of choice when I expect to do battle." Kellen watched Rae scan the room, stopping when her father marched through the door. "How on earth did Gayle manage to persuade him to come? Ah, well, he's always had a soft spot for her. Of course."

Kellen wondered if Rae was aware of the tone of loss in her voice. "This is our reception. Why wouldn't your father want to attend?"

"He's not much for doing the 'family scene.' Granted, we haven't had much family scene to attend."

Kellen was uncertain how she should interpret the wry tone. She watched the admiral kiss Gayle on the cheek and shake hands with Alex before rounding the table and approaching her and Rae.

"Congratulations, again," he murmured. "Mrs. de Vies wouldn't take no for an answer. May I sit by your side, Kellen? It's my privilege as your father-in-law."

"I've never heard this expression." Kellen turned toward Rae for an explanation.

"It's an ancient Earth term," Rae said. "It means that my parents are now your parents too."

Refusing to let her inner turmoil show in the company of Rae's friends, Kellen merely dipped her head. *Ancient tradition? Gods of Gantharat, it's impossible to keep track of all these human traditions. How am I supposed to know if they're valid or just for appearances? Is this "father-in-law" term legitimate? Is this man now my "father" as well?* Her thoughts whirled as she motioned toward the empty chair next to her. "Then, Ewan, it's a privilege for me too to have you here next to me."

The steely gray in the admiral's eyes lightened at her words. Taking her hand in his, he kissed it with universal old-fashioned chivalry. "The pleasure is all mine, Kellen."

The catering staff brought in the first course, steamed vegetables with several small bowls of different sauces, and soon everybody was eating and talking. Kellen enjoyed the meal, relieved to find more evidence that SC food was not too alien for her palate.

Having grown most of their vegetables and roots on her estate, she wasn't used to synthetic or cryo-preserved foodstuff. During the spring, summer, and fall, she and Armeo rarely ate meat, but it had been introduced as a source of food again, having been almost unheard of before the Onotharian occupation. Hunting was one of the few ways for Gantharians in sparsely populated areas to get by in the winter season. The Onotharians had taken their opportunity to choose away from them by forbidding Gantharians to own anything high-tech, such as food synthesizers and computerized cookware. Of course, nobody of Gantharian descent could own any weapon without the required paperwork. To hunt for wild game, the populace could use only low-impact rifles.

Kellen looked at the end of the table where Armeo sat with David and Dorinda. He was laughing and doing the food justice, sometimes glancing her way. She felt both pride and relief that he was settling in so well. *What if I have to uproot him again? He'll end up hating me if I can't provide him a home.*

"He's checking to make sure you're okay." Rae's whisper made Kellen jump. "He's doing so well, but I think he's still concerned someone may snatch you away before his eyes."

"Did he tell you that?"

"Not in so many words, but you're all he has. He'll fear losing you for a while yet. If you're happy and secure, so is he."

Kellen considered this. Rae's reasoning was logical. If she settled and found the strength to shape a new life for them, his happiness would follow. Yet she'd begun anew so many times after losing the people she loved; how could she commit to anyone here? *I can't pretend for a second that this fake union with Rae is anything but a sham, a five-year sentence Rae probably can't wait to finish serving.*

The sound of metal against glass interrupted her trail of thoughts. Ewan Jacelon was standing with his glass raised. "Kellen, Rae, I want to join this long line of friends in congratulating you. I hope the future will bring you happiness and fulfillment, with each other and as Armeo's parents. To come here and find my daughter with a ready-made family was a pleasant surprise…one I'd given up on, to be blunt." Kellen noticed that a steely glare from his daughter made him pause. "Please, everyone, join me in a toast to the happy couple. To Kellen and Rae."

"To Kellen and Rae!" Everybody sipped their beverage of choice, only to begin to clink their glasses with utensils.

Kellen looked at Rae, uncertain of what was going on. Obviously she needed to do something, but she had no idea what.

Candles reflected in Rae's eyes, making them sparkle as she smiled. "We're supposed to kiss."

"Kiss?" *This can't be true.*

"That's what they expect." Rae motioned with her head toward the smiling guests still making the noise. "It's our reception, after all."

Stunned, and unsure how to proceed, Kellen looked at Rae and tried to signal her dismay.

Rae's expression softened as she leaned closer. "Just do what I do." She brushed her soft lips over Kellen's, lingering for a moment before she withdrew.

The wedding guests cheered, and several demanded a repeat. Smiling, Rae shook her head. "That's it," she said, reaching for a small fork. Not looking at Kellen, she waved it in the air. "I want to know what's for dessert!"

Laughter erupted, allowing Kellen time to find her bearings. She guessed Rae was buying her time to recover her wits, and she was grateful for the reprieve. She had not been prepared for such an intimate display in public.

❖

Rae sat next to her father on the couch, with Alex on her other side. The two men shared a warm camaraderie while off duty, which had made Rae jealous when she was younger. Ewan Jacelon spoke to Alex on equal terms, with none of the implied criticism he so often intertwined in his conversation, or monologues, with Rae. Only after years of hard work had she realized she had to be proud of herself and let her job make her happy.

Barely listening to the men discuss a political issue, Rae frowned at the sound of insistent, much younger voices. Intense, they were urging Armeo to act.

"It's true, you can't, Armeo. Go ask him. Go on."

"But what if you're wrong?"

"I'm hardly ever wrong." Dorinda sounded just as haughty as Gayle sometimes did when Alex showed his stubborn side and required what his wife called "gentle persuasion." Her tactic was identical, and just like Alex, Armeo folded.

Three young faces peeked around the bulkhead, Armeo's nervous. He took a few steps closer and wiped his hand on his trouser legs, evidently waiting for the admiral and Rae to notice him.

"Yes, Armeo, did you want something?" Ewan Jacelon asked. "You look troubled."

"I have a question, sir." Glancing at Rae, he shoved his hands into his jacket pockets. "Dorinda tells me I've got it wrong. She says since your daughter married Kellen, you're my step-grandfather and I can't call you by your first name, like you suggested."

Rae held her breath, awaiting her father's reply with her hand tightening around her coffee mug. *Damn you if you let him down, Father. Don't ignore him too.* Armeo's eyes were huge in his thin face. The thought of her father condescending to him in front of his friends awoke painful memories of similar situations when she was Armeo's age.

Leaning forward, her father reached for the boy's hand. "Armeo, you know what? I think Dorinda has a point. I wasn't thinking when I asked you to call me Ewan. Normally, you'd call your grandfather 'grandpa' or 'granddad.' Now, I'm going to give you the choice, since you're not a child, but a young man. You can keep calling me Ewan, if you like"—Rae met her father's eyes and couldn't decipher the emotions stirring in his—"but it would make me happy if you'd consider calling me either of the other two."

Armeo's face brightened, and he looked over his shoulder at his two friends.

"I told you so," Dorinda said helpfully.

"So which is it going to be?" Ewan Jacelon asked, a broad smile changing his stern features.

"Granddad. I like how it sounds. Can I tell Kellen?"

"Sure."

"Thanks!" Armeo swiveled and hurried toward the opposite corner of the room where Kellen was talking to Gayle and Leanne.

Rae was astounded. Unable to quite believe what she had just witnessed, she turned to her father, her voice low. "You realize what you just did, don't you?"

"If you're asking if I knew what it means to Armeo, yes. I may have acted like a bull in a china shop with you when you were a little girl, but I'm not completely insensitive. Maybe I've learned from my mistakes." Ewan stroked his beard, usually a sign that he was concerned. "He's vulnerable and needs reassurance, something to cling to. He needs to be certain that not only you will stand up for him and his mother, but that I will too."

"Don't let him down." Rae's throat hurt. "Just…don't."

The admiral shook his head. "I give you my word."

Rae rose from the couch. Feeling out of place and out of sorts in civilian clothes, she caught Kellen's glance across the room. Even at this distance, she could detect a multitude of questions in her skeptical blue eyes.

❖

Kellen stepped out of Armeo's room, careful not to close the door completely behind her. Armeo wanted to read for a while, and for once she extended the time before lights out. She knew he needed to unwind as much as she did after the surprising turn of events during the evening. She could tell it meant a great deal that the admiral had invited Armeo to view him as a grandparent.

The living room in their quarters was dark. Walking into the master bedroom, she found Rae unzipping her dress and tugging it off her shoulders.

"You received a lot of compliments for the dress. It was a good choice." Kellen attempted small talk while she watched Rae remove the pearls, only to curse under her breath when the necklace became stuck in the small buttons on her dress. She walked up to her and freed it, then put it back into its case.

"Yes, seems it was a hit. So was yours. I saw you had a long conversation with Leanne D'Artansis. Pilot talk?"

"Yes. I'm considering what kind of position to apply for. I asked her opinion."

"You did?" Rae stopped on her way to the bathroom. "What did she say?"

"She understood my concerns and suggested I take some simulation tests to find out what ships suited me best." Kellen was puzzled at how devoid of emotion Rae's eyes had become.

"Good. Sound advice." Turning to go into the bathroom, Rae seemed to change her mind a second time, glancing over her shoulder, her eyes dark gray. "What concerns did you mean?"

Kellen began to unclasp her dress. "I've researched the positions available for a pilot on *Gamma VI*. I don't want to stay away from the station for any long periods of time, which limits my possibilities."

"Of course. Armeo."

"Yes, and you. If we're going to make our marriage work, neither of us should be gone for any great length of time. Also, it's dangerous if I pilot a merchant vessel along the border, for instance."

To Kellen's surprise, Rae seemed to stiffen. "You're right. You're absolutely right." She paused. "Why didn't you come to me sooner and discuss this?"

Taking off her dress, Kellen shrugged. "I didn't want to bother you with details. You already knew I was concerned about not having a meaningful job. I thought if I showed you I could find one on my own…" She shrugged. "I'm not a child like Armeo. I don't need my wife to take care of every little thing for me."

"That's not what I meant. I…oh, never mind. It doesn't matter." Turning away, Rae went into the bathroom and closed the door.

Kellen stood motionless for a moment before she hung her dress up in the closet. Sitting down at the dresser, extracting the pins from her hair, she bit her lower lip. Why did Rae act like this? As she removed the rest of her clothes and put on a satin-mesh kaftan, she went back over their conversation in her mind. Rae had asked her about her conversation with Lieutenant D'Artansis, and then...Lowering her hands, Kellen stared at her reflection in the mirror. The red kaftan flowed freely around her, the thin material barely more than an insect's web. Her hair lay in tousled locks around her shoulders, and she had a haunted expression in her eyes that she recognized all too well by now. *When was the last time I relaxed and let go? I can't remember. Ever?*

"The bathroom's all yours." Rae was dressed in a similar robe. "I just rinsed off. I'm tired."

Not sure how to be anything but direct when dealing with her wife, Kellen waited until Rae sat on her side of the bed before she pivoted on the stool. "Did I break protocol when I talked to Lieutenant D'Artansis, rather than you, about my career choices?"

"Oh, God, of course not. Actually, if you'd come to me first, I'd have told you Leanne D'Artansis is the one to approach for such advice."

"Your reaction earlier suggests otherwise." Kellen rose and walked over to the bed. Sitting next to Rae, she looked down at her spouse's hands, then reached out and covered the one nearest her. "Why did my initiative upset you?"

"It didn't..." Rae curled her hand, hiding it under Kellen's. "Damn it, it did. Leanne is your age, shares your profession, and she's very beautiful." Rae looked utterly dismayed. "I was jealous. This is ridiculous! I don't have time for this. We have to focus on the custody hearing and make damn sure the court-ship judge rules in our favor." Rae rubbed the back of her neck with her free hand, her movements jagged, clearly showing her annoyance.

Stunned, Kellen didn't know what to say. She knew she had to try to preserve what little trust they had between them. Armeo's future depended on it. "Surely you must realize how superfluous any jealousy on your part is?"

Raising her head, Rae blinked. "What?"

"Our marriage is little more than a business deal. I guess politics is an even better word. No emotions are involved, which means there's no call for jealousy."

Rae blushed faintly and her eyes turned blank. "I'm well aware just what our marriage is all about. After all, it was my idea."

"I know that. I hope there won't be more displays of public affection."

Rae flinched. "What do you mean?"

"The kiss." Kellen's ire was up and she knew it would've been smarter to remain calm, but her own reaction to the short caress in front of Rae's friends and subordinates still upset her. Completely unexpectedly, the kiss had sent shivers through her entire being and stolen her breath. She definitely believed any signs of vulnerability on her part could get her and Armeo separated, or worse, killed, and she could still feel the soft caress of Rae's lips on hers. "Well?" she insisted when Rae didn't reply.

"I'm sorry our first kiss had to take place in public. It's not how I'd pictured it."

Kellen let go of Rae's hand as if she'd burned herself. "You've imagined a first kiss between us?"

Rae squeezed her eyes shut for a moment and looked like she wished she hadn't opened her mouth. "Only natural, don't you agree? After all, we're married."

"You maneuvered me into this union, and that doesn't give you any right..." Kellen choked when her temper ignited again. Staring at Rae, she hated how her eyes began to prickle with tears of fury.

"Are you implying I'm demanding my marital rights?" Rae thundered. "That's a damn insult and totally uncalled for!" She rose and tugged her kaftan closer around her.

Kellen followed her, walking closer to tower over Rae. "Is it? You've just confessed to harboring precisely such thoughts. Am I supposed to happily oblige?"

"Damn you." Redness seeped into Rae's cheeks. "I can't believe you said that."

Acting before she thought, Kellen grabbed Rae by her shoulders, pressing her lips against hers. As if frozen, Rae stood still between her hands, her mouth half open under Kellen's. Rampaging feelings flooded Kellen's body, and she crushed Rae against her. The smaller body fit well along her lean, muscular frame.

Rae seemed completely stunned for a few more seconds, but then she raised her hands, and Kellen expected a struggle. Instead, Rae moaned as she cupped her cheeks and slipped her tongue between Kellen's lips.

Kellen had never reflected if the art of kissing was universal, but now it was entirely impossible not to return the caress. Meeting Rae's tongue with hers, she tasted her for the first time, wanting to both growl with anger and whimper at the unexpected pleasure. The kiss went on for a few seconds longer before Kellen pushed Rae back at arm's length.

"You're just like the Onotharians, trying to bind me to you regardless of what you have to do to accomplish it. You don't own me!" A lump grew in Kellen's throat from sheer anger, preventing her very breath.

Her eyes a cold, slate gray, Rae spoke low and forcefully. "How dare you compare me to someone like M'Ekar and his peers? How can you even suggest anything like that? I'm stuck in this for five years too, remember? I've put my life on hold just as much as you have. I've risked my name and my career to keep you and Armeo safe. I don't need this from you!"

Rae now growled, not backing away but placing a strong hand, knuckles first, on Kellen's chest. "You can curse your fate for hours on end, but the fact remains, we're stuck with each other and have to fake this union as best we can."

Kellen raised her hand faster than even her own eyes could detect and grabbed Rae's wrist. Clutching it, she kept it pressed against her chest. She didn't take her eyes off Rae's, and her heart raced as her temper flared. "Don't worry. In five years, or sooner if possible, I'll be gone, and so will Armeo."

As if time stopped, Rae ceased to breathe for a moment and seemed speechless. Lowering her gaze toward her hand, she didn't tug; instead she kept it where it was. "Five years is a long time."

Taken aback by the remorseful tone, Kellen loosened her grip a little. "Yes."

"Armeo will be a young man of seventeen. He'll see me as a parent, and you really must consider me made of steel and devoid of feeling if you don't realize that I'll consider him a son long before then," Rae said throatily.

Suddenly ashamed of her outburst and accusations, Kellen regarded the woman in front of her with new eyes. She saw pain in Rae's gaze, and had she been able to, she would have relented. However, she had Armeo to consider, and he took precedence in everything she did. She couldn't afford to soften in front of anyone, least of all someone in Rae's position. Tomorrow she'd be back in her uniform again, back in command, the one who determined her immediate future with Armeo by her side.

"A lot can change in five years," Rae said, stronger now. "You should be the first to concede that whole worlds can go under in less time than that."

Kellen stepped closer to Rae again, pressing the commodore's fist harder into her soft flesh. "That's not fair."

"It's true, isn't it?" Rae freed her hand and folded back the bedcovers. "We better get some sleep."

Despite her anguish at Rae's words, Kellen retreated. Needing to put distance between them, she tugged her kaftan closer and entered the bathroom. The sliding door hissed behind her just as her knees gave way. Leaning hard against the counter, she stared at her reflection, all too familiar. Pale, with the blue blood cells drained from her skin, eyes slits of blue fire, and her upper lip drawn back in a faint snarl. Tereya had once taken a picture of her looking exactly like this while practicing *gan'thet*.

I have to find a way to relax, or I'll go out there and throttle her for saying what she did. "Shower. Medium-hot. Pulsating."

Water began to stream in thrusts from the showerhead and Kellen tossed her kaftan on the floor, desperate to get warm. She hadn't been this cold in a long time.

CHAPTER ELEVEN

Rae opened her eyes, feeling satiny skin under her lips as strong hands held her close. Inhaling deeply, she smelled a soft, alien scent reminiscent of the dark red Tamara lilies that flourished in the meadows on her parents' estate on Earth. Sweet, almost fruity, with a faint trace of something darker, muskier. She finally realized she was captured beneath another body and tried to move, with little result. Kellen was fast asleep.

Rae, on the other hand, had not slept well at all. Pretending to breathe evenly, she had listened to Kellen settle down after her shower, half expecting her to opt for the couch in the living room. Rae lay far over on her side of the bed and stared out the view port most of the night. Only in the early morning was she eventually so tired she fell asleep, and now she had no idea how they'd ended up like this.

Rae pushed long blond strands of hair from her own face and tucked them behind Kellen's ear. The tender movement seemed surprisingly natural. "Kellen? Wake up. You have to move a little bit."

Still no reaction. Rae turned her head, her lips ending up just a whisper away from Kellen's mouth. Soft gushes of air washed over Rae's face as her wife breathed.

"Come on," Rae tried again. "It's almost time to get up anyway." Circling Kellen's waist with her arm, expecting to find fabric, she felt nothing but smooth skin. Realizing the thinlinnen shirt must have ridden up, Rae was about to remove her hand when her spouse gave a soft sigh.

Swallowing against the sudden dryness in her throat, Rae allowed her fingers to linger, to savor the feel of Kellen's skin. She should remove her hand, but it was as if it were glued to the beautiful woman asleep in her arms. Wiggling her other hand free from underneath Kellen, Rae wrapped both arms around her, reveling in the furtive embrace. *Clandestinely touching a sleeping woman. That substantiates her accusations last night, doesn't it, Commodore?* Still, her self-deprecating words weren't enough to make her remove her hands right away.

"Rae..." Another whisper from the full lips so close to hers.

Rae bit back a moan, again trying to wake up Kellen. "Hello there, time to get up."

Moving to the side, freeing Rae, Kellen opened unfocused eyes. "Yes? What time is it?"

Rae glanced at the chronometer. "Ten minutes before the alarm goes off."

Kellen's eyes slowly focused, and her expression became guarded. Still, she seemed reluctant to move. "Rae. About last night..."

Rae groaned at the memory of the mutual accusations. "Oh, damn. I said something unforgivable to you." She looked deep into Kellen's eyes, searching for...something. "Forgive me. I'm not a cruel person. Really."

"I know." Kellen placed two fingertips on Rae's lips. "I accused you of manipulating me for your own purpose. I made you think I meant physically, and then I initiated a kiss. That wasn't honorable."

Curious at Kellen's choice of words, Rae put her hand over her wife's. "I kissed you back." The words hung between them, and Rae knew her embarrassment was clearly visible. Kellen seemed different as well this morning. Where her eyes had burned through layers of resentment and fury last night, they now looked at Rae misty blue and pensive. *Probably just a temporary respite. Soon they'll be shooting daggers at me again.*

"I do appreciate your sacrifice," Kellen said.

"Granted, five years with a stranger is a sacrifice. But, Kellen, you're not a complete stranger anymore." Rae struggled to find the right words. "I mean, I don't know much about you, but I'm learning. Last night, we let distrust and fear get the better of us. I know you don't have much reason to trust anyone, and perhaps me in particular..."

"I can't afford to." Kellen's soft tone mitigated her brusque words.

"Then there's the kiss." Rae forced herself to sound matter-of-fact even though the memory of their passionate embrace made her breathless. "Anger and passion are sometimes closely related. I didn't expect to react the way I did." *Or you.*

Kellen remained quiet for a moment and seemed to consider what to say next with great care, or perhaps she was struggling with the same unsorted feelings and confusion. Rae figured her wife was too proud to show embarrassment, but she could actually feel Kellen cringe. *Damn, let go of her! By the stars, she's half naked. You can't speak of hasty actions in the heat of an argument and be feeling her up at the same time!* Blushing profusely, Rae tore her hands from the silky skin. She sat up and swung her legs over the edge of the bed, just about to rise when Kellen stopped her by placing a hand on her thigh.

"It's important that we don't let our anger show. To the universe, we're…in love and just married. We can't take our personal concerns out with us when we leave these quarters."

Rae knew Kellen was right, but still it made her uneasy to hear her list the reasons like that. *Does a secret part of me wish that Kellen and I could be closer merely for our own sakes?* She shied away from the thought immediately. It was too complicated and too soon. She looked over at her wife who now sat up in bed, looking deceptively angelic with her flaxen hair tangled around her shoulders. *Too beautiful.* Rae's eyes fell upon Kellen's lips. It seemed impossible that just a few hours ago they had kissed her thoroughly. *Too soon. Too much.* She knew she had to say something more about their heated words. They had eaten away at her most of the night.

"Please, forgive me for what I said about worlds changing fast. It was insensitive. And wrong of me."

"Apology accepted." Kellen paused, her fingers gripping the bedcovers. "I was tactless too. It was unfair of me to compare you to the Onotharians."

"I appreciate you saying that." Only guessing how difficult it must've been for her, Rae jumped up. She needed to put distance between them, but she also felt energized by their newfound truce. "It's time to get ready. We have a long day ahead of us."

Kellen slid out of bed in one fluid movement. Walking toward the bathroom, she was a study in white and blond, her bluish skin making her look ethereal, like a forest entity out of an Iminestrian fairy tale.

Rae couldn't take her eyes off her. *I wonder how someone so strong can look so vulnerable. Or...am I the only one who sees it?* Taken aback by this notion and angry at herself for indulging in unproductive thoughts, she strode to the guest bathroom to grab a shower. She made it a cold one.

❖

Kellen strolled into a large room that housed several different flight simulators. Two ensigns nodded at her and saluted the petite woman at her side.

"Carry on, please," Lieutenant Leanne D'Artansis said, and returned the salute. Her long, red-blond hair lay in a snug bun against the base of her neck, and her marbled eyes glittered in colors that ranged between golden brown and green. Her slightly upturned nose boasted an interesting pattern of light freckles, and the only things preventing Kellen from describing her as cute were her firm, ample mouth and her surprisingly husky voice.

"As you see, Kellen, you can try any of the vessels used by the SC forces. They should handle the same way the Onotharian ships you were used to."

"Which one should I start with, Lieutenant?"

"Oh, please, call me Leanne. This is pretty informal, after all. How about the frigate? Then you can move on to the smaller vessels."

"Fine." Reluctantly charmed by Leanne's exuberant charisma, Kellen couldn't help but return the smile.

Leanne strode over to the ensign in charge of the simulators. "Is number 5 available?"

"Yes, ma'am," the ensign replied smartly. "Ms. O'Dal may use it for thirty minutes before the next pilot arrives."

"Good." Leanne turned to Kellen. "Why don't you run the introductory sequence and then try a few of the different scenarios? I'll monitor you from out here."

"Are you sure you have time? You must be very busy."

"Don't worry about it." Leanne quickly positioned herself behind the controls. "The way you speak, I think you love flying as much as I do." A puzzling dark shadow flickered over her features. As if she realized she was showing too much, she quirked one corner of her mouth in a faint smirk. "I'll enjoy putting you through some interesting surprises in there."

Kellen nodded. "I know I'll enjoy the challenge."

She climbed through the hatch that led into a cabin. Inside, the controls looked exactly like the helm of an SC Class One frigate. Having gone over the specifications of the ship, she knew it was similar to the ones she had flown back home.

"Can you hear me, Kellen?" Leanne's voice flowed through the comm system.

"Loud and clear."

"All right. Take her through the starting sequence."

Kellen flipped switches and punched in commands, listening to the familiar hum when the simulator began to power up. She took a determined hold of the large handles and eased the frigate out of the imaginary port. Other ships approached, and she carefully maneuvered around them.

"Excellent. Now prepare for the leap to field-distortion drive one, course Alpha Zero Two."

"Field-distortion drive leap initiated." Kellen punched in new commands and listened to the main deflector reverberate.

She observed her instruments and saw the field-distortion drive form ripples around the ship. It was time to adjust her course. Using the navigational console to her left, she calculated the course to Alpha Zero Two and submitted the data, then leaned back into the chair. Numbers ran down her screen like a digital waterfall as the computer worked on the coordinates she'd entered. A sudden thrust pressed her into the seat before the DVAs kicked in and removed the feeling of the G-forces. "Field-distortion drive one."

"Good job. Adjust your course. There's an asteroid belt in your path."

Kellen smiled at the gleeful tone in Leanne's voice. Watching the long-range scanners, she saw a dense asteroid belt and decided it was too vast to go around. She reduced to impulse speed and grabbed the handles again. Exhilarated, she knew the next set of maneuvers would be fun.

❖

"Commodore, an urgent message from SC Headquarters. Patching it through on a secure subspace channel."

Rae allowed herself a pensive drum roll of her fingertips against the desk before she responded. "Thank you, Lieutenant." She watched the SC insignia appear and rotate before the signal was established.

A man about her father's age came into view. "Commodore Jacelon," he said with a nod.

"Councilman Thorosac."

"I'll get right to the point, Commodore. A matter of grave concern has caught our attention. We've received new intelligence from *Gamma V* and *Gamma VII*. Several Onotharian ships have been deployed to patrol the border. When I approached the Onotharian government, they informed me that Ambassador M'Ekar still has their trust and they take his recommendations at face value. The situation concerns us greatly. I've spoken with your father on several occasions, and he assures me you have everything under control."

His doubtful tone of voice made it obvious the Councilman did not quite trust Rae's ability to handle the Onotharian situation. Normally, Rae admired Thorosac, and she regarded him as one of the most levelheaded Council members. His reservations toward her stung, but she made it a point to hide her pain well. She couldn't afford to show any uncertainty.

"Sir, we believe the Onotharian ships at our borders are diversions to keep us occupied while they try to seize Armeo M'Aido."

"How can you be sure?"

"We can't, but our intelligence and my own experience regarding Ambassador M'Ekar's methods make it very likely."

"So what are your immediate plans, Commodore?"

"We have reinforced security on the station as well as along the borders. We can't act unless acted upon in this matter." Rae leaned forward, determined to make herself clear. "On a diplomatic level, however, the Council can do several things. I'm sure Admiral Jacelon has informed you what the political ramifications would be should Armeo M'Aido fall into the hands of M'Ekar."

"Yes, and I agree. The Council was surprised to hear the M'Aido dynasty was not extinct. We thought Zax M'Aido and his aunt were the last of their line."

"They're that famous?"

"They were close to royalty in the Onotharat Empire. I'm sure the rumors about the child's existence are already spreading. M'Ekar has no doubt commissioned clever propaganda to strengthen his claim to the last M'Aido on his homeworld."

Rae's voice sank to a low rumble. "Armeo is a child, not a pawn to be used in a political game."

"Make up your mind, Commodore. One minute you're asking me to go through diplomatic channels to put pressure on the Onotharians, and the next, you insist we treat the boy like any child."

"He *is* a child! He's a fugitive, a refugee, if you like, who had to watch his home be burned to the ground by people out to destroy him and the woman he sees as his mother. Ms. O'Dal sustained a wound that would have killed her if left untreated."

Knowing her emotional outburst was not helping their case, Rae forced herself to calm down. "Granted, I realize you need to use any means necessary to defuse this situation, Councilman, but Armeo deserves a chance to grow up within the bounds of his family. And as I'm now part of his immediate family, I will not sit idly by if I see he is in any kind of danger. I promised him and his mother, and so did Admiral Jacelon, to keep them safe."

Councilman Thorosac rubbed his chin, as if he considered her statement. "You always were your father's daughter in so many ways, Commodore. I respect your desire to keep your family safe, but so much more than individual interests is at stake here. If the boy falls into the wrong hands—"

"He won't," Rae interrupted. "I will not allow it."

"Brave words. The Council will let you try this case in court, as planned. But I need to warn you. If we find any reason to believe you can't handle the situation, we'll be forced to move the boy into protective custody."

The Council openly doubted her ability to protect Kellen and Armeo. Her fury, rising inside her like an unbending plasma storm, made her speak in a fierce growl. "You cannot do anything of the sort! She is my wife, and, by law, until the judge aboard the *Dalathea* has reviewed this case, I'm Armeo's guardian. His *parent*, in fact." The emotional ramification of her words pierced through her anger and almost made her falter at the overwhelming truth in them, but she kept going. "They're SC citizens, with the same rights as anybody else within these borders. You can't touch them."

"We would not be interested in Ms. O'Dal. She's of little importance. The boy, however, is the catalyst that could throw our sector of space into turmoil. I needn't remind you how our union of planets has fought for decades to sustain a peaceful existence."

"What the hell are you talking about?" Rae knew she was out of line but didn't care, addressing the Councilman the way she would a crew member guilty of insubordination. "Would you separate the boy from his mother?"

"She's not his mother. She's his guardian, and the guardianship can be transferred to the Council, if necessary."

"My father has agreed to also serve as a guardian of the boy. That should be good enough for the Council."

"For now, yes. If you can keep the M'Aido child safe and out of M'Ekar's reach, then your situation will remain as it is."

"And why can't the Council use its influence with the Onotharian government to get rid of M'Ekar?"

"He was married to a M'Aido and pulls a lot of weight in his homeworld. I admit it *is* puzzling how a reckless megalomaniac such as the ambassador can have such unrestricted power. There must be more to it."

"All right. Leave it to me to take care of Ms. O'Dal and Armeo. My father and I are perfectly capable."

Thorosac didn't look convinced. "I hope so. We expect daily reports, Commodore."

Rae clenched her teeth to avoid a rude reply. "Yes, sir."

"Good luck. Thorosac out."

The screen flickered, and the SC insignia replaced the Councilman's face. Rae stared at it while she tried to calm down. She should have expected the Council's stance but was shocked to hear Thorosac actually declare its intentions. His detached tone of voice had made his words sound even more callous. Unless she proved herself worthy of carrying out the task, the Council would take Armeo not only from *Gamma VI*, but also from Kellen.

Not even daring to think about Kellen's reaction to this information, Rae punched a few commands into her computer. Something Thorosac had just said rang a distant bell in the back of her head.

Impatiently, she reached for her communicator and summoned Lieutenant Grey. Mentally picturing the striking tactical officer, Rae blessed the fact that the impressive woman was stationed at *Gamma VI*. Owena Grey was as tough as they came. Her stern expression accentuated something dark, like a restrained, potentially explosive force within. Her stark features made her face as intimidating as it was beautiful. Owena moved with lethal grace, not unlike Kellen, although the Gantharian was not as massive. Rae had always suspected the lieutenant carried a lot of emotional baggage, but as long as it didn't affect her performance, Rae didn't address it.

Ten minutes later, Rae saw through the transparent aluminum walls how Lieutenant Grey walked into the mission room and stopped momentarily to observe the view screens before she continued to the commodore's office. Turning the walls from translucent to opaque, Rae nodded toward the visitors' chair.

"We have a new problem." Rae laced her fingers together on the desk, forcing them to stop trembling from either anger or the adrenaline rush she'd experienced while talking with Councilman Thorosac.

"What can I do?" Lieutenant Grey took out a handheld computer.

"We need to know more about Armeo M'Aido's past, especially on his mother's side. Something I learned just moments ago sparked my interest in that side of the family tree."

"Why the sudden hurry, ma'am? Is this for the custody hearing?"

"No, not quite. I'm fairly sure we'll obtain full custody of Armeo. No, and this is confidential, Lieutenant. It's just as serious, if not more so. The Council may take Armeo into its custody, a ward of the state of sorts, if we can't show enough evidence we can protect him."

Grey's thick, black eyebrows drew together, creating a dangerous look in her dark blue eyes. "They'd take him from Ms. O'Dal? The only mother he knows?"

"Yes. They didn't include her in their plans. No doubt they consider her too reckless, too hard to control. If they try to take that boy away they may find out firsthand how dangerous she can be, eh? But we, Lieutenant, are going to make sure that doesn't happen. Do you read me?"

"Yes, ma'am."

"I want you to use whomever you need with a level 1A security clearance to go through all of the records you can locate on Zax M'Aido and his time as a cadet at the Gantharian Academy of Pilots. I'm missing something here. Focus on his friends and acquaintances during that period. I also want you to find everything you can about the boy's mother…what was her name…Tereya something. Damn, do we even know her last name?"

"It should be easy to discover in the academy records. I remember reading about the rumors at the time of his death. His illustrious family, which was close to royalty on Onotharat, ostracized him."

Impressed with her memory, Rae nodded. "Yes, I read that too. Probably because he married a Gantharian. I know she was Kellen's best friend. I'd like to ask her about Tereya, but I don't want her to find out about the Council's backup plan." Rae shook her head in dismay. "I can only imagine her reaction."

"I spoke with your wife at the reception yesterday," Grey said. "She seems resourceful and ambitious. I can't picture her sitting idly by when her foster son is in danger."

"She never lets her guard down. I think doing that every single day for the last seven years makes it automatic."

They sat in silence for a moment.

"You realize I'll be doing a background check on your wife as well."

"Do whatever it takes. I want answers and I want them fast. I'll deal with the fallout later. I need to be prepared for the unexpected. Right now, I can't view the whole picture. That ties my hands when I need to develop a successful plan."

"I understand. By the way, ma'am, I was on my way here to discuss the current situation along our borders when you hailed."

"Go ahead, Lieutenant. What are our neighbors up to?"

"I've followed the patterns of minor attacks on the border, and they don't make sense. They're scattered, more annoying than dangerous. They start in one sector, calm down, and within the hour ignite somewhere else."

Rae looked at her tactical officer, her mind reeling. "How long has this been going on?"

"The last six hours, with increasing frequency."

"Damn, they're testing our defenses, looking for our weaknesses, and trying to throw us off balance. And if they succeed, they'll move in, cause a diversion, and try to get their hands on Armeo while we're struggling to find our bearings. A dangerous game, don't you think? I know his family has been a political icon for centuries, but this…"

Incensed, she pounded her desk. "They're willing to go to war to get Armeo, and they're willing to kill him if they can't have him. What the hell is so damn important about this boy? I can't figure it out."

"I'll get on it, ma'am," Lieutenant Grey said, rising from the chair. "If there's anything in the records we'll uncover it."

"Thank you. Report to me on the hour."

"Yes, ma'am." The lieutenant stood at attention for a moment, turned on her heel, and walked out the door.

Rae turned the walls back to forty percent transparency, enough to see what was going on in the mission room. Her staff was hard at work, monitoring the ships approaching or departing in the ports. She was well aware that three generational ships had moored in the last few days, increasing the population aboard *Gamma VI* by approximately thirty-five percent. These nomads represented a major source of income for the commercial sectors on the space stations, and *Gamma VI* was no exception. Her duty was also to provide them a safe haven to restock their supplies and make necessary repairs on their vessels.

Something moving in the corner of her eye caught Rae's attention, and she was surprised to see her wife purposefully approach. "Kellen, is everything all right? Have a seat."

"I'm fine." Kellen was dressed in what had become her usual attire since she arrived at the station—the same blue trousers and leather jacket that the crew members wore. She had tamed her long hair into a loose bun, snuggled into the base of her skull. She sat down and neatly clasped her hands, gazing at Rae with a new spark in her eyes. With her chin raised, she still appeared proud and arrogant, but for the first time she seemed almost eager. "I'm here to make a request."

"Go on."

"I've spent five hours in different simulated SC vessels, and now Lieutenant D'Artansis has offered to supervise me if you'll let me try the type of ship I handled best. Here are my transcripts." Kellen handed over a handheld computer.

Rae scrolled down the list, inwardly amazed at some of her daring flight patterns and realizing Leanne D'Artansis might have met her match. "Do you want to try one of our assault vessels? You know you can't go outside the station beacons, but a short spin around the block isn't out of the question." *Don't betray my trust now. You're smart enough to realize this is a test, Kellen.*

"Lieutenant D'Artansis will be in the navigator's seat. She'll determine how far from the station we can go."

"Not far at all." Rae gave her wife a stern look. "You're a target. If you stay inside the beacons, we know what ships are present and where they are. You'll have to wear one of the computerized suits to mask your biosignature. Since not many Gantharians travel this part of space, you'd be too easy to spot." She paused and examined Kellen's record in the assault-craft simulator. "Very well. You have my permission to go off-station for one hour. No more. Enjoy your flight and return safely."

"I will!"

"Good." Rae examined the new expression of enthusiasm shining from Kellen's eyes. "So, are you considering this type of ship? Only members of the military operate them, you know."

"Yes, I realize I'd have to apply for a commission. Right now, it's impossible, but perhaps further down the line. It would give me something to work toward."

Rae's first reaction was to balk at the idea. *Is she serious?* "You'd be prepared to apply to the Fleet?" This was almost too much. She knew trusting Kellen at the helm of a spaceship was the same as providing her an easy way to escape. Only the fact that Leanne would be in the navigator's seat, and Armeo safe back on the station, made it doable. Kellen would never leave her charge behind.

"If I'm going to live here, I'd be honored to serve. Do you think I'm not capable or that I wouldn't serve the Supreme Constellations well?" Kellen's eyes gleamed in defiance.

"You're contemptuous when you speak of the SC Council, and yet you now talk about a possible application for a commission. Can you blame me for being...surprised?" Rae mitigated what she initially was going to say in an attempt to not alienate Kellen further.

Kellen had the good taste to lower her eyes for a moment. "You're right. I'm suspicious of anyone in authority, and for good reason." She raised her gaze to Rae's again. "However, once I commit to something—or *someone*—I'm loyal. My allegiance to Armeo should be proof of that."

Rae thought she detected a hint of honesty and pleading behind the proud declaration. Having Kellen off-station for a moment was perhaps a good idea, since they were about to transfer some of the

Onotharians back to their ship. Armeo was in school under Terence and his bodyguard's supervision. Making a mental note to assign one more guard to the school, just in case there was a breach in security while the Onotharians were in transit, Rae rose from the chair

Kellen stood up and hesitated before she rounded the desk. Rae got up and tilted her head back so she could meet Kellen's gaze.

"Yes?"

"Thank you." Her features softened, and she placed a gentle hand on Rae's shoulder. "I won't betray your trust. I have a lot to return to."

❖

The shuttle bay of the *Ajax* was an impressive sight. Frigates carried eight assault craft in their belly, but a destroyer such as the *Ajax* held twice as many in each shuttle bay.

Kellen walked next to Leanne and gazed at the sleek ships lined up in immaculate rows, waiting to be deployed. Approaching the lieutenant in charge of the shuttle bay, Leanne saluted.

"Sir, I have authorization from Commodore Jacelon for Ms. O'Dal to test-fly a 615 assault craft."

"Let me check, Lieutenant." The man scrolled down his computer, nodding. "I have verification. You can take *Red Dragon 4*. Will you be acting navigator?"

"Yes, sir."

"Good. You have one hour of flight time. Stay within the beacons and stay sharp."

"Aye, sir." After another salute, Leanne guided Kellen to a ship in the front row. "This is it, the *Red Dragon*. I've flown this one on many a mission. It handles like a dream."

Kellen nodded, reaching for the ladder welded to the side of the ship. The flight suit she was wearing felt heavy as she climbed aboard and sat down. Leanne was right behind her, strapping herself in.

"Once the chief gives you the go-ahead, take her out just like you did in the simulator. I'll be monitoring you from here and, if necessary, I'll take over. I don't think I'll have to, though." Leanne sounded chipper. "This is a welcome change from my daily routine, Kellen."

Having yet to find anything similar to a daily routine, Kellen clamped her lips against a sarcastic remark while she began the starting sequence.

The headset inside her helmet buzzed to life. "*Red Dragon 4.* You are clear to take off."

"Affirmative. *Red Dragon 4* clear to go." Kellen punched in the commands and felt a muted hum when the powerful vessel started to move toward the shuttle-bay launch pad. After she lined the ship up, she pressed the stick forward and engaged the computer. Though most of the starting and launch sequence was computerized, she usually liked to keep her hands on the controls and feel the power of the machine reverberate through her body. It was the same thrill as riding her *maeshas* along the grassland around her estate.

The *Red Dragon* shot from the belly of the *Ajax* and moved past other minor ships in Port 1. After exiting the outer perimeters of the station's structure, Kellen punched in the commands for the computer to release all controls to manual. With a deep sense of gratification, she performed a series of flight patterns so she could get a feel for the ship. It felt liberating to be behind the helm, to call the shots, if only for a moment.

"Wow, you're a pro already." Leanne laughed in Kellen's headset. "Let's get a little farther from the station so we don't end up on top of a frigate. I want you to perform the evasive maneuvers we practiced in the simulator."

Kellen took the ship out a few kilometers, making sure they were still well within *Gamma VI*'s beacons. Carrying out the intricate maneuvers, she felt as if the *Red Dragon* were an extension of herself. The ship handled easily, as Leanne had said, and seemed to have unlimited capability.

Scanning the tactical screen next to her, she frowned. "Lieutenant, do you see the readings on TAC 1?"

A brief silence. "Yes. Good eyes, Kellen, but what they hell are they? They don't make any sense. They look like random space white noise."

"Scroll back and see how long this 'white noise' has been out there." Kellen knew she sounded abrasive, but there was something familiar about the readings.

"I'm scrolling. Damn it, the interference has been there for half an hour, the pattern increasing by the minute. I've never seen this before."

Kellen froze, her hand clutching the controls as the readings began to make sense. "But I have. We have to alert *Gamma VI*. These are no space anomalies. These readings are from cloaked Onotharian vessels, and they're right on top of us!"

CHAPTER TWELVE

What the hell…" Rae stared at the information emerging on the screen and slammed her fist into the console. "Damn it! Kellen's right. Sound general quarters!"

Lieutenant Todd punched in the emergency frequency, which relayed his message to the stationwide communication system. "General quarters! General quarters! All hands to battle stations. Secure civilian quarters. All bridge personnel to the mission room. This is not a drill. I repeat, this is not a drill."

Grabbing her communicator, Rae hailed Lieutenant Grey. "Lieutenant, go by the school and bring Armeo to the mission room."

"Almost there, ma'am." Rae barely recognized Owena's out-of-breath voice over the klaxons. "His guard is keeping him in a secure area with the rest of the children until I get there. ETA mission room in five minutes."

"Good." Turning her attention back to Jeremiah, she continued to issue orders. "Launch the *Ajax* and six frigates. Establish a perimeter around the station." Looking down at the message that had sent the mission room into a controlled frenzy, she was amazed how the so-called white noise contained a barely distinguishable pattern. "Cloaked ships. Where the hell did they find this technology?"

"I have the *Red Dragon* on long-range scanners. They're continuing their planned exercises as if nothing's happened. Should I order them back to the station?"

Rae wanted to say yes, but knew they needed eyes out there where the signals were stronger. "No, ask them to keep relaying the data. In theory, the cloaked ships can't use their long-range scanners without blowing their cover, so they should be safe enough." She glanced at the large screens on the far wall. "Is the assault craft close enough for us to get a visual of them?"

"Let me try, ma'am," the ensign on her left said, entering codes into his work console. "Onscreen."

After ten seconds of flickering, the screen showed the small vessel with Kellen and Lieutenant D'Artansis. The ship circled in intricate patterns, still performing the flight test. "Get me audio with the *Red Dragon*." Rae's voice was harsh. "*Gamma VI* to *Red Dragon*. Lieutenant D'Artansis, respond."

"D'Artansis here, ma'am."

"Once we give the order, head for the station without delay. Do I make myself clear?"

"Yes, ma'am."

"Can Kellen hear me?"

"Yes, Commodore," Kellen replied. "Go ahead."

"Don't return to the station on a straight trajectory. Fly in a wide circle and head for Port 2, or you'll end up in the line of fire."

"Understood." A brief pause. "Lieutenant D'Artansis is calculating the coordinates right now. We should also be able to tell you how many enemy ships are present shortly."

"Something you picked up at the Academy of Pilots?"

"Yes."

"All right. The sooner the better."

Jeremiah caught her attention. "The *Ajax* and the *Infinity* are heading out with the other ships. Captain de Vies is in command."

"Good."

The computer screen next to Rae lit up as it received new information. Reading the assessment based on the erratic data, she clenched her teeth. "All right. Now we know. Get them out of there."

Jeremiah opened the comm link to the *Red Dragon*. "Return to base. I repeat, return to base."

"Oh, my God." Rae could hardly believe what she was seeing. On the main screen four ships decloaked before them, two of them of incredible size. They paused well inside *Gamma VI*'s beacons. They didn't resemble any class of ships known to the SC, and Rae could only surmise their firepower was impressive and able to more than match that of any of her SC ships.

"Did they respond?" She turned to Lieutenant Todd. "The *Red Dragon.* Did they confirm?"

"No. I can't get a clear signal, ma'am."

A foreboding feeling erupted, twisting her stomach into a tight knot. *Kellen, respond now and let me know I was right to trust you.* In the meantime, Rae knew what she had to do.

"Jacelon to the *Gamma VI* fleet. Assume defensive positions. Hold your fire until my mark." She punched in new commands. "Port 2. Launch frigates and destroyers, second wave, pattern Theta Four."

Confirmations sounded through the comm system. Rae stared at the unbelievable sight with burning eyes. "Hail them."

Jeremiah carried out the order. "They're responding. Audio only."

Rae nodded. "Onotharian vessels. This is Commodore Jacelon of the *Gamma VI* Space Station. By using illegal cloaking devices, you have violated Supreme Constellations laws. Also, by approaching this station with more than the stipulated number of vessels, you have committed an act of war. Return to the border or my fleet will fire."

"This is Ambassador M'Ekar," an unknown voice stated, its dark resonance making Rae clench her hands into fists. "I don't believe we've met."

"And I'd like to keep it that way," Rae retorted. "Turn your ships around, Ambassador."

"I will do no such thing. Most of your frigates are now dealing with, let's say, tiny skirmishes along your part of the border. They won't get here in time. Your remaining fleet will not be able to match our firepower."

"I wouldn't be so sure if I were you," a baritone voice said behind Rae. For once, her father's presence felt reassuring and supportive. "This is Admiral Jacelon of the SC Fleet. Unlike my daughter, I have had the dubious pleasure of running into you once. Something I'd prefer not to do again. You do not want to challenge us. Turn your ships around."

"Admiral Jacelon." M'Ekar did not falter. "What an honor. I regret not being willing to accommodate you or your daughter. I want the child known as Armeo—"

"Cut communication," Rae hissed. Glancing to her left, she saw Armeo standing behind her father, with Lieutenant Grey by his side.

"Jacelon to Captain de Vies."

"De Vies here."

"Initiate attack pattern Epsilon Four."

"Yes, ma'am."

Feeling her father's hand on her shoulder, she turned around. "Yes?"

"Deploy my ships, Rae. You're going to need all the help you can get until your frigates return."

"Thank you. I guess I don't have to ask if they're ready."

"They've been on standby since we arrived."

Rae opened communications to the admiral's five ships and was relieved to hear they were all ready to launch immediately. On the major screen, she saw flashes from the exchange of fire and debris scattering among her vessels and the Onotharians.

"Any news of the *Red Dragon*?" she asked through gritted teeth.

Jeremiah shook his head. "No, ma'am. I'll keep trying."

"Good."

"Where's Kellen?" Armeo said from behind Rae. She hadn't seen when he had come into the mission room and wondered how much he'd noticed of what was going on. Rae turned around to face the boy and cringed at the look in his dark eyes. "Is she in our quarters?"

"No, she's not. She had things to take care of, but she'll be back soon." It stripped her soul bare to see how quickly he panicked when he was separated from Kellen. All she could come up with was to hug him close, and to her surprise he wrapped both arms around her waist and buried his face against her.

"Why don't you go with Ensign Y'sak here and sit in my office?" she suggested. "I'm going to be very busy for a while, but I'll be right here where you can see me. So will my father. All right?"

Armeo nodded against her, then withdrew and quickly wiped his cheeks. A young man in his early twenties placed a hand on the boy's shoulder. "Come on, kiddo, we can play a game on the computer while we wait."

After she watched Armeo go into her office, knowing it was reinforced with impact-resistant shields and one of the safest places on the station, Rae focused on the screens before her. "Report."

Owena moved over to her console next to Rae, furiously punching in commands. "The *Infinity* is doing well. The *Ajax* sustained some damage to its starboard nacelle, but is still functioning well enough to fight. The second wave is in play."

"Casualties?"

Jeremiah scrolled down the screen. "No mortalities. Twenty wounded. Uncertain of the Onotharian ships' condition."

Suddenly a blinding light on the screen exploded, making Rae flinch. "What the hell was that?" she exclaimed, dreading the news.

"We took out the weapons array of a frigate, labeled *Onotharian 3* by the computer. From what I can see, it destroyed half the ship, ma'am," Jeremiah reported. "We have another five Onotharian frigates on long-range sensors. God, *Onotharian 1 and 2* must be huge, if they carry vessels that big in their belly. I'm scanning as much as I can of them."

"Excellent," the admiral murmured from behind. "Let's take care of them. Admiral Jacelon to Captain Doromar." He hailed his own vessel. "Go in from grid four-two-six, attack pattern Dahlia Six."

"Aye, Admiral."

Rae snapped her head around and stared at her father. "You named an attack pattern after my mother?" She was incredulous.

The admiral had the grace to mimic a guilty look. "Six of them, actually. It seemed appropriate at the time. She can be infuriating."

"I'm receiving a faint signal from the *Red Dragon*," Owena interrupted. "They're at the outer perimeter of the battle zone."

"Can they hear us?"

"I'm not sure. If I trust the signal, they're dead in the water, ma'am." Rae detected an undercurrent in Owena's voice that made her look inquisitively at her tactical chief. She thought Owena's features were even more rigid than usual, but she didn't have time to ponder it now.

"They're on their own until one of our frigates can lock a beam on to them and reel them in."

Hoping Kellen and Leanne were masking their signal and only playing dead, Rae focused on the task at hand. The admiral's ships had surrounded one of the massive Onotharian ships, now firing at it in intricate patterns, the frigates moving like arrows while avoiding enemy fire.

Another searing light hurt her eyes, when what looked like the front of one of her frigates imploded before them. "Damn," Rae whispered.

"Jeremiah, casualties?"

"Four dead, sixteen wounded. Life support intact in the aft compartments. Detecting biosignatures coming to the wounded crew members' aid."

"Four…" Rae felt as if her blood transported ice to every part of her body. "This ends now." She slammed her hand on the control to the secure communication system. "Commodore Jacelon to all vessels. Deploy remaining assault vessels. Attack pattern Omega Twelve. Fire at will."

"Aye, Commodore." Captain de Vies acknowledged the order. "Omega Twelve in place."

Looking like small deadly beetles, the assault craft swarmed the remaining three Onotharian vessels, firing nonstop. The admiral stood close to Rae, who found his presence a source of strength. "I won't allow them to destroy this station or get their hands on Armeo."

Not aware she'd spoken out loud, she jumped when she felt her father's comforting hand on her shoulder. "Damn right."

"The *Red Dragon* is moving," Jeremiah exclaimed. "*Shi'cht*, what's going on out there?"

"Enhance their signal on the screen," Rae ordered. It was usually a bad sign when Jeremiah swore in his Iminestrian mother's native tongue.

A bright red circle identified the small ship where it entered the battle zone, moving in on the largest vessel.

"Hail them! Get them out of there! What the hell is she doing?" Rae barked.

"Their communication system is down." Lieutenant Grey had taken over the console to Rae's left.

"She had orders to return to the station," Rae said. "I should've known better than to trust her."

"Perhaps she knows something we don't," the admiral mused. "You're right in your assessment. Kellen's a loose cannon, but she's not stupid. Nor is she suicidal."

"Damn it, Kellen," Rae muttered to herself, pressing her lips to a fine line. "You gave me your word." *What are you doing? I never should've let you go out there. What was I thinking?* Fear and remorse wrapped themselves like a cold, slippery entity around her heart.

❖

"Make sure you stay on the calculated trajectory," Leanne yelled. Friendly fire had taken out both internal and external communications.

"Yes, Lieutenant." Kellen grabbed the stick and pushed it forward, while she blinked sweat from her eyes not to miss any of the coordinates flickering in the eyepiece attached to her helmet.

Watching the mark appear in the corner of her eye, she threw the *Red Dragon* into a roll, flying belly up against the massive ship above them. She knew they were called Devil Class ships, and the Onotharian fleet possessed only three of them. Her father had managed to obtain blueprints of the prototype, and Kellen was now betting not only her own life, but also Leanne's, that they had been correct.

Seeing a familiar pattern appear in her eyepiece, Kellen yanked the controls toward her, moving in closer to the ship.

"Damn it, Kellen, we're too close," Leanne shouted. "We're going to hit their shields. Our own are down to fifty-five percent."

"I know. Trust me." Kellen scanned the information, feeling a jolt of exhilaration mixed with dread when she spotted what she was looking for—a flaw in the design. *I must be right. It's our only chance.* "Leanne, it's coming up," she yelled. "Hold on!"

The *Red Dragon* might not be able to sustain the blast, but Kellen knew this was it. Firing her two torpedoes at the target, a barely visible node, she shoved the controls as far to the right as they would go. "Let's get out of here!" Kellen punched in commands to take full control of the small ship away from the computer. There was no room for any autopilot safety net now.

"Will the other Gamma vessels make it?" Leanne shouted. "We don't have any way to warn them!"

"Rae must be monitoring us from the mission room. She'll alert the other ships, and their shields will protect them." Kellen prayed she was right. A blinding light lit up behind them. "Hold on, Leanne! We can't outrun the shock wave. We have to ride it!"

❖

"They're firing at *Onotharian 1*!" Lieutenant Grey exclaimed. "Now they're turning away from the enemy ship like a bat out of hell."

"What the hell did she...Damn! Jacelon to all Gamma vessels. Stay clear of *Onotharian 1*. I repeat, move away from *Onotharian 1*!"

"Aye, ma'am," Alex de Vies's calm voice sounded over the comm system. "Are my readings deceiving me, Commodore, or do I have one assault craft too many out here?"

"You're correct. The *Red Dragon* has gone maverick on us. Lieutenant D'Artansis is navigating." She couldn't disclose Kellen's presence on the *Red Dragon*, in case the Onotharians were monitoring the comm channels.

During the brief pause, Rae knew Alex's mind was scrambling to understand.

"Got you, ma'am."

As he spoke, another blast lit up the space between the station and the battle zone. The shock wave traveled toward them and rocked the station enough for the klaxons to go off. "Shut down the damn noise," Rae yelled over the blaring alarm. "Report!"

"Minor damages, no casualties aboard the station." Jeremiah seemed relieved as he read from his screen. "As for *Onotharian 1*... They're dead in the water, ma'am. I don't know what the *Red Dragon* fired at, but it turned the ambassador's ship into a sitting duck."

"What? What about the fleet?"

"Minor damages from the shock wave. Two assault craft are incapacitated. The crews weren't injured."

"The *Red Dragon*?"

"Still operational, it seems. Making its way to the *Ajax*, ma'am."

Rae steeled herself, trying to control her fury. "Commodore Jacelon to Ambassador M'Ekar. I think this is a suitable moment for me to accept your surrender. I see on long-range scanners that my remaining frigates are only minutes away. Now that we know what to look for, we don't see any other cloaked Onotharian vessels about to come to your aid."

"Commodore Jacelon, this is Deputy M'Indo. The Ambassador requests you allow him to transfer to one of our other ships."

"Our readings show your ship has functional life support. Request denied. I will now tend to my own fleet first, making sure the people you injured through this violation get the care they need before I allow you to move a muscle. Take your weapons off-line, lower your shields, and prepare to be boarded. Jacelon out."

Leaning against the console, Rae drew a trembling breath. Her heart was pounding so hard she was sure the ones standing next to her could hear it. The thought of *Gamma VI's* losses were still too fresh to really have an impact. "Final verdict, Jeremiah," she asked in a low voice. *Count the dead, gather the wounded. Notify next of kin. Mourn again.* Staccato words simmered in her mind. She'd been here before. Gone through this more times than she cared to remember, and still she handled it badly.

Outwardly, she stood ramrod straight, full of sympathy for the people who had lost a loved one, always the leader, the fearless commodore. Inside, she bled for every one of them. *I'm never as lonely as I am now, when I have to face my responsibility.* She tried to keep the feeling of utter desolation from her voice. "Jeremiah?"

"Eight dead. Twenty-four injured. Among them, four in critical condition. One frigate, the *Emerald,* is severely damaged and needs towing. The *Ajax* has deployed medical aid to the frigates." Jeremiah stated the facts professionally, but his hollow voice gave him away.

"Eight dead." Rae turned around and looked at the admiral. "I failed to keep them safe." *What could I have done differently? What did I miss? Damn it, eight of them. Eight!* Repressing a shudder, she stared at the handheld computer Jeremiah gave her. The numbers and names scrolled across the screen, and she placed a hand over it for a moment. *They were under my command, and I sent them to their deaths.*

"Don't, Commodore." Her father looked stern, but his eyes held a soft expression that she knew was meant just for her. "You have work to do."

Trust Father to be to the point. Still, Ewan's words, spoken with a completely new tone of compassion, helped Rae get a grip on herself. "Hail the *Ajax.*"

"Captain DarTancor here, ma'am," the Raggazarorder captain responded.

"You have the *Red Dragon* crew aboard. What's their condition?"

"The navigator is in the infirmary for minor burns. The pilot is there for a checkup but seems uninjured."

Relieved, Rae turned to her father, coughing to clear her voice. "I'll go to Armeo and let him know his mother is all right."

"Of course. I have the conn while you talk to him."

"Lieutenant Grey, could you…" Rae faltered. The tall woman standing next her stood motionless, as if she had not heard her commanding officer. "Lieutenant? Owena?"

Owena jerked. "Ma'am?" To Rae's surprise, she saw tears in the other woman's eyelashes. *I've never seen her cry before. Ever.*

"Owena? Are you all right?" A chilling sensation pierced her midsection. "Did you lose someone in the battle?" *Please, no.*

"No, ma'am. I heard the captain. She's in the infirmary." Owena's stark voice betrayed her distress.

Leanne and Owena? Of course. Normally oblivious to such signs, Rae realized she should have known. They always sat together in the officers' mess hall, and Leanne's face was usually an open book. *I'm so oblivious sometimes. The way Owena looks this instant…like someone given reprieve from certain torture.* "Just minor burns, Lieutenant. She'll be fine." Rae wanted to place a reassuring hand on Owena's arm, but the stark look on her face didn't permit such familiarity.

Rae was still numb. She still hadn't fully realized in her heart that Kellen was all right. It still pounded out of control, the only sign of her fear.

Straightening up, Rae walked toward her office. Armeo stood instantly, his hands flat against the desk. Ensign Y'sak snapped to attention, only relaxing when Rae motioned for him to do so. "As you were, Ensign." Turning to Armeo, she saw he was trembling but kept his chin up, meeting her eyes without wavering. "Kellen's all right. She's safe aboard the *Ajax.*"

"You promise?" Blue tears rose in Armeo's eyes. "Is it the truth, Rae?"

"It is absolutely the truth. I wouldn't lie to you."

Armeo held his own for another five seconds. When the first tear ran down his cheek, he threw himself at Rae, wrapping thin, wiry arms around her waist. Holding the boy tight, Rae let her own tears flow as she rocked him. She knew up till now she'd managed to convince herself that her heart wasn't involved. Witnessing Kellen risk her life to save Armeo and *Gamma VI*, and now, holding this boy who clung to her like a child in need of his parents' consolation, had changed everything.

❖

Port 1 was buzzing with activity. Kellen strode toward the gates, eager to find Armeo and let him know she was safe. She saw several security guards stand at attention and guessed correctly that she had a welcoming party. At the end of the walkway, arms folded in front of her, stood her wife.

"Rae." Kellen tried to read the expression on her face, but Rae seemed restrained.

"Kellen. Walk with me back to the mission room." She spoke in precise sentences with short, clipped words.

Uncertain what to think, Kellen lengthened her stride to keep up with Rae's pace. She blurted out an explanation, wanting to get the tension out of the way. "I disobeyed your orders out of necessity."

"It was not your call to make." Rae's anger flared for a second.

"People were dying, Rae! We couldn't communicate with the mission room, but I couldn't sit idly by and play dead when I knew I could help. I'd seen blueprints of this vessel and knew its greatest weakness."

"You what?" Rae's voice sank an octave. "We can't have this conversation here." She gestured to the passing crew members. "You will be debriefed at the mission room immediately."

Kellen opened her mouth to speak, but closed it again. Her actions had ended the battle, but they had also betrayed the trust of her wife.

"I know everyone at the station is safe," Kellen tried, "but Armeo…is he very upset?"

"He was. Right now, he's with Ensign Y'sak and Lieutenant Grey in our quarters. It was getting late, and he needed something to eat in familiar surroundings. Lieutenant D'Artansis will join them there as soon as Gemma allows her to leave the infirmary. Her burns were worse than we initially thought. Second degree and quite extensive."

Kellen shuddered. "They happened when the blast hit us. The console behind her exploded and burned through her suit. I'd disengaged the autopilot and couldn't let go of the controls to help her. She screamed for me to just get us out of there."

"Gemma assures me the lieutenant will make a full recovery."

Kellen already knew this, but it didn't erase the memory of the diminutive lieutenant's muffled cries of pain when the flames began to consume her flight suit. Leanne had ordered her to fly, her voice a growl of anguish that would stay with Kellen for a long time, as would the odor of singed flesh that had nauseated her when she carefully released Leanne from the harness.

After carrying the lieutenant to the *Ajax* infirmary, Kellen had stayed with her until the doctor assured her she was out of danger. Just before the physician had sedated Leanne, the pilot squeezed Kellen's hand and asked over and over for Owena. Kellen realized Leanne meant Lieutenant Grey and assured her she'd get word to the tactical chief. Relieved, she had watched Leanne fall unconscious, finally escaping the pain when the medication kicked in.

The security officer on guard punched in the code to open the door as Rae and Kellen reached the entrance to the mission room. "Commodore. Ma'am." He saluted them both.

Rae shot her a knowing glance as they passed him. "Word is spreading."

"What word?"

"Oh, don't underestimate the grapevine. Soon the whole base will know how you saved the day."

They walked through the mission room, where everybody stopped what they were doing for a moment. Eyes followed Kellen until she entered Rae's office and the commodore switched the aluminum walls to zero transparency. The admiral sat in one of the visitors' chairs, and Todd stood by the far wall.

"Kellen," the admiral said. "Have a seat. You must be exhausted."

"Thank you." Kellen gratefully sank into a chair, her body aching all over. Determined not to let her pain show, she dug deep for strength.

Rae sat down behind her desk and pulled out a handheld computer. After punching in a few commands, she looked at Kellen, her face stern. "Now, return to what you said before. You once saw the blueprints of this vessel?"

"Yes, my father managed to obtain the blueprints for the prototype before he died, and I hid them and all of his other possessions in a secret vault on our estate. He showed me the ship's weak spot—the node that, if hit by a torpedo, would relay the impact to wipe out their weapons and communications arrays. It stuck in my mind because it was one of the last conversations we had." She remembered how she'd leaned over the table in the vault, looking with keen interest at the blueprints. Her father's hand tenderly cupped the back of her neck, as was his habit when he expressed his love for her. He had noticed her interest in the blueprint of the new Devil Class ships and shown her what he regarded as their biggest flaw.

"Your aim was dead-on. You burned every circuit in their weapons array and destroyed the shield." Rae read from her computer. "They sustained a hull breach that reached across ten decks."

"I had to be sure," Kellen said. "I fired two torpedoes into the node."

"So you had long-range scanners but no way of communicating. How did you persuade Lieutenant D'Artansis to go along with the plan?" the admiral asked.

Kellen couldn't judge if he was pleased or shared his daughter's point of view. "I suggested this course of action, and she questioned me to see if I knew what I was talking about. She decided to trust my ability to fly the assault craft and target the node. We waited for the right opportunity, and shortly after the *Emerald* was severely damaged, she made the call. Lieutenant D'Artansis knew if we failed, the Onotharian ship would probably break through our shields."

"You did some brilliant maneuvering out there," Todd added. "I don't think I've seen anyone, except possibly D'Artansis, fly like that. You must have disengaged the computer to make your escape."

"Yes, I did. The computer wouldn't have allowed such a flight pattern." Kellen looked at Rae, exhaustion burning inside every bone of her body. "Please, may I go see Armeo?"

"One more question, and then you may leave." Rae placed the computer on the desk and leaned forward on her elbows, her fingers laced together.

Kellen did not avoid Rae's penetrating eyes. Instead she tried to shake off the fatigue that threatened to disable her. Absentmindedly she wondered if the medication she was still on was causing this extreme reaction.

"How did your father, a farmer and family man, have access to these blueprints?"

Glancing at Commander Todd and the admiral, Kellen hesitated, knowing her answer wouldn't go down well. "I can't share this information."

"You can and you will. It's vital. I need to explain to the Council how you, in their eyes a mere fugitive, can possess classified information."

Kellen ignored her sore muscles and shot up from the chair, sending it flying backward. Clasping her hands behind her back, she glared at Rae. "I'm bound by honor. I'm not going to compromise it."

"You are going to talk, Kellen. You don't have any other choice." Rae pressed her hands onto the desk and rose slowly from her chair. "Listen to me. This situation will continue to blow up in our face unless we have all the information we need to deal with M'Ekar and the Onotharians. We can't act blindly and expect to win!"

"And I can't betray my vows!" Kellen felt her nails dig into her cold, sweaty palms. "You expect me to go back on my word, to dishonor a sacred duty. You have no idea what you're asking. I cannot commit treason, Rae." *Please.* As much as Kellen wished Rae would relent, a part of her knew her spouse wouldn't give in. How could she make her understand?

"I'm not asking you to commit treason!" Rae exclaimed. "Damn it, Kellen. Listen to me. If you don't level with us, the Council will accuse you of espionage and demand we incarcerate you, maybe even extradite you. You'd be separated from Armeo, the very thing you're here to avoid!"

Kellen tensed. She had no way to explain, no valid reason to give them why her secrets must remain just that, secrets. Realizing she was holding her breath, she let it out slowly, wracking her exhausted mind for a way out. "This goes against everything I've lived by. For so many years, I kept my father's secret, knowing we were doomed if anyone found out the truth."

Rae's expression softened. "Your father is dead. You and Armeo are no longer on Gantharat. Would anyone back there be in danger if you revealed the secret?"

"Not immediately. Most of my father's associates were killed along with him when he went on his last mission. They were betrayed."

The admiral rose, took Kellen by the shoulders, and guided her back to the chair. "Please, take a seat. You were swaying," he explained. "Go on."

Kellen knew she had lost. She would never risk being extradited. Her mouth dry, she forced herself to speak, knowing she couldn't turn back. "My father was one of the leaders of the resistance. He led many successful missions against our oppressors."

Rae squinted, as if judging the truth behind Kellen's words. "Bondar O'Dal was a resistance leader?"

"Yes. He died when I was sixteen."

"I know. It's in your file. You've been on your own for a long time."

"Not all alone. I had Tereya. She was the reason my father had to take so many precautions." Kellen rubbed her aching temples.

"What was so special about Tereya?" Rae sat down again as well, still nailing Kellen with her resolute gaze.

"My father carried an ancient title, part of our family for a long time, now passed down to me."

"What are you talking about?" Rae asked, new lines around her eyes making her look as tired as Kellen felt.

"My father was a Protector of the Realm, a duty and honor I've tried to fulfill since his death." Kellen was surprised at the relief that flooded her system after she disclosed her long-kept secret. She could see the confusion on Rae's face and the understanding that slowly dawned in the admiral's eyes. Almost nauseated from unburdening her secret, whether the others understood the magnitude of it or not, she slumped back in the chair. She searched Rae's eyes for a reaction, but the commodore looked over at her father, who seemed stunned.

"Oh, my God," Ewan Jacelon inhaled. "Armeo. I should have realized…"

Kellen nodded. She knew it was time to tell the rest and experienced both dread and relief. If nothing else, this would make everyone see how important it was that Armeo remain with her. Wouldn't it? "Yes. He's the reason…the only reason, ever since his mother died."

"And you're the only one left of your kind, of your dynasty, aren't you?" the admiral mused out loud. "Your adamant protection of Armeo. It all fits."

"What are you talking about?" Rae demanded, her eyes now a stormy gray.

"Rae, I ask you…may I go to him now?" Kellen whispered. She barely managed to remain erect in her chair. "I need to reassure him."

"Of course." The admiral stopped his daughter when Rae looked as if she was about to say something. "Commander Todd, I need to talk to the commodore. Would you escort Ms. O'Dal to her quarters?"

"Yes, sir."

"Thank you," Kellen whispered, unable to read the set features of her wife. "Until later, then," she said.

"Yes." Rae looked discontented. "I don't know how long I'll be."

With a feeling of defeat, Kellen walked toward the door. She gripped the door frame with an ice-cold hand and looked back over her shoulder, unable to resist a last glance at Rae, who didn't meet her eyes. Instead she was leaning over her computer, punching in commands at a furious pace.

Kellen left the commodore's office and tried not to limp too badly on her way to the elevator. Her bodyguard followed at a respectful distance, and for once, she was grateful for his presence, since she wasn't sure she'd make it all the way to their quarters.

❖

Rae could see from her father's expression that something out of the ordinary had occurred. "All right, can you tell me what all that was about?"

He was silent for a moment, as if assembling his thoughts. Then he said, "Over the centuries Kellen's title, Protector of the Realm, has belonged to those who shielded the Gantharian royal family in times of trouble. Only my interest in the history of alien worlds made me recognize its significance. If her father bore it before her, and lived a clandestine life as a mere farmer, he was protecting someone at the time."

It didn't take Rae long to understand. "Tereya." She stared at her father.

"She must have been the last of the O'Saral dynasty. Presumably they all perished during the first year of the occupation."

"And now, Kellen protects Armeo," Rae murmured. "Damn."

"It's her sacred duty. These families lived clandestine lives. Nobody knew exactly who they were, and they became almost mythical figures in the Gantharian lore. A Protector was almost as illustrious, almost as fairy-tale inspiring, as the O'Saral Royales themselves. It is important that we keep Kellen's secret at the top-level security clearance."

"I see. She must have been thinking of that today," Rae murmured. "To be away from him during a fierce battle, aware if we lost, she might lose him as well." Rae thought of Kellen's exhausted appearance earlier. *The last of the Protectors. How utterly alone you've been for so many years, Kellen.* To think that Kellen was only sixteen when she shouldered the enormous responsibility, with no one to turn to, was mind-boggling. *How can I make you see that you have me now? Will I ever earn your trust?*

"It's starting to make sense, isn't it," the admiral said. "The ambassador's perseverance, the backing he receives from the Onotharian government...for a mere boy, we thought." He stared at Rae, shaking his head. "Not a mere boy at all, but a prince of two kingdoms."

CHAPTER THIRTEEN

Thoughts whirled in Rae's head while she watched the sleeping boy. His tangled hair framed a face totally relaxed, as he had finally fallen asleep after Kellen had sat with him for over an hour.

"Was he very upset? I tried not to frighten him when he asked for you and you weren't here."

"He was angry at me for not telling him before I went to perform the test flight," Kellen admitted. "He can be quite protective."

Rae motioned for Kellen to join her in the living room. It had been a long day, and only when she was certain the security detail was in control of the alien ships did she leave the mission room in Jeremiah's capable hands. She was going to relieve him early in the morning.

Backup forces were on their way from the *Gamma V* and *Gamma VII* stations. The SC Council had deployed military as well as diplomatic vessels. They would reach *Gamma VI* within three days, and it would be up to Rae to hold the fort until then.

The ambassador was under house arrest aboard his own vessel. Apparently called the *Kester*, but still officially referred to as *Onotharian 1*, the ship had a seriously damaged weapons array and shield emitter. Rae had informed the ambassador that one well-aimed torpedo would blow him and his flagship off the space chart, which she would not hesitate to do unless he fully cooperated.

Now she turned to her wife, mixed feelings fighting for control. She sensed barely harnessed turmoil behind Kellen's blue eyes. "Let's sit down and talk," she said. "I've been on my feet all day."

Kellen sat down, ramrod straight and by no means relaxed. She was still dressed in the flight suit and looked every bit the toughened space pilot.

"I believe your initiative saved the station," Rae said quietly, "and the lives of many of my crew members. Thank you."

"I went against your orders." Raw emotion pervaded Kellen's voice.

And this bothers her all of a sudden? "Yes, but Lieutenant D'Artansis made the call to go along with your plan. She, as a senior officer, is supposed to use any advantage while engaged in battle. Her decision was controversial, but still by the book."

Kellen squinted, fatigue making her pale, her skin shimmering a faint blue. "You're not angry anymore?"

Rae paused to study the strong features of the woman next to her. Kellen looked as if she was reluctant to exhale. "From a professional standpoint, no. I'm in awe of your courage and grateful for the outcome. On a personal level…" She searched for the right words. "You scared me, Kellen. You vowed to obey orders and to stay safe. When you went ahead and did exactly the opposite, I had no idea witnessing you risk your life would be so hard."

"I had to do everything I could to save the station. I have a duty toward Armeo, but it was more than that. I saw the frigate implode and knew people were dying. Leanne was very brave to take a chance on my plan. It was a split-second decision for her. And yes, we could have been killed." Kellen bowed her head for a moment.

"So you can understand why I was upset?"

"You counted on me to obey orders."

"That's the technical part of it." Rae gave a wry smile. "And yes, I did, against my better judgment, since I'm slowly getting to know you." She hesitated but then reached for Kellen's hand. "It was gut-wrenching to watch you out there, but I'm proud of you."

Kellen clenched her teeth, her jaws working as her eyes filled with blue tears. "You are?"

"Yes."

"I…" Kellen's tears spilled over, running down pale, blue-tinged cheeks.

"Damn, you must be exhausted." *I've never seen her cry like this from anything else but fury. This is different. Very different.* Rae raised her free hand and wiped them away. "Don't cry. You're safe and so is Armeo, thanks to you. Relax. Right now, this minute, everything is okay."

"You don't understand. Eight people from this station are dead because of Armeo's presence. If I hadn't brought him here…"

"Shh, don't. You didn't bring him here, remember? I did." Rae scooted closer, framing her wife's face with her hands. "Tomorrow I'll be busy all day, taking care of this mess, but right now everything is fine." Acting on impulse, Rae leaned in and kissed Kellen's trembling lips gently. "Trust me." She brushed her lips over Kellen's mouth again.

Suddenly limp, Kellen let her head fall onto Rae's shoulder, and she buried her face against her neck. "I trust you," she sobbed quietly. "I do."

Rae ached inside at the pained tone, and she understood it had taken all of Kellen's courage to say the words. *Is it fatigue speaking, or does she mean it?* Rae detected something raw and true in Kellen's choked voice. "Tomorrow we'll talk more about your past and Armeo's heritage. My father briefed me about some of it, but you'll have to fill in the blanks. Right now we need to go to bed. Come on." Rae circled Kellen's waist, frowning when her spouse flinched. "What's wrong? Are you hurt?"

"Just sore," Kellen admitted. "The G-forces from the shock wave were really heavy."

"Did you see Gemma?"

"No, the physician aboard the *Ajax* scanned me and gave me a…a fresh ticket?"

Rae couldn't resist smiling. "A clean bill of health. I think you need a hot, soothing aqua shower." Rae helped her stand up. Walking into the bathroom, she punched in commands for hot water, setting it to waterfall mode, and then turned to Kellen. "There you go. I'll have a shower in the guest bathroom while you enjoy this one." A shadow flickering across Kellen's face made her hesitate. "Yes?"

"Would it be presumptuous if I asked you to stay?" Kellen blushed faintly. "I don't want to be alone."

"No, not presumptuous at all. Need some help?"

Kellen nodded. "If you don't mind."

"Here. Let me do this, then." Her breath catching in her throat, Rae reached for the locking mechanism on Kellen's collar. Without hesitation, she tugged at the fastener at the front of the flight suit. She pushed her hands inside and eased it down, sliding it off her wife's shoulders.

Rae was secretly appalled when she saw the bruises where the safety straps had dug into the flesh. "Oh, God, Kellen." Going down on her knees, she pushed the flight suit down slender legs, glancing at the scar from Kellen's previous injury. To her relief, it looked no worse than it had that morning. As she unbuckled the soft velver-hempen pilot boots, Rae spoke gently. "Here, step out of them. That's it, and then the suit." She pushed it off Kellen's feet. Looking up, she saw how her spouse shivered in her underwear. "Into the shower you go."

Kellen reached to pull the gray thinlinnen top over her head. She managed to lift the fabric halfway, only to stop, moan, and lower her arms. "I'm too sore." She tried again and failed, looking utterly dismayed.

She's like me. Hates needing help...or someone. "Let me do it." Rae stood up and eased first Kellen's right arm inside the thinlinnen top and then the left. She tugged it over her head and ripped it off, tossing it toward the recycling hamper, where it would enter the station's elaborate system of reprocessing.

Distinct blue-black bruises marred the lean-muscled body, drawing exact lines where the straps had pressed into the pale bluish skin. Disregarding any signs of embarrassment on her part, Rae tugged down Kellen's SC Fleet–issued disposable briefs, throwing them the same way as the shirt with a flick of her wrist. She nudged Kellen toward the shower.

"Stay in there as long as you need. I'll be here when you come out."

Kellen nodded and stepped into the shower stall. Hot water sprayed over her muscles, and her facial expression changed into one of bliss as she closed her eyes.

Rae found it impossible to move. Watching through the glass wall, she saw Kellen merely stand there, her face turned up into the streaming water that cascaded down strong, feminine curves. Her eyes feasting on the breathtaking sight, Rae began to undress. She shivered when cool air reached every part of her. Carefully, Rae entered the shower stall and stood close to Kellen, without touching her. "You're so sore. Let me help you wash your hair."

Blue eyes snapped open. "Rae?"

"Expecting someone else?" Rae removed the hair clips from Kellen's severe twist. Placing them on the narrow shelf to her right, she untangled the long tresses and let them fall onto Kellen's shoulders. She filled her palm with shampoo before returning it to Kellen's head, where she worked up lather, then rubbed her wife's scalp gently and watched the brilliant eyes close in pleasure. "How does that feel? Good?"

"Yes."

Taking some body soap from another dispenser, Rae slipped her hands down to Kellen's shoulders, mindful of the bruises. She slid the silky soap along Kellen's arms, and slowly the wiry muscles relaxed. "That's it." Rae traced the shoulders again, stepping closer to reach her back. "You better turn around."

Kellen complied wordlessly, as if she put all her trust in Rae. She rested her palms against the wall while Rae soaped and massaged every inch of her back. Moving her hands to Kellen's hips, she had to bite her lower lip to not moan out loud as she inadvertently brushed against the rounded bottom before her. Rae slowed her motions and allowed her hands to spread the foam over the generous curves. Unable to resist, she squeezed the cheeks while pretending to wash them thoroughly, her hands becoming more insistent than she intended.

Kellen gasped and surprised Rae by turning into the touch. She pushed herself off the wall and ended up with her back fully pressed against Rae.

Moving of their own volition, Rae's hands circled Kellen's waist. Rae needed more soap and allowed one hand to quickly reach for the dispenser, returning with some, which she spread over a taut stomach.

Rae buried her face into wet hair where the water had rinsed out most of the shampoo and unabashedly rubbed herself against Kellen while she reached up to cup her full breasts. The soap made her touch slippery, but she still felt the hard, blue-red nipples prod her palms. When her fingertips closed around them, rolling them into even firmer peaks, Kellen gave a strangled whimper and began to tremble.

"Like this?" Rae breathed, tugging gently at the pebbled surface. "Like this, Kellen?"

"Yes..."

Kellen arched into the touch and pressed her bottom against Rae, who struggled to ignore her own sudden stab of pleasure, instead focusing on Kellen. "You feel so good," she managed, and took a handful of soft flesh, massaging it before she returned to the nipples.

Only when Kellen moaned and shifted restlessly against her did she continue to spread the soap again. As she moved past Kellen's stomach and reached her hips, she shifted and placed herself on her wife's right side. Kellen fumbled for support, holding on to her with one arm.

"That's right," Rae murmured. "Hold on to me. I won't let you fall."

Kellen looked at her with eyes displaying equal parts desire and alarm. "Rae?"

"Kiss me."

Kellen lowered her head and brushed her lips against Rae's. Opening her mouth, Rae let her tongue enter and caressed its counterpart. Her heart raced, forcing her heated blood through wide-open veins, and all Rae could think was how utterly delicious her wife tasted. Barely able to breathe, she slid her right hand down, cupping the wiry curls at the apex of Kellen's thighs. She felt, rather than heard, her groan. Rae's fingers had begun to move and softly massage the quivering woman in her arms, when suddenly Kellen pushed her head back over her arm and devoured her mouth, examining every part of it with her tongue.

As the water rinsed the soap from their bodies, Rae felt closer to Kellen than anyone else in her life and was eager to explore every one of her wife's secrets. Gently moving her fingers between the swollen folds, she felt the breathless woman flinch as she reached the erect bud just inside. Rae circled it carefully, avoiding direct touch. Still Kellen whimpered and began to shiver.

"Too much?" Rae whispered. "Am I…hurting you? Tell me. I'll do anything you want." It was true. Rae couldn't think of anything she wouldn't do for Kellen right now. *I want to make her feel so good. She's so damn beautiful. So sexy, it kills me.*

"No," Kellen groaned. "You're not hurting me…it's just been so long and I don't know how to…"

"I'll be careful." Rae turned Kellen around and into an embrace with her free hand, kissing her between smiles as tenderness blended with desire. "I'll be very careful." She leaned down to kiss the large, puckered nipples, soothing them with her tongue. Not about to delay, she knelt before Kellen and nudged her legs apart. She nuzzled the damp curls and then turned her head, placing long kisses on Kellen's thighs before she returned her attention to the sensitized area between them.

"Rae?" Kellen's voice was shaking. "Please…"

Rae didn't want the proud woman to beg. She parted the drenched folds, revealing the source of Kellen's pleasure. She thought her tongue might be gentler than her fingers and wasn't prepared for Kellen's violent reaction. As Rae leaned forward to flick her tongue over her sex, Kellen gave a loud cry, tossed her head back, and spread her legs farther apart. Grabbing the bar next to her, she leaned against the wall, her eyes closed. Rae had stopped the intimate caress but now returned, pressing her mouth fully onto the engorged ridge of nerves. She held on to Kellen's hips and let her tongue work around it, sensing small tremors begin deep inside Kellen and increase as she continued her caresses. Rae explored with sensitive fingers, circling Kellen's entrance, and heard yet another tormented cry from her.

"Rae! I need…I need you…"

Rae knew what Kellen needed and pushed two fingers inside. She felt the tight muscles contract and flattened her tongue against Kellen, giving the swollen clitoris her full attention. She wanted desperately to give her all the pleasure possible. Her own sex ached, moisture pooling between her legs as she kept up her movement, but nothing else mattered except Kellen's satisfaction.

"Oh!" Kellen's legs went rigid, her back arching as her inner muscles clenched Rae's fingers in a tight grip, which lasted for what seemed an eternity before Kellen's legs finally gave out, sending her sliding down the wall.

Catching her, Rae held her lover close. "There…I've got you."

Kellen breathed hard and clung to Rae for several minutes. Rocking her, Rae pressed her lips repeatedly onto Kellen's damp temples and murmured inaudible words of comfort as she waited for Kellen to recover from her orgasm.

❖

Slowly, Kellen opened her eyes, looking up at Rae from where she rested on her shoulder. Warm eyes gazed back down at her, and a tender smile parted Rae's kiss-swollen lips.

"You still alive, darling?"

Kellen flinched at the term of endearment. It was the first time Rae had called her this, and she wasn't sure how to reciprocate. Still trembling inside, she wanted to hide her face, feeling utterly vulnerable.

"Yes, I'm fine." As she returned the smile, she tried to joke. "More than fine."

Rae's smile broadened. "Really? Well, I'm glad. Perhaps we should get out of the shower before we grow gills?" Standing up, Rae helped Kellen to her feet. "I didn't aggravate the bruises, did I?" Rae traced the blue-black marks on Kellen's upper body.

"No." Kellen looked down at her, not sure how to phrase what she wanted to say. Before she could formulate the words, Rae turned off the water, took her by the hand, and led her out of the shower stall. "Let's skip the auto-drying sequence and just use towels." She grabbed two bath towels from the heated towel rack and wrapped one around Kellen before she unfolded the other one for herself.

Kellen secured the towel around her body and then reached out for the one in Rae's hands. She placed it around Rae's shoulders, and before Rae had a chance to object, she used her superior physical strength to lift her up, one arm around her back, one under her knees.

"Kellen!"

Walking into the bedroom, Kellen stopped next to the bed. The covers were turned down, and she placed Rae on the sheets, feeling the cool fabric against her hands. The towel fell back, revealing Rae's pale, slightly freckled skin. To Kellen's surprise, Rae blushed, moving her hand as if to tug at the towel.

"No," Kellen murmured, letting her own towel fall to the floor. "You won't need to cover yourself up. I'll keep you warm. Trust me."

Suddenly not nervous or uncertain at all, Kellen lay down next to Rae, leaning her head against her hand. "You're beautiful," she whispered. "You're the most beautiful woman I've ever seen."

"Liar," Rae said huskily. A faint smile played at the corners of her mouth.

"The truth," Kellen insisted, taking Rae's hand and kissing her way from the fingertips up to the pale shoulder. Amazed at how soft the tough and commanding woman felt, she pressed her mouth against the hollow area beneath her collarbone. Rae moaned, raising her hands to Kellen's hair and caressing the damp strands. Encouraged, Kellen let her tongue trace the fragile bone, licking a blazing trail across to its twin.

"Oh…" Rae moved restlessly on the bed. "You're like fire against me…"

"I am?" Kellen used her tongue again, painting a wet trail between Rae's breasts.

Her breath a prisoner in her chest at the promise of emotions in her wife's voice, Kellen kissed her way down to Rae's breasts. Because they were smaller than her own, she feared they would be more sensitive, but the nipples were just as rigid, just as eager to be touched. Closing her lips over the nearest one, she was startled when the hands in her hair pressed her closer.

"Oh, God, yes." Rae arched.

Kellen reveled in the feeling of her wife's fingers caressing her, tugging at her. Taking her cues from Rae, Kellen sucked hard at the nipple, grazing it with her teeth, keeping up the rough caress until Rae offered up her other breast, urging her to claim it. Kellen caught the nipple between her teeth, almost afraid she might hurt her. She held back, but the demanding hands in her hair urged her on.

"Please, Kellen, don't stop. I need this…you…so much." Rae's voice was hoarse with desire. "I've looked at you, wanted you…but I never thought it would feel like this." When her nipples were crimson, she shuddered and shied away from the caresses. "Too sensitive now, Kellen," she whispered. "Kiss me…"

Kellen moved up and kissed her deeply. Rae in turn wrapped her arms around Kellen's neck and returned the kisses, trembling against her.

"Kellen," she murmured against her full lips. "You set me on fire…do you realize that?"

"Yes." Kellen was on fire too. Her previous orgasm had not been enough.

Looking down at the disheveled woman, she knew there would be another, but she was determined to drive Rae toward the monumental bliss first. She nudged Rae's legs apart and settled between them, rubbing her own sex against Rae's. "Oh! Yes…Yes." Rae closed her eyes and wrapped her legs around Kellen's waist.

Kellen reached down and pressed her fingers between Rae's folds. Feeling the copious moisture, she spread it over the rigid clitoris protruding between them. She looked down at Rae and caught an expression she interpreted as pleasure mixed with pain on her face.

"You're so wet," she whispered. "You want me."

"Desperately," came the husky reply. "I want you in so many ways. I need you to make me yours, to help me come. Please."

Kellen leaned farther down, her aching nipples touching Rae's, and put her lips against her lover's ear. "You want me inside you. My mouth on you…"

"Yes…"

"Devouring you…"

"Yes."

"Exploring every part of you…"

"Kellen! Yes!"

Sitting on her heels, Kellen found Rae's entrance, pressing first one, then two fingers inside. She felt Rae draw her knees up and hold on to them, and watched in awe how she opened herself to Kellen's exploration. Recognizing this as a display of trust and desire, Kellen gained full access and used her other hand to spread the moisture farther down. Rae went rigid as Kellen briefly touched her lower orifice.

"No!"

"You asked me to go inside." Kellen's voice was soft. "Allow me to fill you completely."

"No, no…not there…I mean, not…yet…" Rae trembled, her jaws clenched. "Oh, Kellen…"

Starting to move her hand, Kellen curled the fingers already inside Rae, finding an area that sent jolts through the shivering body beneath hers when she massaged it. Her other hand massaged the area below, but did not enter.

"You can't…oh, God…you…" Completely incoherent, Rae threw an arm over her eyes, sobbing as Kellen did not relent but stayed on the path, heading for the rendezvous with ecstasy.

Kellen didn't allow herself to think why it was so important to reciprocate; she simply knew it was. Working Rae's body as if honoring a secret vow to bring her the ultimate pleasure, she realized her efforts drilled new holes of arousal within her own body.

Rae's skin was flushed, and Kellen wondered if she was fighting to reach her orgasm or struggling against it for fear of letting go. She wanted nothing but to help her wife reach the precious gift of pleasure that Rae had just given her. Examining Rae's sex, so trustingly displayed before her, she identified the engorged clitoris, grateful for the similarity in human and Gantharian physiology.

She leaned down and took the swollen bud between her teeth. Rae froze as Kellen flicked her tongue over it. Kellen held it with gentle strength, not about to let go, while her fingers kept up their thrusting motion and her left hand insistently pressed harder against Rae's other opening.

"Kellen…" Rae's voice was barely audible. "Yes, please…take me. All of me."

Kellen took the clitoris in her mouth and pressed her tongue to it. Entering Rae totally with tender fingers, she used both hands to fill her. She knew she was taking a chance by pushing beyond the last boundary, and she heard Rae give a brief cry before muffling her voice against the pillows. Kellen moved her fingers back and forth, not too slowly, but not so fast that Rae wouldn't feel every one of them as Kellen stretched her.

The orgasm wracked Rae's body with a clearly visible force. Kellen could feel how hard it hit and rode the wave of pleasure with Rae. To her amazement she felt the same waves roll and crash inside herself. Urging her on, she did not let go until Rae went limp and clutched at her. "Oh, let me hold you…"

Kellen removed her hands carefully and reached for a hand sanitizer before she moved up to take Rae into her arms. She rocked her as Rae sobbed against her neck. She wondered if her lover had ever let go like this, if she had ever before let her command mask down long enough to surrender so thoroughly. Kellen pressed her lips onto Rae's short hair.

"I'm sorry." Rae wiped her eyes on the bedsheet.

"Don't be. I don't mind your tears, since they're from pleasure, not pain. You're safe with me." Kellen kissed the damp eyelashes. "I have a confession to make. You were so beautiful when you climaxed, and I in turn couldn't believe how you allowed me to…" Kellen's voice turned into a whisper, and she felt her cheeks warm. "What I'm trying to say is…you pleasured me again."

"I did? I mean, just now?"

"Yes." Feeling the cold air from the ventilation gush over them, Kellen tugged at the covers and slid them up over their damp bodies. "Just now."

Rae placed soft kisses on Kellen's shoulder, wrapping her arm around her wife's neck. "I'm glad. You made such wonderful love to me. Thank you."

Kellen wondered if her responsiveness surprised Rae as much as it did her. She traced the outline of her lover's lips before leaning in to kiss them. "You're welcome."

So many years of abstinence, with only her own two hands for sexual satisfaction, Kellen had been sure she'd never feel the warmth of another body next to her own. *Amazing, how I was able to read her reactions. Even more astonishing how she let me conquer her body. She surrendered to me—and took my breath away one more time.* The implications of these unusual actions and emotions made Kellen recoil instinctively, a reaction that gave her a pang of sorrow.

For a moment she distracted herself with the mundane, cleaning her hands a little more. Ordering lights out.

The darkness hid them then, and Kellen waited for her eyes to adjust. Stars cast a pale light, illuminating the red in Rae's hair. Kellen struggled to speak, her throat suddenly thick with sentiment. "Earlier," she managed, "you called me 'darling.'"

Rae pressed her face closer. "I did, didn't I?"

"It's a Premoni term of endearment."

"And now you're asking, did I mean it?"

Kellen kept her voice calm. "Did you?"

Rae nuzzled the skin on Kellen's neck. Kissing just below her ear, she sighed, the small gush of air making Kellen shiver. "Oh, yes, I did."

A warm glow erupted in the pit of Kellen's stomach, and she forced annoying tears back as she raised her hand to push Rae's tousled hair from her blue-gray eyes. "I'm pleased." The words were inadequate, but they seemed enough for Rae, who scooted closer, kissing Kellen's shoulder.

Not saying anything more, they allowed fatigue and satisfaction to lull them to sleep, arms and legs wrapped around each other.

CHAPTER FOURTEEN

Admiral Jacelon was too old to pull all-nighters, but he couldn't let go of the puzzle he'd been assembling for hours. Determined to prove what he'd begun to suspect, he refocused his attention on the documents he had received from SCI, Supreme Constellations Intelligence. The pieces were finally falling into place, and he felt certain he was correct.

Very little in the records of the O'Saral family documented their history after the occupation of Gantharat began. Onotharat had long claimed the smaller planet, but the Gantharians, backed by the royal family, had resisted fiercely.

When the better-armed Onotharian forces invaded the peaceful planet twenty-four lunar years ago, one of their main targets was the O'Saral family. They killed all younger members of the legendary royal family, and the rest perished in the years that followed.

Tereya O'Saral had been the oldest daughter of King Tyo-Vendel O'Saral Royale. Destined to rule Gantharat one day, the young girl received the best education possible. Her father's decision to send her to an off-planet school with her entourage had no doubt saved her life.

Ewan kept scrolling through the documents, trying to discover why and how Tereya ended up being Kellen's "sister."

❖

"I decided to keep the school open today, with increased security." Rae looked at the faces along the conference table. "The children need to know we're operational and that they're safe. Terence de Brost is aware of the situation, and he's put together a special schedule today to help them work out yesterday's events."

"Excellent," Admiral Jacelon said. "I have information too. I spent most of the morning talking with Councilman Thorosac. It took some doing, but I managed to convince him we're quite capable of handling the matter. Our security detail has incarcerated practically all of the Onotharian officers by placing them on *Onotharian 1*. That way they can't get to their weapons before our crew members disable them." He rubbed his eyes, stroking his face in a familiar gesture, which Rae interpreted as frustration. "I was surprised at how bloodthirsty the good Councilman was. Normally, Thorosac is the leader of the more liberal wing of the Council, but this time…let's just say he wants revenge."

"Did he comment on Ms. O'Dal's contribution to the battle?" Rae hoped Kellen's heroic actions had not passed unnoticed.

"He has a lot of questions, but I told him he'd have to wait for my report. There are still many things we don't know."

"SC personnel control all outgoing communication with Onotharat, so no one on the seized ships can report anything unless we authorize it. As you understand, we don't have enough manpower to monitor the Onotharians properly. Reinforcements from *Gamma V* and *VII* are due in less than two days. In the meantime, the closest SC planet, Corma, is sending ten frigates to patrol *Gamma VI* space until we have made repairs and can spare any ships. We still have to worry about pirates. Good news is the Onotharian 'decoys' at the border have left."

"We haven't detected any anomalous white-noise readings suggesting any cloaked ships, either," Lieutenant Grey added.

"Good." Rae nodded. "Commander Todd, what's the condition of the injured crewmen?"

"Most have been released to their quarters. Fourteen are still in the infirmary, six in critical condition. Dr. Meyer has also visited the *Onotharian 1*, where she treated some of the wounded." Todd looked uneasy. "Seems the ambassador was very confident he'd win this battle without any problem. Dr. Meyer found four children belonging to high-ranking officials with him on his mission."

Rae felt herself go pale. "Their condition?"

"Uninjured."

"Make sure these children have what they need. If necessary, bring them onto the station."

"Yes, ma'am."

Glancing around the table again, Rae detected the familiar fatigue she had so often seen in the faces of her crew the day after a battle. Her father's eyes looked red, and she wondered if he had slept at all. Lieutenant Grey seemed unable to relax the muscles in her jaw, and Jeremiah kept flexing his shoulders. Alex de Vies was a source of strength on a day like today.

"Captain de Vies, do you have anything to add?" She knew her friend usually cut to the core of things.

"Yes, I do. I'm pleased how our pilots handled themselves. The communication between the vessels worked as it was supposed to. In retrospect, we should have launched all the assault craft earlier, but fortunately, Ms. O'Dal waited for the perfect moment to attack. One of the gutsiest moves I've ever seen."

"Any gutsier and she'd be dead," Rae muttered. Noticing Lieutenant Grey turn paler, she wanted to bite her tongue. "Sorry, Lieutenant. How is Lieutenant D'Artansis today?"

"She's doing okay, ma'am. Dr. Meyer gave her medication and used the derma regenerator. She'll be back at work in a day or two." Owena spoke in a calm voice, and Rae had the feeling it took all of the tactical chief's self-discipline to be so matter-of-fact.

"Her actions went beyond the call of duty, Lieutenant," Rae said. "And I intend to recommend Lieutenant D'Artansis for the Second Medal of Merit. I've also mentioned her bravery in a dispatch to the leaders of Corma, her homeworld."

Owena's face lightened up in a rare smile. "Thank you, Commodore. It will mean a lot to her."

"Speaking of that," her father added, "I did something similar. I realized it wouldn't be appropriate for you to nominate your own spouse for recognition, so I took it upon myself to do it. I've recommended Kellen O'Dal for the civilian version of the same medal. I hope this meets with your approval, Commodore."

The memory of Kellen's soft skin against her fingertips and her drowsy voice whispering good morning before they embraced took Rae's breath away. "She'll be stunned," she said. "And I'm grateful."

"Hold that thought." Ewan docked a handheld computer with the screen at the end of the table and picked up the remote control. "I did some research last night, and since everyone here has at least level-two security clearances, I can share it. This incident keeps growing, and it's more multifaceted than we expected."

Stunned, Rae found herself looking at a picture of a very young Kellen with her arm around a shorter, dark-haired girl, both of them in front of an alien animal.

"This is Kellen O'Dal and her 'sister,' Tereya O'Saral. The name probably doesn't mean very much to any of you, but the O'Sarals were legends in their own time. Here's the last picture taken of the family before the occupation. Pay attention to the woman sitting in the middle of the first row."

He changed to the next picture. A blond woman in her mid-thirties, dressed in an ice blue suit and wearing a golden red cape over it, looked back at her—at the camera—with calm eyes.

"Who is she?" Rae asked, although already guessing.

"Queen Deamareille O'Saral Royale. Mother to Tereya and her three siblings, two brothers and a sister, all younger. To the left of Deamareille is her husband, King Tyo-Vendel O'Saral Royale. Only the king kept the O'Saral Royale as an honorable addition to his family name. As for Armeo, should he claim the throne one day, he'll be crown prince until he is of age, which is twenty-two Gantharian lunar years. Only then is he entitled to the name Armeo O'Saral Royale. Of course, as it stands now, if the Onotharians remain in power of Gantharat, it's all a moot point." After Ewan told the history of the royal family of Gantharat, he pressed the remote, and a handsome young man with Armeo's eyes appeared on the screen. He wore a uniform and stood in front of an alien crest.

"Zax M'Aido, age twenty and graduating from the Gantharian Academy of Pilots. Here, he's already secretly married to Tereya O'Saral. When his father, Colonel M'Aido, acting Governor of Gantharat at the time, found out about it, Zax was ostracized and later killed in the line of duty before Armeo was born. Here are similar pictures of Tereya and Kellen." The admiral flipped through two more pictures showing the two girls in the same uniform.

"Tereya and Zax lived with Kellen on her farm, and when Zax died, Tereya stayed with Ms. O'Dal. The two girls raised the boy together, until a fateful day five years later." Ewan clicked the remote again, this time showing a death certificate. "Tereya M'Aido was fatally injured in a vehicle accident on her way home from Vastar, the nearby city. Nobody saw it happen, and the other vehicle involved was never found.

She died hours later at the local clinic. As we know, Kellen has raised Armeo since then, watched over him and kept him safe."

"What about her father? Did you find out more?" Rae asked.

"Yes. Bondar O'Dal, farmer, family man, was much more than that. A widower since his daughter Kellen was eight years old, he disappeared shortly after the invasion of Gantharat, only to emerge four years later, this time with two daughters. Claiming Tereya was adopted, he settled in a relatively peaceful valley in the countryside, growing crops and breeding *maeshas*. You saw the creature in one of the pictures earlier.

"During the next four years, Bondar O'Dal led a double existence. Farmer by day, resistance leader at night. He was a high-ranking member of a small group of people determined to fight the Onotharians. They managed to obtain several sensitive documents over the years, including the specs to *Onotharian 1* when it was still being built. When Bondar was on a mission inside an Onotharian prison, trying to free members of his group, he ran into an ambush and was killed. Kellen and Tereya were sixteen at the time."

"Oh, my God," Alex murmured. "Sixteen isn't very old for a Gantharian."

"No, but they ran the farm with the help of the supervisor Bondar had employed." Ewan glanced up at his daughter, his eyes expressionless. "At the same time they enrolled at the academy, Kellen O'Dal evidently became active in what was left of her father's resistance group. Doing mostly humanitarian missions, smuggling refugees and organizing food transports to remote refugee camps, she also carried out courier assignments. When Zax was killed, she increased her activities, but they almost ceased after Tereya died."

Rae felt her fingertips go cold. Staring at her father, she couldn't believe her ears. "She was an agent for the resistance?"

"Yes. She kept Tereya's secret, and later Armeo's, without any aid or support, as far as we know."

Rae stood and walked closer to the view screen, now showing a picture of Kellen and Armeo. As she stared at the beautiful face, she placed both hands on the conference table, secretly biting her tongue hard. *Oh, Kellen. What other surprises do you have up your sleeve?*

❖

Kellen checked her appearance in the mirror. Knowing she would face not only Rae and her father, but also several other high-ranking officers, she had opted for the black leather suit she wore when Rae tractor-beamed the *Kithanya* to *Gamma VI*. She admitted it was a blatant display of independence to not show up at the debriefing dressed in the neutral SC uniform she had worn since recovering from her injury. It was also oddly comforting to wear her own clothes, and it was an unmistakable way to reaffirm where she originally came from and who she was.

Her eyes shimmered a sharp, translucent blue, with sparkling highlights of a light she'd never noticed before. *Is it because of you, Rae? This light—distinctive and obvious to anyone who takes the time to look close enough.* Mystified, Kellen reached for a large silver-covered titanium hairclip and put her hair up in a twist before she walked out of the bathroom.

The made-up bed caused her to inhale a sharp, painful intake of air, suddenly out of breath when she remembered how she and Rae had turned to each other several times the previous night, reigniting an insatiable passion. Shaking her head, Kellen forced herself to focus on the matter at hand and left her quarters.

She and her guard walked through the busy station and rode the elevator to level one. Removing any expression from her face, she approached the door and nodded to the ensign guarding it. As she entered a small waiting area next to the main conference room, she saw a small kitchenette at the back wall and, suddenly thirsty, she grabbed a Recyc-Flaxen mug and filled it with water.

"Kellen? We're ready for you."

The husky voice made the small hairs on Kellen's arms stand up, but she calmly finished her water. "I'm ready as well."

Rae's eyes were a stormy gray, which Kellen had learned was not a good sign. She scanned Kellen's outfit, raising an eyebrow as she gestured toward the tight-fitting leather attire. "Back to where we started?" she asked.

"It seemed appropriate." Kellen heard how short she sounded but didn't know how to change it since her vocal cords felt as rigid as the rest of her body.

Following Rae into the conference room, she braced herself. Admiral Jacelon, Lieutenant Grey, Commander Todd, and Captain de Vies sat around a rectangular table. The men rose as she entered,

Alex de Vies pointing toward an unoccupied chair next to him. "Hello, Kellen. Please, sit down."

Nodding briefly to the people assembled, Kellen did as suggested. She was relieved to find only familiar faces in the room and, glancing at Rae, she folded her hands on her lap, preparing to be questioned.

Admiral Jacelon put down his handheld computer and regarded her closely, but not with obvious doubt or hostility, as far as she could tell. "Kellen, we have asked you to join us, to confirm some information and possibly elaborate on it as well."

"I will try, sir." Kellen made sure the words came out strong. This was no time to appear weak. She had at least some leverage, having aided in the battle yesterday.

"Good. I've briefed the commodore and her senior crew about what SC Intelligence have found in their records. They have their ways of tapping into data streams, though I can't go into detail how that's done, and came across some documents that shed light on the current situation. Why don't you start by telling us what happened when your father died?"

Steeling herself against the sudden pang of longing that flared in her chest, Kellen said, "My father, Bondar O'Dal, was a member of the Gantharian resistance as well as a Protector of the Realm. He brought Princess Tereya O'Saral home from the Gantharat Hossa asteroid, where she and I went to the music conservatory. We were twelve years old when my father dared bring us back to Gantharat, claiming he had adopted Tereya. He settled as a farmer, breeding *maeshas* and growing crops. He loved us deeply and worked for a free Gantharat. As it turned out, he died for it."

"We understand there was an ambush."

"My father kept his records and documents in a vault beneath the barn floor. That last morning…I have often wondered if he suspected what was going to happen, because he took me to the vault and showed me how to open it. Inside, I saw a table with four chairs. Blueprints were displayed on the walls, and some were rolled up like paper scrolls. He showed me around, explaining his filing system in the computers and the cabinets. That's when I saw the blueprints of the prototype. Father said the Onotharians had long strived to construct a cloaking system for their flagship. One of the members of his group had found a flaw in the design, a fatal flaw as it turned out, which the Onotharians obviously never managed to rectify."

"The node you fired on yesterday." Sitting down at the head of the table, Rae leaned forward on her elbows. "Keep going."

"I had learned of my father's sacred duty toward Tereya when he came to get us on the asteroid and we went underground. During our last conversation, he stressed it would become my duty, in case something happened to him. I asked him what the mission of the evening was, but he refused to tell me. All he said was that several lives depended on the outcome." Kellen swallowed hard, forcing herself to keep going. *It still hurts, Father. Sixteen lunar years and I'm still broken. I haven't healed.*

"Strangers brought his body back. No explanations, just his body, in the back of a terrain hover vehicle. I made Tereya stay out of sight and arranged to have him buried at his favorite place on the estate." Kellen forced herself to go on, although the memory of her father's broken body, the gray paleness of his skin, still caused her nausea. "Later I found out that he and his group had rescued political prisoners from one of the asteroid-belt prisons, but when they returned, the Onotharians ambushed them."

Rae laced her fingers together, her glance unwavering. "I'm sorry we have to bring up such painful memories."

"I understand the necessity for these questions." Kellen tried to keep her voice matter-of-fact.

"We've seen evidence of how you joined another resistance group when you were eighteen."

"The resistance leaders approached me several times before I became of age. I could not leave Tereya home alone, so it wasn't until we both enrolled in the Academy that I saw the first opportunity to make a difference and honor my father without risking Tereya. We stayed on campus in Ganath, the capital, and I went on missions when I knew Zax and Tereya were busy with studies and each other."

"What was the nature of your missions?" the admiral asked.

Kellen hesitated for a moment, her eyes finding Rae's. "As soon as I was able to use my pilot's license, I started transporting refugees and other resistance members, both planetside and to nearby systems or asteroids, using different aircraft put at my disposal. I never asked where the resistance cell got them, and I participated in low-risk missions because of my duty toward Tereya. I also served as a courier, transporting documents off-planet to resistance-owned ships hiding in the asteroid belt."

"Low-risk, you say. I guess everything is relative," Ewan Jacelon said. "You must have put your life on the line for your country on several occasions. Did any of your missions result in major collateral damage?"

Kellen felt her anger erupt as she looked at the faces of the individuals around the table. "The Gantharat resistance makes sure that civilians, whether Gantharians or Onotharians, are safe. We are *not* terrorists. We don't go after soft targets. The Onotharian government, however, doesn't bother to show the same consideration. Many Gantharian men, women, and children have died because of their actions. Even their own people have suffered, since many of them voiced their opinion against the occupation. Onotharat and Gantharat were once allies, and many families have mixed heritage. Now, family members are at war with each other.

"So, to answer your question, no, I have not killed any civilians or innocent people. However, I have destroyed several military Onotharian vessels, and the soldiers aboard died in the process." Kellen was not about to make excuses for taking the lives of her oppressors, and she looked straight at Rae, half expecting her face to show dismay. But to Kellen's surprise, she merely nodded as if she understood. "If you had seen what these bastards did to Tereya…The local Onotharian police force ruled it an accident, but it was obviously not. There's no way I can make you understand how terrible it was to watch her die, and to once again take care of a loved one who was dead from excessive violence." Kellen found it increasingly hard to speak. "She was a beautiful, loving mother. Armeo deserved to have her in his life—and she was eliminated, murdered in cold blood."

Kellen fell silent then, aware that her emotions were running so hot, she could misjudge in some way and undermine her own cause. Thankfully, the admiral began to speak, taking her mind off her agonizing memories and giving her a chance to compose herself.

"Armeo has the potential to become either a pivotal person when it comes to Gantharat's and Onotharat's future or a formidable puppet for any mastermind who gets their hands on him," he said. "I now understand why you are so adamant about protecting him—you and nobody else. I have communicated with the Supreme Court judge presiding on the *Dalathea*, and she informs me she intends to try this case personally. Judge Beqq is one of our leading experts on intergalactic law, and since the SC doesn't acknowledge Onotharat's occupation, Gantharian law takes precedence."

"So Kellen's case is strong?" Rae asked.

The admiral hesitated. "I'm not sure how much weight it will carry. According to Judge Beqq, being a Protector of the Realm falls into a legal gray zone. It's an ancient tradition, originally bestowed upon twenty different families centuries ago, now dwindled to one living person protecting one last member of the Gantharian royal family."

Unable to remain seated, Kellen rose and walked over to the porthole. Staring at the busy port outside, she placed a hand against the transparent aluminum, feeling its cold surface on her palm. "Four dynasties shared the honor when the occupation began," she said. "During the first five years, they fought hard to keep the O'Saral family safe. More than fifty individuals gave their lives, but in the end their sacrifice was pointless. The Onotharians systematically targeted and destroyed the O'Saral Royale. My father had no alternative. He had to keep Tereya's identity a secret. I knew when he died that protecting and fighting for Tereya, and later Armeo, would be my lifelong duty."

She whirled around, eye ablaze and all her muscles engaged. "Make no mistake. I will remain at Armeo's side and keep him safe—or die trying."

❖

Rae had never seen Kellen look more dangerous, or beautiful, as she did standing there before the porthole like a sleek feline defending her offspring against predators, the lights from stars and spaceships behind her.

Rae looked around the table. "Let's adjourn. Kellen has confirmed the information we need, and I now wish to speak to her alone. Dismissed."

Admiral Jacelon quirked a sardonic eyebrow at being dismissed by his daughter, but only stated he was going to catch up on some sleep.

When the door closed behind Lieutenant Grey, Rae remained seated for a moment. Then she slowly rose and crossed the floor, not taking her eyes off the other woman, who looked less like the Kellen she had begun to know over the last few days and more like the angry and defiant alien she had tractor-beamed to *Gamma VI*. Still, the sight of the young woman she had married evoked a surge of emotions within her. She wanted to rush over to her, take her in her arms, and swear everything would be all right. Sensing such actions were out of the question, she resorted to merely gazing at her, thrilled by her beauty.

"My plans haven't changed," she said, inserting strength into her voice, wanting to set things straight. "Our marriage, and consequently our mutual guardianship of Armeo, is still on."

"And your father? Is he still going to be 'the person beyond reproach' we need to convince the SC legal system?" Kellen hissed. "He sounded less certain now that he knows the truth. It's more than he bargained for, isn't it? Armeo's heritage, my position…" Her pupils dilated, rendering her eyes dark shadows. "How can you be sure he won't change his mind when the political situation is so much more volatile than he originally thought?"

Rae folded her arms across her chest. "My father has worked nonstop since the battle yesterday to inform himself of your laws, your history, of all *you* didn't tell us, in order to keep Armeo safe and with the woman he considers his mother. I realize you had to be careful, but once you knew what I was prepared to do to protect you…" Rae clenched her teeth against the stab of pain. "You could have told me the truth."

Kellen clasped her hands, and Rae noticed from the whitening skin how her blunt fingernails dug into her flesh. "You don't have to remind me of what you were prepared to do, Rae. I know you've put your life on a five-year hold."

"That's not what I meant!" Rae stepped closer. "Granted, the first day, I thought of it as an overwhelmingly long time, but how can you suggest after last night that you think it's all about sacrifice?" Appalled at how hurt she sounded, Rae bit off the last word. Turning, she meant to put some distance between them, when a hand on her arm stopped her.

"Rae, don't…don't go."

"I'm not going anywhere. We're going to finish this conversation." She looked at Kellen. "Last night was just about the two of us. You were all I was thinking of."

"And I thought only of you. It hurts to know the plans have changed."

"What makes you think that?" Her head spinning, Rae tried to remember what was said during the meeting.

"The judge your father consulted, the same judge who will be presiding at the custody hearing, thinks Supreme Constellation intergalactic law may not support my role as a Protector. Even if M'Ekar loses the case, I risk losing Armeo to someone else whom the SC deems more fit for this assignment."

"My father has found nothing to indicate Judge Beqq will take a boy from the only family he's ever known! What's more, he will still speak on our behalf, and if you ask me, this entire station is prepared to testify for you after what you did yesterday." Suddenly she realized this was Kellen on the verge of panic. Going into action mode, she struck out in all directions in a desperate measure of defense—one woman against the universe. The habit of a lifetime.

Rae took her gently by the shoulders. "Listen to me, darling. We've learned more of your past, that's true, but you've committed no crimes, nor are you guilty of any wrongdoing. Yet. If you take Armeo and run now, however, the SC will not look favorably on it. They will think you put him in unnecessary danger."

Kellen inhaled deeply. "I was certain..." She blushed faintly. "I was certain you and your father were about to change your minds."

Deciding to gamble, Rae listened to her heart and embraced Kellen tightly. "Do you usually jump to conclusions so rashly?" she asked with deliberate tenderness.

Kellen stiffened. "I don't know. I'm so used to carrying the full responsibility on my own. I *need* to be suspicious, to constantly assume the worst." She slowly wrapped her arm around Rae. "This strategy has kept Armeo and me alive through the years. It saved us from the pirates we ran into on our way to SC space."

"I understand." Rae kissed below Kellen's ear. "I *do* understand, but it's important that you get used to talking to me. If we can't trust each other, Armeo is in jeopardy. I want to keep the two of you in my life, and I don't just mean for the sake of justice."

Kellen pulled back and looked down at Rae. "What are you saying?"

Lifting her hand, Rae caressed her wife's cheek with the back of her hand. "Surely you must realize what's growing between us? Can you blame me for wanting to hold on to that as well?"

"No, I can't blame you. After last night I was confused. For the first time, my main objective wasn't clear. Don't misunderstand. I would still do anything to keep Armeo safe...but the way you make me feel. It's unexpected."

"As in good unexpected?" Rae quirked an eyebrow. She wished she could read the emotions chasing each other in her wife's eyes.

"Yes." Kellen surprised her with a breathtaking smile, making her inhale deeply and forget to exhale. Her sheer beauty was enough to make Rae lose track of more than her breath.

"I need you to promise me something," she urged. "I know you're impulsive, but I'm certain you wouldn't lie to me. Tell me you won't grab Armeo and run. Come to me first, and we'll solve whatever situation may come up together. Don't ever just…disappear."

After a pensive moment, Kellen nodded. "Very well. I give you my word. However, no matter how I feel about you, Armeo comes first."

"Of course he does." Rae glimpsed a strange sadness in Kellen's eyes and let her hand slide down the black leather sleeve of her suit. "How do you feel about me? Or is it too soon for me to ask?"

"You're my first personal indulgence in a very long time. I feel… happy with you."

"Oh, Kellen. I know what you're saying, better than you think." Rae sighed. "Even now, I have to get back to work. I have memorials to prepare." Feeling Kellen flinch, she hugged her closer. "You'll be there with me, won't you?"

"Are you sure?"

"I need you there. This part of my work is the hardest for me."

"In that case, I'll be by your side." Kellen kissed Rae, and it felt more like a kiss of comfort than passion. "I'll find out what's appropriate to wear. When does it start?"

"This evening at 1900 hours." Rae allowed herself to close her eyes and lean into her wife. "Thank you."

❖

As she entered her quarters, Rae dismissed the security guard on duty before she tugged at her dress-uniform jacket. The buttons wouldn't budge, and she cursed under her breath. Kellen came out of Armeo's room, looking composed if a little pale.

"Armeo's sound asleep and—what's wrong?" She crossed the floor.

"The damn collar is choking me," Rae hissed, tugging violently at the offending garment.

"Shh, let me help you." Kellen nimbly undid the many golden buttons on the dark red jacket. Gold epaulettes adorned its shoulder pads, and tiny golden braids formed intricate patterns down its sleeves. "It's a beautiful uniform. You need to be careful."

"Right now I'm not in the mood to be careful," Rae muttered as Kellen carried the jacket away to hang it. Weak in the knees suddenly, she placed a hand on the table next to her.

She had known the memorial would be difficult, but she was unprepared for the anger that had almost choked her while she gave the eulogies. She was so frustrated and incensed with her own failure it made her nauseous. Rae slammed her palm on the table and realized the stinging sensation did not mitigate her fury for a second. She could still see the faces of the people who had lost loved ones in the battle, and she knew from experience these images would haunt her for a long time. They always did. So did her self-castigation, no matter how unproductive it was. Only one thing had been different today. Just as it was time for the last eulogy, her lungs had caved in, not allowing enough oxygen to reach her veins. Desperately struggling for composure, she had ended up focusing on the serene face of her wife, who sat close to the middle aisle, and only then did her voice return.

Rae wondered how she could have gone through the difficult evening without her spouse, her lover. Tugging at the top button of her shirt, she walked into the bedroom and found Kellen in front of the closet, undressed down to her underwear.

"Thank you for standing by me this evening."

"It was difficult for you." Kellen removed her thinlinnen camisole and stood before Rae in only her briefs. "I also found it hard. I can't seem to get rid of the guilt, even if my intellect tells me I'm not responsible for M'Ekar's actions."

"No, you're not." Rae dragged a hand wearily across her face. "The SC reinforcements will arrive earlier than expected, which is good news. They'll deal with the ambassador. I've ordered every Onotharian off the station. My father didn't agree with my decision, but I don't want anyone of Onotharian descent on *Gamma VI* at this point. Armeo's safety is paramount, and I will not compromise it."

"What about the injured Onotharians in the infirmary?"

"They have fully functional infirmaries on two of their vessels, and Gemma assured me they could be moved." Rae unbuttoned her uniform trousers, her hands moving in a jagged pattern. *Is it adrenaline or am I totally screwed up? Damn buttons.* "Granted, I can't be sure about the motley crew in the residential and commercial area of the station. Any one of them could be a spy, I suppose. We're still on a SEC 5 alert. I'm not taking any chances."

Kellen placed her hands over Rae's. "Let me help you." she said. "A lot has happened in these last few days, and my guess is you're hurting over the loss of your crew members."

"Of course I am!" Rae exploded. "I'm not a machine that can just keep going. I send people out into dangerous situations every day, and most of the time they make it back safely. This time...Eight of them! Eight young people with their lives ahead of them..." Recoiling, she bit her lower lip to prevent more words of self-doubt from breaking free.

"You're not responsible for their deaths," Kellen said as she carefully tugged at Rae's flaxoid linen shirt and freed it from her uniform pants.

"Oh, but that's where you're wrong," Rae argued hotly. "No matter the circumstances, I'm in command of this station, and I'm always responsible for what's going on. Always."

Kellen seemed to consider this statement. "I understand. Let me rephrase. It wasn't your fault. Your responsibility—but not your fault."

Busying herself with the buttons on the starched shirt, Rae wanted to take solace in Kellen's attempt to comfort her, but knew she had a long way to go before this pain would disappear, if ever. During the years, she had lost her fair share of crew members to piracy and accidents, and she knew every one of their faces. They still haunted her in her dreams, and when the onslaught of these nightmares kept her awake, she'd recite the names of the fallen soldiers like a prayer.

Kellen's soft hands on hers yet again startled Rae. "Let me," she murmured gently.

Not sure why the mere unbuttoning of her shirt began to calm her, Rae closed her eyes, inhaling Kellen's unique scent. Her wife pushed the shirt down her arms, removed it, and tossed it onto a chair before she proceeded to the SC-issued bra. Kellen helped her take off her boots, and soon her trousers pooled around her feet and she stepped out of them.

Shivering in only her panties, Rae didn't resist when her lover embraced her. "Kellen..."

"Yes?"

"The way you touch me. I can't believe how much I need to feel your hands…"

"Like this?" Kellen's hands slid up and cupped her breasts. "You need my touch on you, our bodies meshing together…the unity?"

"God, yes."

"So do I."

Rae felt Kellen's lips move into a smile against her temple, and she sank farther into the strong arms. "Take me to bed?"

"With pleasure." Kellen dragged the covers aside and nudged Rae to lie down.

Gratefully, she settled against the pillows and watched as her wife finished undressing. When she noticed not only the bruises from the assault-craft straps, but also several new dark marks on Kellen's bluish skin, Rae felt her cheeks warm. "Oh, God, did I cause those?"

"What?" Kellen looked surprised at the traces from the previous night. "Don't worry. They aren't painful."

"I had no idea I…we…were that forceful last night."

"Neither did I. Let me examine you." Kellen removed the covers and looked down at Rae's body. "Turn over."

Rolling her eyes, Rae turned over on her stomach. When Kellen didn't speak, she glanced over her shoulder. "Well?"

"As I suspected." Kellen tugged at the white thinlinnen panties. "Lift up."

Rae's heart began to throb faster as she lifted her hips, mystified. "What are you doing? Is there anything…oh…"

Removing the underwear, Kellen pressed her lips against the small of Rae's back. "I accidentally scratched you here." Her lips traveled to the left, a bit farther down. "And sucked the blood to your skin here." Her warm, smooth tongue soothed something that didn't hurt to begin with. "And I've massaged you too vigorously here." Her insistent hands gently caressed Rae's buttocks, making her tremble and bury her face in the pillows.

Full breasts rubbed tantalizingly against her back and one leg slid between hers. Turning her head to the side, for air, she panted as her thighs were pushed farther apart.

"You didn't hurt me last night," Kellen whispered close to her ear. "You made love with me."

"And you with me," Rae said huskily, her head spinning. "You drive me crazy, do you know that?"

"How do I drive you crazy?"

The voice in her ear was a low purr, the leg between hers mercilessly pushing against her swollen sex. Rae began to roll her hips, pressing down on the silken thigh. "Your beauty, your resolve...and your fire...your tears, even..."

A hand slid around Rae's waist and worked its way down her stomach, cupping the dark auburn curls at the apex of her thighs. Knowing Kellen could feel how ready she was to be explored, Rae managed to hold back a moan, but she whimpered out loud when two fingers pushed farther inside. Undulating against the relentless hand, she closed her eyes, focusing on the pangs of pleasure beginning to mount inside her. As they slowly spread down her thighs and up her abdomen, she began to moan, knowing she was quickly losing control. Dragging one leg up and bending her knee, she pressed her body against Kellen's, seeking more of the warmth, more of the safety in having her lover behind her.

"You're going to make...me...oh!" Her inner muscles contracted, and she felt them grab Kellen's fingers in a viselike grip as she arched, coming hard in her wife's arms. For precious seconds, her body went rigid and the orgasm blazed through her like wildfire. She felt strong arms wrap around her, tearing her into a fierce embrace.

Registering on some level that Kellen had yet to experience the same release, Rae rolled on top of her and parted her legs with a quick flick of the hips. Rubbing her aching mound into her lover's, she looked down into Kellen's eyes, registering every small change. She smiled out of sheer pleasure, placing soft kisses on Kellen's full lips.

Mesmerized by the sounds emanating from Kellen, Rae rocked against her, making sure she kept up the pressure. She quickly became caught up in the rhythm and pulled one of Kellen's legs up over her shoulder. Having unlimited access, she now rubbed frantically against her wife. It seemed the increased fire of the caress was too much for Kellen. She gave a sudden cry and went rigid beneath Rae, tossing her head back in abandon. Rae looked at her with burning eyes. She didn't want to miss a thing. *Oh, stars, you're like a liquid blue flame. You're beautiful. I can't get enough of this heat, of your legs around me, pulling me in. Into you...Oh, Kellen.* She continued to rock, slowing the pace gradually until they finally came to a halt. Kellen's hair, untangled from its usual severe hairdo, tumbled around her shoulders and spread across the pillow.

"You've never looked more beautiful." Rae was unable to stop looking or move off her wonderful lover. She took yet another leap of faith, voicing her previous thoughts. "I can't get enough of you, darling."

Kellen drew a trembling breath. "I can't get enough of you either. You're all-important to me…and our lovemaking is too. I ache inside when you're unhappy."

Rae stared at Kellen, deeply touched. Unable to find the right words, she kissed her softly before she slid down to lie along her right side. "I guess we should try to get some sleep. Tomorrow's going to be another long day."

"Yes." Kellen shifted, turning on her side and facing Rae. "Sleep well."

Raising a hand to push back the long blond hair from her face, Rae cupped Kellen's cheek and smiled languidly. "You too."

CHAPTER FIFTEEN

A ll rise! The honorable Judge Amereena Beqq presiding!"
The imposing figure of Kosaric, the bailiff, compelled Rae
and everyone else to their feet as his fluorescent yellow eyes scanned
them carefully. Of Savorian descent, he exuded authority.

The woman who entered from the chambers behind the main
courtroom aboard the vessel *Dalathea* was a striking human-Cormanian
hybrid. In her early fifties, with a river of red hair flowing down her
back in long curls, she wore a traditional twillmix black cloak, a custom
that began on Earth more than five centuries earlier. It flowed around
her, its bloodred Cormanian fairy-silk lining whispering against the
black retrospun cotton dress underneath. Before sitting down, she let
her gaze sweep over the people gathered to seek her ruling.

Agador Gosh, Kellen and Armeo's legal representative and
Jeremiah's civilian friend from the private legal firm in the commercial
sector, had requested closed doors for the custody hearing because of
its classified nature. Not counting the parties involved, only six people
were present, all with the required security clearance. Four high-ranking
Council members were witnessing the testimonies via view screens
routed through a secure subspace signal.

"Be seated." Judge Beqq's resounding voice carried easily though
the large room. "We have gathered to determine the fate of a young boy,
Armeo M'Aido. Evidence has been put forward by both parties, and
now I want to begin by hearing the young man."

Rae heard Kellen breathe deeply. This procedure was unexpected.
She thought Armeo would be heard last. Rae wanted to kick herself.

She ought to have anticipated an unconventional approach from Judge Beqq.

She glanced at their legal representative, and he gave a nod she supposed was meant to reassure her. "Some judges find it more informative to hear the child first," he murmured. "To prevent everyone else's point of view from influencing him, Commodore."

Trying to sound confident, Rae said, "Go on. You'll be fine," and nudged Armeo gently.

As soon as he had settled into the chair in the witness box, the judge said, "Armeo, I'm going to ask you some questions. You don't need to be nervous, because I only want to know your opinion about a few matters. However, even though you're not under oath, I do expect you to be truthful with me. Do you understand why we are here today?"

"Yes, Your Honor, I do. We're here to make sure I can stay with Kellen and Rae." Armeo glanced toward his guardian.

Beqq looked serious, her dark green eyes mere slits. "Are you aware this might not be the outcome?"

"Yes." Armeo returned the penetrating gaze. "I'm aware mistakes can happen."

Rae bit her lip, amazed at how the boy managed to sound respectful and defiant at the same time. She lowered her gaze and saw Kellen grip the side of her seat hard. Scooting over to the chair Armeo had vacated, Rae put her hand over her wife's, stroking it furtively.

"So, not allowing Kellen O'Dal and Commodore Jacelon custody of you would be a mistake?"

"Yes, ma'am. Kellen has been a mother to me since my birth mother died. I love her and she loves me."

"And Commodore Jacelon? How do you feel about her?" Judge Beqq raised an inquisitive eyebrow, which did not seem to faze Armeo in the least.

"I haven't known Rae for very long, but she has provided a home for us. She says my safety is important, and she loves Kellen."

Feeling her cheeks flush, Rae resisted the urge to groan out loud. She knew this trial would intrude into their private lives, and even if she tried to remain pragmatic about it, she was cringing. *Damn uncomfortable.*

"So, you love your guardian as if she were your mother, and you're settling in with Commodore Jacelon. Is this a correct assumption?"

Armeo nodded. "Yes, Your Honor. I also have a new grandfather since Kellen married Rae. Rae's father has given me permission to call him 'granddad.'"

A faint look of amusement flickered over Beqq's features before she continued the hearing. "How would you react if custody were given to the Onotharian representative?"

The boy's eyes took on a haunted expression. Kellen squeezed Rae's hand. "How can she torment him with such questions?" she hissed.

Armeo shook his head. "You can't do that, ma'am. The Onotharians have committed many crimes and have also attacked this station. You can't hand me over to them. I have to stay with Kellen. She's my guardian and Protector. I belong with her and Rae." He spoke calmly, but Rae could see his hands tremble.

"I can promise you this, Armeo. The only thing that matters when I make my ruling is what's best for you. Not for your guardian, or for the Onotharians, but for you. I have to ask you to trust me."

"Your Honor, it isn't easy to trust *anyone* when people are prepared to kill on my account."

Rae closed her eyes at the pain in Armeo's voice. She had been so busy the last few days trying to sort out the mess after the battle while awaiting backup, she had forgotten how quickly the grapevine worked on the station. Of course, the children at school heard their parents talk and then repeated it among their friends. He knew all about the battle and the casualties.

"You're right," Judge Beqq said. "Go and sit with your guardian. You did very well on the stand."

Armeo rose, crossed the floor, and sat down next to Rae. She put her arm around his shoulders, and he rubbed his cheek against her shoulder. He wasn't prone to show such need for comfort in public, and the motion strengthened his hold on her heart.

"The court calls Kellen O'Dal to the stand!"

Kellen rose and, after being sworn in, she took the stand, seemingly collected. As she listened to Kellen give her testimony and then repeat everything she had revealed at the debriefing yesterday, Rae hoped her statement would have the same impact on Judge Beqq as it had on her senior staff. Gazing over her shoulder, she saw her father seated behind her. He acknowledged her with a brief nod.

"It is obvious you care for the boy, having raised him since he was five years old," Beqq stated.

"With all due respect, Your Honor, this is not correct." Kellen sat ramrod straight in the witness booth, her hands folded on her lap. "I helped his mother rear him from birth, and have been his sole provider since he was five. He has seen me as a parental figure all his life."

Beqq leaned back in the leather chair. "I see. Have you thought about how you will handle this child's extraordinary legacy once he comes of age?"

Kellen sent a worried look toward Armeo. "I have told Armeo of his past and his heritage. He of course began to question me about his birth parents when he was old enough, and I have always been truthful. However, I do believe in a child's right to have as normal a childhood as possible..." Kellen turned her luminescent blue eyes on the judge.

"Therefore, I turned his education into a game, something we did for fun, to make sure he learned the essential things for an O'Saral. I've been careful not to pressure him into making a commitment regarding his future too soon. Armeo's heritage comes with many duties and obligations—and also grave danger. As far as we know, he may have to live in exile for his entire life, unless the situation on Gantharat changes dramatically."

"A wise decision." The judge nodded. "There's no question Armeo loves you. How would you describe his relationship with your spouse and her family?"

"Armeo is very intuitive. My hostile approach when we ran into Commodore Jacelon's SC vessel did not influence how she treated him. He was impressed by her kindness and consideration, even if she initially assumed I was a space pirate."

"And now?"

Kellen's eyes softened marginally. "I know Armeo's heart so well. He is starting to bond with the commodore and her father. After the admiral suggested Armeo refer to him as 'granddad,' my child has found the one thing lacking from his life—a valuable male role model. Armeo might be the last of the O'Sarals and the last of the M'Aidos, but having Commodore and Admiral Jacelon take such an interest in him will benefit him if he should buckle under such a heritage, especially when he's older."

"Since you bring up continuity, what are your own feelings for Commodore Jacelon? You married very quickly, after knowing each other for only three days. How do you predict your future together?"

Rae went cold, and the court officials and people present seemed to hold their breath.

"Not being familiar with your laws, I had no idea marrying a SC citizen could provide sanctuary for Armeo and me. Rae…Commodore Jacelon explained to me that I probably wouldn't be able to apply successfully for asylum and custody of Armeo, given the circumstances. When she offered me marriage, since I found her an attractive and remarkable person, I accepted." Kellen looked straight at the judge.

"Your Honor, I won't lie. It wasn't love at first sight, but it was certainly respect, attraction, and mutual need. Commodore Jacelon has showed me the possibility of a long and stimulating relationship, and I'm determined to make it work, not only for Armeo's sake, but also for myself. While back at Gantharat, I thought I was destined to live in solitude with Armeo on the estate, and I accepted it…but now that I'm married and experiencing the benefits of a loving relationship, I don't think I could ever go back to such a lonely existence."

Rae's eyes stung from unshed tears at her wife's words. Constantly surprised by Kellen's unexpected depths, she stored the words away in her memory, knowing she would bring them out later and reexamine them when she needed reassurance.

"Thank you, Ms. O'Dal. You're excused."

Kellen rose and moved gracefully across the floor toward Rae and Armeo. Sitting down next to Rae, she seemed tense but in full control of her emotions. "It was difficult."

"I know. You did great." Rae stealthily patted her wife's knee. "Better than great."

Kellen shook her head, looking doubtful. "Better?"

"You were honest and informative," Rae murmured, glancing sideways with a half smile. "Very informative."

Kellen redirected her attention toward the judge as the bailiff called out Rae's name. It was time for the commodore to take the stand.

❖

Listening to Commodore Jacelon, her wife of six Earth days, describe the events that had taken place since a small alien vessel attacked the *Ixis* nine days earlier was unnerving. Kellen pulled Armeo closer, ignoring his surprised glances. She wasn't sure why her nerves played such tricks on her. She hadn't expected Rae to say anything negative, and she tried to understand Rae's motives for being so blunt about her initial resentment toward Kellen. Perhaps Rae's honest statements would make her description of the reluctant attraction toward a perfect stranger more credible. The judge would know if her new wife was exaggerating her feelings for Kellen to impress the court.

Having relayed the details of how Kellen had fired on Ambassador M'Ekar's vessel, Rae now looked completely relaxed as she awaited the next question.

"How do you predict your future with Kellen O'Dal?"

"I see challenges down the road, both of a marital nature and because of Armeo's heritage. However, I'm prepared to take on the responsibilities of bringing up a child and working on keeping my marriage healthy and long lasting."

"Do you love your spouse?"

Kellen noticed a tiny crease on her spouse's brow. Realizing how Rae must detest having to account for her private matters to the court, she dreaded the answer.

"Ms. O'Dal intrigues and mesmerizes me. She's a very beautiful woman who anybody would be proud to call their wife. Like you stated before, Your Honor, we've only been married for a very short time. The first time I profess my love should be in private, and my wife should be the only one present, don't you agree?" Rae's smile was obviously meant to disarm, but the expression in her slate gray eyes was uncompromising.

Judge Beqq did not comment on the challenge. "And the boy? How do you regard Armeo?"

"Armeo will steal anyone's heart in an instant. He made friends right away when he started school on the station. Once Kellen and I were married, I knew I'd play a vital part in Armeo's life. He seemed to look to me for support while he was worried about Ms. O'Dal's injury and also when she was involved in the battle two days ago. I'm sure I have a lot to learn about children since I haven't any personal experience, but I'm also certain Armeo and I will learn about each other—together. I will never let him down."

"I see." Judge Beqq punched in a few comments into her handheld computer. "I have here an affidavit from your father, Admiral Jacelon, stating he is prepared to become the boy's overall guardian, to act as his protector in *this* realm." The woman's choice of words clearly hinted at Kellen's ancient title. "Are you and your father in agreement on how this would work out?"

"Yes." The single word was forceful. "My father has grown very fond of the boy and truly sees him as the grandchild I have never provided. I know my father will never abandon or fail Armeo in any way. Neither will my mother once she has the opportunity to meet him. My mother is Diplomat Dahlia Jacelon, operating in Sector1:3."

Amereena Beqq smirked. "I'm well aware of who your mother is, Commodore. I've had the pleasure of running into her on several occasions." Kellen thought she glimpsed a somewhat exasperated look on the judge's face.

After a few more routine questions, Rae was excused. Judge Beqq sat quietly for a few moments, entering data into her personal computer. Kellen watched her nod toward the bailiff, then turn her attention to the only Onotharian present.

"The court calls upon Counselor M'Undee to deliver Ambassador M'Ekar's statement and demands. Rise and remain by your desk."

Heads turned toward the undersized, thin Onotharian civilian, now browsing through his computer while rising to his feet.

"Your Honor, Council members, Admiral Jacelon." The man bowed, and still Kellen knew the gesture was merely for appearance. The Onotharians only respected their own kind. "I am Ambassador M'Ekar's representative since he is currently under…house arrest aboard his vessel, the *Kester*. If it pleases the court, the ambassador has recorded his statement to be played on a view screen."

Kellen turned quickly to meet Rae's eyes. Her wife looked calm but dug her teeth into her lower lip before she muttered, "What the hell is he up to now?"

Judge Beqq drummed her fingertips on the desk before she nodded her consent. "Very well." Wooden panels slid open at the far wall, revealing a large view screen. "You may proceed. Give the recording to the bailiff."

Looking slightly intimidated by the Savorian man towering over him, M'Undee handed over the computer chip. "Thank you."

The bailiff pushed the chip into a console next to the bench. On the screen, an image of an Onotharian man in his late sixties appeared. He wore a deep blue robe with a silver pattern in the sleeves and the lapels. His long, dark gray hair, intricately braided, was tied with silver threads. The man oozed wealth and authority.

Her immediate feeling of rage shot bile to burn Kellen's throat. She wanted to throttle the man on the screen, the criminal responsible for so much death, in the past as well as in the last few days.

"Your Honor, I, Ambassador Hox M'Ekar of the Gantharat-Onotharat System, am using this media to testify as to why Armeo M'Aido should be returned to his family on Gantharat."

Kellen's nails dug into her sweaty palms. The ambassador looked unaffected by the last day's events, and Kellen knew he was still hoping he would gain custody of Armeo.

"My late wife was one of the last M'Aidos, and sadly our only son died at the tender age of three. She was never able to overcome his death completely, but took great solace in following her nephew Zax's accomplishments and adventures. When he decided to marry a woman we thought was a mere Gantharian commoner, his father made the unfortunate mistake of disowning him. Later, when Zax was killed, his death destroyed his father and, ultimately, my wife." M'Ekar displayed a sorrowful expression.

"After a long period of mourning, I came across information that led me to my only remaining blood relative—Zax's young son, Armeo. To my horror, the woman keeping him away from his next of kin was leading an unlawful existence, participating in hostile activities directed toward the Onotharian Empire." The ambassador paused, pinching the bridge of his nose as if in pain. "We decided to rescue the boy, take him from her by any means necessary. Kellen O'Dal did indeed live up to her reputation of being dangerous, to Armeo and anyone who approached her. She set fire to her home, grabbed the poor boy, and ran, killing two of my agents in the process, along with her employees— three innocent farmhands."

Kellen gave an almost inaudible whimper, covering her mouth with a trembling hand.

"He's lying!" Armeo hissed next to Rae, his eyes dark blue pools of anger. "That's not how it happened! The men burned down our house...*they* killed our workers!"

"We tracked O'Dal through intergalactic space and came close to apprehending her several times. She acted with a recklessness and hostility that defies description. Taking out pirates and vessels approaching her with peaceful intent in the same bloodthirsty manner, she stayed one step ahead of us. We did not dare corner her, for the sake of the boy."

"I never…" Kellen heard her voice break and suddenly felt Rae's hands on her shoulders, pressing her down into the seat.

"Calm down, Kellen. You knew he'd play it like this. Think of Armeo. Calm down."

M'Ekar's voice kept going. "When we learned of her latest deception, marrying a prominent SC woman, someone you'd think not easily fooled, we became desperate. Armeo is important for Onotharat, that's true, but most of all, he deserves to be with his own kind. Kellen O'Dal is dangerous. She's a Ruby Red Suit fighter. She can kill a man with her bare hands and never think twice about it. Your Honor, I implore you. Do not leave an innocent child in the hands of this cold-blooded warrior. He deserves better than that. He deserves to come home to his own. Thank you." With a low, static-filled sound, the recording went black.

Kellen held on to her seat with one hand and Rae's hand with the other. On the other side of his new parent, Armeo sat motionless and stone-faced. Knowing she would have to wait to embrace him until the hearing was over because of the strict rules of the conduct in the courtroom, she focused on breathing evenly, exercising her training to remain calm.

Judge Beqq waited until the bailiff removed the computer chip from the console before she spoke. "I will keep this statement in my possession until I've reached a decision. I must consider several things and will let you know my verdict tomorrow morning at 0900 hours. This court is adjourned."

Everybody rose as the tall woman left the courtroom. Kellen turned to Armeo, wanting to wrap him in her arms and tell him everything would be all right. To her surprise, the boy looked behind them, extending his hand toward Admiral Jacelon.

"Granddad, can he do that? Can he demand I come and live with him since he was married to my father's aunt?"

Taking the boy's hand, Ewan shook his head. "The ambassador is in a bit of a bind, my boy. The Supreme Constellations is holding him prisoner after he's committed an act of war against us, which doesn't make the judge see him in a favorable light. Several people have testified, in writing and in person, to Kellen's advantage. You have me and you have Rae. You'll be fine."

Kellen found herself absorbing the reassuring words, needing them as much as Armeo did. Yes, she was the boy's Protector, and it was her sacred duty to keep him safe, but never before had she felt more like his mother, in the truest sense of the word. Knowing she would embarrass Armeo if she hugged him now, she steeled herself and forced back the treacherous tears burning behind her eyelids.

"I need to go back to work," Rae said. "Why don't we go somewhere for lunch first? You can rejoin your friends in school afterward, Armeo."

The boy lit up. "I can? Can we eat at Hasta's?"

"You liked her food, eh?" Rae ruffled Armeo's unruly hair. "Of course we can."

The admiral and the boy began to walk toward the exit, but Kellen found herself unable to move. Fury mixed with fear made her limbs freeze, and she watched everyone vacate the room, leaving her and Rae behind.

"You really look like you need something to eat and drink. You didn't touch your breakfast." Rae's voice reached through her inner turmoil. She gently took her arm. "You did great on the stand, and so did Armeo."

"It may not be enough."

Rae squeezed her arm and moved closer. "You may not be informed about SC law, but I am. And what I don't know, our legal representative does." She lowered her voice. "You have to trust this will work. Judge Beqq will *not* send Armeo away with M'Ekar. The thought is ridiculous."

Inhaling deeply, Kellen tried to force the panic away. It kept her from thinking straight, and she knew it was vital that she did. "All right," she said huskily. "I'll try to stay calm and wait for the verdict." She could sense Rae was not quite pleased with her response, but it was all she had to offer. "And I *do* need to eat something."

Her eyes softening, Rae nodded. "Then we better catch up with Armeo and my father."

Walking out of the courtroom, Kellen wondered if Rae understood how unnerving it had been to look at the hateful man responsible for their situation. She didn't dare ask herself what she would have done had he been there in person.

❖

"Admiral Jacelon, Commodore Jacelon, we have received disturbing information." Councilman Thorosac folded his hands in front of him. The view screen also showed four other Council members—two men and two women of different descent.

Rae felt a foreboding chill run down her spine, but merely acknowledged the man with a nod. "Go on, Councilman." To her left, her father, the only other person present at the emergency meeting, lit a cigar. The ventilation system began to hum faintly.

"We understand from the four Council members who witnessed the hearings that the court ship *Dalathea* docked at *Gamma VI* this morning and the custody hearings regarding the child commenced immediately."

"That's correct. Judge Beqq will deliver her verdict tomorrow morning at 0900 hours."

"I see." Thorosac paused, glancing at the woman next to him. "SC intelligence has reported a new development taking place in the Gantharat system. We're now facing a very dangerous situation."

The admiral leaned forward. "Marco," he said, "we go back a long way. Don't beat around the bush. Tell us what's going on."

Thorosac's face was solemn, his gaze firm. "The Onotharians have vast resources and use them relentlessly, if required. Our agents have evidence that they've fired up their propaganda system with a media campaign. They're claiming Ambassador M'Ekar was only responding to a Supreme Constellations act of war against the Onotharian Empire, including the Gantharat System."

"What?" Rae's head snapped up.

"Yes, Commodore. The Onotharian government claims the SC is holding Armeo M'Aido, the unknown last member of the Gantharian royal family, hostage."

CHAPTER SIXTEEN

Rae stood in her quarters by her father's side and watched Kellen and Armeo as they sat together at his new computer. The blond head leaned against the dark one as Kellen pointed at something on the screen. "He has homework." Rae spoke quietly as she witnessed the unexpectedly endearing scene. "He has a very analytical mind, but Gantharian grammar drives him crazy. However, his intergalactic language is better than mine when it comes to pronunciation."

"The O'Sarals are known for having several geniuses in their dynasty. The M'Aidos as well." Her father felt around in his breast pocket and looked relieved when he found his cigars.

"Not in my quarters, Father."

"Sorry, I forgot."

Rae turned her attention back toward the open door to Armeo's room. Apparently the boy had said something to amuse Kellen, who tossed her head back and laughed out loud. The sound ran through Rae's veins, enticing her. Her nipples hardened and the muscles in her thighs tensed. Dressed in a loose, light blue dress, her wife looked more casual and at home than ever before. Rae yearned to wrap her arms around both of them from behind, simply to claim them as hers all over again.

Taken aback by her possessive thoughts and the protectiveness surging through her, she turned abruptly to her father. "Are you sure I can't persuade you to stay for dinner?"

Raising his hand, Ewan waved the unlit cigar in front of him. "Not tonight, Rae. I have documents to go over and also two subspace meetings. Why not save it until tomorrow? I'm certain we'll have things to celebrate."

Rae wanted to believe him. "I hope so."

"Tell Kellen and Armeo good night for me, will you? I don't want to interrupt them." Ewan stunned his daughter by kissing her cheek before he left. "Have faith."

The door to her quarters hissed closed as her father left, and Rae walked over to Armeo's doorway and leaned against the frame, listening to them talk. Not really paying attention to the words, she let Kellen's sultry voice and the boy's brighter way of speaking wash over her. Sometimes the two would resort to sentences in their Gantharian native tongue, filling in where intergalactic language didn't suffice.

Kellen's hair glistened, the long waves reflecting the light from the computer screen. Falling well below her shoulder blades, it made Rae's fingers itch to comb through it.

Armeo suddenly slammed both palms hard onto the desk before twirling full circle on his chair. "Yes, that's it! I got it!" His eyes sparkled. "Rae, I didn't hear you come in." Rising, he threw himself into her arms. "I finally managed to break down the longest sentence ever written. Mr. Terence will be so relieved. He spent forever trying to explain this to me."

Rae hugged the boy and ruffled his hair. "Good job." Clearing her throat she looked at Kellen. "I didn't want to disturb you when you were concentrating." She let go of Armeo, who sat back down.

"Okay if I play a game until dinner?" he asked, sounding hopeful.

"Of course. Half an hour." Kellen rose in one fluid movement and took Rae by the hand. She led her into the living room, where she nudged her against the wall next to Armeo's door. "So you were watching us?" She leaned in for a kiss.

"Yes," Rae breathed in a whisper. "I stood listening... wondering..."

Kellen framed Rae's cheeks with both hands. "Wondering?"

"Wondering what I possibly could have done to deserve this... you..." Rae murmured against Kellen's lips. "Looking at the two of you, I thought...never..."

"What do you mean?"

Tears rose in Rae's eyes despite every effort to not let her emotions take over. "I can never let anything, or anyone, take you away from me." Swallowing her tears, she allowed Kellen to hug her. "I won't."

Kellen nuzzled Rae's hair and stroked her back gently. "I don't want to leave you either. Armeo and I…we want to stay." Catching her lover's eyes, Kellen blushed faintly. "For the first time since Tereya died…I feel I belong somewhere. Not just for what's best for Armeo. For me."

Afraid she would begin to cry, or whimper out loud, Rae pressed Kellen toward her, claiming her delicious mouth, deepening the kiss to muffle herself and to convey every single emotion surging through her. Kellen returned the kiss, opening her mouth to Rae's eager tongue, mimicking its caress.

A distinct ping from the kitchen sounded a few times before Rae's brain registered it. "Is that dinner?" she murmured.

"Yes. Well, almost. We need to add the last of the vegetables, and then it will be ready in twenty minutes."

"Home cooked. Mmm…" Rae purred.

"Want to help?" Kellen dragged her toward the annoying timer.

"Not particularly," Rae confessed. "But I want to watch."

As she followed Kellen's every movement while she prepared the last of their meal, Rae couldn't keep her thoughts from straying to the court hearing. Would this be the last time they sat down to eat as a family?

❖

Judge Amereena Beqq punched a few commands into the computer console before her. "I have now thought long and hard about what is best for the young man, Armeo M'Aido of the Gantharat System."

Rae felt a small, cold hand take hold of hers. Squeezing it gently, she tried to convey confidence to Armeo. The boy leaned into her, holding on to Kellen with his other hand.

"From a legal point of view, this case sets a precedent. SC law is clear. While dealing with a foreign nation in matters like these, the homeworld law applies. As we all know, Onotharat is the occupying force in the Gantharat system. However, the Supreme Constellations has never acknowledged the occupation and regards it as unlawful. This suggests that Gantharian laws apply. Granted, Armeo is half Onotharian, but he has resided on Gantharat his entire life, as a Gantharian citizen.

His mother was a member of the Gantharian Royal family, Crown Princess Tereya."

Glancing at Kellen, Rae saw her hold her breath and begin to tremble.

"Gantharian law presents its own set of problems," said the judge. "New, modern laws are mixed with ancient dictates, some very sketchy and open to a wide interpretation." Her terse tone of voice made it clear what Amereena Beqq thought of such an arbitrary legal system. "Kellen O'Dal has inherited an ancient title from her father—Protector of the Realm—which is mentioned in Gantharian law, but only in a historical sense. For the last century, the bearers of this title have not had to execute their obligation, until the occupation. Now it is time to decide if this title is official or a mythical thing of the past." She rose from the tall chair.

"All rise!" The bailiff's voice carried through the courtroom, sending them all to their feet.

"Armeo M'Aido, approach the bench." The judge's voice was kind.

Armeo let go of Rae's hand and walked beside her. The bailiff placed a hand on the boy's shoulder, guiding him to the center of the floor, where he faced the bench.

"I will now pass my ruling." Judge Beqq glanced at the small crowd. "In this custody hearing, between the parties present, I have ruled in favor of Kellen O'Dal and Commodore Jacelon. Armeo M'Aido will remain in your care, and any claims by Ambassador M'Ekar are denied." She gave a warm smile. "Armeo, do you understand this? You are to stay with your guardian and the commodore."

"Thank you, Your Honor," Armeo said huskily, blue tears forming in his eyes. "Thank you."

"I have stipulated a few conditions in this document." Judge Beqq raised a handheld computer. "One, Admiral Jacelon will act as overall guardian, to protect Armeo until he is legally of age. This is also a safeguard, should anything happen to Ms. O'Dal or Commodore Jacelon."

Rae felt tears begin to run down her own cheeks, and she fought to remain in control. She failed completely when Armeo turned around and ran back to them, throwing himself into Kellen's arms and reaching for Rae a moment later.

Allowing both her wife and her son to enfold her, Rae realized how tense she had been. She relaxed into their arms and was vaguely aware of her father's congratulations and the Onotharian counselor's objections.

"I intend to appeal this outrageous ruling, Your Honor!"

"It will serve no purpose." The judge dismissed the protesting man. "SC court-ship rulings are final. Such are our laws."

Rae finally let go of Armeo and Kellen and turned toward her father. "We both know this is just the beginning, but it was an important step. Have you heard more from Councilman Thorosac?"

"Yes, and I need to talk with you right away," the admiral replied. "I have new classified information."

"Very well." Rae looked at Kellen and Armeo, who stood close together, waiting for her. "I have to attend a meeting," she managed, knowing she was disappointing them. "We'll celebrate when I come home later."

"I understand," Kellen said. "I'll take Armeo back to school so he can share the good news with his friends."

"Sounds fine. See you later, then." About to turn around, Rae changed her mind and bear-hugged Armeo. "I'm so happy."

"Me too, Rae," he murmured against her shoulder.

Letting go of him, she leaned forward and kissed Kellen on the cheek. "See you later, darling. Keep your communicator close."

"Of course." Kellen's eyes still glistened with tears, but her shoulders showed less tension, and a faint smile played on her lips.

Turning toward her father, Rae took a deep, cleansing gulp of air and slipped back into her professional role, motioning toward the door. "All right, shall we, then?"

"After you."

❖

She had never known it could hurt physically to go from euphoria to a sinking feeling of pure dread in a matter of minutes. As she stared at the computer screen showing the SC Council meeting, Rae felt like she had been stabbed.

"I motion we do not allow an alien woman to retain custody of this child!" one of the councilmen exclaimed. "The Onotharians demand he be returned, and it's in our best interest to accommodate them."

"Councilman Timma, with all due respect," Thorosac interrupted. "Judge Beqq has ruled on the case, and the boy stays where he is. I know why you're so eager to play into the Onotharian hands. Your homeworld has a long-term understanding with them, since you import most of your fuel from them."

Several other voices interfered, demanding to be heard by the elders in the Council.

"Damn," Rae whispered, turning toward her father. "I knew the Council was divided on the issue, but I had no idea it would come to this."

"Several planets depend on Onotharian assets," he said. "Councilman Timma is only representing one of several. There are enough of them to cause trouble."

"Will they be able to sway the Council?"

"It doesn't look good. If they do, there's no telling what—"

Loud voices from the Council meeting interrupted him, and they turned their attention toward the screen. A tall BaDalchian woman had taken the podium.

"The Onotharians have long claimed that what you refer to as an occupation is instead a legitimate reclaiming of their territory. The Onotharian Empire is vast, practically the same size as the SC, and they would be a valued member of our union. Having the last of the M'Aido dynasty as well as the last of the O'Sarals on SC territory renders us an unexpected and very useful asset, which we should not waste!"

Rae ground her teeth at the woman's callous way of describing Armeo. "Damn her! To all intents and purposes, she's talking about my son!" She clenched her fists, flinching when her father put a steadying hand on her shoulder. "He's nobody's asset."

"Councilwoman Migra, the child is first of all a young boy who is now in custody of one of our most decorated officers, Commodore Jacelon, and her spouse, who in turn is his Protector, according to ancient Gantharian law."

"Gantharian law!" Migra spat. "A fairy-tale title without substance! We need to seize this boy and restore him to his own people in exchange for the Onotharians' collaboration and gratitude."

"Are you suggesting we use the boy as nothing but a trade-off?" Thorosac sounded outraged and incredulous. "Councilwoman Migra, if you insist on traveling down that path, I will have you removed from these chambers for breaking the Humanitarian Convention!"

The woman paled, taking a step back from the podium. "I'm merely a representative for my homeworld and…"

"Now she backtracks," Rae snarled. "Good for Thorosac. He nailed her."

"Still, several others share Migra's opinion," her father said. "We need to be aware that winning the custody hearing today may only have bought us a little time. The Onotharians have committed an act of war against us, and if we're going to retaliate…"

Rae heard a tap on her office door. "Enter."

Commander Todd walked in, carrying a handheld computer. "An important message for you, Admiral, via a secure subspace channel."

"Thank you." Ewan Jacelon took the device and punched in his authorization code. Reading through the short message, he pinched the bridge of his nose for a second. "It's as I suspected. They're preparing for war and want me to assume command of this sector. We're the only defense between the SC and Onotharat."

Rising from her chair, Rae stood at attention and saluted her father. "Sir!"

Jeremiah Todd followed her example. "May I inform the station, sir?"

"By all means. You will also prepare for the arrival of twice as many military vessels as arrived yesterday. We will have to reroute trade vessels and generational ships to *Gamma V* and *VII*."

"Aye, sir." Jeremiah left the round office.

"Will you need this particular office space, or do you prefer something else, sir?"

"Rae, I may be your commanding officer, but please refer to me as your father when we're alone. I was just starting to enjoy the truce between us."

The wistful tone in her father's voice surprised her. "Of course, Father. Thank you."

"And no, I don't want your office. I want you to set up headquarters for me in the conference room. I'll need plenty of space to brief the captains who will arrive shortly, and to strategize."

"Not a problem." Rae was secretly relieved. Relinquishing her office didn't appeal to her.

"Who do you recommend I use to monitor this situation and report any trends to me?" Ewan pointed at the screen where the Council members argued their respective opinions.

"Lieutenant Grey's next in command, Ensign Murad. He's a keen young man who won't miss anything."

"Excellent. Now, I want to spend a few hours celebrating with my grandson. I have a feeling I'll be busy in the upcoming days."

Rae gave a strangled sound, her throat constricting. "How the hell am I going to explain this to him?" She gestured toward the screen. "He thinks it's a done deal now."

"Don't say anything yet. Not until we know." The admiral pressed the button to turn the aluminum walls opaque and put his arm around her shoulders. "Leave Armeo to me for the time being. You'll have your hands full trying to explain to Kellen. She's not going to take this well."

"Oh, God, that's an understatement."

Ewan let go of his daughter and gave her a rueful smile. "I'll keep Armeo in my quarters until you tell me the coast is clear. If necessary, he can spend the night."

Rae felt her cheeks warm and tried to mask her embarrassment by leaning over her computer screen. "Thank you, Father. I'll page you later."

Turning the walls transparent again, Rae watched the main screen, which tracked the many military ships as they approached her station. She knew an evacuation of civilians was imminent if the SC declared war.

❖

"No! I will not allow it to happen!" Kellen refused to sit down, pacing back and forth in their living room. She tugged at the buttons of her jacket and impatiently tossed it over a chair. "The court awarded *us* custody of Armeo, and I would sooner take him aboard the *Kithanya* and leave…"

"I know, but you can't! The only people who care if you live or die are on this station. If you take Armeo and run, you'll be alone, and what kind of protection will that offer?"

Kellen stopped pacing and stared at her wife. "I was his sole Protector for seven years."

"That was different. You have to admit, as soon as someone really went after Armeo, you needed help. There's no shame in that." Rae reached for her, but Kellen stepped back.

"I'm not ashamed. I didn't ask for anyone's help. You dragged me to *Gamma VI* against my will…" Tears of fury rose in her eyes. Her resentment toward the scheming Council members made her lash out at Rae, and she hated not being able to stop herself.

"I know I did!" Rae's temper flared. "I'm glad I did, because if I hadn't, you'd be dead from the infection in your wound and Armeo would be mourning you, all alone, and in the hands of God knows what people."

Moving so fast that Rae had no chance to react, Kellen slammed her against the bulkhead. "Damn you!"

"Damn me for what? For being right? For caring about you and Armeo?"

Kellen pressed herself against Rae, immobilizing her wife as the turbulent feelings rampaged inside her. All of her nerve endings ignited when Rae didn't lower her gaze.

"Damn you for making me care," Kellen murmured. "Damn you for…this…" Kellen kissed Rae wildly, parting her lips without hesitation. She let her tongue seek out Rae's, challenging it to a fight for dominance.

"Kellen," Rae said huskily against her mouth. "You can't leave. I won't let you."

"I'd be long gone before anyone noticed." Kellen realized her voice had lost its conviction.

"That's where you're wrong. I'd know." Rae framed Kellen's face with her hands. "I'd know instantly and come after you. Don't you see? I could never let you go."

"Why?"

"Because you're my wife. It would break my heart if anything happened to you."

Kellen willed her rock-hard muscles to relax. She still pressed Rae against the wall, stroking along her arms, but she knew her touch had changed from frantic to loving. "What does that mean?" she asked, her voice little more than a whisper.

"If you stick around, we can find out." Rae's lips drew a moist line along Kellen's neck, just above the neckline of her dress. Her hands slid down to cup Kellen's breasts, massaging them until the achingly hard nipples ignited a dark pleasure between her legs.

Kellen's throat ached and she found it difficult to speak. "I don't want to leave you."

"Why?" Rae challenged in a gentle voice.

"I would miss you. I would miss this." Capturing Rae's lips, Kellen kissed her again, this time with a passion tinged with tenderness. Nibbling along her lover's lower lip, she didn't relent until Rae whimpered her name and broke free.

"Trust in me, Kellen." Rae's chest rose and fell unevenly. "Don't leave." She slipped her hands around Kellen's back and held on to her. "Stay with me."

"I don't wish to abandon you." Kellen lifted her and carried her toward the bedroom. "My heart tells me I belong with you." She dipped her head and kissed Rae, feeling both desire and remorse. "Right now, all I can think of is how I want to make perfect love to you."

Rae's arms tightened around Kellen's neck. "Oh, yes."

Kellen placed Rae on the bed and hovered over her, all her senses heightened. She gazed into her eyes, dark gray, hinting toward blue. "Beautiful," she managed, her vocal cords betraying her when she had so many things to say.

Giving herself over to the passion, she lowered her body onto Rae's, claiming her in a searing kiss. Right now, in this bittersweet instant, she knew this was where she belonged.

Kellen sat up in bed next to her sleeping wife, her thoughts far away as she considered the information Rae had given her the previous evening. After they had picked up Armeo from the admiral's quarters, they returned to their own and went straight to bed. Unable to sleep, Kellen turned the information over in her head and examined every angle. *She's asking a lot. Unconditional trust in her and faith in virtual strangers. Is she using the growing bond between us to subdue me?* A quick glance at the still form curled up next to her softened her cutting thoughts. *No. She cares. It's in her touch.* Still, having gone over every detail of their situation, she knew the only thing that made sense would not please Rae.

Kellen gently shook the sleeping woman's shoulder. "Rae. Wake up."

Rae stirred, shuddered, and tugged at the blankets. "Kellen?" She looked up with sleepy eyes. "What time is it?"

"The alarm will go off in half an hour." Kellen slid down, making it easier for Rae to meet her gaze. "I've analyzed the situation and know what I have to do to keep Armeo safe and also help my people."

Rae rubbed her face. "What are you talking about?"

"I'm keeping my word to tell you first." Kellen didn't falter. "You have to let me return to Gantharat."

Chapter Seventeen

Rae, now wide awake, stared at Kellen, certain she had misunderstood. "What the hell are you talking about?"

"There's a good chance I can find the evidence my father and I collected against the Onotharians over the years, but to locate it, I have to go back."

"You'd never get past the Onotharians. They're getting ready to wage war on the SC." Pushing the covers off, Rae got up and put on a blue kaftan. "Where did you and your father keep this evidence?"

"In the vault under the barn."

"You told us the Onotharians destroyed your estate, burned it to the ground."

"They did, but the vault may still be intact." Kellen rose on her knees in the bed, and the sheet fell off her naked body. "If I could…"

Rae's temper blazed and she flew toward the bed, sitting down next to Kellen. Taking her by the shoulders, she barely refrained from trying to virtually shake some sense into her. "Do you really think I'd let you go on a suicide mission like that? We'll find another, safer, way to sway the Council."

"And what if we can't?" Kellen raised her voice. "What if this is our only chance?"

Rae felt Kellen tremble. "You're cold." She tugged at the bedcovers and wrapped them around Kellen, hugging her. "Listen. I can't allow you to go, especially not on your own. Armeo needs you, and so do I."

Kellen remained rigid for a moment but then relaxed against Rae. "Don't dismiss the idea completely. My father and I had extensive documents that prove a long list of atrocities the Onotharians have committed since the occupation. Records of how they sent innocent people to the asteroid-belt prisons and tortured them. Tactical information and blueprints of even more powerful vessels than the *Kester*. I don't remember details, and it wouldn't matter if I did. You need well-documented proof to sway the Council."

"You can't even be sure the vault is still intact."

"No, but there's a good chance it is. Don't you see? If you could present the Council with such evidence, the Gantharians would stand a chance. As things are now, with so many SC homeworlds swaying toward Onotharat, we both know Gantharat won't experience freedom for a long time, if ever.

"Onotharat might even become a powerful member of the SC. That would be catastrophic, not only for Armeo, but also for the Gantharian refugees enjoying SC shelter and the peace-loving worlds who'd vote against an Onotharat membership. I can't let this opportunity pass us by!"

Her passionate words didn't leave Rae unaffected. She kissed Kellen's cheek. "All right. I'll discuss it with my father, but if he decides to act on it, it'll be an undercover SC Intelligence operation. I won't be able to tell you about it."

Kellen withdrew, her jaw set. "The mission, if it takes place, would be more likely to succeed if I were a part of it. I know the territory, and only I know how to bypass the security measures around the vault."

Rae knew Kellen's points were valid, but her heart screamed no at the thought of sending Kellen back into hostile territory on such a high-risk mission. "I'll brief my father at the morning meeting," she said. "He's taken command of this sector and has the final word."

"Very well. I hope he'll see the possibilities of this information." She pulled Rae closer. "I don't mean to worry you. I'm starting to depend on the growing feelings between us. I'm not disregarding how I…we feel." She kissed Rae's forehead. "I want you to know how much you matter to me."

Rae's throat clenched around a growing lump that was choking her. Her pulse increased when Kellen didn't break eye contact as she towered over Rae, holding her firmly.

"You have a way with words," Rae whispered. "And you have a way of catching me off guard too."

Tipping her head back, she studied Kellen's serious expression. Kellen's hair lay in tousled waves around her shoulders. Illuminated by the stars from behind, she looked ethereal, out of this world. Rae smiled at her thoughts. Of course Kellen would look otherworldly—she was.

Rae caressed Kellen's cheek, then brushed her thumb over her lower lip. "Sometimes I think this is a dream," she said huskily. "I think I'll wake up and find these quarters empty. I know you and Armeo haven't been here long, but I can't imagine either of you gone. You see, you matter to me as well." *How could I ever risk losing you when you look at me like this?*

Rae heard Kellen's breath catch and felt her face brush against her short hair. "I'd stop at nothing to find my way back here."

Rae turned her head and searched for her lover's lips. Lost in the deep kiss, she found her own body reacted instantly. "Oh, yes." Curling her arms and legs around Kellen, she allowed her to untie the belt to her kaftan. Kellen's hands roamed her sensitized skin and made Rae cry out as they quickly moved toward the parts of her body that still ached from last night's passion.

"You're ready for me," Kellen whispered, her fingers parting slick folds. "You want me."

"Yes, I do…" Spreading her legs and drawing her knees up, Rae knew if Kellen didn't take her that instant, she would self-combust from sheer frustration. "Do it. Please."

Kellen's long fingers filled her, pressing relentlessly against a spot that sent Rae into convulsions, grasping at Kellen for support. Before long the orgasm washed over her, relentless and almost frightening in its intensity.

Kellen caressed her until Rae stopped trembling. Placing kisses along her forehead, she parted her own legs in what Rae interpreted as a gesture of trust and need. Rae rolled over and ended up half on top of Kellen, her hands roaming the curves of the beautiful woman beneath her. "That's right, darling. Your turn now."

Deepening the kiss, Rae heard Kellen's cry of pleasure as she claimed what her lover offered so willingly.

❖

Rae sat on her father's right and focused on the computer in her hand. She glanced up as he leaned back in the chair at the head of the conference table, and recognized the barely harnessed impatience on his face. Drumming his fingers against the table, he waited until his senior staff assembled. As his next in command, Rae worked until the last minute, reading a variety of reports. Browsing through the information, she froze when she read the tactical officer's deductions.

"Good afternoon, everyone," Admiral Jacelon said. "Commodore, I believe you have some news for us."

Rae nodded briskly. "Yes, sir. Half an hour ago we received new intelligence. The Onotharians are gathering around our border, sending large units from Gantharat bases to intercept a potential retaliation from the SC.

"The latest report suggests there's a rift in the Council regarding how to proceed. The majority want to respond with force and ultimately help liberate Gantharat. The rest think we should accommodate the Onotharians by handing over Armeo M'Aido. This act would possibly ensure the trade between the Onotharians and the homeworlds that depend on their minerals."

"What does the Council chairman think?" Jeremiah Todd asked.

"Fortunately, Marco Thorosac views the recent events as clear aggression toward the SC," Rae answered. "When they vote, however, the Onotharian-friendly forces within the Council might prevail."

"There's more," Owena said. "Ultimately, such a development would change the center of power in this part of the galaxy. Given their history, the Onotharians would have no qualms about using their well-oiled propaganda machine to form alliances within the SC once their membership had been approved."

The admiral nodded. "And if that happened, we could very well be seeing the same things happen to our smaller planets that occurred on Gantharat."

"Asteroid prisons, government-owned media, and an elaborate informer-based society," Rae filled in. "The pro-Onotharian Council members don't seem to realize their need for minerals could eventually destroy the Supreme Constellations."

"Or they close their eyes to it," Jeremiah said, his voice filled with dismay. "So, what can we do? *Gamma VI* is the last outpost between the Onotharian forces and the rest of the SC. No matter what, we'll be right in the line of fire, so to speak."

Admiral Jacelon rose to his feet and placed both hands on the conference table. He regarded his senior staff unsmilingly. "We have a rare window of opportunity. For now, the debates still run high back at SC headquarters. They'll argue this issue until they can put it to a vote, so we have to find enough evidence to show conclusively how the Onotharians operate. Once that's done, if everything goes our way and the Council decides to keep the Gantharian prince with his family and refuse the Onotharians, the regrettable outcome will most likely be war."

An ominous silence filled the room.

"Damned if we do and damned if we don't," Alex murmured.

"Perhaps it was inevitable," Rae said. "The Gantharians requested SC intervention when the occupation began, but for similar political reasons we chose not to get involved."

"Fate comes back to bite us in the a—" Jeremiah quieted after a glance from Rae.

"True," she said. "Earlier today I learned of an opportunity, which then seemed too farfetched and dangerous, but now begins to feel like the proverbial last hope. Ms. O'Dal told me that the vault where she and her father kept evidence regarding how the Onotharians have treated the Gantharian people might be intact." Rae described what Kellen had suggested.

"It almost sounds too good to be true," Jeremiah said. "How great are the chances the vault didn't burn out?"

"According to Kellen, the vault was built to withstand such an attack."

Owena punched some commands into her computer. "We don't have any intelligence on how the O'Dal estate survived the fire. SC intelligence was able to tap into Onotharian satellites orbiting Gantharat two weeks ago, but at the time clouds from large hailstorms covered the northern hemisphere where Ms. O'Dal lived."

"So our unit would go in blind if we decided to obtain the records," Alex said. "Sounds like a suicide mission to me."

Feeling unsettled when she heard her own recent words repeated, Rae laced her fingers together and said, "This couldn't be a standard operation by just any security detail. I admit, I reacted to this idea much the same way you did, Alex, but I've thought about it all day."

Her father sat down slowly. "You've come up with a plan." It was not a question.

"An embryo of a plan," Rae cautioned. "I'm going to need all of you to make it doable." She paused, not taking her eyes off her father. "It's not just about Armeo anymore—I don't think it ever was. It's about the future of Gantharat and ultimately, the Supreme Constellations.

Powerful forces are at work here, and who knows which planets in this union will decide to go along with the pro-Onotharian worlds, with time?"

"So, tell us what you have up your sleeve, Commodore." Alex smirked.

"We don't have much time. The away team needs to get to Gantharat the fastest way possible. Maximum field-distortion drive gets you to Gantharat in about three weeks. Too slow." Feeling jittery, Rae rose and paced as she voiced the thoughts that had whirled through her brain most of the day. "Also in the name of speed, we need someone with local knowledge to join the away team. Since that person needs to know how to bypass any booby traps around the vault, I'm sure you realize it has to be Ms. O'Dal." Rae thought she saw a glimpse of sympathy in Owena's eyes.

"How would the team get to Gantharat in such a short time?" Jeremiah asked. "Even if we had tachyon-mass drive, a multitude of Onotharian forces patrol the sector. And we don't have time to outfit any of our frigates with this technology."

Rae knew her next in command was right. Tachyon-mass drive was still a controversial way to travel; such propulsion polluted space, and strong forces within the SC had always lobbied against it.

"I'm aware of that. However, there's another way. Commander Todd, do you remember the two pirate vessels we intercepted about two months ago?"

Jeremiah's face lit up. "Yes, I do. I see where you're going, ma'am."

"Then I assume they're still in our possession?"

"I would think you'd already made sure of that, Commodore." Todd smiled briefly.

"Correct." Rae turned to the admiral. "We have two captured pirate vessels outfitted with tachyon-mass drives, sir. Each can carry four assault craft, and we can easily reinforce their weapons array with SC torpedoes."

"How many would be a part of the away team?" the admiral asked, a slight frown appearing between his eyebrows.

"Four pilots, two navigators, and two tactical officers for the pirate vessels. Eight pilots and eight navigators for the assault craft. Also four maintenance crew members and four security officers—and of course Kellen O'Dal. Their biological signatures would be masked. Everyone would appear to be pirates, which would give them a good chance to slip through the Onotharian net. Also, traveling at that speed makes the vessels harder to detect and pursue."

Admiral Jacelon looked at her under raised eyebrows. "And who'd head up this operation?"

Rae returned her father's steady gaze. "I would, sir."

❖

Armeo's eyes were brimming with unshed tears as he stared at the two women on the couch. "Why can't I go with you?"

Kellen's heart ached at the obvious pain in the boy's voice. "Because it's too risky. You have to stay behind with your grandfather."

"What if you don't come back? Or Rae?"

"Something could always go wrong. I won't lie to you. It's dangerous but also very important."

Armeo walked out of reach and stood by the porthole. His body rigid, he seemed oddly untouchable. Kellen wondered if, for the first time, she was glimpsing the man he would one day become.

"We've always been together," he muttered. "You've never left me behind before."

"And I wouldn't do so now either, if it weren't necessary." Kellen allowed the boy his space while she tried to explain. "I have to return to Gantharat and find the documents beneath the barn. Now, this is a secret, so you can't tell anyone, not even Dorinda."

"Dorinda says her dad is going too."

"Yes, Captain de Vies will pilot one of the ships."

"Dorinda isn't very upset. She says her father goes on missions all the time."

Kellen considered this. "You know, perhaps since he does, Dorinda doesn't realize this is a very special mission. She'll need you around to be her friend when she understands what's going on."

"Yeah?" Armeo looked at her, his eyes so like Tereya's it made Kellen's heart twitch. "Maybe it's better I stay here to help her and Granddad."

"Yes, I think so. Your grandfather will be very busy. He's taken command of this sector and will need your support."

"When are you leaving?"

"Early tomorrow morning."

Turning his head, Armeo met her gaze with his chin raised. "All right. I'm not happy about you leaving without me, but I'll do as you ask." The regal tone in his voice would normally have made Kellen smile. Tonight, she was closer to tears than to laughter. "Say you'll come back," he said, his voice suddenly unsteady again.

"I'll do my very best, *shindar'sh.*"

After a few moments, he returned to her and wrapped his arms around her waist. They stood in silence, and Kellen sensed he needed no more information at this point, merely for her to make good on her word.

❖

Rae stood in the large opening that led into a cargo area on Deck 41. She rarely visited this part of the station and hadn't seen firsthand how many confiscated vessels were stored down here, awaiting reconstruction or disassembly.

"Over here, Commodore." Lieutenant D'Artansis waved her over. "These are the tachyon-mass drive ships we intercepted."

Leanne was busy making sure the spaceships were ready to launch. Several mechanics and engineers were at her disposal, and Rae could see three tool carts around one of the port nacelles.

"Problems?" She motioned with her chin toward the two women with their heads buried inside an open hatch.

"Nothing that won't be fixed when it's time to go, ma'am."

"Good. Maintenance will bring aboard what we need in an hour. We've renamed the ships. I will captain the *Liberty,* and I want you to pilot it."

"Understood."

"Captain de Vies will command the *Freedom.* The admiral and I will brief the away team at 0400 hours, so I suggest you try and get some sleep before then."

"Yes, ma'am. I just have to make sure the...which one is this? It used to be called *X'yash.*"

"This is the *Freedom.*" Rae tipped her head back and looked up at alien writing underneath the vessel.

"Well, I want to make sure everything's working on the *Freedom* before I go to bed." She hesitated. "And, ma'am..."

"Yes, Lieutenant? Is there something I can do for you?"

"You've already done it, ma'am." Leanne's multicolored eyes sparkled, but her face was serious. "I'm grateful that you're deploying both Owena and me on this mission. I would've found it difficult if either of us was left behind."

"You're aware of how high-risk this is?"

"Yes, ma'am. That's why." Looking absentminded, Leanne patted one of the *Freedom*'s aft struts. "I think you've guessed we're... together."

Rae stepped closer, giving Leanne a smile. "Yes, I have. If I didn't think you could handle it during a deployment, I wouldn't have considered assigning you both."

"In fact, I think our performance is dependent on it. Had Owena been left behind at the station...I'm afraid my thoughts would've been with her, knowing how much she worries. I know we all do that with our next of kin, but this...what Owena and I have, it's almost as new and fragile as..." She stopped and blushed from her neck up to her strawberry-blond hairline.

"As Kellen's and my relationship?" Rae placed a gentle hand on Leanne's shoulder. "You're right. I've never seen Owena so close to losing it as when we were in the mission room during the last battle. When she learned you were all right, she actually began to breathe again."

"She's not really big on trust."

Neither is Kellen. "She'll get there."

"I know. Time will tell her I'm worth trusting."

How extraordinary. Kind of a mirror relationship, in some ways. Feeling connected with Leanne, and certainly protective of the young pilot, Rae regarded her fondly. It was impossible not to be charmed by her. True kindness emanated from Leanne like mist on a lake. "Time to get some shut-eye, Lieutenant."

"Just one more check of the hydraulics for this strut. It's not quite there yet."

Rae knew Leanne could have ordered any one of the mechanics on duty to take care of the problem, but understood her urge to deal with it herself. It had also to do with deployment jitters. *We all have them, and we all deal with them in different ways.* "All right. See you early tomorrow, then."

Rae returned Leanne's salute and walked around, scanning the two ships that would take them through enemy territory. Sleek, and with an alien design that stirred her curiosity, they were supported by thin legs with large clawlike feet. Having read the specs, she knew the metallic alloy used for the hull enabled them to travel at an unfathomable speed through space. The pirates had emptied their computer of all useful information when two *Gamma VI* patrols intercepted them, and now her computer experts were downloading SC data to replace the missing files.

Checking the chronometer on her wrist, Rae knew she would probably not get much sleep tonight. She had too much to do to ensure the mission's success. Kellen was spending the evening with Armeo, and Rae would have loved to join them, talk with the boy, and if possible reassure him. Suddenly needing to hear Kellen's voice, she walked over to a remote corner of the hangar and grabbed the communicator from her shoulder.

"Jacelon to Kellen O'Dal."

The communicator came to life after a brief moment. "Kellen here. Is something wrong, Rae?"

"No, everything's fine. How did it go with Armeo?"

"He's gone to bed and I think he's asleep. Did you want to talk to him?"

"Yes, but don't wake him up." Rae hesitated. "Was he very upset?"

"He was angry because we're leaving him behind."

Closing her eyes, Rae leaned against the bulkhead. "And now?"

"I promised him we'd do our best to come back." Kellen's voice had a catch in it. "He seemed to accept it, but I think he doubts me for the first time in his life. Who can blame him?"

"That must be confusing for him...and painful for you."

"It is." After a rustling sound, Kellen's voice sounded closer. "Will you be home soon?"

"In a couple of hours."

"Oh."

"I have to make sure everything's ready to go, but I shouldn't be too long. I need to get some sleep before we deploy."

"Why don't you page me when you're on your way, and I'll warm some food for you?"

Kellen's thoughtfulness made Rae smile. "Thank you, darling. That would be lovely. I'll do that."

Placing the communicator back on her shoulder, she remained where she was, watching the activity around the two pirate ships. Soon they would embark on a mission most people would consider doomed to fail. She could feel her body preparing for battle, the sudden rush of adrenaline flooding her as she examined one possible scenario after another.

As she walked toward the ship she would command tomorrow, Rae felt her stomach lurch at the magnitude of her responsibility. The outcome of this mission could alter the history of many worlds within, as well as outside, the SC. After climbing its ladder, she strode into the *Freedom*, making room for the crewmen she passed. A narrow corridor led to another aluminum ladder. For all its technology, the pirate ship didn't provide any comforts such as elevators.

After her second climb, she found the unusual bridge. A thronelike captain's chair with computer consoles embedded in its armrests and small screens attached to its sides sat in the center of the bridge. Six chairs that faced different computer consoles encircled it. Slowly sitting down, she was startled when the consoles buzzed to life next to her.

Rae carefully familiarized herself with the controls, eventually realizing that she could access every part of the ship from the chair. Once she was confident she knew how to operate the vessel, she shut down the computer. She glanced over her shoulder at the silent computers as she left the alien bridge. Tomorrow it would be buzzing with activity when they prepared to deploy, but right now she could sense the ship's spirit, feel it reverberate through her. Rae prayed it would carry them to Gantharat and back home again, with their mission well accomplished.

❖

As Armeo sat up in bed, not quite awake yet, his heart hammered painfully against his ribs. He threw the covers to the side and rose, walking into the dark living room of their quarters. A faint light came from the bedroom where Rae and Kellen slept. He still shivered from the nightmare, now fading in his memory, and tiptoed over to the half-open door, afraid to wake his guardians but needing to see that they were still there.

To his surprise, the commodore was still awake, reading from a handheld computer. Kellen was asleep next to her, curled up with her head on Rae's shoulder.

"Armeo? Are you okay?" Rae asked.

"Yes. I didn't mean to disturb you," Armeo whispered, feeling embarrassed to be caught spying on the two women.

"Come in." Rae put the computer down and patted on the bed next to her. "Sit down. Can't you sleep?"

Sitting down, Armeo shook his head. "I was asleep, but I had a bad dream."

"You did? What was it about?"

"I can't remember. It was dark and...no, I can't remember it anymore." Lowering his gaze, he plucked at the SC-issued woolen-down blanket, tracing the pattern of stars woven into the fabric. "Why are you awake?" he asked.

"I've got so much to do and so little time," Rae explained. "I think maybe you're worried since Kellen is leaving you behind."

"Not only Kellen." Armeo felt a lump in his throat and was swallowing repeatedly to get rid of it when Rae slowly reached for his hand. "You're going too."

"Yes, and I'm going to take really good care of Kellen and make sure she gets back to you, sweetheart."

Surprised at the term of endearment, Armeo looked at Rae, reassured by her soft smile. Her eyes radiated the same warmth when she looked down at Kellen's head on her shoulder and then at him.

"You're very important to me," she said. "So is Kellen, and we're a family now. I know she feels very bad for not being able to stay with you, but we can save a lot of lives if we succeed."

"That's what Dorinda says too." Armeo held on to Rae's hand, taking comfort in the touch. "She says her dad is the best captain in the SC and that he'll make sure both ships return safely."

"She's right, you know. Alex de Vies is one of my best friends, and he's the best captain you can imagine."

"So you'll all come back, then? Everyone?" He knew it was an impossible question, but something made him ask anyway. *Rae's the commodore. She can do anything.*

"I can't promise things will go well, Armeo. But I can give you my word that I'll do my utmost to bring all my crew members home again. All of them."

"Thank you." Armeo looked at Kellen who slept, unaware of their conversation. "I love Kellen."

"I know you do."

"Do you love her?"

The commodore seemed to consider the question carefully. "I told Kellen earlier that I can't imagine my life without her, or you, in it. What does that tell you?"

Armeo examined Rae's expression carefully, finding nothing but honesty in her eyes. "It tells me you're truthful." Lifting their joined hands, he rose and placed a quick kiss on the commodore's knuckles. Rae's surprised look didn't escape him. "I think I'll go back to bed now. Good night, Rae."

"Good night, Armeo."

CHAPTER EIGHTEEN

Red lights flickered and klaxons howled, alerting the hangar crew. Sealing the doors leading into the space station, the officer in charge initiated the launch sequence for the two vessels about to embark. Automatic magnetic tracks guided the *Liberty* toward the hangar doors, located at the bottom of the station.

Rae followed the procedure from the captain's chair aboard the *Liberty,* knowing Alex de Vies did the same on the *Freedom.*

"Go to half-impulsion," she ordered as soon as the vessel cleared the doors. "Take us to the outer perimeter, beacon five."

"Aye, ma'am." Leanne punched in the commands, steering the sleek ship past several SC vessels.

Glancing over her shoulder, Rae saw Owena at tactical. Kellen stood beside Ensign S'hos, monitoring the data stream. She exchanged a nod with Rae.

Leanne's hands moved swiftly across her console. "Half-impulsion, bearing two-one-two, toward beacon five."

"The *Freedom* is right behind us, ma'am," Owena reported.

"Good." Satisfied both vessels were out of the hangar, Rae thought about the poignant goodbye the two families had gone through less than half an hour ago. Armeo obviously tried to hide his fear, but when Dorinda took his hand, the boy cried inaudibly, blue tears streaming down his face. Rae knew Armeo was more aware of what was at stake, and his tears had affected all of them, including Dorinda. The girl clung to her father, imploring him to come back soon. Alex de Vies didn't take his eyes off his wife while she assured their daughter that the days would pass quickly. Gayle joined their embrace, ruffling Alex's hair and smiling tremulously.

When they reached beacon five, the two ships set a course toward a space corridor cleared of all other traffic. Following it would take them well beyond Supreme Constellations space, where they would have to rely on Kellen's navigation. She had spent the last twelve hours plotting a course parallel to the one she had followed to reach SC space. Together with Ensign S'hos, Kellen was already punching in commands for future reference.

"Admiral Jacelon to Commodore Jacelon."

"Jacelon here. Go ahead, sir."

"We've received directives from the Supreme Constellations Council, Commodore. Unless you return within fifteen days with solid evidence of what we claim the Onotharians are guilty of, they plan to make Armeo a ward of the Supreme Constellations, with complete authority over his future. We both know what this means—an imminent risk the Council will acknowledge and approve the Onotharian occupation of Gantharat. We must avoid this at all cost."

"Understood, sir. We're ready to launch. Unless we run into trouble, our ETA in the Gantharat System should be within one hundred and ten hours. We're prepared to engage the tachyon-mass drive."

"We'll monitor you from here as long as our long-range sensors can track you. Be safe, Rae. Godspeed."

"Thank you, sir. I'll report in before we're out of range. Jacelon out."

"Ready to engage the tachyon-mass drive, ma'am," Owena stated. "The *Freedom* is powering up as well. Forty-five seconds until launch."

Rae checked her computers, trying to disregard the alien design. "All hands prepare for tachyon-mass drive. Shuttle bays, secure ships and cargo. All crew members to their duty stations. Begin countdown."

"Beginning countdown, ma'am," Owena acknowledged. "Twenty seconds and counting."

A computerized voice recited numbers in a falling sequence, and Rae tugged her seat belt tighter around her. Glancing toward Kellen's workstation, she saw her and the ensign strap on harnesses attached to the console.

"Five-four-three-two-one—tachyon-mass drive active." The computerized voice went silent, but a low hum originated from deep inside the vessel. Reverberating throughout every bulkhead, the energy seemed to hold its breath before it unleashed into a thrust, propelling them through the space corridor at an illegal speed. Invisible to the human eye, a tachyon-particle resonance bubble formed around the two ships, creating an impenetrable defense against space debris and smaller asteroids.

Rae, her back pressed into the chair, briefly closed her eyes when tremendous G-forces threatened to overcome her before the DVAs managed to catch up. When it no longer felt as if her intestines would become one with the chair, she looked around to make sure that the others were all right. "Report."

"All systems are functioning within their reference values. Shuttle bays one and two report all personnel and equipment made it through the jump. All sensors are operational, and long-range scanners show no enemy contacts out there. We're on our way, ma'am."

"Excellent. One hundred and ten hours may seem like a long time, but we need every one of them to prepare. However, it's also important that we rest if we get a chance. Lieutenant Grey, you have the bridge. Ms. O'Dal, you and Ensign S'hos will navigate and enter new coordinates into our flight plan. Also plot alternative routes, because I'm sure we're going to need them. Lieutenant D'Artansis, I want you at the helm as much as possible. I'll relieve you later."

Unbuckling her belt, she rose from the chair and glanced toward the view screen. Rae was used to seeing the distant stars become reduced to long silver streaks when a ship leaped to field-distortion drive; traveling by tachyon-mass drive turned them into faint marks, barely visible. The difference would take some getting used to.

The SC's prohibition against this type of propulsion didn't stop pirates from building ships like these, able to outrun any of the SC patrol vessels trying to catch them. The *Gamma VI* station had the two ships in their possession only because they had surprised the pirates while they were making repairs behind a small nebula. Now, Rae was glad they hadn't dismantled them as planned.

❖

Six hours later, Kellen pushed herself farther into a narrow crawl space, dragging a toolbox behind her. As she crept through the passage, she hoped to quickly find out what was causing the fluctuation in power.

Ensign S'hos had discovered a minor deviation in the readings half an hour ago. Knowing from her recent journey how small matters like these could escalate, Kellen had taken it upon herself to make repairs.

As she inched through the crawl space, she vaguely smelled something burning. Another yard into the vessel's elaborate machinery, she detected faint smoke coming from a set of relays. Realizing the potential danger, she clutched the small toolbox and disregarded the pain in her knees and elbows from sliding along the unforgiving steel grid. The smoke now increased in density, its sickening smell making her cough. Engaging her communicator, she opened the tool box with her free hand.

"O'Dal to the bridge. We have a small fire in the port crawl space, among the relay clusters. Extinguishing it now."

"Lieutenant Grey here. Can you determine the cause of the fire?"

"Give me a minute, Lieutenant." Kellen took a small fire extinguisher from the tool box and sprayed the circuits closest to her. More smoke billowed from the fried parts and stung her eyes. Reaching into the tool box, she found an oxygen mask and strapped it on. It should have worked automatically but seemed to malfunction; no oxygen streamed through the mask. Straining to see through the smoke, Kellen figured the mask would at least cover her nose and mouth. When she leaned in to inspect the burned area, she flinched. "We have a problem, Lieutenant. There's a foreign substance attached to the burning relays. I've seen similar material before. It's a substance that self-combusts at a given time, depending on how it's administered. We have to notify the commodore."

"I heard." Commodore Jacelon's voice was a low growl through the comm system. "Are you all right? Can you extinguish the fire and assess damages?"

"Yes, and I have enough spare circuits and relays with me to replace the most important ones. However, my oxygen mask isn't working. Have Ensign S'hos ventilate new air into the crawl space on my mark." Kellen knew she would have to wait until the fire was out before she could ask for oxygen. She used up two small extinguishers before she was satisfied. Tears ran down her cheeks from the smoke, and she coughed despite the protective mask. "Ventilate the crawl space."

After a few seconds fresh air streamed through the shaft, taking the smoke and stinging smell of burned circuitry with it. Kellen began the painstaking work of replacing the damaged parts and running her diagnostic tools over the remaining ones. Only when she was satisfied everything would run smoothly did she begin to close her toolbox.

Suddenly, stopping, she reached for a flashlight and switched it on. As the beam trailed the wiring between the relays, she looked for other signs of sabotage. After she found two more places with the self-combusting substance, Kellen again tapped her communicator. "Commodore, I have disturbing information. I've found more of the substance that hasn't ignited yet. I'm sure I'll find more. I'll need liquid nitrogen in spray cans to stabilize it before I can remove it."

After a brief pause, Rae spoke. "Damn. Then we can expect even more. Another crew member will join you with the nitrogen, and I'll have two others inspect the starboard crawl space."

"We don't have much time," Kellen stressed. "If they all burn, we don't have enough spare parts to make repairs. We need to neutralize this substance immediately."

"Locate as many as you can. Mark them with fluorescent tags. You'll find them in the toolbox. Ensign Santino will follow you and neutralize the substance. He'll provide you with an oxygen mask." Jacelon paused. "And, Kellen, be careful."

"Affirmative. I'll be cautious. O'Dal out."

Slowly moving forward, Kellen began to place the fluorescent tags where she found evidence of sabotage. When she was almost at the end of the crawl space, she heard a shuffling sound behind her and realized Ensign Santino had arrived. Bracing herself on her elbows, she pushed back, trying to reach the young man as quickly as possible.

"Throw me the oxygen mask, Ensign," she called. "Make sure your own is functional. We need to start neutralizing this substance immediately. Are you familiar with the procedure?"

A mask with a small tube hanging from its side slid toward her across the metal grid floor. "Yes, ma'am." He glanced down the crawl space. "It's going to be a close call, ma'am."

Kellen grabbed the two cans of liquid nitrogen that rolled toward her. "All the more reason to hurry, Ensign. Let's begin."

Working in unison to beat the odds, they sprayed the nitrogen where the fluorescent tags indicated sabotage. Kellen didn't allow herself to ponder who was responsible for this situation. She prayed the second team in the other crawl space would also get the job done in time, or they would become as immovable as an old *maesha*.

"I think that was all of them, Ensign. Now, let's remove the substance. Use a knife or screwdriver, but make sure you don't damage the relays or the circuits."

Slowly they made their way toward the exit, scraping off the substance and using a small suction device to remove it completely. Her elbows raw with pain from leaning against the metal grid, Kellen clenched her teeth and kept working. When they were done, she heard Ensign Santino exit through the hatch behind them, his grunt of relief replaced by a familiar throaty voice.

"Good job, Santino. Kellen, let's get you out of there. You look like hell." Rae reached inside the hatch and helped her special crew member as she moved out of the narrow tube. Outside, Kellen slowly stretched and carefully extended her arms. Grimacing against the pain, she looked in dismay at the blue blood that trickled down her wrists.

"Have you contacted the *Freedom*, Commodore? It's likely they've also—"

"Yes, Captain de Vies has been informed. God, look at your elbows." Jacelon took Kellen gently by the arms and examined them.

"I need bandages," Kellen reflected calmly. "It wasn't very comfortable in there. I'll bring extremity shielding next time."

"Let's hope there's no next time," Rae said as she glanced into the crawl space. "Ensign S'hos is our designated medic on this mission. He has a med kit on the bridge. Santino, let's get you checked out as well."

The young man nodded, clutching his left shoulder. "Yes, ma'am."

"What about the other team? Have they found any signs of sabotage in the starboard crawl space?" Kellen asked as they made their way through the pirate vessel.

As if to answer her question, Rae's communicator beeped. "No sign of sabotage in this part of the vessel, ma'am. The blueprints suggest there's a small crawl space above the bridge. Do you want us to check that out as well, Commodore?"

Rae paled. "Yes, Lieutenant, and make it quick. Report back ASAP. Jacelon out." She slammed her fist into the closest offending bulkhead. "Damn! Where else have they managed to get to us?"

On the bridge Ensign S'hos quickly tended to Kellen's scraped skin. Clearly taken aback by the distinct color of her blue blood and its dramatic effect against her skin, he moved the derma fuser an inch above the wound with trembling fingers, cleaning and closing it simultaneously. Rae stood next to her, and Kellen wondered if she realized she had placed a hand protectively on her shoulder. Rae seemed lost in thought, her attention turned inward. Suddenly she looked at Owena, who was approaching them.

"For the self-combusting substance to ignite now, it must've been applied less than twenty-four hours ago. I gave the order to start preparing the two pirate vessels at 1030 hours yesterday. It's now 1345. Only accredited personnel had access to the hangar."

"That means one or several of them were paid off, or otherwise coerced, to commit treason," Owena said.

Her eyes switching to a dull gray, Jacelon didn't hesitate. "Open a secure subspace signal directly to Admiral Jacelon's console. Brief him on what's happened. He'll take the appropriate measures from there. We're also going to conduct diagnostics of every system aboard this vessel. I'll contact Captain de Vies."

Owena returned to her work console, punching in commands as she attempted to contact *Gamma VI*. "I can't get through. All the secure lines are occupied. What the hell's going on back there?"

❖

Rae discussed all the plausible reasons for the communication activity at *Gamma VI* with Alex de Vies, most of them foreboding. Her old friend had also tried to reach the mission room as well as the admiral's personal console, but with the same frustrating results.

"Do you want to try any other channels, or turn back?" Alex asked.

"Neither," Rae said, after some consideration. "I'm not presumptuous enough to think I'm indispensable at *Gamma VI* right now. My father is more than capable of dealing with any situation that might arise. Our two ships are all that stands between the Onotharian Empire and the SC. We'll go through with our plan."

"I thought you'd say that." Rae could hear the concurrence in Alex's voice. "My crew searched the *Freedom* with a fine-tooth comb. No sign of sabotage."

"Perhaps the saboteur was interrupted, or figured if he put this ship out of action, we'd turn back rather than continue in a single ship…"

Rae's voice trailed off. "I still can't understand how the Onotharians, or an Onotharian-friendly individual, could get to the *Liberty* so quickly."

"I've sent an encoded subspace message that will bypass any other queued messages awaiting the admiral's attention once he logs onto his personal computer."

"I did too. We'll be in range for another twelve hours. Let's hope we can contact *Gamma VI* before then. I've also had my crew examine the ship, but who knows if the saboteur has anything else in store for us?" Pressing her hand against stiff muscles in her neck, Rae briefly closed her eyes. "In the meantime we'll stay on course, on maximum tachyon-mass drive."

"I've got your back covered, Rae. You know that." Alex's voice became gentle. "We've been in tougher circumstances than this, my friend."

"Yeah, I know. I just can't quite remember when. Jacelon out."

Sitting in the miniscule compartment that served as her office, Rae scrutinized her team's recent report. They hadn't found any other signs of sabotage, and given the time frame, it was unlikely the saboteur would have had time to create more havoc.

Rae heard a knock and a familiar voice. "Rae, I need to talk with you."

"Enter."

Kellen stepped inside, the door immediately hissing closed behind her. "Have you been able to contact *Gamma VI* yet?"

"No, and neither has the *Freedom*. I just briefed Alex regarding this report." Rae waved her handheld computer in the air. "His team hasn't found anything to suggest sabotage."

"Good." Kellen leaned forward across the desk and rested her chin on her hands. "I have a theory as to why we can't contact the station. It's unlikely that all the lines would be busy, correct?"

"Right." Rae leaned back in her chair. "What are you thinking?"

"We're traveling at supersonic speed, away from the station. I think the waste particles emanating from the *Liberty* and the *Freedom* create a disturbance. Having gone over some facts in the SC database you'd installed on the bridge, I discovered that the SC banned this propulsion system not only because of the toxic antimatter, but also because of communication issues."

Rae's mind reeled. "So, again, we're left with a damn-near-impossible choice." She rose. "I think you're right, which means we have to do it Alex's way. He sent an encrypted subspace message to my father's personal work console. I've done so already and will repeat it shortly." She saw a ghost of a feeling flicker across Kellen's strong features. "Yes?"

"Please, send a special greeting to Armeo? I know it's not ship's business, but…"

"Of course, I will. If I know Armeo, and I'm beginning to, he hasn't left Father's side for a minute. We can enter a short greeting to him without raising any suspicion if the enemy intercepts the message."

"Thank you, Rae. It means a lot to me," Kellen said with a catch in her voice. "This mission *could* fail, and I want Armeo to be certain I was thinking about him."

Rae encircled Kellen's waist. "How are your elbows doing?"

"They're fine. Look." Pushing up her uniform sleeves, Kellen displayed new, bluish skin where Ensign S'hos had used the derma fuser.

Worried about Kellen's cautious tone, Rae squeezed her gently. "We'll make this mission successful," she vowed. "We'll go home to Armeo and stay together like a family. Don't go into this mission sounding defeated, darling."

Kellen seemed to hold her breath for a moment, then leaned forward and kissed Rae thoroughly. Surprised, Rae parted her lips to allow the brief, passionate kiss. Swaying where she leaned against the desk, she searched Kellen's eyes for the reason for the embrace.

"Very well." Her lover nodded. "You're right. I can't go in fighting, thinking I'll be under enemy control."

Still thinking Kellen's words sounded ominous, despite her courageous attitude, Rae took her spouse by the shoulders. "And you'll obey orders and not go in half-cocked…"

Kellen cupped her cheeks gently. "You're my commanding officer on this mission. I will not willingly disobey orders. However, I also must honor the vows I swore as a Protector of the Realm as well as a Ruby Red Suit *gan'thet* master."

Rae's heart went cold. "That might pose a problem."

"I don't think so." Kellen released her and stepped back, folding her arms across her chest. "This is a covert operation, conducted in an unconventional way, far from Supreme Constellations space. We're using unlawful means of transportation, and we're about to violate what the Onotharians claim is part of their sovereignty. I think my allegiance to you, as well as to my other duties, will not only be useful but also something you can rely on."

Kellen's intense blue eyes regarded Rae steadily. Knowing her answer could destroy the ground they had broken together, Rae still had her doubts but admitted to herself that she had a point.

"I'm afraid something might happen to you." It wasn't what Rae had intended to say, but nevertheless true.

"Are you sure your feelings aren't more about your fear of how bringing me on this mission might affect your performance?"

"What are you talking about?" Rae snapped her head up.

"We are…growing fond of each other. You have brought me, your spouse, on a dangerous mission out of necessity. Perhaps you're afraid you will lose your edge, that I'll distract you."

It was not far from the truth, Rae grudgingly admitted. "You're right, in part. I *am* afraid something will happen to you, for several reasons. The first one is…I don't know how I could ever break that kind of news to Armeo."

"And the second?"

"Is about how I couldn't stand to lose you." Rae cleared her throat while pushing sudden images of a wounded Kellen from her mind's eye. "We just have to accomplish this mission in one piece. The alternative is unthinkable."

The blue eyes softened. "Instead of regarding my past and skills as a liability, why don't you look at them as an asset?"

"I do. It's just not that easy." Rae tried to organize her scattered thoughts. "The success of this mission depends very much on you. It's your homeworld, your vault, your assembled information, and your familiarity with the surroundings. Many things can go wrong before we even get to Gantharat. While we're there, the entire away team will be in danger, and getting home will be even harder if the Onotharians detect us." Rae tried to keep her voice under control. "I confess I'm afraid my emotional attachment to you might cloud my judgment."

"Me too," Kellen said. "When it was just Armeo and I against the universe, it was…easier. Now, it has become more complicated."

"Regrets?" Rae searched her lover's eyes for the truth.

"None. I believe what we call *va'yeshmir,* destiny, brought me to *Gamma VI,* to you." Kellen pushed a stray lock of hair from Rae's forehead. "I know you want to trust me, but I also know you find it difficult, perhaps because of our cultural differences."

"We come from such different backgrounds. Because I was born into a strict military way of life, with my father as my role model, I do things according to the law and by the book. It comes naturally to me. Even this mission, covert and as unorthodox as it may seem, is in accordance with SC law, and with Judge Beqq's ruling. Using these vessels is the only exception to the rule, one I have to live with. You follow another code of honor, but when you think about it, our approach to things isn't that different."

A doubtful expression flickered across Kellen's face. "Don't fool yourself, Rae," she murmured. "You said it yourself. You're bound by rules and regulations stipulated by the SC. You abide by the law. I, however, have only one objective—to protect the realm, to protect Armeo, at any cost." She made a wry face, and Rae saw a sudden tremor reverberate through her. "Admittedly, I've become conflicted since we were married. I won't abandon my duties, but my heart is also with you."

Suddenly Rae understood what Kellen meant. "So, if you were faced with a situation, where you had to choose...choosing Armeo would be your only option, but it would cause you pain."

"Indescribable pain," Kellen whispered.

Rae didn't have any simple answers and couldn't say very much to such an honest confession. "Armeo will and shall take precedence. He's your first priority, and I acknowledge that."

"He should also be yours." Kellen's words were harsh.

"What?"

"If something happens to me and you have the chance to complete this mission without me, you too must sacrifice me to keep the last of the O'Sarals safe. You married me, the last Protector of the Realm, which means you adopted these duties as well, as my wife."

Feeling her chest constrict, Rae leaned her forehead against Kellen's shoulder for a second. "I should've realized that from my father's report."

"I inherited this sacred duty and prepared for it all my life. I know it must seem overwhelming to you to learn of it in this manner."

"I love Armeo." Rae's voice was huskier than usual. "He stole my heart the night he paged me when you were in pain. Sacred duty or not, I'll always look out for him. You…" She caressed Kellen's pale cheek. "I can't promise I'd be able to sacrifice you, if the situation arose." Her throat hurt. "You mean too much to me."

Kellen stared at her, conflicting emotions obviously fighting for power in her eyes. "It seems my concerns are also yours. We'll both have to make sure such a situation doesn't occur. I'll work on several backup plans for the approach to Gantharat."

"Good." Letting her arms circle her lover's waist, Rae nudged her toward the door. "It's late. Why don't we try to get a few hours' sleep? I have to relieve Lieutenant Grey at 0300 hours."

"All right. I know you said you'd also take over from Lieutenant D'Artansis later in the day. Why not let me do that?"

About to object, Rae changed her mind. This entire operation almost breached protocol and regulations. Letting Kellen take the helm wouldn't be such a stretch. "Okay. I'm sure she'll appreciate it."

They left the miniscule office and walked toward the aft where the sleeping compartments were located. Rae climbed inside one of them, which reminded her of an old-fashioned bunk bed, making room for Kellen to join her before they closed the leatherlike curtain. The small sleeping area went dark, and Rae moved closer to Kellen. Wordlessly, she wrapped her arms around her wife.

"Thank you," she whispered, her lips only a breath away from the generous curve of Kellen's neck.

"You're welcome." Kellen pressed her lips against Rae's hairline. "Now try to get some sleep."

Rae closed her eyes, Kellen's familiar scent engulfing her, making it possible to relax for the first time all day. She felt a hand slowly massage her back, its loving movements lulling her to sleep.

CHAPTER NINETEEN

"What the hell is this? Some sort of diplomatic invasion?" Admiral Jacelon strode across the mission room toward Commander Todd. "How many ships are on their way?"

"Sixteen frigates and four cruisers, sir."

"Damn." Ewan stared at the screen. The SC Council had taken him by surprise, sending a massive diplomatic delegation that represented most of the homeworlds in the union of planets. He looked at Jeremiah Todd in horror. "Can *Gamma VI* sustain this many people on top of all the military ships currently here?"

Todd made a face. "Let's hope they brought their own java, sir."

The admiral huffed. "You got that right. What's their ETA?"

"Two hours, sir. They've been transmitting data continuously for the last half hour."

"Great. Here comes bureaucracy in its prime." The admiral detected movement to his left and saw his grandson approach, walking slowly as if hesitant to disturb him. "School out already, Armeo?" He extended an arm, and the boy lengthened his stride.

"Yes. Dorinda's with her mom. They're going to the commercial section. Mrs. de Vies says it's best to stay busy when you're worried about something." Armeo looked doubtful. "May I join them? I'll take Y'sak."

The admiral smiled inwardly at Gayle de Vies's remedy for a concerned mind. "Why don't we assign one more guard to be on the safe side? You could pick up some cigars for me, perhaps, while you're at it."

Armeo's expression brightened. "Sure! Just write down what kind you want."

The admiral placed a hand on the boy's shoulder and led him into his makeshift office. As always astounded by the strong feelings of affection this child evoked in him, he logged onto his console to reach the security department. Commander Todd had conducted careful background checks on the four security officers responsible for Armeo's safety when he was in school and out of the admiral's sight.

A sound alerted Ewan that he had a long-distance incoming subspace message. It turned out to be several. Surprised, he realized they came from the two pirate ships under his daughter's command. The *Liberty* and the *Freedom* hadn't been in contact for a while, but Ewan knew they were past the point where long-range scanners could detect them. With increasing concern he read the reports about the sabotage attempts on the *Liberty*.

"Is something wrong?" Armeo's voice brought the admiral back. "Is it from Kellen and Rae?"

"Yes, it is, son. Kellen left an encrypted note for you. Here, I've run it through the decoder. You can read it yourself."

Armeo lit up and leaned closer to the computer screen, reading out loud, "'Please let Armeo know I am doing well and so is Rae. We miss him very much and cannot wait to be home with him again. *Meo shindar beo'sh, Armeo.*'" He turned his glance to Ewan. "That's Gantharian. It means 'I love you.'"

"There, you see? They're doing fine." The admiral opened a channel to the security department and requested an additional guard. "When he arrives, you go have fun in the commercial sector. We'll have dinner in the commodore's quarters in two hours."

"I'll be back by then," Armeo said. "Are you cooking, Granddad?"

"As a matter of fact I'm a great chef, but right now I'm so busy I hardly have time to eat. However, when Rae and Kellen get back, I'll make my special pasta dish. How about that?"

"Sounds great." The boy sucked in his lower lip between his teeth for a moment, a gesture that the admiral had learned to interpret as deep worry. "Ten days. It seems like forever."

Ruffling Armeo's hair, the admiral said, "I know. I think so too."

A young ensign appeared in the doorway. "Sir, Mrs. de Vies and her daughter are at the door asking for your grandson."

"All right, Armeo, run along and be careful. If anything out of the ordinary happens, you have the device I gave you."

"Okay, sir." Armeo held up the small pager, which contained a communicator as well as an emergency beacon that would make it possible to track him. "Here it is."

"Good. Have fun."

Watching Armeo cross the mission room, the admiral grinned broadly. His new grandson had stolen his heart completely.

❖

The *Liberty* reeled from a sudden explosion close to her starboard bow. Using the tachyon-mass drive, the vessel was highly susceptible to impacts. The DVAs went off-line in an instant, tossing the crew around.

"What the hell was that, Lieutenant Grey?" Rae shouted over the klaxons. "All hands, secure your stations. Damage report!"

"Ma'am, I detect an antimatter trail on our port bow. A ship is closing—" Another explosion cut Ensign S'hos's words short.

The harness that kept her in the captain's chair dug into Rae's shoulders and around her waist as the *Liberty* was tossed into a spin. She heard an explosion go off on one of the lower decks. "And the *Freedom*?"

"Long-range scanners are down. Shields at twenty percent. Deck 4 sustained damages, but so far no casualties."

"Lieutenant Grey, target the other ship's propulsion system and fire at will."

"Torpedoes away." Owena's voice was cool. "A direct hit, they're slowing down."

"What kind of ship is it?"

"Pirates, ma'am. They carry no official signatures." Owena punched commands into her console. "They're not alone, Commodore. Here come their buddies."

"Defensive pattern Epsilon Five. *Liberty* to the *Freedom*. We're under attack. Are you in range?"

A short static made her worry their communications array had been destroyed, but then she heard Alex's response. "Not yet, Commodore. We'll be close enough to take the third ship out in about four minutes. You have to hang in until then."

"Third ship? Do we have visual yet, Ensign S'hos?"

The screen flickered, and then two sleek vessels came into view. "Where's the third ship?" Rae asked. "Why hasn't the one we fired on slowed down?"

Kellen's hands flew across the console where she assisted Ensign S'hos. "The third ship is right behind us, on a parallel course. The vessel we hit is using an auxiliary tachyon drive to match our speed."

"Microfractures on Decks 3 and 4. We have to put the brakes on, ma'am." Owena's voice was urgent. "We're heading for a hull breach if they give another full volley!"

"Damn!" Rae raised her voice. "*Liberty* to the *Freedom*. Drop out of tachyon-mass drive. I repeat, drop out of tachyon-mass drive. We're going to maximum field-distortion drive."

"Affirmative, Commodore. Dropping to maximum field-distortion drive."

"On my mark, Lieutenant D'Artansis." Rae regarded the vessels on the screen carefully. "Where exactly is the ship behind us, Lieutenant Grey?"

"Five degrees off our port bow."

"It'll be a close call, but that'll have to do. Reduce to field-distortion drive." The *Liberty* lurched as the forceful propulsion system went off-line. Clutching her seat, Rae fought to remain where she sat.

An ear-deafening screech sounded as something broke on a deck below. "Damage report!" Rae yelled.

"Hull breach on Deck 3. Shields are holding, but down to thirty-five percent."

"Evasive maneuvers! Get us away from the third ship."

D'Artansis threw the ship into a maddening pattern, clearing the pirate vessel's path as well as the *Freedom* trailing it.

"Pirate vessels are still on tachyon-mass drive and several light years away." Ensign S'hos's voice trembled, but the young man remained by his console. Kellen was still clenching the handlebars until Leanne resumed a less turbulent course.

"The *Freedom* is right behind us, ma'am," Owena reported. "She's intact, no casualties. As for our ship..." She paused, reading from her computer screen. "One crew member on Deck 3 sustained minor injuries when the hull breached."

"We have a window of opportunity to regroup before the pirates return. Slow down to full-impulsion so we can launch an attack." Rae hit the open ship communication button. "All hands, prepare to deploy assault craft."

"Ma'am, we're one pilot short. Ensign Am-pah sustained a fracture to her left arm."

"Damn, we need every ship out there," Rae hissed. The pirates could return any time. Glancing over her shoulder she looked at Kellen, who returned her gaze with a nod. "Very well. Make sure Ensign Am-pah's injury is attended to. Ms. O'Dal will take her place."

Kellen was already on her way to the narrow ladder. Rae wanted to make her swear she'd be careful but knew this kind of personal remark was impossible.

Obviously relieved and impressed, the lieutenant in charge of the shuttle bay spoke again. "Understood, ma'am. Ensign Ferris will navigate for Ms. O'Dal."

Rae knew Ensign Ferris was in his late forties, seasoned from all the years he'd patrolled the SC border.

"Excellent. Be ready to launch in five minutes." Even that was a stretch. She turned to Ensign S'hos. "Anything on long-range scanners?"

"The pirate vessels have dropped out of tachyon-mass drive and are turning. Two of them are on a circular trajectory that will take them on an assault path above us. The remaining ship is backtracking, facing us directly."

"Bold moves," Rae murmured. "Any signs they're scanning us?"

"No, not yet, ma'am. I think the lead insulation the former owners of our ships installed around the shuttle bay to keep us from scanning their cargo will keep any of their sensors from penetrating us."

Rae hoped S'hos was right.

"Assault craft ready to deploy," he said.

"Good." Rae paused for a moment. "*Liberty* to the *Freedom*. Prepare to launch assault craft. Defensive pattern Beta seventy-seven."

"My thoughts exactly, Commodore," Alex replied. "Deploying now."

The shuttle bay doors hummed as they opened to allow the deadly ships to depart. Rae pictured them as they left their mother ships and turned in a narrow circle, only to slide underneath the belly of the larger vessels and hide, ready to strike.

"Pirate vessels three minutes away and closing," S'hos reported.

"Assault craft pilots, attack pattern Delta on my mark. Ensign, do we have visual?"

"In a few seconds, ma'am."

Rae looked at the view screen at the front of the bridge and saw the pirate vessel heading right for them.

"Any sign of the ones coming in from below?"

"Yes."

Dividing the screen into two parts, S'hos showed images of the three ships approaching. Black and sleek, with weapons on all sides, they approached like giant vultures.

"Jacelon to de Vies. Let's deal with these fools."

"Affirmative, Commodore."

Rae saw the *Freedom* break away in a sudden burst of energy, rolling past the two pirate ships that approached from below. Then she felt the *Liberty* mimic the movement in the opposite direction and watched Leanne's hands fly over the controls as the battered ship obeyed her commands.

"Assault craft, *mark*."

Rae kept her eyes on the main view screen directly ahead, watching the two-seat ships leave their hideout like two small swarms to engage the enemy. Firing at the pirates' weapons arrays and propulsion systems, they seemed to take them by surprise. Rae was pleased to see the three pirate ships now scatter as they tried to evade the torpedoes directed toward them.

"Ma'am, she's getting heavy. I can't hold her," Leanne called out. "Something's wrong with the hydraulics."

"You have to keep her together, Lieutenant. Engineering, we have problems with the hydraulics…we need it fixed right away."

"We're on it, Commodore. We have a silicon leak from the manifolds leading to the port nacelle. The good news is we erected aluminum walls around the hull breach."

"Good job. Be careful with the leak. We can't slow down. We'd be sitting ducks."

Leanne struggled with the controls, but it was obvious the *Liberty* was in trouble, her flight path increasingly irregular.

"You're not looking too good, Commodore." Captain de Vies's voice came across the comm system. "Watch out. You have a pirate on your tail now."

"Surprise, surprise," Owena muttered. "Assault Craft 1, return to—"

"I'm here, Commodore," a familiar voice interrupted before the screen lit up with a blinding light, making Rae's eyes sting as the *Liberty* reeled from an explosion. When it cleared, she saw debris hurdling through space around them.

"Kellen, what's your status?" Rae held her breath, panic erupting in her midsection.

"Assault Craft 1 here, Commodore." Kellen's voice was calm. "One of the pirate ships destroyed."

"Thank you," Rae said, pressing her palms hard against the armrests. "Now go help the others."

Rae watched how the complete destruction of the lead pirate vessel seemed to discourage the other two. Facing the eight assault craft along with the two larger ships, the pirates circled them twice, engaged their tachyon-mass drives, and left the SC-manned ships behind. Relief surging through her, Rae lowered her tense shoulders and noticed for the first time just how painfully the harness dug into her upper body.

"Their flight path suggests they're heading for the Onotharian Empire." Ensign S'hos looked up at the commodore. "If they tell the Onotharians we have SC assault craft aboard, ma'am…"

"They're pirates and not likely to volunteer information to any authority that would throw them in jail," Owena said.

"Unless they sell the information." Rae rubbed her temples. "We might face a welcome party once we reach Gantharat. I think we've lost the element of surprise."

"The assault craft are returning to the shuttle bays, Commodore," Ensign S'hos reported.

"Good. Prepare for tachyon-mass drive. Lieutenant D'Artansis, resume our initial course, but only for the first thirty minutes. Then turn to the alternative trajectory Ms. O'Dal calculated earlier. We need a different approach to Gantharat."

❖

Ewan walked through the gate that led to Port 1. About to greet the man whom he disdainfully referred to as "the head honcho" of the diplomatic delegation, Admiral Jacelon stopped in mid-stride, making the two lieutenants walking a few steps behind him almost trip over their commanding officer.

"Dahlia!" he exclaimed. "What the hell are you doing here? You're supposed to finally take some time off."

The tall, slender woman before him placed a hand on her hip, obviously enjoying the moment. "You'd think I wasn't welcome, Ewan. Is that how you greet your wife?"

Ewan groaned inwardly, yet he gazed appreciatively at his wife of more than forty-five years. Dahlia wore her light auburn hair in a low, intricately braided bun and was impeccably dressed in a twill-mix black pantsuit, its coattail reaching the back of her knees, over a crisp, retrospun white shirt. Her features were more defined with age than the first time he saw her in his parents' house at a dinner function, and reflected her dynamism. If anyone ever mistook her finely shaped nose and elegant high cheekbones for fragility, Dahlia's clear gray eyes would make them rethink that assessment. She now met his gaze, unblinking as she awaited his reply.

"Of course I'm delighted, but surprised, to see you, darling." He stepped closer and kissed her cheek. "I take it you're part of the diplomatic delegation?"

"Yes. The SC council needed high-ranking diplomats to help deal with the mess. It was a chance to combine business and pleasure."

"And the pleasure part in it?"

Dahlia Jacelon winked at her husband. "Seeing you and Rae…and I understand I have a new grandson. I can't fathom the idea Rae is married. Not to mention having a stepchild. Are they around?"

"Rae and Kellen deployed on a mission three days ago. I'm taking care of Armeo."

Leaning down for her leather briefcase, Dahlia shot him a glance. "You are? How's that working out? Normally you're not very fond of children."

He didn't deny it. "Armeo has a way of getting under your skin." Ewan offered no other explanation, but he could see his wife's piqued interest.

"I'll be in charge of the diplomatic negotiations with the Onotharians until the SC Council determines which path to take. Is M'Ekar still in your custody? I need a conference room to conduct these talks."

"And you'll have it. First things first. Let me show you our quarters. You can freshen up before you dig your subtle claws into the ambassador." Motioning toward the exit, he reached for her large suitcase. "This all you're bringing?" Dahlia was famous for traveling in style.

"Are you joking? My two assistants are taking care of my other bags, all six of them. This is just the bare necessities."

Ewan realized he should've known better. "Of course, dear."

Dahlia glanced at him. "Don't pretend to sound like the henpecked husband. What's going on? What's this deployment Rae has gone on? How can her wife, a civilian, go on a mission?"

Well accustomed to how his wife rattled off questions like an ancient machine gun, the admiral shook his head. "It's highly confidential. I'll brief you when we're out of earshot." Offering his arm, he said, "I decided to let Armeo stay in the commodore's quarters, where he has his own room. I've been sleeping on the couch, but I'm sure Rae won't mind if we use the master bedroom until she and Kellen return."

As they approached the commodore's quarters, Armeo came from the other direction, escorted by two security guards. The boy carried several bags, which Ewan guessed were his purchases from his shopping spree with Dorinda and Gayle.

"Granddad!" Armeo lit up and rushed toward him, obviously missing the distinguished woman who stood next to him. The boy stopped in front of him and held up some bags. "I found your brand of cigars and bought you a present."

"Hello, Armeo. A present for me? I can hardly wait." He paused. "By the way, the lady standing next to me…"

His eyes round with surprise, Armeo blushed a faint blue before he handled the situation in what Ewan suspected was strictly according to his upbringing. Armeo let go of the bags, straightened his back, and reached for Dahlia's hand, where he placed a kiss on her knuckles. "Forgive me, ma'am. I'm pleased to make your acquaintance."

Dahlia looked stunned, and she held on to Armeo's hand when he tried to withdraw it.

"Armeo, this is my wife Dahlia. She's Rae's mother—your grandmother." Armeo surprised Ewan by taking a step backward and almost stumbling over a small table. His eyes shimmered, but Ewan didn't see any actual tears. Proud of how Armeo handled the situation, he did his best to act casual.

Dismissing the security guards and picking up Armeo's bags, Ewan punched in a code next to the door and ushered the other two inside. Dahlia took a new hold of Armeo's hand and gazed down at him with an unusual mix of awe and tenderness in her eyes. Used to dealing with royalty and all kinds of heads of state, his wife was not easily swayed. Ewan wondered if it was the fact that he probably was the closest they'd get to a grandchild or Armeo's heritage that influenced her.

"Hello, Armeo," Dahlia managed. "I've looked forward to meeting you."

"I have as well, ma'am…Should I call you ma'am…or?" Looking thoroughly confused, Armeo turned his head and searched Ewan's face.

"Call me Grandma, or Dahlia, whichever you want." His wife beat Ewan to it. There was a definite catch in her voice. It was as if her face had softened, making her features less sharp, and her voice assured Ewan of her sincerity. Normally Dahlia knew just how to use her body language and voice, and now, it was the "real thing," as Rae would have put it in her younger days, when she accused her mother of always faking it, always being the diplomat and never saying what she truly meant. Ewan knew this wasn't always true, although many times it was, and it hurt his wife when Rae withdrew from them.

"Grandma," Armeo said, as he pulled his eyebrows together. "I wish I'd known you were coming. I didn't get you a present."

"Don't worry about it, kiddo," Dahlia said, still holding his hand. "I think getting a grandson is hard to beat."

Ewan witnessed what very few people ever had a chance to see— his wife's slate gray eyes turning into a soft blue as she scrutinized the boy. The thought of the child going shopping for his grandparents no doubt struck a chord with his wife. Dahlia's love for beautiful things, and Rae's contempt for dead objects, had added to the rift between mother and daughter. Ewan remembered Dahlia coming home from journeys to distant SC worlds, bringing gifts from the most exotic of places, only to see resentment in her daughter's eyes for being gone so long. He had been busy building his own career at the time, but he hadn't been blind to either's pain. *I didn't do much to help them, did I?*

He saw the light in Armeo's eyes and knew instinctively how the boy was already opening up to Dahlia, as was his nature.

"How old are you, Armeo?" Dahlia asked.

"Twelve. Gantharians live to be about one hundred and thirty. Mr. Terence helped me figure out I'm about nine or ten human years. That's why I'm shorter."

"Who's Mr. Terence?"

"My teacher at school. He's great. We all like him a lot."

"Sounds excellent." Dahlia smiled. "So you've been shopping?"

"Yeah, Dorinda and Aunt Gayle took me to all the stores in the big shopping precinct in the commercial sector."

"I love to shop too. You have to show me the mall one of these days when I'm not working."

Ewan groaned at the understatement. At the same time, he wondered if Dahlia would have time to carry out her suggestion, since he knew she'd have her hands full with M'Ekar. He winced at the thought of anyone being subjected to his wife's undivided attention in a matter of this magnitude. *Ah, hell, M'Ekar deserves it. And more.*

Glancing at her husband, the diplomat raised an eyebrow with an inquisitive look in her eyes. "Yes?" Ewan hoped that none of his thoughts were readable.

"How about something to eat? You can freshen up while I order something from Hasta's. Then Ambassador M'Ekar is all yours."

"Ah, Hasta's." Dahlia sighed. "I can't wait to try some of her pasta dishes, but for now I better stick to some soup and salad. I retain water when I'm in space."

Ewan walked over to Armeo, who was rummaging through his bags. "You mentioned something about a present, son?"

"Here, Granddad." Armeo held up a small wooden box. "It looks like something...something I used to have."

Ewan opened the box and saw silk paper wrapped around a small item. "Now I'm curious." He winked at Armeo, knowing he had to do everything he could to keep the boy's spirits up, even fake enthusiasm for a gift, no matter what it was. "Let's see now..." He carefully unwrapped the silk paper.

Inside, a small object glimmered in his hand—a ring with an elaborate pattern and an inscription. Large and manly, it fit perfectly on his right ring finger. "What does the inscription mean?" he asked huskily, looking at the pattern of a stylistic eagle.

"It says *Norontammer'h*, 'granddad,' in Gantharian. I used to have a ring like this that belonged to my father. It had a crest on it, and the inscription on the inside said *O'Saral Royale*. It was too big for me and we kept it in…a secret place on the farm. I didn't have time to bring it with me when we escaped."

"Did it have an eagle, like this?"

"No, not an eagle, but almost. It had a *boyoda*, a birdlike animal with a wingspan of more than two meters. It lives in the mountains on the northern hemisphere of Gantharat." Ewan watched Armeo's eyes turn several shades darker. "I miss it. I miss the view from my bedroom." He winced, sending the two adults a quick glance. "It's not that I don't like it here. I do. And I love watching the ships come and go…it's just…"

"I understand." Ewan cupped Armeo's chin. "I really do. I will treasure this gift and wear it every day." He wasn't lying. The ring symbolized something he couldn't put his finger on. *Perhaps I'll have a chance to do it right with this child and, by not failing Armeo, I might be able to keep the truce with Rae.* Clearing his throat awkwardly, he tried to cope with the unexpected emotions flooding his system. "Now, can you help your grandmother carry her bags into the bedroom and show her where she can wash up?"

Armeo lit up. "Sure. Here, Grandma, it's this way." He lifted the larger suitcase with complete effortlessness, impressing Ewan, who knew how much his wife usually packed. "Rae and Kellen sleep in here."

"In a minute, child." Dahlia watched Armeo disappear into the bedroom, then turned to Ewan. "The mission they're on is dangerous, isn't it?"

"Very. A lot is at stake, not to mention Armeo's future."

"Yes. I've read the classified information sent to *Gamma VI* by the SC Council. The pro-Onotharian wing pressured the ambivalent members. Councilman Thorosac did his best to keep the discussion rational, but several planets depend on cheap merodynite crystals as their main source of energy…"

"I know. Monetary arguments override moral values." Ewan's jaw tensed, and he knew his voice betrayed his contempt.

"I'm here on a special assignment." Dahlia walked closer. "Thorosac is beyond concerned where this situation is heading. If the Supreme Constellations forms an alliance with the Onotharians or, worse, lets them in as a full member of the union, it'll be a disaster."

"Rae's gone to get indisputable evidence of the Onotharians' atrocities against the Gantharat System. Hopefully it'll make the SC Council refuse to grant the Onotharians membership."

Dahlia briefly closed her eyes. "She's on her way to Gantharat, isn't she? That's why Kellen O'Dal is on this mission too." As always, his wife's powers of deduction were flawless.

"Yes."

"How much does Armeo know?"

"He's a smart kid. He knows his heritage, but he's not aware of his desperate situation right now. It's enough that he worries about Kellen and Rae."

"His fears aren't exaggerated."

"No. I'm afraid not. The way politics are developing, their mission is a last-ditch attempt."

CHAPTER TWENTY

It looks like Earth." Rae studied the sight of Gantharat, green and blue, parts of it obscured by clouds as it revolved on its axis.

Two moons and a belt of asteroids orbited Kellen's homeworld, but its beauty was lost on her at the moment. Concentrating on the task at hand, she could think only of their plan as the *Liberty* approached the Gantharat System. Kellen had spent the better part of three days working on it. She hadn't slept much, and now she ran a new diagnostic of the *Liberty*'s long-range scanners, which still showed no activity to suggest the Onotharians knew they were coming. But it was too early to be confident.

"The coordinates, Ms. O'Dal." Rae didn't raise her glance from the many computer screens attached to the captain's chair.

"We'll come in on a low trajectory, heading two-four-eight, and then the chain of mountains will guide us." Kellen knew the landscape well and had opted for one of the dormant volcanoes that bordered her estate as a good place to land. They couldn't risk keeping the vessels in orbit.

"Send the calculation to the *Freedom*, Ensign S'hos," Rae ordered. "Lieutenant D'Artansis, enter the data. Half-impulsion."

"Aye, ma'am." Leanne D'Artansis took the sleek ship into a soft turn, perfectly aligning them with the flight path. "Course corrected."

"The *Freedom* is right behind us," Ensign S'hos reported.

Kellen glanced at the young man next to her. S'hos had used the derma fuser once more on her elbows, making sure the skin healed without scarring. Being a native of Drebruria III, he was a small, dark-skinned man. Drebrurians were renowned not only for their humble outlook on life but also for their analytical skills. S'hos certainly exemplified both traits. He had gone through the SC Academy in record time and now held a senior position despite his youth. Kellen genuinely liked S'hos and was impressed by his low-key way of carrying out his duties, as well as his willingness to learn from her, a civilian.

"Ms. O'Dal." S'hos now interrupted Kellen's train of thought. "I'm picking up broadcasts from the Gantharian networks, some of it in Premoni. I've heard them mention your son several times."

"Let me listen." Kellen plugged in an earpiece and held her breath as she listened to the male voice on the major broadcasting service.

"...not only has his existence been kept from us, his loyal subjects, but he is now in the hands of the greatest threat ever existing to the Gantharian people. A phalange within the Supreme Constellations is unlawfully claiming the child, and only the controversial actions of our representative will help us reinstitute our only surviving monarch..."

Kellen ripped the earpiece from her ear. "Commodore, the Onotharians are well underway with their local propaganda, making it sound as if hostile people within the SC are holding Armeo against his will. I know how this works. The Gantharians are by no means fools, but the Onotharians are good at what they do. I've seen what their tactics can achieve."

"All the more reason to stay out of view when we're planetside," Rae said. "How much longer, Lieutenant D'Artansis?"

"ETA the chain of mountains and the...was it the Besiac volcano, Kellen?" Leanne asked.

"Yes."

"And you're sure it's dormant?"

"Very sure."

"Just checking. ETA in two minutes." Leanne, at the helm, sent Kellen a reassuring grin. Kellen tried her best to return it, but she was already switching into battle mode. Focusing on the task at hand came easily, and she was not accustomed to using irony and friendly banter as a way to relax, as her travel companions were.

"All hands, prepare for landing. Shuttle bay, ready assault craft for launch shortly after touchdown."

Leanne's hands moved quickly across the alien console, and all Kellen felt of the landing was a small surge and a faint jolt when the DVAs adjusted to Gantharat gravity.

"And we have touchdown," Leanne informed them.

"The *Freedom* has landed as well," S'hos added.

"Any sign we were detected?" Rae turned to look at Owena Grey.

"None. The pirate scrambler is effective to a degree. So far, no sign of Onotharian ships."

"There could be cloaked ships out there, ma'am," Ensign S'hos said.

"I've scanned on all frequencies and don't detect any disturbances or patterns that indicate cloaked vessels." Kellen punched in another set of commands. "Nor are there any movements other than wildlife within a two-thousand-meter radius."

Rae stood. "Let's go then. And make it snappy."

Captain de Vies, with maintenance, two security guards, and enough crew members to serve as backup, would stay by the ships in case of an emergency. Kellen hoped they wouldn't need them.

She raced through the narrow corridors, slid down the ladders without touching the steps, and scurried up the assault craft she would fly in order to lead the others to what was left of her estate.

Right behind her, Rae entered the navigator's seat and strapped herself in. "Jacelon to de Vies. We're ready. What's your status, Captain?"

"Ready to launch in two minutes, Commodore. Awaiting your go-ahead."

"Affirmative. Launching in two minutes, then. Jacelon out."

Kellen adjusted the harness, checking her instruments and the eyepiece attached to her helmet. Wearing the standard-issue SC flight coverall, she rolled her shoulders, content to feel the familiarity of her own combat outfit underneath.

"Everyone's set to go." She heard Rae's throaty voice in the headset. "No more delays. Open shuttle bay doors."

The large doors hissed open to show the ground, black from ancient dried lava. "Assault craft, deploy. Formation Delta Two Delta behind Assault Craft 1."

Kellen punched in the command for the start sequence, and the small vessel hummed to life. Exiting the shuttle bay, she flew out and immediately began the steep climb out of the volcano.

Their timing was excellent. Dusk had begun to fall, and the sky was multicolored orange and purple. Kellen made a sharp turn, flying low to avoid the sensors that picked up everything larger than birds traveling through the Gantharian atmosphere. Glancing at her left view screen she saw the other shuttle craft forming a double *W* behind her.

"So, this is your home." Rae's voice was soft in Kellen's headset.

"Not anymore," Kellen replied harshly. "My home is with you and Armeo. I can't relate to a geographic site. It's not a home."

"As happy as your words make me feel, I still think you're wrong, darling." Rae's voice was tender. "This is where you were born. This is where you originated. It may not be home right now, but it was once— and might be again, one day."

"I don't think so. I could never subject Armeo to such danger again."

Rae didn't answer. Perhaps she realized there was no point and it wasn't the right time to discuss the matter.

Keeping an eye on the sensors, as well as taking visuals through the shuttle windows, Kellen adjusted their course to avoid flying in plain view of local residents. She began the breathing pattern her *gan'thet* master had taught her, to enter the preferred state of mind before battle. Not missing a beat, she reduced speed and flew along the soft contours of the landscape.

"ETA one minute," she informed Rae in a monotone. "Former main structure to your right, sixteen degrees."

Kellen tried to convince herself seeing her burned-down property wouldn't affect her. She couldn't afford to let it break her concentration.

❖

Rae gazed out the small window of her hatch at the charred acres and dead trees of Kellen's once-prosperous farm. The Onotharian agents had torched not only the different structures on the property, but also the crops and the grazing fields for the *maeshas*. The darker, slightly elevated areas, Rae assumed, were where the buildings had once stood.

Kellen landed the assault craft and immediately opened the hatch above their heads and unbuckled her belt. "We have to hurry. They're bound to discover us sooner or later."

Rae was already halfway out of her seat, pushing up and reaching for the handlebars to her right. As she swung her legs over the edge, she felt with her feet for the ladder. The two women made their way to the scorched ground. New grass was beginning to work its way through the ashes, which Rae took as an omen. "Life prevails," she murmured out of earshot of the others.

Glancing around at the sixteen crew members, Rae saw determination mixed with something she couldn't put her finger on. Owena Grey stood behind Leanne, her ice blue gaze unwavering as she met her commanding officer's eyes.

"All right, people. We don't have much time because at this time of the year, the nights last only a few hours. Six of you secure a perimeter around the shuttles and what's left of the barn." Rae pointed at a large pile of burned rubble. "The rest of you, bring the equipment and come with me."

"It's worse than I imagined," Kellen muttered next to her. "The entrance to the vault is in the north corner of the barn."

"It's not completely burned down, but close."

Kellen nodded. "There's where the villa used to be." She pointed slightly to the right of the barn.

"Oh, my God, Kellen. There's absolutely nothing left of it." Rae put her hand on her wife's lower back for a moment as they kept walking. "I'm sorry, darling."

Kellen looked around, her pain evident in her eyes, but didn't reply.

They walked around the rubble, about five hundred yards from the forest line across the field. Rae didn't notice any movements there to suggest enemy presence but knew that could change quickly.

"In here." Kellen pointed. "We might need to blast our way through to save time. If the hatch to the vault is intact, a plasma-pulse weapon won't damage it."

"Lieutenant." Rae motioned for Owena to join her. "On my mark." She raised her weapon. "Now."

Simultaneously, two plasma beams met and pierced the rubble, turning it into fine dust. When a tunnel began to form, Rae ordered Leanne and one of the other pilots to join in. Slowly the tunnel expanded until Rae thought she could see the floor through the smoke and dust.

"Is it big enough?" she asked Kellen. "We need to get you in there, and I'll be right behind you. Once you get the hatch open, we'll form a chain and pass the documents for safe storage in the casings over there. Captain de Vies, Lieutenant Grey, and I are the only ones privy to the codes once they're locked."

She motioned toward a rectangular chest containing narrow titanium-carbide rods. "Now, here are the hydraulic props. You press this sensor and one prop will hold up several tons. Put them wherever you think best, and I'll do the same. Lieutenant, once I'm inside, you send in two crew members to reinforce the tunnel. We can't afford to be trapped, and we can't waste time."

"I understand, Commodore." Owena nodded and walked over to the crew.

"You ready?" Rae rifled Kellen a sharp glance.

Kellen nodded and approached the newly formed tunnel. She grabbed a piece of wood for leverage, almost toppling over when it fell to pieces beneath her hands. The next one held her weight, and she disappeared into the rubble.

Rae bent down and used the same beam to haul herself into the stack of wood. She practically welded a tunnel by firing the plasma-pulse sidearm, and the stinging, sour odor where plasma had hit the half-burned rubble was almost more than she could bear. Coughing, she crawled farther inside, installing hydraulic props where needed. She was pleased to see that Kellen had placed hers at the most critical points already.

It was reassuring to see the soles of Kellen's boots appear in front of her. Rae stopped when she noticed Kellen wasn't moving forward anymore.

"What's wrong?"

"Two large planks are crossing the tunnel. We have to find a way to move them so we can reach the vault." Kellen looked back over her shoulder. "Hand me your weapon."

Hesitating for only a second, Rae unlocked the clasp and gave her plasma-pulse weapon to Kellen, who felt across the first plank, obviously judging where to aim the laser beam. "Cover your eyes," she warned. "We're a bit too close for this."

Hiding her face in the crease of her arm, Rae listened to the crackling noise when the plasma pulse singed through the wood. Chips of wood rained over her, a few of them landing on her head. Feeling their heat, Rae groaned and quickly brushed them off before her hair went up in flames. Then Kellen moved a few feet forward. Rae was about to follow when Kellen's voice stopped her.

"Wait!" A pause. Rae heard a cry, immediately followed by a strange crack, followed by a thud. Rae disregarded Kellen's words and crawled forward. Kellen was breathing heavily, resting her head on her outstretched left arm.

"What happened?" Rae found the tunnel wide enough for her to slide up next to Kellen.

"I had to divide the second beam with as little force as possible." Kellen's voice was strained. "I'm sorry. It's been a while."

With no idea what Kellen was talking about, Rae examined the second wooden board, now broken in two. She noticed traces of blood where it had split into jagged edges. Finally understanding, Rae reached for Kellen's right hand. The skin on her knuckles had torn from the force she had used to break the plank.

"You crazy woman," Rae whispered, her heart sick at the pain. Forcing herself to focus, she holstered the weapon and reached into her side pocket for a temporary bandage. "We can't have you bleeding all over the evidence." She taped the skin together. "Ensign S'hos sure has his work cut out for him with you on this trip," she quipped, feeling her smile become rigid.

"As I said, it's been a while, and I didn't have enough space to do it right." Kellen rolled over on her stomach and proceeded forward. "I see the hatch. It looks burned, but we should be able to open it if we can free it from the debris."

They crawled up to the hatch and found several half-burned planks obstructing one corner.

"My turn," Rae said, and aimed the plasma-pulse weapon toward the debris. "Firing!" A hissing sound was followed by a foreboding screech when the rubble began to shift. "Take cover!" Rae clasped her arms around her head, expecting the burnt planks to fall on top of her any second. When this didn't happen, she looked up and saw a large pole jammed into the ruins above her. She reached for more hydraulic props and put them in place to secure the area around them. "Quickly now, Kellen. Move up to the hatch."

Kellen slipped past her, digging her elbows into the ground to push herself forward. Rae thought for a fleeting moment of the injuries Kellen had sustained to her arms on the *Liberty* and wondered if all this crawling aggravated them.

Kellen reached the hatch, brushed aside the dust, and uncovered a black square made of a shiny metal alloy. Rae watched her press her palm against it and heard a soft hum as it slid aside into the floor. Punching in a long code and using her handprint again, Kellen jumped back when the hatch began to move. A gush of musty air caused dust to swirl around them and made Rae cough. Sliding in the opposite direction from the smaller hatch, the door disappeared inside a casing in the floor. Kellen reached inside and flipped a switch, turning on a greenish light. "We can go in now."

"All right. Hang on for a moment." Rae engaged her communicator. "Jacelon to Grey. What's the situation out there?"

"Everything's quiet. The guards at the outer perimeter don't have anything to report."

"Good. You can begin to form the chain now."

"Yes, Commodore. Is the hatch open?"

"Yes. We're going in now. Be careful crawling inside. Leave a meter between each member of the chain. This pile of rubble is unstable. Install more hydraulic props before you bring us more of the casings."

"Understood."

Kellen had begun to ease into the opening and now disappeared out of sight. Rae crawled forward, sliding her legs over the edge, only to jerk in surprise when familiar hands took hold of her.

"You're on a steep and very narrow staircase, with no railings. Be careful walking down. It's sixteen steps."

"All right. Let's go."

Kellen hadn't exaggerated. The staircase was hard to descend. Scraping her hands on the walls when she tried to maintain her balance, Rae peered toward the green lights. When she reached the floor, she looked around in amazement.

Bookshelves and folder cabinets covered three of the walls. On the far wall a computer blinked on standby, and in the middle of the floor stood a table, cluttered with maps and blueprints.

"You know what we need and where it is."

"Yes. This way." Kellen motioned toward the far wall. "If you'll make backup copies of what's in the computer, I'll start compiling what hard copies we need to bring."

Not bothered by Kellen's commanding tone, Rae sat down on the metal stool in front of the computer console and found herself staring at a completely alien keyboard. "Eh, Kellen. I'm sorry, but I don't know where to begin."

"Oh, I forgot." Kellen leaned over her and pressed two buttons. "Voice recognition—Kellen-Red-Red-Zero-Four. Allow new user.

Language: Premoni. Confirm." She pressed a few more buttons. "It'll obey your commands now."

"Thank you." Impressed to see such elaborate technology, Rae began to download the entire contents of the hard drive on discs she had brought with her. Each disk could hold 500 exabytes of data, so it would take a while to download it all.

When she confirmed that the data stream was uninterrupted, she got up and walked over to Kellen, who moved quickly from one cabinet to another, hauling folders out and tossing them on the large table.

"Commodore? Everything okay?" A black ponytail swung down like a grackle's wing from the opening in the ceiling as Owena Grey hung over the edge.

"Yes, send down some more of the casings so we can pack the hard-copy documents."

"Aye, ma'am."

Soon black leatherlike casings landed at the bottom of the stairs, and Rae began to shove documents into them, not bothering to sort anything. She would have plenty of time to do that later. As soon as one casing was full, she climbed halfway up the steep stairway and gave it to Owena, who sent it back through the chain of people waiting in the makeshift tunnel.

When she checked the computer and exchanged the discs, Rae knew it would be at least another fifteen minutes before they had everything they needed. In the meantime, Kellen had begun to unfold large rolls of maps that sat in baskets by one of the shelves. "Here's everything from specs and blueprints of the Onotharian fleet to the blueprints of Ambassador M'Ekar's palace. My father collected these during the second year of the occupation, when we were still living underground."

"Underground? Do you mean literally?"

"Yes. Vast tunnels run beneath our capital. It's a Gantharian tradition, you could say. Every one of our children's fairy tales has a secret tunnel in it, or other secret passages. In fact, M'Ekar's palace has four official entrances and sixteen secret ones."

"You're kidding."

Kellen gave a rare broad smile. "I'm not."

Rae laughed, nudging her with her hip. "We're almost done. One more disc and we can leave."

Rae watched Kellen zip up the last of the maps and check to make sure they hadn't forgotten anything. She walked back through the room, her steps slower and a serious expression on her face. "Rae?"

"Yes? What's wrong?"

"Nothing. Not really. I know we don't have much space aboard the assault craft, but can we fill up one more casing of documents? It has nothing to do with obtaining evidence to bring down the Onotharians…" Kellen's voice had a catch in it, and she squeezed her eyelids shut tightly, as if to keep tears from forming.

"What is it?" Rae walked closer.

"My father stored a book that's been with our family for generations as Protectors of the Realm. It lists not only our family and the duties we've performed, but also all the other Protector families and what their duties have been."

Gently squeezing Kellen's arm, Rae could feel her wife's quickening pulse. "Bring it. I think, apart from it being important to you and Armeo personally, we're going to need it to validate what we find. Here's the last casing…"

A deafening explosion shook the ground, making the green-tinted light go out for a few minutes.

"Kellen!"

"Here, I'm fine. The light will come back on."

True to Kellen's words, the lamps began to shimmer, but flickered, as if they would go out at the slightest disturbance. Rae reached to her belt, ripped her flashlight out, and stuck it into her breast pocket to have it ready.

"Lieutenant Grey?" she called up the stairs. "Report!"

No reply. Reaching for her communicator, she hailed the lieutenant without result. A loud beep from the computer made them jump. "I'll get the last disc." Kellen rushed over to the small box next to the computer and ejected the disc. Placing it with the others in the special bag Rae had brought, she snapped it shut. "Done. We have to get out of here."

Rae began up the stairs, using her flashlight to examine the exit. What she saw stopped her cold. "Damn!" She looked down at Kellen's pale face. "The tunnel has collapsed. The hatch is completely blocked by debris." She ran a hand over her face and sat down on one of the narrow steps. "There's no way out."

❖

Owena emerged from the tunnel with the last of the casings, only to find a weapon pressed against the back of her neck before she had a chance to rise to her feet.

"Careful...Lieutenant, is it?" a male voice snarled in her ear. "No hasty movements or my trigger finger won't hesitate. Understood?" The weapon pressed painfully at the base of her skull.

"Yes." Owena's voice was cold, noncommittal.

"Good. Get up. Slowly."

Owena rose, quickly assessing the situation. Out of nowhere, Onotharian men and women dressed in black jumpsuits under long leather coats, holding impressive high-energy rifles, had appeared and now held the crew at gunpoint. Leanne was standing only a few feet away, still clutching a document casing, her green eyes aflame.

"M'Gared, go ahead. Time to seal this entrance for good."

Owena took the chance to turn her head and look at the man behind her who was giving orders. Tall, with black hair, his complexion deeply tanned, he looked striking where he stood, the wind blowing his long leather coat around him like a cloak.

M'Gared, a tiny woman with an unpleasant smile, approached the entrance to the tunnel, a large, long weapon steadily placed on her shoulder.

"No, don't," one of the young ensigns from the *Freedom* called out.

M'Gared only laughed and winked at the man behind Owena before she fired. A roaring sound filled the area when the missile hit the tunnel. Its impact threw debris up into the air for a few seconds before it came crashing down when the large pile of rubble collapsed.

Owena felt rage and remorse. Acting on impulse, but also trying to take advantage of the element of surprise, she kicked the weapon out of M'Gared's grip. Her hands gripped the trigger mechanism and she twirled, aiming it straight at the man who ordered the destruction.

"I don't think so," the Onotharian smirked, having dragged Leanne, the closest SC soldier, in front of him. He pressed his sidearm hard enough to Leanne's temple to bruise her, the weapon humming ominously. "That was a very foolish thing to do, Lieutenant. Drop the weapon."

Owena felt someone poke her in the back and she kicked backward, at the same time throwing the high-energy rifle to the ground. At the sight of the petite woman she felt as if her heart would explode in her chest. Leanne's eyes burned with rage, and she did not give the Onotharian man an easy time. Fighting him, she was in danger of being killed even if Owena had obeyed his command. Owena tried to make eye contact with her lover, wanting to convey her thoughts without giving M'Aldovar more leverage. If he knew they were more to each other than mere colleagues, he'd have one more advantage.

Leanne stared at her, and Owena could see the tall man was almost strangling her. "That's it," the Onotharian said. "No need to get all feisty, now is there?" He pushed her away so quickly, Leanne fell to the ground on all fours.

Owena wanted to lift her up but stood her ground, biting hard into the tip of her tongue. *Get up and get out of the way, Leanne.* Her eyes went to the collapsed tunnel, and a long shudder ran down her back. As far as she knew, Kellen and the commodore had been on their way out as well. Had they been in the tunnel when the missile hit? Dead or alive, the two women were trapped inside.

"So, Lieutenant, I think we have somewhat of an intergalactic incident here. Don't you agree?" The man behind her swung her around by the shoulder.

Without thinking, Owena grabbed his hand and squeezed his wrists, enjoying his grimace of pain before he raised his weapon and pressed it against her temple, his face less than an inch from hers.

"Don't be a fool." The man spat on her. "What's your name, lady warrior?"

"Lieutenant Owena Grey of the Supreme Constellations Naval Service. Serial number one-six-five-alpha-five-alpha." Owena wiped his saliva from her face with a disdainful look.

"How correct of you, Lieutenant. Allow me to introduce myself. I'm Trax M'Aldovar, Commander of the Onotharian Secret Service."

"I'm not surprised," Owena growled, the pain from the weapon making her furious. "You certainly dress the part." M'Aldovar didn't respond to her mockery. "My team will collect the information you've stolen. An Onotharian court of law will determine your fate. You have been informed."

Owena shook her head, looking at M'Aldovar with something similar to pity. "You will not succeed in your mission, Commander."

He gave her a violent shove as he brushed by her. Pleased to have rattled the Onotharian enough for him to forget to search her, Owena reached the small communication device in her pocket and pressed her thumbprint on the sensor. She hoped her hands weren't so dirty that the device couldn't scan her correctly. They needed to get a distress call to Captain de Vies.

CHAPTER TWENTY-ONE

One of the Onotharians shoved a high-energy rifle painfully into Owena's lower back. She cursed under her breath as she joined the rest of the team outside the pile of rubble. Glancing at Leanne, Owena felt red-hot anger erupt in her chest when she saw a red swelling on her lover's right cheekbone.

Ensign S'hos leaned closer. "Ma'am, they came out of nowhere. We had no readings on our sensors to suggest any cloaked vessels."

Farther away, behind the burned-down barn, Owena saw four small ships hover just above the ground. Equipped with blue reflector lights, they moved ominously in small circles. She had never come across any intelligence that described small Onotharian ships with cloaking ability.

"Listen up!" The man with the plasma-pulse weapon raised his voice. "Begin walking to the ships in groups of three."

"Where are you taking us?" Owena demanded.

"Shut up." The cool and emotionless voice was contradicted by another painful shove of the weapon. "Move."

Knowing they had little choice, Owena slipped her hand into her pocket and pressed her thumb against the sensor again. They needed air support now, before the Onotharians had herded them into the ships. Then a rescue attempt might be too late.

❖

Rae stared at Kellen while her mind examined their current situation. She pushed thoughts of running out of oxygen to the back of her mind. They still had hours before this became a concern. "You mean we're trapped in here?"

"The vault has only one entrance," Kellen said. "However, my father also installed an extra exit. It can't be opened from outside, but if we're lucky and the tunnel hasn't collapsed...Over here."

Rae dragged the casing with the discs with her, tugging the shoulder strap over her head and securing the locking mechanism. In a remote corner Kellen tried to drag a bookcase along the wall. Despite her superior strength, it wouldn't budge.

"*H'rea deasav'h!*" Kellen cursed as she renewed her efforts. "It hasn't been used in a long time."

Rae positioned herself at the end of the bookshelf. When Kellen began to tug, she shoved against the cool metal surface with her shoulder and dug her heels in. At first the shelf seemed to be stuck, but then it unlocked and moved out of its shallow socket.

"It's moving," Kellen grunted. "Again."

Disregarding her aching shoulder, Rae pushed, her feet slipping on the dusty floor. When a thirty-centimeter gap appeared, Kellen let go and tried to press herself through. She disappeared, and several unnerving seconds went by before Rae could hear her voice.

"It's safe to come through, Rae. It's pitch black. Turn on your flashlight."

Rae switched it on and attached it to her wrist, then barely made it through the gap before the shelf slid back into place. She felt a tug and stumbled forward, afraid the casing with the discs would get caught. "Now it went easy enough," she noted with exasperation.

The tunnel smelled of earth and decaying root systems, but when Rae let her flashlight scan the closer surroundings, she saw it was in reasonable shape.

"All right, lead on." Rae watched Kellen's pale features in the dim glow of the flashlight before she turned around and began to walk. As Rae followed, she wondered what was happening to her crew outside. Had Owena and any of the others still been in the tunnel when it collapsed? Pushing the destructive thought away, she focused on Kellen, scanning the floor of the tunnel with her flashlight to avoid tripping.

The tunnel became increasingly narrow, and in some places they had to walk sideways so they wouldn't get stuck. In several places roots had penetrated the tunnel from above, forcing Kellen to duck.

"I suppose this was how your father honored the secret-passage traditions of your people, and combined it with necessity for an escape," Rae mused.

"Yes, my father was particular about always having more than one option or solution to the matter at hand. He made sure Tereya and I knew exactly what to do in case something happened to him. He showed me this exit from the vault, but this is the first time I've walked through it. He didn't want us to use it unless absolutely necessary, to prevent anyone from finding out."

"Where does it exit?"

"Behind the stables…or what's left of them." Kellen's voice trailed off. "I kept eight *maeshas* in there. They probably all burned."

Placing a hand briefly on Kellen's back to show her support, Rae spoke softly. "I know it's heartbreaking to think about. Let's just hope the stable hasn't collapsed on top of the exit." Rae motioned with her chin toward the ceiling of the tunnel. "I'm afraid bad things are going on up there."

They moved as fast as possible through the narrow passage. Protruding roots tore at Rae's uniform and ripped the resilient material. After another ten minutes they reached a narrow staircase made of stone, and Kellen let her flashlight sweep up the steps.

"It looks undamaged," she murmured.

"Yes, let's go." Rae took the lead and began to climb the stairs. Counting them as she ascended, she realized the tunnel that led from the back of the vault had taken them deeper underground. It took forty-eight steps to reach the top, where a small ledge allowed them to stand side by side below the hatch.

"How do you open it? Just push?"

"No, there's a safety device, a handprint sensor. It will engage a hydraulic system and unlock it." Kellen brushed dust and dirt from the area to the left of the hatch. A faint light appeared, and Kellen pressed two buttons to activate the sensor. The outline of a hand appeared on the surface of the sensor, showing Kellen where to place hers. As Rae waited impatiently, she began to plan where to attach the small explosives she wore in her belt. Glancing around the rim of the hatch, she was startled by a sudden hissing sound when the hatch unlocked. It unhooked from large clasps and opened about three centimeters.

Rae climbed one more step and pressed her face to the opening, squinting at the sun on the horizon.

"I can't see much," she muttered. "Let's push it open a little farther."

When they put their shoulders underneath the hatch and pushed, the heavy door slowly swung open. They were about two meters from the large pile of burned rubble that had once been Kellen's stables. Rae pulled out a scanning device and gripped it tight as she interpreted the readings. "I see at least twenty-five life signs in close formation fifteen degrees left."

"Look." Kellen tugged at Rae's arm and pointed up and to the left. "Onotharian ships. Those are hunter-class vessels. They must be equipped with cloaking technology."

Rae holstered the scanning device and heaved herself up over the edge, careful to stay low. Crawling, she hid behind what looked like the door to the barn. Made of metal, it had been distorted and scorched by the fire, but not destroyed. She hoped it would protect them from the Onotharians' sensors.

Kellen mimicked her motions, edging close to her.

"We have to alert Captain de Vies," Rae said in a low voice. Not daring to use the communicator, she felt in her pocket for her pager and pressed her thumb on the fingerprint sensor. "Let's hope Lieutenant Grey found a way to reach him already. From what I could detect using the scanner, the Onotharians are taking our people aboard their ships."

"They'll end up in one of the asteroid prisons," Kellen said huskily. "It'll be the last we see of them if they do. We can't let them recloak and take off, Rae."

"We won't. Come on." Rae rose and moved quickly along the far side of the barn. She reached for the small plasma-pulse weapon on her hip. She knew she couldn't take out all of the Onotharians but was determined to create a diversion to buy Captain de Vies more time.

As they reached the last corner of the barn, Rae inched forward and quickly counted the Onotharians holding her crew at gunpoint. She raised her hand toward Kellen, who moved in behind her, using her fingers to indicate nine Onotharians were within sight.

Rae watched as a tall man dressed entirely in black herded her crew toward one of the ships. Realizing it was just minutes before Owena, Leanne, S'hos, and the rest of the away team were lost to them, she made a split-second decision. "Here. Cover me." She handed Kellen her second plasma-pulse weapon and leaped into action.

Sprinting across the area between the barn and the house, Rae fired at the guards who stood by the ramp that led up to the ships. They fell to the ground instantly, and the surprise attack seemed to stun the Onotharians enough for Rae to advance farther. She heard the familiar hissing sound of a plasma-pulse weapon from Kellen's direction, and the tall man grabbed his shoulder as he staggered to the side.

Owena, standing closest to the man, threw herself at the guard behind her and overpowered him with a forceful kick toward his knee while she ripped the plasma-pulse rifle from his hands. Turning in a violent spiral, she launched a kick that sent him flying.

Rae ran toward the only undamaged part of Kellen's home, the north side of the veranda. Hiding behind the railing, she fired continuously, taking out four more guards. Leanne was tossed to the ground when a guard crashed into her, but she pushed free and grabbed for his weapon. Still on the ground, she fired toward the closest Onotharian ship, creating a plume of smoke from its port nacelle. Rae gasped as the shadow of yet another tall man fell over Leanne.

"D'Artansis, look out!" Rae yelled as the man she had pegged as the Onotharian leader directed his weapon toward the pilot. Leanne spun and threw herself to the left, dodging the beam by mere centimeters.

His face radiating cold outrage, the man scanned the direction the voice had come from. Rae knew she was in trouble when he spotted her. Kellen laid down cover fire but missed when all of a sudden the Onotharian leaped through the air and landed on his feet farther to the right. He raised his weapon again, firing at Rae's position.

She rolled to her left, seeking shelter behind two barrels. Splinters of wood exploded next to her when the Onotharian blasted them into pieces. Blood ran down the side of Rae's neck, but she ignored it and checked her weapon. She had enough power to make a last attempt.

Crawling back to the left side, where the railing began, she saw through it how her crew were fighting the Onotharians with their bare hands. Knowing they were fighting a losing battle unless someone with firepower assisted them, she risked poking her head up and aimed at a female Onotharian who held S'hos at gunpoint. As the laser-pulse beam from Rae's weapon hit the woman in the chest, Rae saw S'hos fall to the ground and remain there.

"No!" Rae kept firing, taking out two more guards before another blast from the Onotharian leader hit her shoulder. Dizziness threatened to overcome her and she struggled to stay vertical. Using her uninjured arm, Rae tried to reach the relative safety behind the barrels. The laser-pulse fire kept coming, hitting her leg and then her midsection. She felt no pain now, only numbness, which surprised her, since she'd been shot before.

Suddenly all the noise seemed far away. People were screaming, in outrage, in pain, but she wasn't concerned. Rae held her weapon close and curled up around it. Something warm gushed from the side of her neck, but she didn't care. Light-headed, she drifted in and out of consciousness. *There is someone I'm supposed to mourn. Who is it?* A contour of a face kept eluding her. *Who is she? She holds my heart and I can't remember. Strange.*

Brutal hands tugged at her uniform, dragging her someplace where she tasted dust and dirt. Suddenly, they tossed her aside and she found herself staring into the barrel of an alien weapon.

"Commodore. I suppose I should be flattered the SC would send one of its highest-ranking officers on a mission to my domain."

Rae squinted in an attempt to focus on the man's face, but the bright sun behind his silhouette made it impossible to make out his features. She panted, shallow movements of her diaphragm, trying to breathe despite the pain. Raising her plasma-pulse weapon, she felt the bones snap in her hand when a large boot kicked the weapon away from her.

The pain from her injuries hit all at once when the numbness lifted. Doubling over, Rae struggled against the haze that threatened to overpower her senses.

"M'Aldovar!"

The voice, deep and clear, echoed between the mountains surrounding them. Cold with rage, it thundered, shouting the alien name. The man hovering above Rae turned to his right. Rae lifted her head to warn Kellen. Unable to quite fathom what she saw, she stared at the vision before them.

No longer dressed in SC-issued attire, Kellen stood in the whirling dust, lit up by the setting sun in all shades of orange. Dressed in her

Ruby Red Suit, she held her rods in a deceptively passive position.

"O'Dal," the man sneered. "I should've known." He raised his weapon and fired at Kellen.

Moving faster than Rae's blurry eyes could track, Kellen raised one of her rods and the beam ricocheted off it with a low hum. Rae blinked. Fighting was still going on over by the ships, but the pain immobilized her, and she could only stare at her wife, now moving in on the man she called M'Aldovar. *Did she wear the Ruby Red Suit under her coveralls? I never saw it. Of course, she wouldn't go into battle without it.* A part of her brain, still untouched by the pain, appreciated the lethal beauty and grace before her.

"I've looked forward to this day, O'Dal." M'Aldovar fired his weapon again.

Kellen crossed her rods, again sending the beam in another direction. "No more than I." She ducked in a low, fluid motion, aiming at the man's kneecaps. One rod hit its goal. M'Aldovar grunted but managed to stay on his feet.

"You're vermin, M'Aldovar." Another sweeping jump seemed to defy gravity. Kellen's body twisted and pivoted, the red suit glowing in the sunlight.

M'Aldovar raised his weapon to fire, but this time Kellen kicked it out of his hand, and it landed only a meter from Rae. Crouching, Kellen changed direction before the man had a chance to collect himself. She sprang upon him with vehemence shining in her eyes. The rods split the air, one landing on M'Aldovar's left temple, the other stabbing him in the solar plexus.

As he fell to the ground, the Onotharian fumbled along the edge of his left boot and yanked out a sharp object. Rae saw him aim it at Kellen and knew she had to act, no matter the pain.

She clawed her way toward the dropped plasma-pulse weapon on the ground next to her. Groaning as pain seared through her, she extended her uninjured arm, determined to reach it—or die trying. She finally managed to wrap her fingers around it. Her arm trembled as she raised it. Rae aimed at the fallen man and fired.

M'Aldovar stiffened as the beam hit him sideways in the chest. A gurgling sound came from his throat before his body hit the ground.

Kellen stood motionless in a defensive position for a few seconds. Rae wanted to call out to her, to tell her to make sure M'Aldovar was out of action. Before she was able to even attempt to shout, Rae saw

Kellen raise her rods, with a resolute expression on her face and her lips like thin, pale lines. Almost faster than Rae could detect, Kellen leaped, turned her body in a perfect arch above M'Aldovar's still form, landed securely on her feet, and slammed the rods onto each side of his neck. A sickening sound, like someone breaking a dead twig, reached Rae, but she could not wrap her dazed brain around it.

A new effort to speak made her cough, and something warm flooded the back of her throat. Behind her she could hear her crew battling the Onotharians. The noise changed, sounding farther and farther away. Slowly everything faded to black.

❖

Kellen regarded the fallen man with great satisfaction. In the deadliest of *gan'thet* maneuvers, she'd snapped M'Aldovar's neck. She moved her rods in the traditional victory pattern before tucking them into her belt, then glanced over at Rae, expecting her to rise. When she didn't move, Kellen felt her heart stop beating, then race out of control. She knew, without a doubt, that something was terribly wrong with her wife, and she forced her suddenly rigid legs to move, throwing herself to the ground next to Rae. Blood trickled from the corner of Rae's mouth, and Kellen couldn't detect any visual evidence she was breathing.

When she felt a pulse on Rae's neck, her heart fluttered in temporary relief. "Rae, look at me. Rae?" She cupped her spouse's cheek, appalled at how cold and clammy it felt. Then she unbuttoned the tight collar and groaned in horror. Rae's blood coated her fingers. Examining its source, she wanted to cry with fear when she saw the deep laceration on the side of Rae's neck. Blood had soaked the shirt she wore underneath her uniform, drenching it as far as Kellen could see.

Someone knelt next to her, making Kellen reach for the plasma-pulse weapon in Rae's hand.

"How is she?" Leanne held on to her own injured arm. "Oh, saints, it looks bad."

"We need S'hos here. He has medical training." Kellen's voice trembled. "Is the situation under control?"

"Yes, for the most part. We have the guards at gunpoint and have immobilized three of their ships." A sound in the distance made Kellen turn her head. "Look!"

Leanne following her gaze. "And here comes Captain de Vies, as delivered by saints and angels."

The *Freedom* and *Liberty* approached rapidly, circling the area once before they landed on the other side of the stables. "S'hos!" Kellen called. "We need your help!"

Another young ensign walked up to them, her face swollen with tears. "I'm sorry, Ms. O'Dal, Lieutenant D'Artansis." She wiped sweat from her forehead, unknowingly smearing dust over her face. "Ensign S'hos…he took a pulse beam straight to the chest…He's dead, ma'am."

Kellen began to tremble. S'hos had been one of the few who was friendly toward her. He had taken care of her injuries and made bashful small talk with her during the journey to Gantharat.

"The commodore's bleeding out, Kellen. We have to put pressure on her carotid." Leanne's voice was low and urgent. "Also, we have to get out of here. We don't know if the Onotharians had time to call for backup."

"Rae!" a male voice exclaimed. Alex de Vies knelt next to Kellen, looking down at her. "Damn, she's in trouble. Let's get her aboard the *Liberty* immediately. Ensign Hammad has medical training. I'll assign her to go with you." Rising to his feet, he approached the men and woman keeping the Onotharians at bay.

"Good job, people," Captain de Vies said. "Disable the last of their vessels and secure the prisoners. Then load the last of the casings and let's be on our way. I think we can count on this place swarming with Onotharian hunters very shortly."

Kellen had pushed the palm of her hand against Rae's wound, to her despair feeling blood trickling between her fingers the entire time. "Leanne," she said huskily, "could you put pressure on her neck while I carry her aboard?"

"Certainly." Leanne placed a gentle hand on the side of Rae's neck. "She's lost a lot of blood."

Not about to comment on the obvious, Kellen lifted her wife in her arms, cradling her. Looking over her shoulder, she glimpsed an object lying discarded on the porch. "Captain de Vies, please grab the casing over there." She nodded toward it. "It's important. Rae risked her life for it."

"I'll take care of it." Alex ran over to get the casing. "I'll keep it with me until we're back on *Gamma VI*."

Kellen began to walk quickly toward the *Liberty*, not taking her eyes off Rae, who was barely breathing. "Should I put her down? She's getting worse."

"No, keep moving," Leanne urged next to her, breathing heavily. "Ensign Hammad is over there waiting for us. We'll give her oxygen and medication when we're on the ship."

Almost running now, Kellen took the ramp in four long strides. The *Liberty* did not have a sick bay; instead they put the unconscious commodore on the mess hall table. Ensign Hammad, a petite woman with piercing brown eyes, had brought an oxygen tank. She placed a mask over Rae's nose and mouth, and to Kellen's horror it immediately became pink from the blood in Rae's airways.

"I'll give her a general pain reducer. Keep up the pressure on her neck, but let go a bit every ten minutes to allow circulation." Hammad worked swiftly as she spoke, injecting the commodore twice. "Now let's see." Removing Rae's clothes, the ensign revealed the major scrapes and bruises all over the compact frame. They discovered two minor high-energy weapon burns—on one of her legs and below her ribs on the same side. She had also taken a hit in her right shoulder.

Kellen suddenly noticed a large blue swelling on Rae's right hand. "She's fractured something." Husky and barely audible, her own voice sounded foreign to her. "The bastard."

Ensign Hammad was examining the deep wound on the side of Rae's neck. "There's a large wooden splinter in here. I'll need to extract it, but we have a problem."

"What kind of problem?" Leanne asked, standing on the other side of the table and wrapping a blanket around the practically naked woman.

"It's trickling now, but it will probably start gushing when we remove the only thing obstructing it."

"Can you have a deep-tissue fuser ready when you remove it, to fuse the vessel instantly?"

"I'll try. I'm not a doctor."

"We know, Hammad, but you're all we have. If you don't do this, the commodore won't make it."

Kellen trembled as she listened to the other women's discussion. "Do it," she said. "As her wife, I'll make the call." She moved to the opposite side, next to Leanne, who quickly squeezed her waist. "Don't let her die. Just do what needs to be done."

Ensign Hammad grabbed a large set of tweezers in one hand and the deep-tissue fuser in the other. "All right, let's get started, then."

❖

Dahlia stopped inside the door of the officer's mess hall aboard the *Kester.* Dressed in black, the deep red scarf around her neck her only splash of color, she knew she looked striking and professional.

Over by a large, elliptic table, Ambassador M'Ekar looked at her with disdain written across his face. "I have demanded to talk with someone in authority for days now," he complained, "and they send me a *woman?*"

"Charming," Dahlia mumbled to her assistants. Turning back to the ambassador, she introduced herself. "My name is Dahlia Jacelon, and to ease your mind, I assure you I'm in authority."

"Oh, for all the saints, not another one." M'Ekar tipped his head back in obvious frustration. "How many of you are there?"

Dahlia gestured for the ambassador to take a seat. "Admiral Jacelon has briefed me." She paused and gave the man a curt smile. "And no, the name is not a coincidence. We're all related. I take it you've encountered my daughter, indirectly at least."

"What can you do for me?" M'Ekar didn't respond verbally to Dahlia's last comment, but his eyes clearly relayed his contempt.

"You must have misunderstood. I haven't come here to *do* anything for you. I have come to interview you on the matter at hand. You have some explaining to do if you nourish any hope at all about going home."

The man drummed his fingertips on the table between them. SC military police guarded them, and Dahlia sensed their presence did not sit well with the ambassador. From the information she had received, Dahlia knew M'Ekar was sixty-nine Earth years of age. He wore his silver-gray hair down to his shoulders, and his all-white, obviously handmade suit—a long, formfitting jacket over masterfully tailored trousers—emphasized his sharp features. Dahlia thought he must have been handsome in his youth, but life had hardened him. His cynical attitude showed in his calculating eyes, like shining granite, as if he was watching her every move, waiting for her to slip up so he could crush her.

Not impressed about what she had read in the extensive file her husband and SC had put together on the man before her, Dahlia listened to M'Ekar's fanatical raving for exactly twenty seconds before she interrupted. "What are your motives for wanting to rear Armeo M'Aido?"

M'Ekar stopped in mid-sentence. "He's of my wife's blood. I'm all he has."

Dahlia punched in a short note on her handheld computer. "When did you last see him?" She knew the answer but was interested in his reply.

"I've never met the boy. The O'Dal woman kept him from me."

"So when did you learn of his existence?"

"Less than a few months ago. When I heard that Zax and the girl he foolishly fell for had a son—"

"Did you know who the mother was?"

"Not at first. When I learned of her true identity, I was sad Zax had not told his father or his aunt of her nobility."

"What difference would that have made?"

"For him to marry a nobody, a Gantharian country girl…It was beneath him. It reflected badly on the M'Aido name."

Glancing at her computer screen, Dahlia spoke in a soft voice that didn't hide her sarcasm. "Could you not accuse your wife of committing the same faux pas?"

M'Ekar squared his shoulders, flashing an outraged look at her. "What are you talking about?"

"You judge Zax's choice of wife, and yet your own wife, Elinda M'Aido, married you, a country boy from the Onotharian rural areas."

"It does not compare," M'Ekar insisted, two burning spots of red appearing on his pale cheeks.

"Exactly how did you find out about Tereya O'Saral's true identity?"

M'Ekar hesitated briefly. He didn't squirm, but small drops of sweat began to form on his upper lip. Dahlia wondered if the house arrest aboard the *Kester* was what made the old fox so transparent. All reports described M'Ekar as utterly ruthless and the toughest of negotiators. He had remained as ambassador on Gantharat for many years now, and he hadn't achieved such status by putting his emotions on display like this.

"I admit I held the young woman and Ms. O'Dal under close surveillance."

"When did that start?"

"When my wife's nephew was killed."

Puzzled, Dahlia leaned forward. Something was amiss in M'Ekar's story. "Then how can you say you weren't aware of the child's existence?"

"I knew there was *a* child. I was not sure it was Zax's. The two girls lived a pretty wild life, being orphaned early on. Tereya could have had more...partners, in her life."

Concealing her contempt for the man in front of her, Dahlia only nodded and kept taking personal notes. Her assistants recorded these interviews, but she always made notes on her own as well when something special sprang to mind. This lifelong habit had saved negotiations on many occasions.

"And then you realized who she was...not a promiscuous Gantharian country girl, but the last of the O'Sarals. Apart from Armeo, of course."

"Exactly," M'Ekar answered quickly, the sarcasm obviously wasted on him. "My agents confirmed it, finding enough DNA to prove it conclusively. After that, the boy's DNA showed his double heritage."

"Wait. Back up a bit, Ambassador. Do you mean you checked Tereya's DNA strands? How could you do that? And the boy's?"

M'Ekar now rose from his chair and paced back and forth. "We obtained samples of her blood at the hospital. And the child...We ordered a school health official to assist in this important determination process."

"Dodgy methods, Ambassador." Dahlia looked at him, knowing her eyes betrayed nothing. "Something in your story doesn't add up. I'm not a criminal investigator, but I know when someone's lying to me."

She rose from her chair and placed both hands on the table between them. "Rest assured, M'Ekar," she said confidently, knowing full well it was a crude insult from a diplomat to deliberately not use his title, "I will get to the bottom of this. You may think your homeworld's influence means you are safe and soon to be released. I want to emphasize how foolish it is for you to delude yourself. You are not going anywhere. I'm working directly for the elders of the Council, who are not as easily swayed in your favor as the representatives of the planets dependent on your empire's resources."

M'Ekar looked as shaken as it was possible for a man of his stature. "Are you leaving?"

She hoped her harsh words and barely concealed threat to keep him for an extended period of time would make him more eager to feed her information the next day. Sooner or later he would slip up. "Oh, don't worry. We'll see a lot of each other during the upcoming days. This was merely an introduction. Good day."

Walking toward the door, Dahlia glanced at the ambassador. He did not look pleased.

Chapter Twenty-two

Owena appeared in the doorway to the makeshift sick bay. "Lieutenant D'Artansis, take the helm. Lieutenant Ng'Ar has medical training and will help out in here. We need to get out of here before the Onotharians send reinforcements. There's not much time."

"Aye, ma'am." Leanne gave Kellen's arm another squeeze. "She'll be okay."

Kellen looked down at her wife's bleeding, bruised body. The compact frame now seemed fragile and beyond repair. "She has to," she whispered as Leanne and Owena left the mess hall.

"I have the splinter in sight," Ensign Hammad reported, looking into a device inserted into the deep wound. "I can reach it with the forceps, but it's a risky procedure."

"I have the deep-tissue fuser ready, Ensign," a new voice said.

Kellen glanced up and saw Lieutenant Ng'Ar standing ready with the fuser. Short and stocky, he oozed confidence and a much-needed calm.

"Remove the splinter when I tell you to," he instructed. "And move your hands quickly out of the way."

"Understood, sir." Hammad closed her eyes for a moment and seemed to brace herself. "Ready."

"Good." Lieutenant Ng'Ar moved close to the ensign, placing the deep-tissue fuser's nozzle only millimeters above the torn skin. "Pull."

Ensign Hammad pressed a button on the device to engage the forceps's claw and quickly backed out of the way, holding the offending piece of wood.

Lieutenant Ng'Ar moved the fuser in small circles inside the wound. "This should take care of the rent in the artery," he surmised. "There's nothing else we can do. How's her blood pressure?"

Kellen studied the portable monitor that sat on a chair next to the table. "Eighty over seventy." She had to steady herself when the *Liberty*'s propulsion system began to roar and whine. When the ship lurched to the left, the inertial dampeners couldn't keep up with its rapid movements. Kellen grabbed the table, which was bolted to the floor. Holding on to the unconscious woman, she stared with dry, burning eyes at the lieutenant. "Be careful with the fuser! We're banking again!"

Lieutenant Ng'Ar stretched his free arm around the commodore's body and curled his fingers around the railing that surrounded the edge on the opposite side of the table. The *Liberty* turned violently, almost stalling, before it finally straightened up.

"Damage report." Owena's voice echoed through the shipwide comm system.

"How is the commodore?" Ensign Hammad was struggling to rise from the floor.

"We managed to keep her from flying off the table. Blood pressure again, Ms. O'Dal?" Lieutenant Ng'Ar asked before he turned to his subordinate. "You all right, Ensign?"

Hammad nodded and began to wrap a thermo blanket around the commodore.

"Still eighty-five over seventy."

"Keep an eye on it. It should rise. The commodore has lost a lot of blood, but we can replace some of it with synthetic plasma. We stored some at the bottom of the cool-shelves in the galley, Ensign."

Hammad rushed toward the kitchen and returned with several containers. On top of each container was a device meant to attach to the patient. He gave one to Kellen. "Anywhere you can find a vein, ma'am. Just press the blue tag against the skin and it will do the rest. I also brought saline and glucose."

Kellen's fingers trembled as she searched Rae's uninjured hand for a vein, finding them thin, like silk filaments, and almost invisible due to blood loss. Hoping she was doing the procedure correctly, she pressed the blue tag onto the back of Rae's hand, and to her relief the locking mechanism made a sucking noise and attached to the skin. The readings on top of the container showed infusion was underway.

Hammad found a vein on the commodore's left foot and attached the blue tag. She smiled toward Kellen. "Two units of synthetic plasma going in." As Hammad looked over at Lieutenant Ng'Ar, her smile faded. "How is she doing, sir?"

"Step up here and scan the wound. The scanner imbedded in the fuser says it's doing its job, but I want to make sure. Blood pressure, Ms. O'Dal?"

"Ninety-five over eighty and climbing." Kellen took a medical scanner and moved it over the wound. She turned it toward Hammad so the other woman could interpret what was on the display.

"The rift is closing, sir."

"Excellent."

Kellen and Ensign Hammad cleaned the wounds and healed as much as they could with regular derma fusers. When only the fractured hand remained, the two women looked to Lieutenant Ng'Ar, who was inserting the deep-tissue fuser into its casing.

"The bones will have to be reset." Kellen gestured toward the battered hand. "We can't just knit them together the way they are now."

"You're right," Lieutenant Ng'Ar said.

"I'm not qualified to do that, sir," Ensign Hammad cautioned. "I've seen it done, but…"

"That makes you the most qualified in this room, Ensign. We can't risk waiting until we reach *Gamma VI*." The lieutenant's cherubic face looked grim. "Do your best. Set the bones and knit them together. It will ease the commodore's pain if the bones are aligned. The way they sit now, the jagged ends are likely to hurt the tissue around them, as well as rub against each other."

His round face softened. "Just do it, Ensign. Dr. Meyer can always perform surgery to correct minor misalignments once we get back."

Kellen watched as Ensign Hammad took Rae's bruised hand and carefully manipulated the broken bones by pulling the fingers one by one, blessing the fact Rae was unconscious and oblivious to the pain. Hammad ran the bone-knitter across the fractures, and then Kellen helped wrap the hand in a cooling orthosis to secure it and keep the swelling down.

"I'll arrange for some belts to strap the commodore to the table. We need to keep her very still when we go to tachyon-mass drive."

Lieutenant Ng'Ar walked over to the door. "Keep an eye on the oxygen saturation and blood pressure. I'll be quick."

As she looked at Rae's white face, Kellen felt her chest constrict. Knowing this was a high-risk mission was one thing; standing here watching Rae in this state was something entirely different. Because she always took pride in her self-control, Kellen was painfully aware of how fear flooded her system.

Leaning over her wife, she placed a soft kiss on her cold, sweaty forehead. "Please, Rae, don't give up. We have what we came for and are on our way home." She tucked the thermo blanket closer around her beloved to keep her from falling further into shock. Her voice was a husky whisper. "I can't lose you. Do you hear? I can't."

Rae gave no sign that she heard her. Lying motionless, she seemed distant and untouchable, as if she would never wake up.

Owena's voice, grave and clipped, came through the comm system. "All hands prepare for tachyon-mass drive. Space corridor secured. Engaging drive in two minutes."

Lieutenant Ng'Ar returned with three long leather-mix belts. Wrapping them around the commodore and the table, he tightened them so her limp body couldn't move.

As she looked around her, Kellen saw nothing she could use to attach herself to the table. Ensign Hammad took a seat next to Ng'Ar, just inside the door, and was about to follow his example and put on the belt hanging from the bulkhead when she stopped halfway. Removing her weapon harness, she tossed it to Kellen. "Here, ma'am. Use that."

"Thank you." Kellen fastened the weapon harness to the railing around the edge of the table. Wrapping it around her waist and tightening the clasp, she leaned over Rae's unconscious body, covering it with her own while she waited for the drive to engage.

The hum accelerated to a loud whining sound, and then the *Liberty* speared through space. The weapon harness dug into Kellen's waist as her feet left the floor. Her sweaty palms slipped on the railing; she was sliding down Rae's body. Clutching at the edge of the table, Kellen dug her nails into it, desperate to stay with the motionless woman beneath her.

The *Liberty* reached full tachyon-mass drive. Reverberating around them like a caged animal about to leap toward freedom, the starship plunged through space on a preset trajectory. Kellen felt nauseous. Bile rose in her throat as the vessel's tremors became faint and barely noticeable.

Ensign Hammad unclasped her belt and walked over to the table. "Here, let me help you, ma'am." With gentle hands she helped Kellen move off the table and unfasten the gun belt. "Are you all right, Ms. O'Dal?"

"I'm fine." Kellen glanced at the monitor next to the table. "Her blood pressure is stable."

"You're bleeding, ma'am." Lieutenant Ng'Ar came up to them. "Let me bandage it."

"Of course." Numb, Kellen allowed the others to guide her to a chair beside the table. The lieutenant quickly cleaned a stinging wound on her forehead. She didn't care about the minor pain. Her eyes were fastened on the face of the woman lying very quietly next to her.

"Wake up, Rae," she mouthed as she felt a single tear dislodge from her eyelashes. "Please, wake up."

❖

Admiral Jacelon regarded Commander Todd with a cold gaze as invisible shivers began at his spine and reverberated throughout his body. "You're sure?"

"Yes, sir. Our spy vessels have transmitted disturbing data collected from SC probes in the Gantharat System."

"What the hell's going on, then?" Suddenly feeling every one of his years, Ewan wanted to sit down but remained on his feet, squaring his jaw. He knew that the spy vessels, a highly controversial asset, monitored the neighboring systems and gathered intelligence from miniscule probes hidden among space debris and in asteroid fields. Transmitting on rotating subspace channels, they were virtually impossible to detect or intercept.

"Two days ago, an Onotharian covert team attacked our away team, sir. They moved in with cloaked shuttles. We've never seen those before."

"And where is our team now?"

"We have no data regarding their exact status, but I can tell you that the *Liberty* and *Freedom* are on a flight path back to SC space. That's the good news, sir." Todd looked ill at ease.

"Yes?" Ewan prodded.

"The Onotharians are gaining on them. Using a propulsion system similar to the tachyon-mass drive, they're hot on their trails, sir. The *Liberty*'s flight pattern suggests it is damaged, and the *Freedom* is right next to her. Captain de Vies wouldn't abandon the commodore's vessel."

Ewan ripped the protective cover off a cigar. "I know. So the Onotharians are gaining on them? When will they reach them?"

"If they maintain course and speed"—Todd checked his computer—"in less than forty-eight hours, Admiral."

"Damn," Ewan whispered. "And we don't know their tactical status?"

"No, sir."

He stood motionless for a moment and rapidly examined and discarded solutions one by one. Walking over to the porthole in the conference room, he regarded the ships moored at Port 1. His eye focused suddenly, and he rubbed his forehead, going over the details one more time. *Is it possible?* Ewan turned toward Todd and raised an eyebrow. "This is a long shot, but I have a solution. It's slightly unorthodox, and my daughter would have my head for bending the rules…but in love and war…"

Todd looked curious. "Yes, sir. Just let me know and I'll be right on it."

"Even if this plan jeopardizes your career? Some people in the Council might not look favorably on it." Ewan wanted to make certain Jeremiah understood the consequences.

Todd didn't hesitate. "For the commodore? Even then."

❖

"My honor is at stake here!"

Dahlia regarded the ambassador, unimpressed by his tendency toward dramatic exclamations. "Very possibly, but lives are also at stake, and I'm appalled by your lack of concern."

The tall man paced back and forth on the opposite side of the conference table. Dressed in black, he seemed more agitated than during earlier sessions.

Dahlia did not take her eyes off him. He had declined to have his aide de camp present, and she wondered if he now regretted his decision. *If he knew that one of the lives at stake is my daughter's, he'd be thrilled.* Dahlia forced back the dread, the disgusting feeling of something wobbly in her stomach, that had been present since Ewan had informed her of the current situation. Part of her wanted to send some impossible telepathic message to Rae, to implore her to come back safely. *How ridiculous. Even if there were such a thing as telepathy, it wouldn't exist between us. We can't communicate when we're in the same room, let alone across light-years.* She didn't know if it was something in her eyes that triggered the ambassador's explosion, but she was in no mood to humor him. *I may lose my daughter because of you, you bastard. If that happens...nothing can save you then.*

"I have the Onotharian law on my side," M'Ekar spat. "I have the unwavering trust of my president, and no matter how many sad stories you try to sell me—"

"This tirade of yours isn't very constructive." Dahlia silenced his ranting with a gesture of her hand. "Let's focus on our mutual goal—a way of getting you out of SC space in one piece and possibly continuing the talks between our worlds."

The man looked at her, apparently bewildered. "What the hell are you talking about?"

"You have several options, Ambassador. The most preferable for both parties is that you relinquish any demands you have of guardianship of Armeo. Only then will you be escorted to our borders and returned to your own people."

Slamming his fist against the conference table, M'Ekar gave an impatient roar. "Damn, woman, you don't understand. What you suggest is out of the question!"

The guards moved swiftly, jerking the ambassador back from the table. "Not so close, Ambassador," the senior security officer reminded the dignitary.

"What don't I understand? You've been tiptoeing around the issue, stubbornly refusing to negotiate despite whatever opening I've presented you." Dahlia leaned back in the chair and watched the man thoughtfully. She couldn't put her finger on something. M'Ekar behaved more erratically than a seasoned diplomat should. Tilting her head, Dahlia laced her fingers together as she asked her next question. "You never did explain why you waited so long to move on Armeo. Nor did you account for the so-called accident that killed his mother."

M'Ekar kicked the chair next to him away from the table and sat down, glaring at her. "I had to wait until it was safe to take the child. I didn't want a baby on my hands. The child was being monitored..."

"So you knew from the start he was an M'Aido...and an O'Saral. Did you have his mother killed?"

His eyes glimmering with a dangerous, yet haunted, expression, M'Ekar laughed joylessly. "Adroit, Madame Jacelon. You tricked me."

"Does that mean you gave orders to have Tereya O'Saral killed?" Dahlia fought to stay calm.

"I did nothing of the kind. Do you think a man in my position would stoop to such a thing?"

"Yes, I do, actually. In my experience men—and women—in your position do things like that, and worse. Perhaps you didn't give the direct order. I don't suppose we'll ever know. However, I'm certain you made it very clear to your subordinates what you expected of them— verbally or not." She motioned for her assistant to lean closer. "Maya, do you have the document ready yet?"

"Yes, ma'am. Here." The assistant pushed a handheld computer over to Dahlia.

She glanced down at the screen and then up at the ambassador. "Seems we have a standstill in the negotiations," she mused. "You're not giving us anything that we're asking for—which means you're going to the brig on the *Kester*."

"I demand to return to my quarters, like before." M'Ekar raised his voice. To Dahlia's surprise, his hands began to tremble as he smoothed his long hair over his shoulders.

"That will be impossible. We'll save manpower if we put you and your closest cohorts in crime behind bars."

"Madame!" The ambassador rose again, sending the chair clattering to the floor behind him. "This threat is beneath you as an SC negotiator. At my level—"

"At your level, Ambassador, you should be humane enough to not murder innocent young women and persecute children. Nor should you treat an entire planet full of people as if they are only pawns or playthings to suit your own agenda." Dahlia knew she was thundering, but she was fed up with this callous man. "You have a chance to save your own neck, M'Ekar—why not take it? It's the best offer you're going to get."

M'Ekar stared at her with the force of malice glimmering in his eyes. Then he seemed to shrink in size as his shoulders slumped, and he leaned against the backrest of the chair next to the one lying on the floor. "Damn it, madame, you don't understand."

"Then for God's sake, tell me."

Remaining on his feet, M'Ekar sent her a resigned look. "I'm not the one operating the strings here—and neither are you. The child's future does not rest in my hands or in yours. Our respective rulers are determined to fight this to the bitter end. Armeo M'Aido has become the symbol of this fight, and you and I know he will never be free. Considering his heritage, he will always be subjected to threats and manipulation. It's not about him. It's what he can bring the one who controls him."

Cold shivers ran down Dahlia's spine at the finality in the man's tone. M'Ekar's theatrical mannerisms had vanished; instead his voice held a tired, knowing quality as he calmly raised the fallen chair and sat down again. She believed him.

"Madame Jacelon, your daughter acted in haste when she married the O'Dal woman. Manipulating the SC court to appoint the two of them as guardians for the boy may seem the humane thing to do, but in the long run…" He wiped beads of perspiration from his forehead. "In the long run, it could be the death of millions."

"How long before they reach us, Ensign?" Owena looked up from the captain's chair. Having assumed command of the *Liberty*, she had hardly slept during the last thirty-six hours. She had tried to lie down on the narrow bed in the small quarters she shared with Leanne, only to find fragmented images of the stealth attack appear in her mind's eye. A fatal high-energy weapon beam—Ensign S'hos tumbling to the ground. M'Aldovar dragging the wounded commodore across the dusty yard in front of the burned buildings, laughing callously while he kicked her. M'Aldovar pressing a weapon to Leanne's head. An Onotharian pulse beam striking her arm.

It had taken Leanne more than three months to wear down Owena's defenses. After they'd met, and she finally allowed the pilot to get close, Owena's life had changed forever. She now found herself vulnerable. She wasn't always comfortable with this state, but she couldn't turn back. Even at moments like these, when they were both involved in a high-risk mission, she didn't regret loving Leanne with her heart and soul.

Leanne had seen right through her. Instead of the intimidating tactical chief who scared her junior subordinates with her mere presence, Leanne regarded her as someone in need of love, in need of her. Owena was stunned. She had always fended for herself, ever since her childhood and adolescent years on Tobrin, a Measter-class desert planet where mining companies offered good credits to those who'd risk their lives in the mines.

Leanne, in turn, had been born into and later ostracized from a family consisting of only women who frowned upon her chosen profession, thinking it was beneath someone stemming from nobility. Their rejection had broken Leanne's heart, but she had still followed it, left Corma, and never returned.

Owena looked toward the helm console and saw her lover bent over the controls, probably double-checking the data. Her arm was wrapped in bandages, and she wore a large patch on her forehead. Ensign Hammad was busy with the commodore, but Lieutenant Ng'Ar had made his rounds, checking the crew over. Fortunately, there was only one fatality and no one had sustained any serious injuries. Owena shuddered. No one except the commodore.

Leanne had managed to convince Kellen to occasionally leave the mess hall where her wife still lay unconscious. Only when they explained they needed her help to plot a course home did she agree to leave her side. Owena sat with Rae when Kellen was on the bridge, and when she returned, her eyes thundercloud blue and her expression pained, Owena had asked what was wrong.

"I'm fine." Kellen repeated her standard phrase. She brushed past Owena only to stop and quickly turn around, her face suddenly contorted, as if she was about to cry and fought not to. "I stepped on to the bridge, and I...I expected S'hos to be there. I had forgotten..." Her voice sank to a whisper. "I had forgotten."

Owena could guess how Kellen felt and wanted to place a hand on the other woman's muscular shoulder, to offer some comfort, but Kellen looked as if the slightest touch would make her explode. "I know. It's hard...Ensign S'hos was very young."

It was as if Kellen hadn't heard her. "He...he tended to my wounds. S'hos showed me nothing but kindness...and I had forgotten he died. Because of me."

Owena flinched. "What? No, no...S'hos is dead because he carried out his duty as an officer in the SC forces, knowing it was dangerous."

"This is hardly normal, everyday SC business," Kellen retorted hotly. "Going into hostile territory with hardly any backup, in pirate vessels...You can't convince me that a young man such as S'hos had any idea what he was getting himself into."

"Oh, but I can." Owena deliberately inserted a gentle forcefulness into her voice. "The commodore briefed everybody carefully before she assigned the duty stations. Had she detected any uncertainty in anyone coming on this mission, she would've chosen someone else. S'hos was young, but trust me, he knew the risks."

Kellen's eyes drifted to the motionless body on the table. They had brought a mattress from one of the quarters to make Rae as comfortable as possible. Several intravenous infusions were hanging from makeshift ropes from the ceiling.

"She hasn't shown any signs of waking up, has she?" Owena asked.

"No. Her vitals are promising, but she's still comatose." Kellen walked over to the table and sat down on the chair she had used since they left Gantharat. "I need to be here when she wakes up."

"Of course. I want you to calculate the course adjustments in another six hours. Leanne will relieve you then, just for a minute."

"Very well."

"They'll intercept in four hours, ma'am." The ensign at ops now interrupted her thoughts. "I think it's time to engage the evasive flight pattern Ms. O'Dal plotted earlier."

"Let's wait a little longer, Ensign. That way, they'll have much less time to recalculate their course." Owena rose from the chair. "D'Artansis, remain on this course, maximum tachyon drive."

"Aye, ma'am." Leanne's hands moved across the console. "Something's draining power off our port nacelle. I can only maintain a ninety-seventh degree of the drive."

"That way they'll gain on us." Owena grabbed the communicator from her shoulder. "Bridge to engineering. We have power drainage of the port nacelle."

"We're on it, ma'am. Two ensigns are down in the port crawl space going through the circuits that burned on the voyage out. The problem is escalating."

Wanting to drive her fist through something, Owena held her breath for a moment. "Good. I want frequent reports, Lieutenant. Every twenty minutes."

Four hours. Owena Grey closed her eyes briefly. Tactically, she was the best person to handle this situation. Still, she wanted nothing more than to have Rae Jacelon, with her experience and sixth sense, on the bridge right now.

"Ensign." She redirected her attention toward the ops station. "You're right. Time to punch in those coordinates and see if we can't buy us some more time."

Looking relieved, the young woman exploded into action. "Aye, ma'am."

They had more than seventy hours to go before they reached *Gamma VI*, sixty to reach the SC border. A few extra hours perhaps wouldn't amount to much, but they had to try.

Chapter Twenty-three

D e Vies to O'Dal." Captain de Vies's voice startled Kellen when it came through her communicator, muddled by static. "The Onotharians are only a few parsecs away. Report to the bridge and readjust our course. Sensors detect an asteroid belt two light-years ahead."

Kellen let her hand caress Rae's bruised arm. She showed no sign of waking up from the coma. Pulling the communicator toward her, Kellen replied. "Yes, sir. I'm on my way. O'Dal out."

Pressing past several maintenance and engineering crew members in the narrow corridors, Kellen made her way to the *Liberty*'s bridge. Owena Grey nodded to her as she approached the ops station. A young female ensign stepped aside, allowing Kellen to begin recalculating their flight path. Having traveled this part of space before, she remembered the asteroid belt well. It was violent, rotating around an axis in a serpentine way. She knew of several ships that had been instantly destroyed inside it.

Pushing away fatigue, Kellen punched in new commands, using the computer with the pirates' immaculate mapping of the sector to plot a new, bold course. Hesitating, knowing it would amount to a bumpy ride, she quickly went over the numbers again to make sure they were error free. "Lieutenant Grey, I have the new flight path. It will take us through an asteroid belt, and it will be dangerous."

"I'm sure it will." Owena straightened her back. "Lieutenant D'Artansis. Enter the flight path into the helm computer. Ensign Ymer, transmit the data, encrypted, to the *Freedom*."

"Aye, ma'am," the young ensign next to Kellen acknowledged and retook her position at the ops console. After a few minutes, she looked up. "*Freedom* confirms receiving the data."

"Good." Owena cleared her throat. "*Liberty* to the *Freedom*. Are you ready to engage?"

"Ready when you are, Lieutenant. You're aware this course will be a fraction away from disaster?"

"Yes, sir."

"Let's be on our way, then. Adjust course. De Vies out."

With a slight hum beneath the deck, the *Liberty* changed course and began to follow the complex trajectory toward the asteroid belt.

Kellen held her breath, awaiting Owena's dismissal. She wanted nothing but to return to the mess hall. When Owena finally turned her head and nodded, Kellen crossed the bridge in long strides and disappeared down the narrow ladder.

The blue-green light in the corridors made everyone look nauseous and tired. Kellen knew the crew was exhausted from constantly repairing the damages the ship had sustained on the journey toward Gantharat. Farther up the corridor, Kellen saw Lieutenant Ng'Ar stacking black casings in a small storage room. Realizing he was handling some of the casings she and Rae had filled with hard-copy evidence, she stepped closer.

"Surely this can't be all of them, Lieutenant?"

"No, it isn't, ma'am. Half of the evidence is aboard the *Freedom*. If one of the ships is destroyed before we reach *Gamma VI*, we won't lose everything."

Kellen nodded and was about to move past the big pile of casings when she saw a familiar object. She had forgotten about the ancient book, her family's records as Protectors of the Realm. Removing it from the pile, she glanced at Ng'Ar, who looked curiously at her. "This is my private property. You can clear it with the commodore later."

Compassion flickered across the man's features. "Of course, ma'am."

Resuming her walk toward the mess hall, Kellen hugged the book to her chest. This was her past, her heritage. In the mess hall lay her future. The book's soft leather cover held a familiar scent—dry, dusty, and a little stale—and its corners dug almost painfully into her flesh through the loose coverall. She ran her fingertips over the indentation in the wide spine, sighing in relief when she found the royal seal intact. In the mess hall, nothing had changed. Ensign Hammad was checking the monitors and watching carefully for any changes in the commodore's condition.

Kellen sat down on the chair next to the table. "I'm back, Rae," she whispered. "I have something I want to read to you."

❖

Dahlia walked into the commodore's quarters and placed her briefcase on the floor next to the clothes rack. Closing the door behind her, she noticed the dimmed lights from the living room. A quick glance at the chronometer on her left wrist told her it was past 2300 hours.

She strode toward the living room, her thoughts turning back to her last session with Ambassador M'Ekar. The sight that met her when she stepped into the room instantly jolted her back to the present.

Ewan sat on the couch reading from a handheld computer, his arm around Armeo's shoulders. The boy had fallen asleep against him, his homework scattered on the floor beneath him. Ewan, occasionally glancing down at the child, tenderness shining from his eyes, didn't notice her at first. This was a side of her husband Dahlia didn't often see, and she wondered if Rae ever had.

"Hi," Dahlia greeted him quietly. "Has he been upset?"

Ewan looked up, smiling. "Not really. He's brave. I don't think he wants to cry in front of me either, even though I told him it was okay. He's probably trying to live up to his own expectations of how a young man should behave."

"We ought to put him to bed," Dahlia suggested, hesitating. "Damn it, how do you act around a young man who wants to be independent and yet so obviously needs support and comfort?" *How did I act around Rae? She was so self-sufficient too, or at least that's how I saw her. She never seemed to need help from anyone.* Cringing at the memory of her own awkward attempts to approach her daughter, Dahlia focused on the present.

Ewan rubbed his forehead, looking just as puzzled as his wife felt. "I don't know. Rae was never this vulnerable. Or at least I didn't see her that way."

His words echoed her thoughts only too well. "Perhaps she was, and we both missed it." Dahlia dug deep for courage and approached the two on the couch. "I'll give it a try." She leaned over Armeo. "Hey, kiddo, time to hit the sack." *Galaxies, I sound too perky.*

Sleepy blue eyes looked up at her. "What…? Grandma?"

Wincing at the title, but with a persistent tenderness growing inside her, Dahlia held out her hand. "Let's get you organized and into bed, all right?"

Wordlessly, the sleepy child took her hand and walked toward the bedroom.

"Why don't I turn down your bed while you're in the bathroom?" Dahlia thought quickly. Should she remind the boy to brush his teeth? Giving a mental shrug, she decided to let him do it his way. He was after all twelve years old, albeit a younger twelve than his human peers.

Armeo returned about five minutes later, dressed in a thinlinnen jumpsuit. Standing in the doorway, he seemed reluctant to walk toward her. Dahlia studied him. "Would you rather I left you alone? Or asked your…grandfather?"

"No." The solitary word seemed to burst from the boy's lips. "I…I just don't like to fall asleep alone."

"Why not?"

"I dream…nightmares. I dream of Kellen and Rae…of them being injured and not able to come back home."

Of course. Dahlia wanted to kick herself. Despite being an accomplished diplomat, she didn't possess the skill to talk to children. "Why don't I sit with you until you fall asleep, then?" she suggested, surprised at the warmth in her voice. Regarding herself as a standoffish and matter-of-fact woman, recalling how distant she had felt from her own daughter, Dahlia held her breath while she waited for Armeo's reply.

"Thank you. I'd like that." He padded over to his bed and slipped beneath the sheets. "Could you tell me what Rae was like when she was little?"

Dahlia laughed. "Kind of hard to picture the commodore as a little girl, isn't it?" Her mind wandering and losing her gaze in the distance, she smiled. "Believe it or not, until her tenth birthday, Ewa Rae Jacelon was what you call a girly girl. She loved pink fairy-silk dresses, white satin bows, and little velvet-mesh gloves. Then, right after her birthday, she became a tomboy. She began to wear blue thermilon clothes and nagged me to buy her a black leather-mix jacket. I wouldn't, but she maneuvered her father to do it. I admit she looked rough and tough when she walked off to school dressed that way. She put the fear of deities into all the other children in her class, of course. She defended the weak and defenseless even then. She would play soldier all the time. Guess it was in her blood."

"I have a problem with my 'blood,'" Armeo said in a low tone of voice. "I already know I have to choose what to do—soon. I'm the last of the O'Sarals. Kellen is my Protector. My destiny is sealed. I'll become the O'Saral Royale—or so it seems." His voice trailed off. "So her full name is Ewa Rae Jacelon?"

"Yes, and she hated it early on. She didn't mind being called Rae—she hated the Ewa part, a version of her father's name. She and her father didn't always agree on things."

"I never knew my father." Armeo's voice became slower as sleep began to overtake him. "I hardly remember my mother. Only little things."

"You have Kellen. She's a mother to you in the most important of ways."

"Yes." Armeo yawned. "How many days until they come home?"

"Your grandfather told me we can expect them in about twenty-four hours. They'll make it back here."

Suddenly awake, his eyes huge and round, Armeo sat up in bed, took Dahlia's hand in his, and squeezed it hard. "You promise?"

"I wish I could. How about this?" Dahlia stroked stray locks of dark hair from Armeo's forehead. "We keep them in our prayers and send them the most encouraging thoughts we possibly can, to carry them home."

"Yes," Armeo whispered, still holding her other hand. "I can do that."

"Of course you can."

Armeo settled onto the pillows, closing his eyes. Dahlia regarded the small hand in hers. Soon, hopefully, it would belong to a resourceful young man ready to shoulder his duties on Gantharat. The diplomat kept her gentle hold of Armeo's hand as he drifted to sleep, curious why her heart ached for a child who was essentially a stranger. He was indeed remarkable.

❖

For their valiant contribution and dedication during the Second Merealian Wars, in the year of the Honorable Concession, the House of O'Dal was recognized as Protectors of the Realm, holding forever the sacred duty of guarding the Royal Family of Gantharat. If necessary, they will sacrifice their lives to ensure the continuation of the O'Saral line. Heramian and Kajana O'Dal will form this dynasty, and their children, Beseto and Kellen, will carry on the tradition, and so will all O'Dal generations to come.

"I was named after Heramian and Kajana's daughter, Rae." Kellen's voice was clear as she read from the ancient pages, carefully browsing the leather-bound chronicle.

Today is a day of sorrow. We lost the beloved, the indispensable Messler O'Dal and his spouse, Heiden. They gave their lives for the Royal Family while traveling through the Merealian Mountains. Their children, Endine and Bondar, will be cared for, but our mourning will be long and hard. The O'Sarals' safety is compromised, and we will need to take them to a secret shelter.

Turning several pages, Kellen held her breath when the names became familiar.

Our hearts rejoice this winter morning, when we welcome to the O'Dal dynasty a girl, Kellen, daughter of Bondar O'Dal and his wife, Gillia.

She let her finger trace the beautiful calligraphy, making out her parents' names.

> We are heading for times of trouble, and our proud family is now reduced to these three names. The O'Sarals need us more than ever, and we pray we can rise to the occasion.

Kellen turned to Rae. "This is why, you see…This is why I have to stay by Armeo's side as long as I live. Rae…" Her wife's hand lay motionless in hers. Kellen turned her attention back to the book.

> Gillia O'Dal, beloved wife of Bondar, died in the year of Precious Prominence, when Onotharian forces descended from the skies, claiming Gantharat as a province. Drawing her arms, she fought the intruders until the youngest members of the Royal Family were safely out of harm's way…

Kellen drew a trembling breath. "My father left a personal note farther down the page."

> My wife, my everything. You will live on through your daughter, who is the mirror of your beauty. Gillia, my beloved, you will be missed.

The touch was so faint it almost escaped her. Kellen snapped her head up and lost her breath momentarily when Rae's fingers loosely wrapped around her own. The book of chronicles fell to the floor when she rose to lean over her. "Rae? Can you hear me? Squeeze my hand if you can," she implored.

Feeling no reaction, Kellen began to think she had imagined the faint movement. Then Rae turned her head, opening drowsy eyes into barely visible slits. "Don't move. *Shindar'sh meo,*" Kellen breathed. "You were hurt badly on Gantharat. You've been unconscious for days."

"Kellen." Rae licked her lips, and Kellen could feel her body tremble as she tried to move. "Flight path…Where?"

"We're on our way back to *Gamma VI*. We got what we came for. Please, Rae, lie still." Kellen tried to hold her down without hurting her. "We don't know how bad your condition is. Lieutenant Ng'Ar repaired your neck artery."

Rae closed her eyes again and slumped back onto the mattress. "Thirsty."

Kellen reached for a mug of water sitting next to her and held it to Rae's dry lips. She took two small sips.

"I'm so glad you're awake," Kellen whispered, trying to control her rampaging feelings. "Are you in pain?"

Rae shook her head. Stroking the mussed hair back from her pale face, Kellen leaned down to kiss her forehead. "Just rest. I'm here to take care of you."

"You…"

"Yes."

"You." Rae's lips trembled as she tried to convey something.

Kellen tried desperately to understand. "I'm fine. I wasn't injured."

Drawing a ragged breath, Rae coughed. "No. I…You."

"What do you mean, Rae? Tell me." Kellen leaned closer, placing her ear against Rae's lips.

"…you." She sounded distressed and frustrated.

Not sure what Rae meant, Kellen was determined to say something, to not let this opportunity slip away. Rae might not make it all the way home; none of them might. Placing her cheek against Rae's, Kellen rubbed it gently. "Rae, listen to me. I want you to know I'm happy I married you. I'm grateful. I…" She kissed the smooth cheek next to hers. "I love you, Rae. I'm in love with you."

When she didn't hear a reply, Kellen raised her head and gazed down at her beloved. Rae was unconscious again.

❖

"Evasive maneuvers. Pattern Delta Delta Four!" Owena held on to the armrest with one hand while she strapped herself into the seat with the other. "Bring us out behind that rock, Lieutenant!"

"Aye, ma'am." Leanne sounded confident while her hands flew across the helm. "We're losing the DVAs any second now."

"All hands to battle stations. Prepare to deploy assault craft." Owena closed her eyes as a blinding light lit up the view screen. "*Freedom*? Captain de Vies, respond. What was that light?"

"We sustained a heavy blow to our shields, Lieutenant, but we're still in one piece," came the calm voice of the *Freedom*'s captain. "They're tailgating you. We're coming in right behind them. Don't slow down, Owena. Lure them farther into the asteroid belt."

"Aye, sir." Owena glanced at the computer screen. Five midsize Onotharian vessels, sleek and fast, approached from different directions. "D'Artansis, you heard the captain."

"Yes, ma'am."

Owena knew Leanne was pushing the *Liberty* well beyond her capability because she could hear the foreboding sounds of metal in agony reverberating throughout the vessel.

One of the larger rocks in the asteroid belt appeared, and Owena watched Leanne force the ship to circle it, flying dangerously close to the surface. "Hold on, folks," Leanne murmured as she jerked a small joystick closer while she punched in new commands. "This'll be a tough one."

The ship went into a roll as the faint gravity of the rock pulled them in. Looking at the view screen with darkening eyes, Owena realized Leanne knew it was their last gamble. Outnumbered by ships with far more firepower, all they could do was keep up this cat-and-mouse game until an opportunity presented itself.

A screeching noise came from the belly of the ship. "We can't open the port shuttle bay doors, ma'am!" the ensign at ops yelled.

Thinking fast, Owena knew she had only one option. "Bridge to shuttle bay two. Open doors manually."

A brief silence. "Aye, ma'am. I'm on it." The male crewman's voice was calm, as if her order had not been a death sentence.

"I want visual from shuttle bay two on one of the smaller screens." Owena pressed her lips together. Shortly an outlook over shuttle bay came into view. While the *Liberty* stomped and lurched through D'Artansis's evasive maneuvers, Owena didn't take her eyes off the bulky man on the screen as he approached the manual override for the massive door. Wearing a space suit with a harness attached to a lifeline, he had oxygen and pressure.

Grabbing a lever, the crewman used his entire body weight to open the door. The decompression tore at him as all air left the shuttle bay. The crewman, Owena cursed under her breath for not remembering to ask his name, hung by the lever as his body slammed against the bulkhead.

Suddenly he lost his grip, sliding along the wall toward the open door, with his safety line taut behind him. His waving hands found a fire extinguisher and clawed at the hose until he got a secure grip and held on.

"All assault craft. Deploy." Owena heard her voice grow darker. "As soon as the last one's out, close the doors. I don't want to hear the automatic closing mechanism isn't working."

"Understood, ma'am," the ops ensign replied smartly. "I'll see to it myself."

Owena stared at the brave man on the screen, his body slamming repeatedly into the wall as the smaller ships passed him. She bit down hard on her lower lip. "Medics, stand by. We have a casualty in shuttle bay two. Await recompression."

❖

Kellen reached underneath Rae's shoulders and legs, lifting her gently and placing her on the floor, where Ensign Hammad had arranged another mattress. The two women fastened belts around the unconscious form, securing her to the bulkhead.

The *Liberty* lurched. Consoles in the corridors outside the mess hall exploded, and this time the DVAs went off-line. Kellen went airborne, shielding her head before she crashed into the ceiling. Grabbing hold of the light fixtures, she held on, turning and twisting to see if Rae was all right.

Rae was hanging from the three belts, the infusions ripped from her veins. Blood trickled from her arms and legs. Blessing the fact that they had strapped the bedding and blankets around her, Kellen slowly made her way toward the outer bulkhead.

Another explosion reverberated through the ship, propelling Kellen through the mess hall. The tables were attached to the floor, but chairs tumbled around the room. Desperate to get to Rae, to protect her from the flying objects, Kellen let go and jumped. She landed on her feet close to Rae, but as she reached for the table next to her, for leverage, the *Liberty* reeled again.

"All hands prepare for impact." Owena's voice over the comm system was grave. "We're on a collision course with an asteroid. The ship is out of control."

It was instantly dark when the lights went out. Her outcry became a whisper when Kellen found the first belt around Rae beneath her fingers. Holding on, she inched herself up along Rae's body, covering it as the universe went crazy around them.

❖

Owena squinted through the smoke and muted light from an emergency source. "Reroute all power to the main deflector. We need to keep the shields up!" Coughing, she slapped the communicator on her shoulder. "Grey to de Vies. We're not going to make it, Captain. Almost all systems are failing. What's your status?"

"We're right behind you, Lieutenant." The man sounded adamant even through the static. "We're not leaving your side. Get the *Liberty* under control, Lieutenant!"

"We're trying, sir."

She watched Leanne's hands fly, struggling with the controls. The *Liberty* twirled past the asteroid with only twenty-five meters to spare.

"Damn it, D'Artansis, you're going to sever the ship." Alex's voice crackled over the comm system.

"She just saved our asses...sir," Owena said through hard-gritted teeth. "Please, Captain, stick to the plan. Get your part of the evidence back to *Gamma VI*. You can still outfly them."

"There's still a chance for you, Lieutenant Grey."

The main view flickered to life. "We have visual, Lieutenant." The ensign at ops hung on to her console, clutching at the titanium bar. Owena glanced up, cold dread filling her.

"Damn. Do we have long-range sensors?"

"In a few seconds, ma'am." A brief silence. "Onotharians attacking from two flanks. We're caught between them and a dense part of the asteroid belt."

"It doesn't matter. Check your readings again. Tactical?"

"Oh, God, ma'am. A ship's decloaking. They've brought reinforcements."

A jolt rocked the already battered ship as a tractor beam locked onto the *Liberty*. D'Artansis's hands danced across the helm. "I can't break free, Owena!"

"Try sending a tachyon pulse through their tractor beam."

"We don't have enough power to do that," the tactical officer responded.

"Damn! Grey to de Vies. Do you have the Onotharians on your sensors?"

"Yes, Lieutenant."

"Get out while you can, Captain."

"We're not leaving you."

Owena bristled, and the stressful situation made her growl. "Now's not the time for heroic actions, sir. Get the *Freedom* out of here. You still have a chance! It's your duty, sir. Don't let this mission be for nothing."

Captain de Vies's voice came through the static loud and clear. "I'm sorry to inform you, but it's too late. We're caught in the same tractor beam. We're entering the Onotharians' ship as we speak."

Owena swallowed against an ever-growing lump in her throat. *Oh, shit.* "Plan B, then, Captain?"

"Yes, Lieutenant." De Vies sounded matter-of-fact. "It's been an honor, Owena. Don't delay. Godspeed."

Owena unbuckled and rose from the chair. "All hands. We've reached the point of no return. At least we'll take some of them with us." She pressed a sensor to open a small hatch on the elaborate armrest. Icy blue diodes flickered in alien patterns. She held her index finger above the smaller sensor inside. "Initiating self-destruct sequence in three-two-one. Engage."

CHAPTER TWENTY-FOUR

Self-destruction sequence initiated. All hands to escape pods."
The computerized voice resonated throughout the *Liberty*.
"Three hundred seconds and counting." Kellen raised her head, horror
filling her, quickly followed by profound sadness. They didn't have
time to reach escape pods. They would enter the Onotharian ship's
cargo doors any minute.

Kellen curled her body around Rae's, closing her eyes as she
awaited the blast that would end their lives. Her thoughts flew to Armeo,
and she tried to transmit her feelings for him through the light-years
between them. "I love you, Armeo. I love you and Rae and…I'm sorry.
I let you down…I'm so sorry. Forgive me?" She hid her face in Rae's
hair, all her fury gone, feeling only deep regret. *I tried, Armeo. I swear
on my parents' sacrifice, I did my best. I'm sorry it wasn't enough.*

As tremors shook the ship when the tractor beam sucked them
toward the massive Onotharian vessel, Kellen pressed her lips against
Rae's forehead, suddenly seeing images of her father riding his favorite
maesha, Dinster, across the green, rolling fields behind their estate,
the chain of mountains towering in the distance. Sunlight flooded the
idyllic scenery. Kellen cupped her lover's cheek as she squeezed her
eyes shut. Her heart full of wistful love, Kellen's mind went almost
blank as she anticipated the nothingness when the tachyon-mass drive
overloaded and turned them all to space dust.

❖

"One hundred and thirty seconds to self-destruct and counting."

Owena clutched the armrest of the chair. The faces around her on the bridge, solemn, sad, but collected and panic free, regarded her closely. She could not afford to fall apart during the last half minute of their lives. *Do they need any last words from me? I hope not, because I don't know what to say.*

Leanne abandoned the helm and walked the few steps over to her. "I guess professional decorum is a moot point, Owena," she said huskily, a slow smile on her face. Leaning down, she brushed a tender kiss across her lover's lips. "I love you, darling. We've had fun this last year, haven't we?"

"We've had the best of times."

"You're my heart."

"I know. I knew I'd come to love you the moment I saw you." Owena had to tell Leanne. She couldn't send Leanne to the afterlife without knowing just how she felt. "I was afraid...to let you close, but now...I'm glad I did. I adore you."

Leanne's tears began to flow. "Oh, damn the stars, Owena. I love you. And yes, I wanted more time with you too. I wanted to show you Corma."

Owena tried to smile, her own tears resisting gravity by clinging to her eyelashes. "In the next life. I'll find you. You have my word."

"I know I do. Now...speak to the crew, Owena."

Owena instinctively recoiled. "What does it matter?"

Leanne cupped her cheek, her eyes gentle, all-seeing. "It matters."

"A hundred seconds to self-destruct and counting."

"All hands, this is your...acting captain." Owena found new strength in the love so abundant in Leanne's serene eyes. "We almost made it. We can follow our ship down and know for certain we took several of their best fighters, and one of their prized ships, with us. I want to..." Her throat convulsed and she bowed her head, swallowing against the onslaught of emotions. "I want to say, it's been an honor to serve with you all. You've made a tremendous effort, each of you. On behalf of the commodore, I want you to know we couldn't have asked for a better crew. Grey out." She whispered the last words.

"Sixty seconds to self-destruct and counting."

Leanne kneeled before Owena. "I'm not afraid."

"I am." Owena took Leanne into her arms, feeling the petite body tremble against hers, or perhaps it was she who shivered. "I dreamed of more time with you."

Leanne's face lit up with the softest, most loving, of smiles. "And I'm grateful for every single moment, which was more than I ever expected. I never thought I'd find anyone like you."

"Oh, Leanne...I love you."

"I know. I love you too."

"Ma'am," the ops ensign said, "the Onotharian vessel is trying to hail us."

"Which one?" Owena raised her head from Leanne's shoulder.

"The one that decloaked."

"We're not interested. There is nothing they can say..."

"Owena, they might..."

A boom resounded through the *Liberty,* interrupting Leanne. Owena realized they had docked inside the Onotharian vessel's shuttle bay, or possibly its cargo bay. "Guess we're inside," she murmured. "Well, the blast from our self-destruct will destroy this ship."

"They're still hailing us," the ops ensign reported.

"Damn it. Why not? Audio only." Owena awaited the ensign's go-ahead sign. "Lieutenant Grey of the Supreme Constellations vessel the *Liberty* to Onotharian vessel. The game's over."

The computer almost drowned out her voice. "Fifteen seconds to self-destruct, and counting."

"Commander Todd to the *Liberty* and the *Freedom.* Disengage self-destruct sequence. I repeat, disengage self-destruct sequence. This is an SC rescue operation."

Reacting instantly, Owena did not allow herself to consider if it was a trick. She was only vaguely aware of the impossible in what was happening. *If I'm wrong, I can reinitiate and weld the doors shut before they realize it.* Slamming the all-stop button on her right console, she opened a comm channel to the *Freedom* with her other hand. "Grey to de Vies. Cancel self-destruct. I repeat—"

"I have, Lieutenant. We heard them too." Alex's voice was hoarser than usual.

Owena awaited the computer's confirmation with her heart hammering painfully in her chest, drawing all of her energy. The seconds ticked by as the computer kept up the countdown for a few more agonizing seconds. "…five, four, three…" After a brief silence the emotionless female voice spoke again. "Self-destruct sequence aborted."

Taking a deep, trembling breath, Owena ripped the communicator from her shoulder. "Lieutenant Grey to Commander Todd. Jeremiah, do you care to explain this?" Her voice sounded harsh even to herself, and tears formed in her eyes and blurred her vision.

"I'd love to, Owena. Can it wait until we have you safely in our shuttle bay?"

"Of course."

"Why do you have the conn? Where's the commodore?"

"She's wounded and unconscious, sir." Owena rediscovered her formal attitude toward a superior officer. "Ms. O'Dal and Ensign Hammad are tending to her around the clock."

"Glad we showed up, then. We have a fully equipped infirmary aboard this vessel."

"See you soon, Commander. Thank you."

She heard Todd clear his throat. "You're welcome, Lieutenant."

Leanne resumed her position by the helm, supervising their entrance into the shuttle bay of the *Kester*'s sister ship, *Ursa*. Glancing at Owena over her shoulder, she gave her a broad smile.

❖

M'Ekar regarded the couple facing him. Not sure if he was supposed to be flattered to be in the company of two Jacelons at the same time, the Onotharian remained seated, knowing full well his action was a serious faux pas in the presence of a human woman.

"We finally meet face-to-face, Admiral." He gave a regal nod. "I have had the…pleasure of your spouse's company for endless days now. I can't possibly think of anything else to say."

Dahlia crossed her legs, leaning comfortably against the armrest on her chair. "It's not what you can or can't tell us, Ambassador. We have information for you."

M'Ekar's interest was piqued. "Yes? Has my government finally taken action to get me out of this godforsaken place?"

The SC diplomat looked mildly surprised and then shook her head, a patronizing smile on her thin lips. "Your government? They haven't shown any interest in your well-being. No. Instead we've received a subspace message informing us that Commodore Jacelon and her crew have collected evidence of Onotharian crimes against Gantharat and other homeworlds."

Feeling all the blood drain from his face, M'Ekar wiped the cold sweat that broke out on his forehead. "By the Gods, do you have any idea what you've done?" he whispered. "You haven't listened to me, Diplomat Jacelon!"

"You've told me several times of the risk of millions dying should my daughter succeed in her mission. For all your dramatic words, you have yet to come up with an example or proof of what you're saying."

M'Ekar slammed a fist on the table between them, denting the metal surface. "Damn it, woman! It should be obvious. The only thing that can come out of this is a full-scale war."

"We're aware of the possibility." Diplomat Jacelon nodded. "However, the SC has to do what's right. If your people gain access to Armeo M'Aido, the power balance will be compromised—and not for the better.

"With Armeo as a front figure, the Onotharians would be able to rule Gantharat with hardly any interference by the resistance movement..." M'Ekar couldn't disguise his surprise and knew Dahlia Jacelon noticed, giving him a knowing look. "Yes, we know about the resistance movement in great detail, thanks to Ms. O'Dal. The documents she's bringing back to *Gamma VI* will confirm everything." Leaning forward, she locked her eyes on him, her steady gaze relentless. "As for Armeo, tell me, what did they offer you for his safe delivery?"

M'Ekar's first reaction was to deny everything, but a new, discouraging scenario was forming in the back of his head. "Madame Diplomat," he said, "my home consists of many worlds, but that fact does not satisfy our leaders. They want more."

"You've been part of the current administration for decades, Ambassador. The better part of your life, in fact," Ewan insisted. "You've been solely responsible for the oppression of the Gantharian people."

M'Ekar leaned back in his chair and chose not to comment on the unfavorable statement. "I possess vital information that I know would interest the SC Council."

Dahlia's casual expression changed into one of unbending steel. "Are you offering to sell out, Ambassador?"

"I am offering...a mutual tradeoff, madame."

She rose and walked over to sit on the end of the table, leaning on her left hand. As she towered over the tall ambassador, M'Ekar secretly acknowledged the effect her strong persona had on him and barely resisted the urge to push his chair back.

"You can't go back, can you?" Dahlia's voice was smooth. "You've failed your leaders by not delivering the child and thus giving them the edge they need. Considering your penal system, your situation is dire, should you be allowed to return with your tail between your legs."

His chest suddenly tightened, making it almost impossible to draw a new breath. Realizing he was experiencing claustrophobia for the first time in his life, M'Ekar slumped back against his chair. The endless sessions he had endured with Dahlia Jacelon's cool voice surrounding him, extracting the information she wanted, clever, cunning, only giving him enough slack to hang himself, had worn him out. She was right. He could not go back. His destiny was sealed.

❖

As if her body came to life after having been suspended in everlasting pain, Rae slowly opened her eyes and found herself in unfamiliar surroundings. The dim light didn't hurt her eyes as it had the last time she tried to focus. Carefully turning her head, she moved her arms, wincing at the pain.

"Don't move too quickly, Rae. Be careful."

The low alto voice. She would know it anywhere. Rae smiled even before she found the blue eyes gazing down at her. Kellen looked exhausted, her skin bluish pale and her long hair completely disarrayed.

"You look like hell." Rae tried for a smile, but was uncertain if she was successful. "Where are we?"

"We're aboard the *Ursa*. Commander Todd showed up to save us. We made it safely into SC space and will arrive at *Gamma VI* in twelve hours."

"Excellent." Though speaking hurt her throat, Rae had more questions. "The crew?"

A shadow darkened Kellen's eyes. "Eight wounded, including you. One fatality."

Not able to hold back a brief whimper, Rae steeled herself. "Who?"

"Ensign S'hos."

The thought of the young man, so eager to please, so dedicated, gone from this universe, was almost too much. "Oh, no. No." Coughing, Rae felt more pain stir, this time on the side of her neck. "No." She held her left side to alleviate some of the pain.

Kellen reached out and held her in a gentle embrace. "I know. I know." Helping Rae get comfortable against the pillows, she kissed her forehead. "Everyone is devastated."

Rae fought to regain her calm. "The evidence?"

"All accounted for."

"The discs?"

"In Captain de Vies's possession. He's briefing Commander Todd right now. They'll be down to see you soon."

"What happened to the ships?"

"Our vessels are in cargo bay one. This ship is one of the Onotharian fleet's largest. The ships pursuing us thought the *Ursa* had arrived as backup for them, but when the commander fired on them, they scattered."

Rae tried to remember the last few days, her mind whirling at the extremes her crew had gone through to get them all back. "I remember you reading to me, talking with me..." Her voice trembled. "You never left my side."

Kellen stroked her forehead, then cupped her cheek. "Not unless I was needed on the bridge. I had to be with you, to make sure you were still breathing. I couldn't lose you."

Raising her right hand, placing it on top of Kellen's, Rae leaned into the touch. "I heard you."

"You did?"

"I heard you say...you love me."

Suddenly blue tears welled up in Kellen's eyes, spilling over and streaming down her cheeks. Absorbed by the fiber-coated high-neck shirt, they soaked it as more kept coming. "I was so scared." Her jaw muscles worked as she spoke haltingly. "I saw your broken body. I witnessed what M'Aldovar did to you."

Grunting, Rae used her right elbow to move up against the pillows. Reaching for Kellen, she pulled her onto her uninjured shoulder. "What did you do?" she said softly.

Kellen went still. Not even breathing, she leaned her forehead against Rae's shoulder without putting any weight on it. She began to tremble. "I killed him. I snapped his neck."

Letting a few seconds pass, Rae knew that whatever she said now was crucial to their future together. "You saved my life. Thank you."

Kellen didn't seem to hear her. "I used my skills, and the tradition of being a Ruby Red Suit *gan'thet* warrior, as my excuse...and I killed him."

"I heard you. Now, listen to me. You saved my life. He would have shown me no mercy, darling. I saw the callousness in his eyes. He would have killed me, and what's more, this M'Aldovar also would have put every one of our crew members aboard a shuttle heading directly for an asteroid prison." Rae disregarded the pain in her neck. Turning her head, she kissed the wet cheek next to hers. "They would have made us all disappear. You saved us."

"Captain de Vies came. He was the one organizing the crew's extraction from the planet."

"Good. He completed his assignment, then."

Raising her head, Kellen blinked the tears away. "You have previously considered me a security risk, a loose cannon. Don't you despise me for taking a life?"

"No." The answer came readily. "It was an act of defense. Once we deliver the evidence to the Council, a lot is going to change for your countrymen. The people of Gantharat will experience freedom."

"There may be a war."

"Yes." Rae coughed again, holding her ribs. "Damn, that idiot screwed me up."

"Let me call the nurse so she can give you more pain relief."

"No, it'll make me drowsy, and I need to stay focused when Alex and Jeremiah arrive." Grateful for the supporting hands helping her find a better position against the pillows, Rae gave a deep sigh while she tried to relax. "Kellen..."

"Yes?"

"You know the truth, don't you?" She examined her spouse's eyes for the answer.

"Which truth, Rae?" Kellen frowned, obviously puzzled.

"You told me you love me." Rae drew a few shallow breaths to alleviate the pain. "You deserve an honest reply." Unprepared for the haunted, desolate expression on Kellen's face, Rae bit her lip, cursing inwardly for causing such a reaction. "Surely you must know how I feel?"

"I had hoped..." Kellen squared her shoulders and elevated her chin, looking steadily at Rae, although her hands trembled. "I've hoped you might...someday, you'd learn to love me too."

"Kellen, listen to me." Rae's voice cracked as tears rose in her eyes. "I love you. I love you more than anything. I've never known anyone like you, and I hope I'll never give you reason to doubt how I feel again. Promise me you'll tell me and give me a second chance, if I do."

Sobbing only once, Kellen took both of Rae's hands in hers and placed her forehead against them. "I give you my word. I give you... myself." Kellen's voice sounded sincere. "I pledge my allegiance to our marriage; I commit myself to you in life and in the afterlife. Where you walk, I shall accompany you. Where I walk, you will be with me, in body, or in spirit. We are joined...in life, in dreams, and among the gods of Gantharat. You are now an O'Dal, a Protector of the Realm, and I am now a Jacelon, with the duties that come with carrying your name. You share my fate, and I am forever a part of yours. Until death, after we pass, and in the next life."

"These are the Gantharian wedding vows, aren't they?" Rae whispered. "They're beautiful. 'Until death, until we pass, and in the next life...'"

Kellen smiled, her lips trembling. "The circumstances prevented me from reciting them at our wedding aboard the *Ajax*. I've longed to say them to you."

"And now you have."

The softest of kisses brushed over Rae's lips before Kellen leaned back, a new expression of ease and pride mixing with the fatigue on her face. "And now I have."

❖

Kellen knew the Onotharian vessel, escorted by a dozen SC frigates, must look impressive as it headed for Port 1 and moored successfully. She stood in the entrance hall of the *Ursa*, her hands resting on the handlebars of the wheelchair where a reluctant commodore sat. Rae had initially balked at the prospect of meeting her subordinates and her father "in a weakened state."

"It's this, or be carried off the ship on a stretcher, Rae," Kellen murmured when she felt a movement in her spouse's shoulder, as if she was about to stand up.

"I dislike this sign of weakness," Rae muttered.

"Of weakness?" Captain de Vies said. "You're on the right side of death purely for one reason—your wife's amazing martial-arts skills. So count your blessings."

"All right, all right. I'm counting. I know when I'm outnumbered," Rae grumbled good-naturedly. "Funny how your friends can decide to team up against you."

"Very funny," Commander Todd agreed merrily, joining them as a soft thud reverberated through the ship when Lieutenant D'Artansis engaged the magnetic pull. "I handed over the conn to Lieutenant Grey. I have to get back to the mission room right away."

The large doors hissed open, revealing crewmen operating the seal on the door that led into the gate. When they pulled a lever, the second set of doors opened. "Very well, we might as well get it over with. Wheel me in."

Kellen knew Rae was impatient, but she was also aware how quickly her condition worsened when the pain relief wore off. "Yes, ma'am," she ribbed her, pushing the wheelchair through the doors that led into a corridor.

As they approached the gate, she spotted Armeo standing next to the admiral, gripping his hand.

"Oh, God." Rae's voice was a mere whisper.

Following her wife's gaze, Kellen noticed a tall woman standing next to Rae's father. She experienced an unexpected bout of nerves when she heard Rae mutter under her breath, "What the hell...Mother?"

Kellen kept pushing the wheelchair toward the small group of three, barely noticing when Dorinda rushed into her father's arms just to her left. Stopping a few meters in front of the entwined couple, she had just managed to push the button operating the brakes, when Armeo mimicked Dorinda.

"Kellen!" He buried his face in her midsection, wrapping wiry arms around her waist. Suddenly she remembered chubbier arms, a shorter boy, but the same dark blue eyes greeting her after countless missions. "I've been worried. I missed you so much."

"I know, Armeo. I've missed you too, but I'm home now."

"Don't leave again, at least not right away," Armeo implored. "I want us to be together now."

"So do I." Kellen's eyes met Rae's over his head. "All three of us."

Armeo turned within her embrace, about to pounce on Rae when Kellen held him back. "Careful. Rae's been injured. She's still in pain."

"Not so much that I wouldn't want a hug," she said with a smile. "I've missed you, kiddo."

Armeo leaned down and put his arms carefully around Rae. "Thank you." He lowered his voice, whispering in her ear, though Kellen could still hear his words. "You brought her back to me, like you said you would."

Kellen heard a tone of regret in Rae's voice as she replied. "Actually, sweetheart, it was the other way around. Kellen saved my life and brought *me* back."

"Then I owe you my deepest gratitude, Ms. O'Dal," a husky voice with the same intonation as Rae's said to Kellen. "I'm Dahlia Jacelon."

Extending her hand the human way to greet the older woman, Kellen drew a shallow breath, uncertain how to proceed. "Please, call me Kellen."

"I'm Dahlia and you're my new daughter-in-law, so I understand," Rae's mother said. "Guess this is an excellent opportunity to welcome you into the family, such as it is."

Recoiling as an unfamiliar feeling of shyness flooded her, Kellen only nodded. To be in the presence of a maternal figure, even though it wasn't her own, so shortly after reading the O'Dal Chronicle Book unsettled her. Gillia O'Dal's spirit was still strong within her, and watching Dahlia Jacelon stirred up emotions of need that Kellen found hard to fight.

"Damn it, Dahlia, you're scaring the poor girl." The admiral turned to his daughter, stroking his mustache repeatedly, as if he desperately needed to keep his hands busy. "Welcome back, Kellen. We're so grateful and happy that you're both safe. This young man has been a brave soldier, but we've all been very worried." He suddenly reached for Kellen, who found herself wrapped up in a hearty embrace as her father-in-law placed a kiss on her cheek, his beard tickling her skin.

"Sir…Ewan…thank you. Thank you for taking care of Armeo."

"He's done very well," Dahlia said, and Kellen wasn't sure if the sophisticated woman meant her husband or Armeo. "I apologize if I seemed slightly surprised."

That was not how Kellen would have described it. She doubted anything could throw the obviously accomplished diplomat.

"I hadn't realized just how young and beautiful you are," Dahlia explained. "The way everyone described you, I expected…something, someone else." She dismissed her own lack of words with an impatient gesture, making Kellen wonder, slightly concerned, what people had been saying about her. "And Rae…" She turned to her daughter. "Are you sure you're all right? Commander Todd briefed us about your condition a few hours ago over a subspace link."

"I'll be fine, Mother."

Dahlia hesitated, as if the image of the frail-looking woman in the wheelchair had removed all of her professional resolve. Kellen wondered what the history between these women was, since Rae in turn looked so apprehensive.

Then Dahlia Jacelon knelt next to the wheelchair, apparently not caring in the least what the floor did to her trousers, and took Rae's hands in hers. "Rae." Kellen watched the diplomat in Dahlia give way to the mother. Ewan had taken out a cigar and was about to light it when the sight made him lower it slowly, a stunned look on his face.

Smoothing back her daughter's hair, she tucked it behind her ears with evident tenderness. Kellen felt a pang of sympathy at the sight of Rae's astonishment. "You're safe." Dahlia's words, though clipped, still held all the emotions of a woman who had feared her only child was forever lost to her. "Thank all deities. Oh, Rae."

Looking pale and tired, Rae tilted her head into her mother's touch. "Mom. I'm glad you're here…"

"You haven't called me 'Mom' in a long time."

"I know."

"Let's get you and Kellen installed in your quarters," Ewan said, momentarily cupping his daughter's neck, a tender gesture Kellen had not seen him bestow on anyone else but Armeo before. "You must be tired, and you'll need to rest a few hours before the first briefing."

Kellen began to object. "It's too soon! Rae's in no condition to—"

"I'll be fine, darling," Rae interrupted gently. "This is how it has to be. We need to present evidence within a few hours to keep the deadline the Council gave us. If not, it will all have been for nothing." She turned to her father. "How long exactly until the first briefing? Have you interrogated M'Ekar further? Is that why Mother's here?"

"Yes, and they've been exchanging a lot of interesting information lately."

"I can only imagine. I want to sit in on some of those 'talks' in the next few days. I'd like to hear what he has to say in his defense," Rae growled.

Kellen heard the pain enter Rae's voice, and she released the brakes and pushed her into the closest elevator, nodding to the de Vies family, who entered the elevator next to them. "Rae, after the briefings, there's no rush. Once the Council is aware of what we brought..."

With a hand clutched over the injured side of her neck, Rae shot her father and Kellen a dark look. "I hope you're right."

They reached their quarters, and Kellen noticed Dr. Meyer approach from the opposite direction, carrying a bag over her shoulder. Glancing at Rae's parents, she saw Dahlia wink at her. "We thought Gemma better look at her right away. If I know my daughter, she'll be eager to resume command of her station. Perhaps the doctor can talk some sense into her."

Gemma reached them just as Armeo unlocked the door. Walking inside, he held the door open for the rest of them, a broad smile on his face.

"What's this about keeping you in check?" Gemma ribbed the commodore. "I thought your goal in life was to keep me busy, by the looks of it."

"Very funny, *Doctor,*" Rae said and attempted to rise from the wheelchair when they heard Armeo inhale sharply, followed by a strangled cry.

Kellen whirled around and stared in disbelief at the man who clutched Armeo. One arm choked him around the neck, while the other held a high-energy sidearm against his temple.

"Y'sak," she gasped, staring at Armeo's bodyguard in disbelief.

"What the hell is this?" Dahlia thundered. "Release the boy!"

Rae stood up, her arm pressed against her midsection. Pain flickered over her features, surpassed only by rage. "You! We trusted you…Get your hands off him!"

"I'll give the orders here!" Y'sak hissed, pressing the disrupter harder against Armeo's head.

Kellen saw everything in slow motion. Y'sak, tugging at Armeo, shouting at Rae and Dahlia to shut up. Armeo's thin face, white, his eyes growing huge. Ewan reaching for his weapon. Y'sak, in turn, firing his sidearm, which went off with a blistering sound.

Chapter Twenty-five

Y'sak's high-energy weapon didn't miss.

"Dad!" Rae cried out. Doubled over in pain, she moved toward Ewan, who sat on the floor, blood oozing from his shoulder.

"Stay right where you are, Commodore," Y'sak ordered. "If not, you'll be next."

In the corner of her eyes, Rae saw Kellen reach toward her belt and unhook the two short *gan'thet* staffs that dangled from her hip. Never taking her eyes off the security guard, who once more pressed his weapon against the terrified child's temple, Kellen moved furtively to her left.

Rae stopped and faced Y'sak. She realized she had to divert attention away from Kellen, who was obviously in full battle mode. Rae knew she didn't have a chance of stopping her wife from performing her duty. "You won't get away with this, Ensign." It was hard for her to speak. The medication had worn off and she was in severe pain. Ignoring her pain, she reached for her communicator.

"I said don't move and shut up!" He was breathing heavily and tugging at Armeo. The pale boy didn't take his eyes off Kellen, as if he was waiting for something.

Dahlia and Gemma ignored the danger and helped Ewan to a chair. "It's nothing," he said in a strained voice. "Singed my shoulder, that's all. Damn it, are you out of your mind, soldier?"

Kellen exploded into action. Raising one staff above her head, keeping the other in a defensive position, she launched at Y'sak. "Armeo, get down!"

Rae prayed the boy would react fast enough. She stared at her lover, seeing the *gan'thet* mastery in her every muscle when Kellen spun around, her right leg splitting the air. The rods glistened as they traced a pattern in front of Kellen, too rapid for the human eye to see.

Armeo ducked, breaking the stunned man's hold of him. When Kellen hit Y'sak's shoulder, she crashed him into the wall behind the door. The sidearm fell to the floor next to Armeo, who grabbed it with both hands. Scrambling on all fours over the floor, Armeo reached Rae, who pushed him behind her, relieving him of Y'sak's sidearm. She tugged at her communicator, fury and pain mixing in her voice. "Intruder alert, commodore's quarters. I repeat, intruder alert, commodore's quarters."

"Affirmative."

Rae barely registered the confirmation when, his back to the wall, Y'sak snapped his hand downward and produced a stiletto from his sleeve. He waved it in front of him, and the blade hummed to life, glowing around the edges. His eyes grew increasingly wild and desperate.

"Ensign Y'sak, what's going on?" Rae managed, swaying where she stood. "Talk to me."

"You know this man?" Dahlia's eyes blazed. "Is he part of your crew?"

"He is...*was* assigned to guard Armeo," Rae hissed. "Ironically, this is the guard he felt most comfortable with."

"Shut up!" Y'sak yelled, stabbing the laser knife in Kellen's direction.

Rae bit back a cry of warning out of fear of distracting Kellen. One slash of that laser knife could kill her. Rae watched Kellen edge closer to him, moving sideways with her staffs ready. When Y'sak suddenly threw himself at her, she crossed her staffs and absorbed the energy when he wedged the knife between them. Twisting, she used the force behind Y'sak's assault to twirl him in a semicircle above her body, then slammed him into the table.

She jabbed one staff onto his lower arm and sent the stiletto flying out of his hand. Having rendered him harmless, she jumped onto the table and towered over Y'sak, one foot across his throat and her staffs raised and ready for the final blow.

"Kellen, no. We have him now," Rae shouted, but her words didn't seem to reach the *gan'thet* master.

"Please, Kellen. Don't kill him," Armeo pleaded. When his words had no effect, he raised his voice. "Protector! Stand down."

Kellen seemed to slip out of her *gan'thet* warrior skin. She stared at Y'sak, whose face turned purple while he fought to breathe, apparently still considering whether to kill him. But then she relented, removing her foot enough for the man to gulp for air.

Rae recognized the closing, traditional victory pattern when Kellen slowly lowered the rods. Lithely jumping off the table, Kellen resumed her defensive stance, fastening her gaze, intense from barely harnessed emotions, on Armeo. "Very well."

Rae kept the sidearm directed at Y'sak, while she barked orders into the communicator. "Jacelon to Security. Where the hell is backup?" She didn't dare take her eyes off Y'sak.

"ETA in thirty seconds, ma'am." Over the comm system Rae could hear the sound of the security officers running.

"Gemma, how's the admiral doing?" Rae didn't dare look for herself.

Y'sak stirred on the table, which gained him a rod across his throat, hovering only millimeters above him. "Don't move," Kellen said in a dark, cold voice.

"Just a flesh wound. I can start treating it immediately. How about you, Commodore?" Gemma replied.

"I'm vertical." Rae glanced at Kellen. "Search him. We don't want any more surprises."

Kellen fastened the rods onto her belt and slid her hands along Ensign Y'sak's tense body. "No more weapons." Her voice was cold and dull, containing no detectable emotions.

"Sit up, Y'sak. Slowly," Rae ordered icily. "What the hell's going on? We've trusted you with Armeo…"

"You weren't supposed to come back!" The young security officer sounded frantic. His pupils were the size of pinheads, and Rae became certain he was under the influence of some drug. "I made sure you wouldn't return."

"You sabotaged the *Liberty*." Rae shook her head in disbelief. Dizzy, she pulled a chair away from the table, grateful to sit down, yet still directing the high-energy weapon toward Y'sak.

"You weren't supposed to make it to Gantharat." His voice trembled. "Once you'd failed, the SC Council would've demanded we return Armeo to the Onotharians."

"Why would you do such a thing?"

"It's your fault she's dead! If you hadn't decided to engage in your personal little war…and for what? A brat you'd never seen before! Or a sexy woman half your age? You chose *them* over your own crew, your own people! You betrayed us!"

"You're out of line, Y'sak." Rae set her jaw. "Who died?"

Y'sak's face distorted with obvious pain and rage. "I lost my sister in the battle after the Onotharian vessels decloaked," he spat.

"Your sister?" Rae tried to think despite the pounding ache. "Only one woman died in the battle. Rosita Sanchez."

"Rosita wasn't her name," Y'sak said in a contemptuous tone. "That's what her husband called her. Her real name was R'oshta. She was all I had."

Rae allowed her voice to soften marginally. "I didn't know. I don't remember seeing you at the memorial service."

"I wasn't about to listen to meaningless clichés about my sister from some big shot who never knew her!" Y'sak lowered his voice. "I told her husband my opinion. He's never liked me. He didn't care if I was there or not! And now he's leaving with their daughter…"

The door to the corridor, still only half closed, flung open. Security officers flooded the room, the first one visibly taken aback when she saw the intruder. "Y'sak!"

The young man sat motionless at gunpoint on the dining room table. His eyes distant, he had obviously withdrawn and wasn't about to respond.

"Remove Ensign Y'sak. Take him to the brig. I'll deal with him later." It hurt to speak. Rae was now biting her lower lip to not moan aloud from the physical anguish. "Right now I have more pressing matters to deal with."

"Aye, ma'am." The security officers half dragged, half carried the apathetic Y'sak from the commodore's quarters.

❖

M'Ekar looked up from the document presented to him on the handheld computer with an outraged expression. "Are you serious?"

Dahlia Jacelon's elegant features revealed no feelings. "This is the only deal you will get from the Council."

"Sticking me on a remote Vester-class planet is the best you can do?" he said.

Rae, who sat next to her mother, was secretly delighted. Vester-class planets were hot and humid, plagued by bloodsucking mosquitoes.

"Jasin does enjoy a brief tourist period during the cold season," she said. "It could be worse, Ambassador. Councilman Thorosac could have suggested one of the sparsely populated desert planets."

M'Ekar clenched his teeth for a moment, his jaw muscles twitching. "The document states I will be escorted with an appropriate entourage to this…place, within a few weeks."

"Yes." Dahlia pointed at a clause farther down. "It also states you'll be outfitted with a computer chip, surgically installed in the medulla prolongata, at the base of your skull."

"What?" M'Ekar tossed the computer on the conference table. "I refuse to be treated like this!"

"Of course that's your prerogative, M'Ekar." Rae nodded. "You can refuse this offer and we'll escort you to the border. Whatever happens to you after that doesn't concern us." She smiled without joy. "Then again, I wonder how popular you'd be when you returned to Onotharat without Kellen and Armeo, and not as victorious as you led your government to believe."

M'Ekar leaned back, drumming his fingers against the armrests. "I can't go back. I staked everything…my future, the future of Gantharat, on this."

"You bet on the wrong horse, then," Dahlia said, with complete aplomb.

"You have no idea about the consequences of your actions," M'Ekar said in a tired voice. "The Onotharian Empire didn't become as vast and prosperous as it is by falling back when things went awry. Our leaders are merciless and goal-oriented. Don't kid yourself, Commodore. Armeo isn't safe. And he won't be until he assumes his title and drives the Onotharians out. If you had let him return with me, I could have protected him…"

"As a puppet for the Onotharians to show at their convenience? I don't think so." Rae shook her head.

Dahlia continued. "As soon as you've fulfilled your end of the agreement stipulated by Councilman Thorosac, you will be escorted to Jasin. A vast net of beacons monitors the planet and the sector around it. If they pick up any signs that you have deviated from your allowed habitat, the chip in your medulla prolongata will engage and simply shut you down."

"What?"

"The chip will emit a signal, rendering you unconscious," Dahlia explained. "And if the local law enforcement doesn't find you within an hour, the condition will be permanent."

"That's barbaric!"

Rae nodded thoughtfully, adding simulated surprise to her tone of voice. "Coming from an Onotharian, I take that as a compliment."

"That can't be part of the SC laws and directives. Your culture isn't as—"

"As violent and savage as yours?" Dahlia completed his sentence. "In fact, this precaution is well within SC laws and directives. Granted, we don't implement it very often, but in your case, it was the only way we could persuade Councilman Thorosac to agree."

Slumping back into his chair, M'Ekar looked at them with a sly expression in his calculating eyes. "I have a request."

"A request?" Dahlia sounded as if she couldn't believe she heard the man correctly.

"Will I get a chance to meet the boy before I depart? After all, I am his only living relative."

Squinting, Rae tried to see beyond the hated façade. M'Ekar sounded sincere enough, but something inside her recoiled like a snapping rubber band. "No." Her eyes never left his face. "Over my dead body. You are his great-uncle by marriage, hardly a relative."

The corners of M'Ekar's lips turned down in an ugly mask of discontent, but he made no further comments.

"That takes care of that," Dahlia summed up. "Study the document, Ambassador, and let us know when you're willing to commit to the terms."

Without looking back, Rae and her mother stepped out of the room and walked side by side down the *Kester*'s main corridor. SC personnel moved purposefully around them, preparing the ship, as well as its sister ship the *Ursa*, for its journey to the Supreme Constellations main shipyard, a vast facility orbiting the Crova Moon in the Corma System. Alex de Vies would captain the *Kester* with Leanne at the helm.

Rae thought of how her favorite pilot had sounded almost as if she were pleading when she in an uncharacteristic nervous tone had volunteered for the job yesterday. Unusual dark shadows under Leanne's eyes testified to her latest ordeal. Being wounded twice in such a short time took its toll.

"I'm cleared by Dr. Meyer to resume my duties. I'd like to take the *Kester* to Crova, unless you've decided on another pilot." Her restless hands had plucked at the hem of her jacket. "The truth is, I've stayed away from Corma far too long." Leanne stepped closer to Owena, who stood by her side. "Seems the Cormanian Parliament is awarding me the Third Meritorious Band. That's pretty special, ma'am. They don't do that often."

"I know, Lieutenant. I have more news for you regarding decorations." Rae had enjoyed the moment. "You will receive the Second Medal of Merit in less than a month for your courage during the battle when the Onotharians first decloaked. I believe it's my father who will do the honors."

Leanne's cheeks colored a deep red. "Oh, Commodore. I didn't...I never..."

Rae laughed. "Well deserved, Lieutenant. And just so you know, Owena, your actions on Gantharat and aboard the *Liberty* have earned you the same recommendation. I fully expect the Council to follow my advice."

"Thank you, ma'am," Owena said, seemingly unfazed by the news. Still, her eyes glittered with something resembling happiness.

"Oh, sweetheart, isn't that great?" Leanne was all the more exuberant. Then her face turned solemn again. "I have to be honest with you, Commodore. I have another reason for returning to Corma." She had stopped fiddling but was obviously nervous, biting down on her lower lip before she continued. "I need to make one more attempt to reconcile with my mothers."

"Reconcile?" Rae urged her on when Leanne seemed to falter.

"Yes, ma'am. My family belongs to ancient Cormanian nobility, and I stem from a long line of a strictly female dynasty. We're nowhere near the M'Aidos or the O'Sarals, but the D'Artansis name...well, my mothers thought I shamed it when I joined the Fleet. They made me choose."

And you chose your own path. Rae knew all too well how unwelcome choices could affect a family.

Owena had folded her arms across her chest at this point, her eyes a frosty sea of blue. "I'm going with her."

Leanne shot the tactical chief a tremulous smile. "Of course you are. No matter the outcome with my mothers, we can still spend our leave on the Draggara Beaches."

Rae had never seen Owena's eyes take on such a soft expression before, and it altered the stern woman's expression completely.

"I wish you luck on your endeavor, Lieutenant," Rae said. "Both the journey and your attempt to reach your family." She hadn't told Leanne how much this situation tied in with her own conflicting emotions regarding her parents. The fact that she was actually talking with them without keeping her guard all the way up felt like nothing less than a miracle.

"Thank you, ma'am. It might turn into a huge disappointment, but I still have to try. I've…missed them."

"I understand that. At least you're not alone, Leanne. Owena will stand by you."

Leanne nodded. "To be honest, that's all that really matters, in the end."

"Have you and Kellen made up your minds yet?" Dahlia asked as they exited the Onotharian vessel, startling Rae back to the present.

"We've hardly seen each other the last few days, let alone had a chance to talk," Rae replied. "We've had to attend so many briefings, then there's the vast amount of information we brought back…"

"So you've been stalling?"

Hating the guilty feeling, Rae didn't pretend to misunderstand. "In a way, yes. Once Gemma cleared me to go back on full duty, I've buried myself in work. I…I just don't know how to tell her, Mother."

"Does she even know what's going on?" Dahlia asked, taking a seat in the almost empty rail car.

Sudden tears burned behind her eyelids, and Rae shook her head. "I don't think so. I look at Kellen and Armeo, and I know they've just gone through hell. It's damn near impossible for me to barge in on their newfound sense of security…and wreck it all."

"At one point you have to. Time's running out for you, daughter."

The unexpected term of endearment, spoken with a tender voice, made Rae reach for Dahlia's hand. "I'm aware of that. I'll talk with Kellen tonight. I won't put it off any longer."

Dahlia squeezed her daughter's hand. "It'll work out, somehow. These decisions are hard to make, but you have to give her the chance to choose."

"Is it fair, though?" Rae swallowed against the sudden lump in her throat.

"Nothing in this damn situation is fair." Dahlia raised her other hand and slid a finger along Rae's rank insignia. "Between you and your father, I have a lot to worry about."

"I'm sorry, Mom. Of course." Rae gave her mother a careful smile. "You'll be busy too."

"I know."

Riding the rest of the way in a new, comfortable sort of silence, Rae thought of the woman she had let into her life and into her heart. It was time to quit stalling.

❖

"I assume we have something to discuss, since Armeo's spending the night with your parents in the VIP quarters?" Kellen faced Rae as she brought them Cormanian coffee in tall titanium Keep-Hot cylinder-mugs. "Yes," Rae said in a low voice. "You're very observant."

"So, why not finally get to the point?" Kellen slid one arm along the backrest of the couch, her eyes fixed on her wife. "You've been tiptoeing around me ever since you went back on full duty. You're tossing and turning—"

"All right, all right." Rae held up a hand. "I'm sure you've heard through the grapevine how negotiations aren't going so well between the Onotharians and the SC."

"Yes. Political turmoil and an increasing number of border skirmishes don't look good." Kellen wrapped her cold fingers around the hot coffee mug. "Will there be a war?"

Rae examined her face with a steady gaze. Her eyes felt almost like a touch where they followed the long waves of Kellen's hair. "Yes, I think so. Not right away. The SC Council is trying every possible route to a peaceful solution first."

"And of course you'll be a part of it all."

"Yes, one way or another. This is what I'm trained to do, darling." Rae placed her mug on the coffee table. "I received directives to begin evacuating civilians from *Gamma VI*. The military will occupy most of the residential area. The same goes for *Gamma V* and *VII*."

Kellen's heart picked up speed, the implications of Rae's words hitting all at once. "No civilians at all…not even family members of the ones deployed here?"

"No. Only military staff and some commercial interests such as shops, restaurants, and legal services for the crew. There are going to be a lot of changes, I'm afraid."

Speechless, Kellen could only stare at her spouse. Not sure what Rae wanted her to say, she remained motionless, unaware of how precariously her mug was tilting until Rae removed it from her hands.

"Don't look like that," Rae implored, raw emotions obvious in her voice. "We're not without options."

"What options? You just said…" Kellen pressed cold fingertips against her trembling lips. "Armeo and I are civilians."

"Yes, but listen to me." Placing the mug on the table, Rae moved closer and took Kellen gently by the shoulders. "The problem we have is not only that you and Armeo are civilians. Armeo is safer now than he was a week ago, but you know as well as I do that until he reaches adulthood and either regains his title as an O'Saral Royale or relinquishes all claims to it, he won't be entirely safe. We'll always need to take special precautions until then. My parents have suggested we move him to Earth, since it's located in the heart of the Supreme Constellations."

Wanting to deny the truth in what Rae said, Kellen knew she was right. As Armeo's guardian, she would always have to do what was best for the boy.

"How can you say we have a choice, then?" Kellen said huskily. "I'll live on Earth with Armeo while you're out here fighting a war."

"Yes, that's *one* option."

Trying to suppress the tears burning behind her eyelids, Kellen bit into the tip of her tongue before she spoke. "There are others?"

"My father is, legally speaking, Armeo's ultimate guardian within the SC. My mother has also signed the documents, and her status, her diplomatic immunity, is irreproachable. Due to their positions in the military and diplomat core, my parents reside in a high-level security area on Earth, a region called Northern Europa. It's where I grew up."

Rae moved closer and cupped Kellen's face with her hands.

"We're not at war yet. I've been offered a position to head up Gamma stations V, VI, and VII. It's mostly a desk job, and initially I'll work from Earth. I told the Council I had to talk with you first, but I know they want me to offer you a commission as…well, I guess you can call it subject matter expert regarding Gantharat. You'd receive a provisional rank as ensign and serve directly under me. We really need your help."

Her heart racing, Kellen stared into Rae's stormy gray eyes. "Armeo…"

"I know. We have our sacred duty. We love him and don't want to be away from him. But he's safer on Earth, and I can do some, but not all, of my work from there. He would be staying with my parents in a family environment." Rae tugged Kellen close and whispered in her ear. "If you do this, if you accept the Council's offer, I promise you…" Rae broke off, rubbing Kellen's shoulders, perhaps for emphasis. "I *promise* you, we'd spend as much time as possible on Earth, and I'd never refuse to let you go to him, no matter when you needed to. Your duty—*our* duty toward him—won't be compromised."

"He would stay with your parents?"

"Yes. Their estate is large. We would have our own quarters there. The de Vies family lives nearby. He'd be with his friend."

Kellen inhaled Rae's intoxicating scent, flowery and with a fresh touch of something fruity, and slid her arms around her lover. "I…" Her voice faded.

"You don't have to decide this instant, darling." Kellen felt Rae's hands tremble. "Think about it, okay? I just know I can't lose you. I love you and will do my best to be with you and Armeo as much as I can."

"I love you too, Rae." The words gushed out before she could stop them.

"I know. I want to spend the rest of my life with you. I haven't learned every little detail about you yet, and I can't wait." Rae's eyes shimmered with unshed tears as she looked into Kellen's. "I have no idea what providence sent you to me, but I know this much is true…I can't imagine life without you."

Kellen could only nod. "I'll think about the Council's offer." She leaned back and lifted Rae onto her lap. "When do I have to let them know?"

"In a week or so. We need to know before the evacuation begins." Rae nuzzled her neck. "I realize this is difficult for you, but trust that I'll love and support you, no matter what you decide."

As she slid her hands underneath Rae's fairy-silk high-neck shirt and pushed it up, Kellen felt her mouth go dry at the sight of the pale, freckled skin. "It's been so long," she breathed. Needing to distract herself from the choice she had to make sooner or later, she caressed her way up until she could tug the garment over Rae's head and toss it on the floor. "I've longed…to touch you." Kissing along Rae's shoulder and nibbling at her neck, Kellen smiled against the dampening skin when she heard Rae moan.

"Kellen…"

"Yes?"

"You burn me…again," Rae whispered. "You're fire. Pure fire."

Kellen licked up along Rae's neck before she moved up to claim her mouth, exploring every part of it with her tongue. The passionate kiss seemed to go on forever. Rae tugged at Kellen's shirt, sending the small buttons flying across the coffee table. Pushing it down her shoulders, she revealed naked breasts with blue-red taut nipples, ready to be stimulated.

Breaking free from the kiss, Rae leaned down and cupped Kellen's left breast, raising it to her hot mouth. When she closed over the hard peak, Kellen cried out as she felt small teeth bite gently into her tender flesh. The pain fueled her passion, making her arch into the touch. Holding Rae's head with both hands, she guided her toward the other breast.

"Yes…just like that…" Whimpering, Kellen grew increasingly impatient. She grasped Rae around the waist and laid her down on the couch. Unbuttoning Rae's uniform trousers, she ripped them off, together with her boots. As she knelt between her lover's legs, she studied her closely before she removed Rae's underwear.

Rae lay shivering on the couch, looking flustered and aroused. "What are you doing to me?" she said huskily. "God…I want you so much…" She seemed unable to lie still, shifting back and forth as she placed an arm over her eyes.

"No, not like that. Look at me," Kellen demanded in a low voice. As she pushed Rae's muscular, slender legs farther apart and bent them more, she began to get a good view. "I want to learn what pleases you most."

"Oh, Kellen, all you have to do is touch me."

"Like this?" Caressing inside the trembling legs, Kellen reached the auburn tuft of hair above the drenched folds. She allowed her thumbs to part them, exposing the copious wetness pooling there. "You want me."

"Damn right, I do," Rae managed, her voice throaty. "You're driving me crazy."

Kellen smiled. She was aroused as well and wiggled out of her slacks and underwear, keeping her unbuttoned shirt on. Leaning down, she kissed the area around Rae's sex. She looked up at the rapt expression on Rae's features and decided to push farther. "Reach down and spread yourself for me. That's right. No, keep your legs bent."

Kellen spread the wetness everywhere between Rae's legs, rubbing tender fingers around her lover's entrances. "I can't wait to take you... to make you mine." Kellen carefully slid two fingers inside.

"Oh!" Rae arched and spread her legs wider. "Oh, God."

Curling her fingers slightly, Kellen moved them out halfway and in again. She let her tongue barely touch the erect clitoris between Rae's folds.

Rae began to undulate and met each thrust of the insistent fingers. "More. Please..."

In a swift movement, Kellen added a third finger and used her other hand to caress Rae's anus. Her fingers were slick with Rae's juices, and she kept them hotly pressed against her lover, on the verge of penetration.

Rae breathed heavily and moaned with every breath. "The things...you do to me..."

The sight of the otherwise commanding woman writhing on the couch in abandon made Kellen's own arousal surge. She needed to push Rae to the heights of monumental pleasure that matched her own feelings. Kellen opened her mouth and sucked the sensitized ridge of nerves inside. Licking it furiously, she pressed more fingers inside Rae, feeling an incredible tightness as she did.

Rae threw her head back and gave a short, high-pitched cry. Muscles contracted around Kellen's fingers, as if to draw them farther in. Aroused beyond words, Kellen felt the first twitches inside herself. "Rae...now...come for me. With...me..."

Pleasure flooded every part of her system, and Kellen devoured the sensitive tissues before her, pushing inside Rae again and again, until her own orgasm began to mellow. Slowly she freed her hands and lifted Rae from the couch, again placing her on her lap. Mindful to wipe her hands, Kellen wrapped a velver-down blanket around both of them. She closed her eyes as she rocked the sobbing woman in her arms.

"Nobody has ever touched me like you do," Rae said in a choked voice. "Nobody has loved me this way."

"I've never loved anyone…or acted so freely—ever," Kellen admitted, taken aback at how weak her voice sounded.

Nuzzling Kellen's cheek, Rae tugged the blanket closer around them. "It's amazing how I can let myself go when I'm with you. I can put everything else in my life on hold and just exist in the moment. It's such an amazing gift…from you."

"Only the two of us in the universe…" Kellen became quiet. "It's a Gantharian song." She trusted Rae to understand as she sang in a low voice.

I was lost and so were you,
And I was found where you begin.
I stayed with you,
I dreamed your dreams.
You claimed me,
Professed to love.
Each broken soul must find her own—
The two of us in the universe
Allow the planets to align.

"We learned that in the Academy of Pilots, believe it or not."

"It's beautiful, and you have a wonderful voice." Rae gave a soft smile. "I think the song applies to us very well."

"I do too."

Silence descended as Kellen visualized the *Gamma VI* station revolving on its axis and watched its commanding officer close her eyes, wrapped up in the arms of the woman who loved her. Kellen smiled. "Go to sleep, Rae. I'll watch over you."

"Mmm. You'll be my protector?"

Soft laughter stemming from sheer happiness bubbled within Kellen. "Always."

EPILOGUE

It will begin in a few minutes, Ambassador."

M'Ekar turned around and saw M'Indo standing in the doorway that led out to the large, mesh-covered veranda. The Jasin nights around the planet's equator were filled with night insects, mostly large, bloodsucking mosquitoes. Though a vast, synthetic net saturated with a repellant to keep the damn bugs out engulfed his dwelling completely, *he* was locked in. Allowed only a few of his staff to accompany him, he had grudgingly agreed to live in a modest bungalow. Compared to his mansion on Gantharat, it was little more than a cabin.

"Ambassador?"

"Very well. I'm coming." M'Ekar entered what passed for a salon and sat down on a three-seat couch. Secretly bracing himself, he looked up.

The large view screen on the wall showed the entire semicircle of the Council Chamber. The lowest section of the hall was called the Pit, and the tall podium in its center, the Speaker's Pillar. Councilman Thorosac stood behind the podium, and Council members representing their homeworlds filled every seat in the gallery.

Reminded of ancient theaters on many worlds, M'Ekar smiled inwardly, thinking how many great, and not so great, actors in the political arena had stood in similar places, speaking truths and lies, just like in the Onotharian equivalent.

Thorosac now raised his hand, wordlessly asking for silence. The voices quieted, and then Thorosac spoke.

"Council members, honored guests. Today is a day of great importance. We stand united, for the first time in years, against the

Onotharian Empire, determined to fight for justice and freedom. Our neighbors, the Gantharians, have paid a terrible price for having desirable natural resources and a politically important location."

Several voices shouted agreement. Thorosac raised his hand, again requesting silence. "It is a day of resolve combined with regret. All hope for a peaceful solution to the conflict is gone. Onotharat refuses to draw back their occupation forces from Gantharat, and the Supreme Constellations cannot abandon a people seeking our assistance for a second time." Thorosac paused.

"Three months ago, a young man took refuge in our part of space. He arrived with his guardian, a woman of great courage who has on several occasions proved herself loyal to him and, thus, to the SC. I want to introduce that young man: Armeo O'Saral M'Aido, exiled Prince of Gantharat."

There was complete silence as a young boy entered from one of the doors leading to the podium. Dressed in an Earth school uniform consisting of gray twillmix slacks and a blue leathermix jacket, he walked the few steps across the pit and joined Thorosac by the podium.

"Prince Armeo…" M'Ekar whispered. He'd never met the child, only seen pictures taken covertly by the Onotharian intelligence. Armeo was a handsome boy, with a distinct resemblance to both his parents. His royal blood was obvious in the way he moved, and his keen eyes reminded M'Ekar of his late wife.

Two women followed him. The taller of the two, a striking blonde with shimmering blue eyes, stayed close to the child. Despite being of obvious Gantharian descent, she wore an SC uniform. *What the hell?* M'Ekar barely resisted the impulse to throw something at the screen.

The other woman stood next to the Gantharian, her commanding presence tangible. Wearing commodore rank insignia, the woman scanned the faces in the gallery. *And her! She and her mother made all this happen. Those Jacelon women will pay the price one day. One day, no matter how long it takes, I'll make certain they know who they crossed—and they'll regret it.*

One Councilwoman rose from her chair in the first row, and then the man sitting beside her mimicked her, until a storm of applause thundered in the large hall. Armeo blushed at the reception, but he stood quietly next to Thorosac and waited for the cheering to subside.

Only then did he step up to the sound system that would carry his voice to the Council members and every citizen throughout the SC watching on view screens.

"My name is Armeo," he began, his bright voice so unlike the authoritative Thorosac's. "I have here, within the Supreme Constellations, found a safe haven and friends. I live and attend school at my grandparents' estate while my guardian has been commissioned by the SC military forces to assist in the upcoming war efforts. On behalf of my homeworld…" His voice wavered. Sending the two women a quick glance, he nodded and gave a faint smile. "On behalf of the Gantharian people, I thank you for the sacrifices you are about to make. The Gantharian people need your help. Thank you."

Looking relieved, the boy stepped down. The red-haired commodore placed a hand on his shoulder.

Thorosac went up to the sound transmitter. "Thank you, Prince O'Saral, for paying us a visit and also introducing yourself to the SC population throughout the sector."

The boy waved and left the Pit, but the applause echoed for a long time.

M'Ekar rose and stood by a window. He stared out into the dark jungle creeping close to his house.

"Sir, can I get you anything else?" his manservant asked from the door.

"No. Nothing." M'Ekar had just turned off the view screen where the child, the hybrid who should have been his ticket to unimaginable power, had addressed the Supreme Constellations and its Council. "That damn woman…" The camera had zoomed in on Commodore Jacelon and the Gantharian bitch responsible for his current situation, where they stood triumphantly next to the boy. Knowing they had won infuriated him no end, but all he could do was bide his time.

Constantly monitored and with the computer chip inserted in his central nervous system, he could do little at present. He stroked with a cold hand along his face, feeling his lips form a thin smile. No matter how humiliating his circumstances were, he firmly believed every problem had a solution.

And he was going to find it.

❖

"Did we make a mistake?" Kellen whispered as the small vessel took off from the roof of the SC Council building. Armeo had insisted on sitting next to the copilot in front. "Now everyone will know what he looks like."

Rae rubbed the back of her neck, a gesture Kellen had learned to interpret as a sign of relief after great stress. "It's no secret that he lives with my parents right now. Anyone determined to harm him would know where to go. The security in their residential area is as good as such things come." She leaned over and placed a hand on Kellen's knee.

"I know my father was against it, but Mother agreed he needed to appear in order to create a foundation for the new alliance to help save a planet and its people. As much as I dislike using Armeo as a front figure, the fact remains he is Gantharat's representative, their rightful sovereign. His life will always entail an element of danger." Rae's voice softened. "If it'll make you feel better, we can ask Gemma to chemically change his hair and eye color. She can also slightly change the color of his skin. The procedures are painless and easy to reverse."

Kellen shook her head. "It may be necessary, but let's wait and see. He lives a sheltered life, I know, and I trust in the precautions your mother has taken."

"All right. Just know we always have options."

Kellen smiled as genuine happiness filled her. "So you keep telling me, Commodore."

"Three more days left of our leave in the Reposa System, and then we deploy, darling. Any regrets?" Rae's tone of voice was light, but her eyes changed to a dark gray as she regarded Kellen.

"No regrets."

"How about we use the Vibra-Pool on the patio? Just the two of us, after Armeo goes to bed?" Rae lowered her voice. "I know how beautiful you look when the stars and the moons cast their light across your body."

Kellen's eyelids grew heavy at the thought of spending the evening naked with her wife in a pool that massaged every part of the anatomy. They had tried it once, and the mind-blowing pleasure had nearly rendered her unconscious. She leaned into Rae for a quick, breathless kiss. "I can't think of anything I'd rather do."

Rae removed the communicator from her shoulder. "Pilot?" She winked at Kellen while instructing the pilot to take them back to the famous vacation and resort planet in the Reposa System where they'd stayed for two weeks prior to Armeo's presentation. "You have my authorization to use the military corridor."

Kellen couldn't help but laugh, a thoroughly happy sound even to her own ears, and then she gave Rae a knowing look. "Are you in a hurry, *Commodore*?"

Rae smiled and stroked her thumb across her lower lip. "Damn straight, I am."

About the Author

Gun Brooke combines her lifelong love for science fiction and romance novels by writing both genres—always with romance at center stage. She resides in the Swedish countryside with her very patient family in a village displaying remnants from the Stone Age and Viking era.

Having first written fan fiction, Gun caught Bold Strokes Books' attention when she entered an online writer's challenge, and the international second edition of *Course of Action* is the happy result. Creating character-driven stories about relationships, whether set in the future or contemporary times, now keeps this Swede occupied full-time.

Putting her fascination with the latest technology to good use, she keeps in touch with friends around the world through the Internet and maintains her own Web site, http://www.gbrooke-fiction.com. She has also been known to create Web sites for other people on occasion.

When not working on her next book, Gun loves movies, reading, cooking/eating/talking, and creating computer graphics. She also enjoys traveling and meeting new people, whom she stores in her ever-growing gallery of characters for future stories.

Look for information about her works at www.boldstrokesbooks.com.

Books Available From Bold Strokes Books

Grave Silence by Rose Beecham. Detective Jude Devine's investigation of a series of ritual murders is complicated by her torrid affair with the golden girl of Southwestern forensic pathology, Dr. Mercy Westmoreland. (1-933110-25-2)

Honor Reclaimed by Radclyffe. In the aftermath of 9/11, Secret Service Agent Cameron Roberts and Blair Powell close ranks with a trusted few to find the would-be assassins who nearly claimed Blair's life. (1-933110-18-X)

Honor Bound by Radclyffe. Secret Service Agent Cameron Roberts and Blair Powell face political intrigue, a clandestine threat to Blair's safety, and the seemingly irreconcilable personal differences that force them ever further apart. (1-933110-20-1)

Protector of the Realm: Supreme Constellations Book One by Gun Brooke. A space adventure filled with suspense and a daring intergalactic romance featuring Commodore Rae Jacelon and a stunning, but decidedly lethal Kellen O'Dal. (1-933110-26-0)

Innocent Hearts by Radclyffe. In a wild and unforgiving land, two women learn about love, passion, and the wonders of the heart. (1-933110-21-X)

The Temple at Landfall by Jane Fletcher. An imprinter, one of Celaeno's most revered servants of the Goddess, is also a prisoner to the faith—until a Ranger frees her by claiming her heart. (1-933110-27-9)

Force of Nature by Kim Baldwin. From tornados to forest fires, the forces of nature conspire to bring Gable McCoy and Erin Richards close to danger, and closer to each other. (1-933110-23-6)

In Too Deep by Ronica Black. Undercover homicide cop Erin McKenzie tracks a femme fatale who just might be a real killer...with love and danger hot on her heels. (1-933110-17-1)

Stolen Moments: Erotic Interludes 2 by Stacia Seaman and Radclyffe, eds. Love on the run, in the office, in the shadows...Fast, furious, and almost too hot to handle. (1-933110-16-3)

Course of Action by Gun Brooke. Actress Carolyn Black desperately wants the starring role in an upcoming film produced by Annelie Peterson. Just how far will she go for the dream part of a lifetime? (1-933110-22-8)

Rangers at Roadsend by Jane Fletcher. Sergeant Chip Coppelli has learned to spot trouble coming, and that is exactly what she sees in her new recruit, Katryn Nagata. The Celaeno series. (1-933110-28-7)

Justice Served by Radclyffe. Lieutenant Rebecca Frye and her lover, Dr. Catherine Rawlings, embark on a deadly game of hide-and-seek with an underworld kingpin who traffics in human souls. (1-933110-15-5)

Distant Shores, Silent Thunder by Radclyffe. Dr. Tory King—along with the women who love her—is forced to examine the boundaries of love, friendship, and the ties that transcend time. (1-933110-08-2)

Hunter's Pursuit by Kim Baldwin. A raging blizzard, a mountain hideaway, and a killer-for-hire set a scene for disaster—or desire—when Katarzyna Demetrious rescues a beautiful stranger. (1-933110-09-0)

The Walls of Westernfort by Jane Fletcher. All Temple Guard Natasha Ionadis wants is to serve the Goddess—until she falls in love with one of the rebels she is sworn to destroy. The Celaeno series. (1-933110-24-4)

Change Of Pace: Erotic Interludes by Radclyffe. Twenty-five hot-wired encounters guaranteed to spark more than just your imagination. Erotica as you've always dreamed of it. (1-933110-07-4)

Honor Guards by Radclyffe. In a wild flight for their lives, the president's daughter and those who are sworn to protect her wage a desperate struggle for survival. (1-933110-01-5)

Fated Love by Radclyffe. Amidst the chaos and drama of a busy emergency room, two women must contend not only with the fragile nature of life, but also with the irresistible forces of fate. (1-933110-05-8)

Justice in the Shadows by Radclyffe. In a shadow world of secrets and lies, Detective Sergeant Rebecca Frye and her lover, Dr.Catherine Rawlings, join forces in the elusive search for justice. (1-933110-03-1)

shadowland by Radclyffe. In a world on the far edge of desire, two women are drawn together by power, passion, and dark pleasures. An erotic romance. (1-933110-11-2)

Love's Masquerade by Radclyffe. Plunged into the indistinguishable realms of fiction, fantasy, and hidden desires, Auden Frost is forced to question all she believes about the nature of love. (1-933110-14-7)

Love & Honor by Radclyffe. The president's daughter and her lover are faced with difficult choices as they battle a tangled web of Washington intrigue for...love and honor. (1-933110-10-4)

Beyond the Breakwater by Radclyffe. One Provincetown summer three women learn the true meaning of love, friendship, and family. (1-933110-06-6)

Tomorrow's Promise by Radclyffe. One timeless summer, two very different women discover the power of passion to heal and the promise of hope that only love can bestow. (1-933110-12-0)

Love's Tender Warriors by Radclyffe. Two women who have accepted loneliness as a way of life learn that love is worth fighting for and a battle they cannot afford to lose. (1-933110-02-3)

Love's Melody Lost by Radclyffe. A secretive artist with a haunted past and a young woman escaping a life that has proved to be a lie find their destinies entwined. (1-933110-00-7)

Safe Harbor by Radclyffe. A mysterious newcomer, a reclusive doctor, and a troubled gay teenager learn about love, friendship, and trust during one tumultuous summer in Provincetown. (1-933110-13-9)

Above All, Honor by Radclyffe. Secret Service Agent Cameron Roberts fights her desire for the one woman she can't have—Blair Powell, the daughter of the president of the United States. (1-933110-04-X)